CHRISTINA DODD

Once A Knight

AVON

An Imprint of HarperCollinsPublishers

This is a work of fiction. Names, characters, places, and incidents are products of the author's imagination or are used fictitiously and are not to be construed as real. Any resemblance to actual events, locales, organizations, or persons, living or dead, is entirely coincidental.

AVON BOOKS
An Imprint of HarperCollins*Publishers*
10 East 53rd Street
New York, New York 10022-5299

Copyright © 1996 by Christina Dodd
ISBN: 978-0-06-108398-3
ISBN-10: 0-06-108398-4

First Avon Books paperback printing: October 2007
First HarperTorch paperback printing: July 2000
First HarperPaperbacks special printing: August 1999
First HarperPaperbacks printing: April 1996

Avon Trademark Reg. U.S. Pat. Off. and in Other Countries, Marca Registrada, Hecho en U.S.A.
HarperCollins® is a registered trademark of HarperCollins Publishers.

Printed in the U.S.A.

10 9 8 7

Books by
Christina Dodd

To Carolyn Marino,
my first editor and a lady who,
through her daring and lack of interest
in romantic conventions,
consistently publishes the best stories
and collects the most prestigious awards.
Many thanks.

ACKNOWLEDGMENT

My eternal gratitude to Barbara Vosbein,
a.k.a. Nikki Benjamin, who when I whined and said,
"I have no plot," said, "Here, take mine."
You're a shining example of friendship—and charity.
I owe you a big one. Call anytime.

Once a prince, always a prince.
Once a knight is enough.

—OLD ENGLISH PROVERB
(OR IF IT'S NOT, IT SHOULD BE.)

1

**Medieval England
Northumbria, 1252**

I saw the whole thing from beginning to end, and I pray you note that there aren't many alive today who can say that. Most people, when they hear about it, say it's a legend, a romance, one of those foolish stories women make up to entertain themselves. I give you my vow, I saw it all, and whatever you have heard, it's the truth.

Better than that, whatever you've heard isn't half the truth.

The first of it I remember was the picnic. Oh, there were other incidents, but I was just a lad, a page in Lady Alisoun's household. I slept with the other pages, trained with the other pages, prayed with the other pages, and painfully penned a letter to my grandparents once every moon which Lady Alisoun read. She read it, she said, to see if I was improving in my lessons with the priest. I believed her then, but now I suspect a different truth—that she read to see if I was happy in her care.

I was, although my contact with her was limited to that once-a-month discussion of my progress toward squirehood. I knew I could become a squire. Lots of men and youths were squires. But I aspired to greater things. I aspired to the holy knighthood. It was the greatest honor I could ever achieve. It was my dearest dream, my greatest challenge, and I concentrated my whole attention on my studies, for I was determined someday to be a knight.

So it took that dreadful picnic to alert me that trouble brewed in Lady Alisoun's household.

The first shout came after lunch, when the young men and women of the village and the castle had scattered into the forest that surrounded the open meadow. I would have been with them, but pages were subservient to everyone, and I had been commandeered to help the serving women repack the baskets while the men lounged in the lazy aftermath of a huge meal. Anyway, someone, I don't know who, yelled, "Lady Edlyn's been taken!"

That caught my attention at once, for at fifteen (four years older than me), Lady Edlyn was kind, beautiful— and unaware of my existence.

I adored her.

The shout caught Lady Alisoun's attention, too. She stood up quickly. Quickly!

No one who lived outside of George's Cross could understand the significance of that, but it brought silence to the meadow. Every eye clung to Lady Alisoun's tall figure, alarmed by her haste.

Lady Alisoun never did anything quickly. She did everything deliberately, calmly. Every day, she rose at dawn, attended Mass, broke her fast, and proceeded to the duty of the day. Every year, she celebrated Twelfth Night, fasted at Easter, supervised the lambing in the spring, and went to Lancaster in the autumn. She was the lady, our lady, the one we timed our lives by.

I'm making her sound old—to me, she was old—although looking back, I know she couldn't have been more than twenty-four or twenty-five. Yet Lady Alisoun didn't look old. She just looked perfect, and that was why that one hurried, unwary motion told us so much.

Three serving girls burst from the woods and ran toward Lady Alisoun as if drawn to a lodestone. "A man . . . a man! He grabbed her!"

One silly village woman screamed, and Lady Alisoun spun and bent a stare on her. Silence descended at once; Lady Alisoun expected proper behavior from all on her estate, and for the most part, she got it.

Then she asked the girls, "Who grabbed her?"

"A man . . . a man," one girl gasped.

But Heath, my lady's chief maid, pushed forward and punched the girl in the arm. "Speak. What man?"

"A stranger."

I heard Alisoun's personal maid, a woman with a babe at her breast, mutter a raw prayer.

Sir Walter called, "A strange man took Lady Edlyn?"

He didn't rise from his seat to ask the question, or act in any way concerned, and I again realized how much I disliked him. For all his superior airs, he was nothing but a knight, elevated by Lady Alisoun to the role of her steward. He was supposed to secure her estates, but today he could scarcely unwrap himself from his woman long enough to show respect.

Looking around, I saw the same dislike mirrored on everyone's face.

We held our breaths, waiting for Lady Alisoun's reprimand. She might be the epitome of a lady, but she could reduce a grown man to tears with a few well-chosen words.

She didn't do it this time. She just looked at Sir Walter through those funny-colored eyes, judging him in her mind. I suppose you could wonder how I knew that, but I did, and so did Sir Walter, because that stocky lowland knave scrambled to his feet so fast his woman fell backward and hit her head against a rock.

Served her right, the slut.

Once Sir Walter stood on his feet, a mad rush ensued. He organized search parties, sending the villeins to different parts of the forest to look for the Lady Edlyn. I wanted to go, too. I hopped up and down on one foot, waggled my hand, finally spoke up, but he denied me the honor of joining the search. I should stay with the women, he said, sneering in his offensive manner.

He didn't like me because he didn't think I knew my place. Actually, I did know it. I didn't keep to it, but I knew it.

Sir Walter himself insisted on going with the trackers to the place where Lady Edlyn had been taken. They would seek her and had the best chance of locating her. Sir Walter wanted to be in on the find to impress Lady Alisoun.

When the searchers had dispersed and their loud calls to each other faded, Lady Alisoun sent the women who carried babes or tended toddlers to the protection of the castle. She sent the contingent of remaining men-at-arms to protect them, too, and big, dull Ivo tried to argue with her about that. He didn't want to leave her, but years of obedience had left their mark, and before long, I found myself alone with Lady Alisoun.

She sat alone on a rug in the middle of the open

meadow. She wore white trimmed in blue. It wasn't practical, but that day she served as symbol to her people. She was the old earth goddess and the Virgin Mary all in one, rallying hope for a prosperous summer after two long years of drought. Her white wimple folded back to reveal a blue cap beneath. Her white cotte showed glimpses of her long blue shift through the lacing. When she raised her long, trailing white sleeves, they fell back and the blue lining showed. No one thought of her as being pretty or otherwise. She just was; the lady. She sat with her back straight, her expression serene, her hands relaxed in her lap.

I didn't say anything, and neither did she, so I started once more cleaning up the mess left by two hundred people celebrating the return of spring. All around, clumps of trampled spring grass gave off a fresh scent. Toppled baskets spilled onto the ground, and ants hurried to scavenge the contents.

Lady Alisoun ignored me for a while and I almost forgot about her. After all, I was eleven and I had been left with a surfeit of leftover food. And not just everyday food, either. All the women had used the last of their premium provisions for this special meal and made honey loaf and honey sweetmeat and honey mead. I ate cautiously at first, putting the food back into the baskets with only a taste here and there. Then the birds and the woodland creatures started approaching, drawn by the odors of food and the absence of almost everyone. If I didn't eat it, they would.

Specious reasoning, of course, but as I said, I was eleven.

Suddenly Lady Alisoun asked, "Do you remember my cat?"

I had been dipping my fingers in a stray pot of honey and conveying it to my mouth, so her query caught me by surprise. My start of guilt must have been conspicuous, but she didn't reproach me. She waited while I licked my fingers, gulped and replied, "Aye, I remember her." She didn't say anything else, so I replaced the cork on the pot and ventured, "She was a nice puss."

"Remember how she always brought the mice and piled them at my feet?" Lady Alisoun shuddered. "And I had to show my gratitude by personally picking them up and carrying them to the pantry."

I couldn't help but grin at the memory.

"I miss her," Lady Alisoun said.

Tapestry had died a few weeks before, but I had paid little notice. After all, the castle bounded with cats and dogs, and if I wished to cuddle a creature, I had them underfoot at all times. But Lady Alisoun had been special to Tapestry, and now I realized Tapestry had been special to Lady Alisoun. Stuffing the honey pot into a basket, I wiped my sticky fingers on my tunic and tried to think of the proper thing to say.

Lady Alisoun didn't wait for me. "Did you hear how she died?"

I had. It disgusted me to think that someone could be so cruel, and now fury seized me. That person had hurt Lady Alisoun in the process.

She fixed me in her gaze this time, and repeated, "Did you hear what happened to Tapestry?"

"Aye, my lady." I wiped my nose on my sleeve, then went back to work filling the baskets. Mumbling, I said, "Someone skinned her alive and nailed her to the castle gate."

"Sir Walter thought it an accident that it was my favorite cat."

I stopped and stared. "Wasn't it? Because if some-one knew it was your cat, that means it would have to

*be one of us who lives with you, and none of us would
do that, my lady."*

She accepted my assurance with a courtly nod.
*"Nay, not someone who lives with me, but someone
who knows me nonetheless. I wonder . . ."* She stared
at the forest around us. *"Because Edlyn was wearing
my cloak when she went into the woods."*

I couldn't think of a reply. I couldn't think of anything.
All I could do was realize—Lady Alisoun and I were
alone out here. George's Cross Castle was a good two
leagues due south. George's Cross Village was a good
three leagues south and east. My lady was in danger. In
fact, she sat on the top of the hill, exposing herself to danger, probably as an enticement to whatever villain stalked
her, and I served as her sole protector. I had dreamed of
the day I would defend a lady in peril, but I had hoped to
have more than a pot of honey as a weapon.

The birds stopped calling. The bushes rustled. I
leaped to my feet, a stout stick in my grasp. A man sped
out of the woods toward Lady Alisoun. I rushed
between them, intent on defending her—and Sir Walter
knocked me aside with a blow to the head.

Through the buzzing in my ears, I heard, *"Get out of
my way, you little bastard."*

I struggled back up, ready to claw and bite as I
always did when someone maligned my birth, but Lady
Alisoun's cool tones stopped me.

"You will not ever call him that again, Sir Walter."

I swayed, waiting, hoping he would defy her.

But he didn't. Instead, he answered easily, *"Of
course not, my lady, if it displeases you. But I bring
weighty news! We found her."*

He sounded as if he had done something great, when
actually, if he'd been doing his duty in the first place,
Lady Edlyn wouldn't have been taken at all. Lady

Alisoun knew it, and he knew it, too, for when she fixed him in her gaze, he flushed uncomfortably.

"She's not dead," he added with a little less exuberance.

"I hope not." She stood, ignoring his hand outstretched to assist her. "For your sake." The shouting was converging in one place in the forest, and she started toward it. "How badly is she hurt?"

"Not—" he cleared his throat, "—badly."

He stared after her as if undecided about his next strategy, but I sprang over the remains of the ruined picnic to follow her, and he barreled after me. He tried to grab me and place me behind him on the trails that wound through the underbrush, but I proved too nimble for him. Skipping aside, I managed to clear the thicket and get ahead of Lady Alisoun, and from then until we reached Lady Edlyn, I busied myself with pushing aside the low hanging branches and helping her over the rough spots.

Vying for her attention, Sir Walter said loudly, "As you feared, a man took her while she played games with the others." His voice got deeper and more authoritative. "She's too old for such silliness. She should sit with the women."

Well, I recognized his tactics. I'd tried it once or twice myself! Shift the blame onto someone else and confuse the issue. What he didn't know was that Lady Alisoun hadn't accepted it from me, either. She said, "When I need your advice on the noble girls I foster, Sir Walter, I will certainly ask for it." She released a branch too soon, and it slapped him in the face.

"Good shot, my lady," I mumbled, but she pretended not to hear. She hurried toward the sounds of excited conversation ahead of us.

One thing for Sir Walter, he didn't take a hint. He

came thrashing through the brush like a bear flushed from its den, growling like one, too. "My lady, I insist—"

"Later, Sir Walter."

"But you know what I think." He managed to get ahead of her and planted himself in the path between her and me. "If you had never taken them in, this would have never happened."

I saw what happened next. Lady Alisoun—our calm, serene Lady Alisoun—curled her hands into fists. Then slowly, she relaxed them. I found myself releasing a pent-up breath of excitement.

Did I mention she was a tall woman? Well, she was, tall and slender, and occasionally, she used her height to an advantage. Right now she drew herself up and looked Sir Walter square in the eye. "We have already discussed this."

My opinion of Sir Walter dropped even more as he just blathered on, using that oh-so-lofty masculine tone of voice. "And you know my conviction. 'Tis against the laws of man and God to place yourself between—"

"I have no interest in your opinion." She spaced her words precisely. "If you find you cannot reconcile your conscience with my actions, you are a free man and an able knight. I could recommend your services to other nobles whom you could respect more."

The color drained from Sir Walter's ruddy complexion, and his blue eyes bulged. "My lady! I've lived in George's Cross for more than twenty years, and have been your steward since the death of your parents."

"For those reasons, I would be loath to lose you."

Almost lost in his beard, his lips moved soundlessly. His barrel chest rose and fell, and a vein in his forehead beat in rapid rhythm. That superiority which so annoyed me altered as he at last comprehended his precarious position.

No one dared chide the lady of George's Cross.

She said, "You can tell me your decision later."

I didn't even have time to cackle before Heath ran pell-mell around one of the oaks. She saw Lady Alisoun and skidded to a stop, kicking up a cloud of dirt. Beckoning, she started back the way she came with the cry, "Praise th' saints, m'lady, she's calling fer ye."

Picking up her skirts, Alisoun hurried. She didn't run—in those days, true noble ladies did not run, for it showed a lack of breeding—but she placed her feet one after the other in such elongated steps she caught up with the shorter Heath almost at once.

I was pretty sure I knew where everyone had gathered, and I scooted around to take a shortcut I'd found in my rambles. But for some reason—to gloat, I suppose—I glanced back at Sir Walter. That expression on his face could have frozen a stone. He looked like a man who wanted to wring someone's neck, and he was staring at Lady Alisoun's back.

Right then I vowed to be my lady's defender no matter what might occur.

I kept my vow, too. That's the best part of the story.

Anyway, I got to the lichen-covered boulders in time to see Heath and Lady Alisoun emerging from the woods. The older children hung from the trees for the best view. In a mill of confusion, villagers and servants craned their necks. Everybody spoke in a large, unified buzz.

Then Heath called, "Make way fer m'lady." The babbling dropped into silence and a path opened.

I hurried to catch up, then followed in Lady Alisoun's wake. The people bobbed and bowed as she made her way through them, and an occasional hand reached out and touched her skirt as if she were an icon brought out for a holy day procession. Like I said, she was the sym-

bol of security and prosperity for George's Cross. It was
a burden she had assumed at the age of thirteen, when
her parents died of the flux. She took the time now to
offer a smile here, a word of assurance there.

You just don't see gracious ladies like her anymore.

Finally she reached a cluster of serving women
kneeling around one weeping bundle wrapped in
Alisoun's own cloak. "She's here," Heath announced
to the sobbing woman. "Lady Edlyn, she's here."

Lady Edlyn launched herself at Lady Alisoun without even looking.

Such impetuous behavior surprised me. Lady
Alisoun gave me a sense of safety and stability, but I
would never, never have spontaneously sought comfort
from her. Indeed, Lady Alisoun staggered back under
the weight, then carefully, as if she were unsure of herself, she wrapped Lady Edlyn in her arms. Lady Edlyn
kept burrowing closer, as if she needed to rest in
Alisoun's heart to once again feel secure. I gathered my
courage and interrupted, "My lady, I don't think you
should stay out here. It isn't safe."

"It's safe." Sir Walter had arrived, red and flushed.

But Lady Alisoun looked up thoughtfully and spoke
only to me. "I believe you are right. We'll go back to the
castle at once, where we are protected."

Much time had passed since then. I've lived a long
life, but no other words ever thrilled me like those—I
believe you are right.

If he could have, Sir Walter would have cuffed me
again. "You're speaking to a lad, my lady. I am your
steward, and I say there is no threat anywhere on your
lands."

Before Lady Alisoun could reprove him for so contra-
dicting her, Lady Edlyn jerked out of her arms and
turned on him. "That man who took me hit me!" She

threw back the cloak's hood, lifted the braids off her neck and showed a bruise the size of her fist. "He hit me," she repeated, "and when I woke, he was carrying me like a bag of wool. When I fought, he laughed and hit me again—" she rubbed her mistreated rump, "—and when he got here, he threw . . . me down so . . . hard I lost my . . . breath and—"

She struggled to tell her tale, but her tears got the better of her, and I clenched my fist at this desecration of my first love.

"Enough!" Sir Walter said. "You were attacked, but he's gone, and he took you only because he thought you were Lady Alisoun."

All sound halted and horror etched every face.

Satisfied with the sensation he'd caused, Sir Walter continued, "We saw the marks in the ground. He had a horse waiting. If he hadn't seen Lady Edlyn's face, he'd have taken her, imagining she was the lady."

Lady Alisoun said firmly, "We must go to the castle at once."

I hung close to my two idols as the exodus wound through the forest. Everyone from the village and all Lady Alisoun's servants crowded around her, forming a human shield. We were a silent group, given to sudden starts and furtive whispers, and when we broke into the cleared area around the castle, I heard the collective sigh of relief.

Me, I took my new position as my lady's defender seriously and peered around. As part of the castle defense, the forest that had once pressed close had been cleared away years ago. The massive outer walls of the castle wound along the bald curves of the hill above the sea. The village hugged the hollow in the inland valley below. Only immovable boulders remained in the green pasture grass between them, and I concentrated my

attention there. Was it possible for someone to hide
from sight among the clusters of rock? I didn't know,
and I didn't want to find out. I started walking very
close behind Lady Alisoun and Lady Edlyn, stepping on
the backs of their heels just often enough to keep them
walking briskly toward the lowered drawbridge. Lady
Edlyn finally turned around and whacked my head, but
I just smirked at her and trod even closer.

Ivo and his men started down from the open castle
gate, and when the villagers saw that, they began to
break away, a few at a time. Fear had infected them;
they wanted to get home and bar their doors. By the
time we crossed the drawbridge, only the castle servants
and the men-at-arms remained in our party. Stopping,
Lady Alisoun waited until most of her people had
passed. One last time, she called thanks to the villagers
and lifted her hand in farewell—and something flew
through the air and struck her.

I didn't see it, I just heard it. The twang, the thump
as it pinned her against the wooden gate, the sound of
material tearing as she fell backward, off balance,
under the impact.

What I did see was Sir Walter moving faster than I'd
ever imagined he could. He reached Lady Alisoun's
side, grabbed her under the armpits and dragged her
out of sight behind the gate, all the while shouting at
the men-at-arms to shut the damned gate, damn it, shut
the damned thing now.

Then he dropped her in the grass and ran back
around the gate and out of sight.

Lady Alisoun lifted her forearm, and I stared in
shock. An arrow had penetrated her dangling sleeve,
piercing the material with its small metal tip. The
fletching feathers, moving with the impetus of a long-
bow and unable to exit the hole, had jerked her off her

feet. Now the arrow still dangled, unbalanced, tip on one side of her sleeve, fletching on the other.

Her gaze met mine, and she blinked at me. I'd never seen her bewildered before, and I thought . . . well, I don't know what I thought. It just seemed someone ought to take care of her for a change. So I knelt, slid my arm underneath her head and placed it in my lap.

It probably wasn't comfortable. I was dreadfully bony then, but she sighed and closed her eyes as if she found comfort in my touch. "I do believe someone tried to shoot me," she said. The words sounded calm, but her voice shook.

By now, the women had crowded around Lady Alisoun and the men had returned with Sir Walter.

She opened her eyes, and it was clear to me that Lady Alisoun had finished with her moment of weakness. Pinning Sir Walter with her gaze, she asked, "Are the villagers under attack?"

"Nay, my lady." Sir Walter lifted her arm and jerked the arrow free. "Only one arrow was shot, and it was shot at you."

Lifting it, he showed the crowd. As if they'd rehearsed, the women started crying in unison, and the men wheeled and stomped like great warhorses anxious for battle.

Well pleased with the scene his words had caused, Sir Walter pulled his soldiers away to search for the culprit. Lady Alisoun's own maid pushed her way through the crowd and dropped to her knees beside us. She was a handsome woman, one who'd come to the castle from another one of Lady Alisoun's holdings when Lady Alisoun wished to train Heath for the position of head maid. I'd heard the serving women gossip that Lady Alisoun had brought her out of kindness, because she had a babe but no husband, but I cared nothing for that. I only knew Philippa had been kind to me, and I liked her even more now, for her first thought was for our lady.

"Alisoun?" Reaching out, she ran her hands lightly over Lady Alisoun's body. "Alisoun, did the arrow hit you?"

Sir Walter hadn't stepped far enough away, it seemed, for she had attracted his attention, and he returned in time to hear the question. "It hit her sleeve, you stupid woman." Sir Walter picked up the material and stuck his stubby fingers through the hole. "Can't you see?"

But Philippa held Lady Alisoun's hand up. A little puddle of shiny red had formed in her palm and trickled through her long, thin fingers. Sir Walter gave an exclamation, and Philippa pushed Lady Alisoun's sleeve up. "Stupid woman?" she answered him smartly. "Stupid man. Let's see the damage."

Then Lady Alisoun did the strangest thing. With her good arm, she grasped the neck of Philippa's cotte and brought her face close. I didn't grasp the meaning of their conversation then, but I heard what they said and remembered, and eventually I comprehended every word.

Lady Alisoun said, "I've got to do it, Philippa."

And Philippa whispered, "I brought this misfortune on you."

"Don't you dare apologize!" Obviously, Lady Alisoun's voice came out louder than she wanted. She glanced frantically at Sir Walter, who strained to hear, then lowered her voice. "It's not you, it's him. I've never let a man frighten me, and I'm not going to start now. I made a vow to protect you. Now I'm going to keep it. I'm going to Lancaster. I'm going to hire the legendary Sir David of Radcliffe."

2

"Are you the legendary Sir David of Radcliffe?"

A woman's melodious voice broke his stupor and a toe prodded him in the middle of his back. Cautiously, David opened his eyes a slit. Tall yellow trees flooded his vision. Then he blinked, and the trees transformed themselves into straw spread on the floor around his head.

Groaning, he remembered. Sybil's alehouse. A morning spent deep in a foaming cup. Then blessed, drunken oblivion.

He closed his eyes again. This was just where he wanted to be.

"I repeat myself. Are you the legendary Sir David of Radcliffe?" The lady's voice lowered in disdain. "Or are you dead?"

This query came accompanied by a kick in the ribs, and before he could stop himself, he flipped over and grabbed the slippered foot in one smooth motion. "I'm not dead yet. But you will be if you don't stop kicking me."

The slender, white form above him didn't shriek or flail her arms or gasp in fear. She simply shifted her weight to maintain her balance and signaled to halt the rush of the two men who guarded the door. Muttering and glaring, the burly fellows retreated, and when they had returned to their posts, the woman repeated patiently, "Are you Sir David of Radcliffe?"

He must be losing his touch. He didn't even frighten her. His grip tightened, then he released it. Bringing his hands to his face, he rubbed them over his throbbing forehead. By the saints, even his hair hurt. "If I say aye, will you go away?"

As relentless as the famine which had destroyed his dreams, she asked, "Are you David of Radcliffe, the king's own champion?"

Fury roared through him, sudden and cleansing as a storm across the Irish Sea. He found himself on his feet, shouting right in her face. "Not anymore!"

She considered him without flinching, her cool eyes as gray as a wash of winter fog. "You're no longer Sir David, or you're no longer the king's champion?"

Clutching the scraggly locks at his forehead, he groaned and staggered backward, collapsing onto a bench. This woman could drive him mad. "No longer the king's champion."

"But you *are* the legendary mercenary who rescued our sovereign when the French pulled him off his horse; who kept a dozen knights at bay while the king remounted and escaped?"

"Fifteen."

"What?"

"Fifteen knights at bay." Moving slowly, each muscle aching from the effort, he leaned back until the table supported his back. With painful precision, he lifted his arms and laid them on the boards behind. Straightening out his knees, he dug his heels into the dirt and straw on the floor, slouched down on his spine, and examined his tormentor.

She was tall. He would wager she could stand flat-footed and stare down at the king's widening bald spot. She was delicate. He doubted her fair skin had ever glimpsed the sun, or her slender fingers performed hard labor. And she was rich. Her white velvet gown molded her curves with a loving touch, and the white fur which trimmed the neckline and the long tight sleeves must be worth more than his entire estate.

Bitterly, he once more tasted defeat. Everything he'd worked for, all his life, had turned to ashes, and now disaster stared him full in the face. His daughter would suffer. His people would starve. And he couldn't save them. The legendary mercenary David of Radcliffe had fallen at last.

His chin sank onto his chest and he examined his toes. His breath rasped painfully in his chest and brought the memory of childhood tears abruptly to mind.

"I have a proposition for you, if you are Sir David of Radcliffe," the lady said.

Did she never give up? Blinking to clear his eyes, he admitted, "Oh, in sooth, I am David."

"Very good." Signaling Sybil, that slattern of an alewife, she ordered two brews, then seated herself on the bench at another table. "I have need of a merce-nary."

"For what?"

"I'll be satisfied with nothing less than the best." The noble lady accepted a full horn cup and stared into its dark depths.

"What would my duties be?" He reached for the cup Sybil held, but she snatched it back.

"Ye'll pay yer bill afore ye get more," she said.

"You'll give me more before I pay my bill."

Sybil sneered. "Or what?"

Pretending amusement, he grinned into her ugly face. "Or I'll not drink here anymore."

The men-at-arms who guarded the door chortled, and Sybil flushed with fury. Quick as a snake, she splashed the contents of the horn in his face.

Wiping the ale away, he observed her hasty retreat. She'd gone too far, and she realized it. Women, even free women who owned their own inns, could not treat a knightly baron with such disrespect. He rose and stalked toward her.

"Good sir, I beg yer pardon," she cried when he towered over her and grabbed her wrist. "Me wicked temper's ever gettin' th' better o' me. Please, sir, don't hurt me. Don't hurt me. I'm just a poor old woman wit' a child t' support."

He hesitated.

Sensing weakness, she added, "A girl child."

Disgusted with himself, he freed her and leaned close to her face.

"A wee girl."

Her high-pitched whining made his head throb. "Just get me an ale, and hurry."

"Aye, sir." She bobbed a curtsy. "Now, sir."

He turned away and took two steps before he heard her mutter, "Gutless arse."

He whipped around, but before he could take her by the shoulders and shake her, the lady grabbed a hank of Sybil's hair, forcing the alewife to her knees. "You'll learn respect for your betters, good woman, or you'll explain yourself at the hallmote."

Sybil whimpered. "I didn't know ye favored him."

That wisp of insolence made David want to slap her,

but the lady answered calmly enough. "The king favors him. That should be enough for the likes of you."

Sybil opened her mouth to refute that statement, but she saw something in the lady's face which stopped her. Instead she touched her forehead to the floor. When she came up, dirt blotted her skin. "Aye, m'lady. As ye say, m'lady. It's just hard fer a poor widow t' see bread snatched from her child's mouth by a worthless ol' mercenary wit' a taste fer ale."

Coldly, the lady answered. "I have gold with which to pay."

Both the alewife and the mercenary stared.

"Gold." She jingled the purse at her side. "I'll pay his bill." She looked him in the eye. "I'll pay your fee."

The promise of gold spoke to David as nothing else could. It spoke to the alewife, too, it seemed, for she rose and scurried off toward the pot which bubbled at the fire in the middle of the room. "If we don't conclude our business soon," David warned, "she'll offer a bowl of her pottage, and a gruesome feast that is." He looked again at the lady, noting how the determined set of her chin ruined the almost perfect oval of her face. She was not the delicate flower she had at first appeared, and it occurred to him to question why she sought him alone, without the help of her spouse or family. Because it was his nature to be suspicious, he wondered if she wished to use him in a clan dispute. "What is it you want?" he demanded bluntly.

"Protection."

"For what? Your lands? Your castle?"

"Myself."

Furious that the gold so quickly slipped away, he said, "I'll not intercede between you and your husband."

"I did not ask you to."

"From whom else would a woman like you need asylum? Your mate will protect you from all the rest."

She folded her hands together at her waist. "I am a widow."

His gaze skimmed her again, and abruptly he understood what she wanted him to know. "A rich widow."

"Precisely."

"A new-made widow?"

"Are you interested in the job?"

Her very answer rebuked his curiosity, but he didn't care. "Have you got an inopportune suitor?" he guessed.

She just stared, eyes gray as flint.

So she wouldn't tell him what he wanted to know. Fine. He'd find out what he wanted soon enough. No woman ever kept a secret, and this one, for all her poise, was very much a woman. He rubbed the stubble on his cheek, and dirt from the floor flaked off into his palm. Carelessly he wiped his hand on his hose. "I am a legend, and legends come dear."

"I'll take nothing less," she answered.

He named the exorbitant sum of three pounds of English money.

She nodded.

"Every month," he added hastily.

"That is fair."

Again he examined her. He hadn't previously thought her a fool, but he should have known. All women were fools—but so were men who imagined they could collect such wages on the strength of a vanished reputation.

"One month in advance."

Opening her purse, she counted out the gold and held it before his eyes. "Is this sufficient guarantee of my good intentions?"

But if she didn't know, why should he tell her? She dressed well, she treated him as if he were a worm, she had guards who eyed her protectively . . . aye, she was wealthy, so what was the harm in shearing just a little of that fleece which cushioned her?

Cautiously, he wrapped his fingers around the money, trapping it and her hand. He felt the delicate flesh and the chill of the gold. He thought how easily he could break her and how much he needed that money.

Snatching his hand away, he polished the sensations from his palm as if that would polish away any deception. "I'm not the man you want." He started for the door just as Sybil arriving holding steaming bowls, and he took a particular pleasure in brushing past her.

"Hey!" Sybil squawked. "Come back 'ere. M'lady, I require payment."

"Pay her, Gunnewate," the lady commanded from behind him, and one of her men-at-arms reached for his purse as the other stretched out an arm and blocked the exit.

David stopped and contemplated the arm, then the massive fellow to whom it belonged. "Move, or I'll move you."

The man-at-arms didn't stir. David threatened him with a straight and evil stare. The man stared back, jutting his chin. David placed his hand on the hilt of his knife. The man drew his blade. David stepped back to make room for the fight.

Then the lady said, "Let him go, Ivo."

Without a sign of regret or relief, without hurry or distress, Ivo brought his beefy arm back to his side and left the way open for David to leave.

David couldn't believe it. The big oaf submitted, not under the menace of David's blade, but under the threat of a woman's scolding. It wasn't respect for a mercenary legend that made Ivo obey, but a single word from his mistress. Stepping close to him, David measured himself against Ivo's chest. Ivo was taller, broader, younger, in every way David's physical superior. Speaking into his face, David said, "Arrant coward."

Ivo flinched under the blast of stale, ale-laden breath, and he sneered. "Poltroon." Then he bowed his head and slipped backward along the wall.

Resentment cramped David's gut. He could have used the combat. He needed to take out his hostility on somebody. Instead he marched through the door, prepared to storm off and leave this farce behind.

Instead the sunlight hit him and he staggered. Damn, it was bright. Bright and unseasonably hot, just as it had been for the last two years. The drought. The damned drought had driven him from his home. Would it never end?

The rays beat into his brain through his eyes, and even when he closed them, the lids proved inadequate protection. Clutching his face, he leaned against the wall and mumbled, "Bloody ale."

"It is not the ale, but your excessive intake that is at fault." The lady's precise voice ground at his nerves like a grindstone against Toledo steel.

Bravely, he opened his eyes and shielded them from the sunlight with his hands. "Who are you?"

"I am Alisoun, countess of George's Cross."

She had appeared fair in the dim light of the inn, but now she positively glowed. White gown, fair skin—and were those freckles that marched across her nose? He squinted. Aye, definitely freckles—in defiance, no doubt, of Lady Alisoun's desire. It cheered him to think something escaped the lady's mandate.

Persistent as David's daughter and almost as fearless, Lady Alisoun asked, "Are you not Sir David of Radcliffe?"

"I told you I was, and I didn't lie about that. I told you I was no longer the king's champion, and I didn't lie about that either." He turned away, ashamed, not wanting to see the contempt on her face. "'Tis the king's champion you wish to hire, my lady, not me."

"You have truly lost the title?" Surprise lifted her voice from the deep richness which had marked it before to a more normal woman's tone. "When did this occur?"

"This morning." His stomach roiled as he remembered. "On the tourney field. The legendary David of Radcliffe fell in defeat."

She was silent for so long, he looked back at her.

At last she said, "'Tis tragic that you failed just when I have need of you, but I need a legend, not a one-time hero. I want *you*."

In a voice harsh with pain, he said, "By the saints, woman, don't you see? I'm not the man I once was. Every fledgling knight in Lancaster has challenged me these last days just to brag they fought the greatest mercenary of our times. I defeated every one of them—beardless boys with more bravado than sense. But when I came up against a seasoned knight, I lost."

She excused him. "Your other trials exhausted you."

He paid her no heed. "I suffered abject, humiliating defeat."

She caught his hand and opened it, then placed the coins in it and closed his fingers around them. "Here are your first moon's wages. The innkeeper has been paid as well. Should you decide to accept my employment, I'm at the Crowing Cock Inn. Be there by dawn."

"M'lady," her man Gunnewate remonstrated. "Ye

can't give a scoundrel money like that and think ye'll see him return!"

David glared, wanting to kill him for his insolence, and realized he could see better now. Glancing up at the sky, he saw clouds gathering. Blessed, blessed clouds, here to break the drought.

Lady Alisoun noticed them, too, and demanded her wooden shoes from Ivo. Lumbering like a trained bear, Ivo brought them and went down on one knee to place them over her leather slippers. Answering Gunnewate, Lady Alisoun said, "He is the legendary David of Radcliffe. He shall not disappoint me."

Sir David had better not disappoint her. If he did, this whole wretched journey and uncomfortable visit had been in vain, and she would have to return to George's Cross bringing little more than a rainstorm.

Without expression, Alisoun observed King Henry III hold court in the great hall of Lancaster Castle just as he had done every morning since he'd traveled north. Patiently, she waited for her chance to present her petition, all the while trying to ignore the presence of Osbern, duke of Framlingford, the king's cousin and her most dreaded enemy.

Osbern didn't make it easy. He watched her with a smirk. Anyone who didn't know them would believe them to be lovers. Certainly Osbern had taken care to represent them as such, and his power and influence were such that her dignified haughtiness only fed the rumors.

After all, she was the widow Alisoun of George's Cross, powerful and influential in her own way. Never mind that Osbern's wife had been her best friend, and that her unexplained disappearance still created gossip.

When coupled with Osbern's insinuations and his rather spectacular masculine beauty, Alisoun's extended sojourn as a single woman created speculation and made her long for the safety of home.

Now she could go, for David would fulfill his duty. He had to, for he was the legendary mercenary. He even looked the part. His rangy form and grace proclaimed his strength. The threads of gray in his dark hair proclaimed his experience. Hard heavy brows lent a severity to his expression, and his eyes had seen much. Yet his mouth saved him from the ruthlessness of most mercenaries. He grinned, he grimaced, he pursed his lips in avarice. Every thought that crossed his mind, he expressed with his mouth, and without saying a word.

She liked his mouth.

Seeing that King Henry had finished with the lesser folk, Alisoun stepped forward and curtsied. Not too deeply, for her family's bloodlines were no less ancient and noble than his, but a modest, respectable curtsy.

Hale at forty-five, with a superficial charm that covered his capricious nature, King Henry responded with a nod. "Lady Alisoun, how good to see you at our court again. You attend every morning, flattering us with your attention. Have you some instructions to share this day?"

He had a distasteful inclination toward sarcasm, especially with her. She didn't understand or like it, for she knew full well an unhappy monarch could create problems for her and the lands which she held in her custody. So she smiled with constrained charm and said, "I take my instructions from you, my liege—"

He snorted.

"—And have only a humble request." He looked her over critically, and she was glad she had worn her best scarlet velvet for this interview. It weighed on her like a knight's armor, keeping her safe with its bulk and brazen beauty.

"What request is that?"

"I wish to retire from your most gracious court and return to my duties at George's Cross. I have been away too long, basking in the sun of your presence."

He cocked his head and examined her. "You *are* getting rather freckled."

Laughter rippled through the courtiers.

"I was already freckled," she replied.

Laughter grew and the king dropped his head as if in despair.

She stared at him, and then, in confusion asked, "My liege? Have I displeased you?"

"Never mind. Never mind. So you wish to withdraw, do you? Is there nothing you wish to take back to George's Cross with you?"

Wetting her lips, she tried to appear unaware of his meaning. "What would that be?"

"A husband, of course." His arm swept the great hall, indicating the courtiers who lined the walls.

Her heart sank. King Henry was mad for marriage. He had used it as a diplomatic coup, uniting England with Provence in his marriage. He used it on lesser nobility, too, to advance his cause within the kingdom and out of it. Those successes gave him an immodest estimation of his own good sense—a good sense he had not proved in his rule of England nor in his choice of grooms for her. Now she dwelled at court, renewing the appetites of the men for her wealth and the appetite of the king for an alliance.

Henry persisted, "You see here the flowers of my kingdom, the best of England, Normandy, Poitou, France. Is there not one here who fulfills your demands?"

She could scarcely say that they did not, and so she protested, "My requirements are reasonable, my lord. Surely you agree to that."

He held up three fingers and counted them down. "Wealth, bloodlines, and responsibility. Isn't that right?"

Her throat caught in dismay at the way he beamed in triumph, but she cleared it and answered, "That is correct."

"Then I have a suitor for you."

He had caught her unprepared. "That's impossible! I've been to court every day, watching to see who might petition to wed me, and—"

"Is that why you've been here?" He looked down at his hand, clenched in a fist. "To give me guidance, should any man dare?"

She didn't like this. She didn't like the king's attitude nor Osbern's superior leer. Someone had been whispering malicious rumors in the king's ear, and she knew the culprit. An importune pang of longing for George's Cross struck her like hunger for a wholesome broth after a diet of sweetmeats, but she fought it away. The solemn facade she'd created after so much youthful training remained in place, and she said, "I would not dream of offering you my advice. I am only a lowly woman, and you are the king of England."

"You do remember," he said. "Then listen well, Alisoun of George's Cross. For husband, I give you Simon, earl of Goodney. Can you think of a more suitable mate?"

Unfortunately, she couldn't. Simon of Goodney carried his nobility, his wealth, and his responsibilities well. A distinguished man and a recent widower, Lord Simon held lands in Poitou where the king wished to strengthen his ties.

She'd been paired with him at the table. She'd listened to his nasal voice. Her stomach had churned when he'd breathed and chewed through his open mouth. She'd seen the food which encrusted his eating knife. And she'd dirtied her eating knife with a drop of his blood when he'd groped her breast with his filthy fingers.

Nevertheless, she knew where her duty lay. Regardless of her feelings, she had to protect George's Cross, and a husband would be an asset. More, this precarious and dangerous situation which plagued her would surely vanish in a husband's custody.

But a husband would also increase the possibility of discovery and the chance she would be unable to fulfill her vow. Dread ran in her veins, but, God help her, she could see no relief from her dilemma. "The earl of Goodney is indeed a fitting husband for me, and I thank you for consideration."

"Does that mean you'll not chase him away?" the king demanded.

"Chase him away? I do not understand."

"Five men I've sent to you." King Henry struck the arm of his chair. "Five! And not one has been able to withstand your lashing tongue." When she would have spoken, he pointed his finger into her face. "One even went on Crusade and never returned."

"He was not worthy."

"And the other four?"

"They were not worthy, either." When he would have spoken, she swept over his objection. "My liege, I am no green stalk of wheat who wavers in the contrary breeze."

He seemed to ponder that. "That's true. You're more like a stalk of yellow wheat stiff with overripe grains."

"Exactly." She congratulated him on his apt simile,

then frowned at the stifled giggles that sounded from the crowd. What did the foolish creatures find so amusing?

"How old are you now?" Osbern slipped the question in like a thin knife through her ribs.

She ignored him. It was rude of him to step between her and the king in their conversation. Rude, typical and . . . menacing.

"She's twenty-six." King Henry answered for her. "The oldest widowed virgin in England, and probably the Continent."

Charm oozed from Osbern's dashing figure, giving him a sheen most men envied. His short dark hair shone almost purple, like a blackbird's wing. His blue eyes blazed with the heat of interest. His sleek body rippled with muscle when he moved, and when he smiled at Alisoun.

Dear Lord, how she hated him. Hated him, and feared him.

"Not still a virgin, surely," he said.

King Henry froze, then turned slowly to face his cousin. "Do you have personal knowledge of this?"

In that drawling, detestable tone, he said, "Personal knowledge of the Lady Alisoun would be—"

"Death." King Henry interrupted. "I would kill the man who claimed to have deflowered the finest example of English womanhood."

Osbern didn't move. Only his eyes moved, flicking from King Henry to Alisoun and back again, and she saw realization dawn. His desire to insult and implicate her had taken him beyond the bounds of courtesy and into the realm of royal displeasure. He might be Henry's elder by five years, but Henry was the king and now Osbern would have to scrape. With the grace that characterized his every movement, he swept a bow to

Alisoun, a bow that somehow included King Henry and the whole court. "No doubt the Lady Alisoun is yet fit to bear the very symbols of purity which distinguish the Virgin Mary herself, and I would fight the man who insinuated otherwise."

King Henry seemed to accept the apology, but Alisoun did not. How could she? She had guarded her reputation and her virtue as a sacred trust, and her name would now be on the lips of the gossips because of one short visit to the court. A mere apology could not wipe the stain away.

But she had been too well trained to waste time mourning what couldn't be mended. Instead, she answered the king. "Five men you have ordered me to wed, my liege, but I am a mature woman with simple requirements of my spouse, requirements which have not wavered through the years of my widowhood. I am a noblewoman of royal descent, so my husband must be noble. My wealth is considerable, so my husband must be wealthy. I am responsible and dedicated to maintaining my wealth and position, so my husband must be equally dutiful. I tested those men who were noble and wealthy to see if they could be molded into fit and responsible mates. Invariably, they fled, but Simon, earl of Goodney will show his nobility by his consistency. I thank you, my liege, for—"

Running footsteps interrupted her. Before Alisoun could see him, she could hear him—Simon of Goodney, shouting in nasal tones, "Stop. My liege, stop! I refuse! I will not marry that woman."

3

The damned witless woman had left without him.

David stood in the common room of the Crowing Cock Inn, cursing all women and Alisoun of George's Cross in particular. He'd learned from his wife what idiots they were, but yesterday Alisoun had behaved like an average, rational person. Like a *man*.

Now here he stood with her money in his pocket and no way to deliver his services.

Well, if she didn't want him, he wasn't going to chase after her. True, she'd said dawn, and some might even say the sun was now approaching its zenith. But Lady Alisoun ought to realize that when a man drank as much as he had the day before, it would take time to sleep it off. Aye, how could he attend the silly woman with a head that ached and a stomach that rebelled? He'd been doing her a favor by hugging his pillow this morning. Furious, he swung his leg over the bench by a table and bellowed, "Bread!"

A girl scurried to do his bidding while her innkeeper-father watched with approval. "Will ye be needing more than bread?" the man asked. "We have a hearty venison stew."

David looked around the Crowing Cock Inn. No dark, louse-ridden inn would do for Lady Alisoun. She stayed with the best and no doubt thought she deserved it. "Aye," he snarled. "I'll have a bowl, and some fine cheese as well."

"At once, sir." The innkeeper himself brought the cheese while the girl presented the bowl. The innkeeper examined David. "Godric, master of this house, at yer service. Ye're Sir David of Radcliffe."

Ah, they still remembered him in the streets. David preened until Godric added, "Ye're Lady Alisoun's mercenary, are ye not?"

David stopped his spoon just inches from his open lips. "Lady Alisoun's mercenary?" He slammed the spoon onto the table and stood up. "Lady *Alisoun's* mercenary? I'm my own man, and no woman owns me." Glaring around him at the nearly empty common room, he saw the serving girl cower and Godric wring his hands.

"Of course, sir. Foolish of me, sir."

"That's better." David started to sit, discovered halfway down he'd knocked the bench over when he'd stood, and barely caught himself before his arse hit the ground.

Godric raced up and settled the bench beneath David, all the while muttering, "Dreadful seat. Horribly unsturdy. Should have had it fixed." He waited until David had inhaled several bites of the stew before he asked anxiously, "You won't tell my lady Alisoun that I displeased ye, will ye?"

David wanted to spit the concoction at the stupid

man. Then he faced the truth, swallowed and sighed. He'd been thrown out of lesser inns than this with just one look at his clothing. Godric should have done the same, or at the least demanded to see his coin before he served him. So it had to be Lady Alisoun's influence. "Why'd she leave so early?" David asked gruffly.

Godric winced. "She didn't show it, of course, but I believe my lady felt uncomfortable crossing the tap-room yester evening. I tried to discourage the gossip, but the mortification must have been more than she could bear." He nodded sagely. "What woman wouldn't be chagrined?"

Obviously, Godric thought David held her confidence, and David hesitated to disillusion him. So he nodded back just as sagely and stuffed bread into his mouth.

"To be rejected so rudely!" Godric tutted. "And in front of all the court."

Perking up at the thought of Lady Alisoun being taken down a peg, David chewed and swallowed. "And by whom? A nobody, that's who."

Startled, Godric protested, "I wouldn't call him a nobody. Simon *is* earl of Goodney, with so much gold in his possession he has cobwebs over the coins, and he has a pedigree to make our sovereign blush. But that he should refuse King Henry's order to wed the fair lady makes him nothing more than a pestilent knave."

"By the saints." David was awed. "Simon of Goodney refused her." Godric flinched at David's surprise, and David spoke hastily to ease his sudden suspicion. "I still can scarcely credit it, with him as thrifty as a Spaniard with a bottle of port."

"Oh, aye." Godric plucked the towel that hung from his belt and polished the table. "'Tis a fact well known among innkeepers."

"What about her other suitor?" When Godric looked confused, David explained, "The one who plots to abduct her. Did you hear how he reacted to Simon's disclaimer?"

"I hadn't heard of Lady Alisoun's other suitor." Godric leaned closer. "Who is it?"

Good question, and one that Godric obviously couldn't answer. David would have to find out another way. Acting virtuous, he said, "If it's not common knowledge, mayhap my lady prefers to keep it that way."

Disappointed, Godric drew back and David returned his attention to the bowl. Ever the clever innkeeper, Godric retreated to leave him at peace, and as David's stomach filled, his honor twitched to life.

Lady Alisoun had given him gold coin. He had taken it, and she did have the right to name the time and place he should fulfill his obligation. By the sound of it, she might have waited for him if not for Simon of Goodney. He supposed he should roar with merriment that the lofty Lady Alisoun had been humiliated, but he'd had his own encounter with the great Lord Simon and knew the extent of his conceit. "In fact," he murmured into the empty bowl, "if Simon of Goodney refused her, that's a strike in her favor."

"Quite right, Sir David." Hovering close as David finished, Godric whisked the bowl away and presented a dish of water.

David looked at it suspiciously, but when Godric indicated he should wash his fingers, he did so. After all, he *had* learned manners when he'd been at court as the king's champion. It had just been long since he'd had to utilize them.

Godric handed him a towel. "One must suppose she is too fine for the likes of him."

Rising much refreshed, David scratched at his belly

and stretched. "Have your stable boys bring my destrier. I'll ride after Lady Alisoun now."

"She'll be well protected with you at her side."

Godric's flattened, outthrust palm appeared in the periphery of David's vision, and David thrust a coin in it. Godric impressed David when he didn't bite it to ascertain its authenticity, but slipped it into his purse where it clanked with its mates. Oh, to be able to stay at such an inn! To afford its luxuries for his daughter! He coveted Lady Alisoun's privileges, coveted them mightily.

Godric said, "I worried when she left with those carts, laden as they were with the purchases she had made, but your presence will set my mind at ease."

"How many carts?" David asked.

"Three."

"Three!"

Godric peered at him. "Lady Alisoun is efficient. She combined her homage to the king with her twice-yearly buying trip."

David shook his head. "Women."

Godric straightened and for the first time exhibited a little manly impatience. "Aye. Women."

In the yard of the inn, two boys clung to the stallion's reins while Louis tossed his head. One of them went flying and the other's eyes grew big as he rode the leather strap. David caught the reins in his own grip and brought the warhorse to a standstill. The still-clinging stable boy dropped to the ground like a flea off a dog while the other scrambled out of the dirt and harm's way.

Looking up into Louis's magnificent face, David explained, "We have to join Lady Alisoun."

With his normal good sense, Louis tossed his head and neighed, then tried to leap backward. David hung onto the reins and swore, taking his bad temper out on the horse with the comfortable security of knowing that the horse would return the favor.

King Louis hadn't always been so capricious. In his younger days, the massive white stallion had been part of the legend of David. Unfledged knights related the story of how David had named his destrier after the French king, which so enraged the English-bred animal he had battled to establish his good standing and thus secured in the annals of history.

But six years of relative inactivity had left him with the attitude that tournament and combat were for younger horses. He wanted the comforts of his own stall. He preferred to have his personal stableboys caring for him, and he resented being called to duty when he should be lauded for his past glories.

All in all, Louis had much in common with his master.

Since David had ridden him to Lancaster, Louis showed his hostility by refusing to be mastered even by the one he adored. David had tried reasoning with him, but most of the time both of them had resorted to brute force.

Like now. David whacked Louis on the shoulder. Louis caught him a glancing blow to the shin. David's high, heavy leather boot protected him from serious injury, but he swore and danced around while Louis bared his teeth in a grin. Then, satisfied, the stallion allowed David on his back. With a wave at Godric, David rode Louis north toward George's Cross.

David knew the well-traveled road. How could he not? George's Cross was considered the last bastion of civilization in the wilderness of fells and woods on the Irish Sea. His beloved Radcliffe was beyond that civilization, and David had had to ride through George's Cross on his way south to Lancaster. Fishermen, sheep, and merchants had mingled in the prosperous hamlet.

He had looked—he looked hard—but saw little evidence of the two-year drought which had wiped him out. Perhaps the drought had been less virulent farther south; perhaps the people of George's Cross had had a cushion of plenty on which to fall back. He was glad to be going there, but at the same time envy gnawed at him.

Lady Alisoun had inherited George's Cross and other estates from her parents, then inherited the dower's portion of her husband's estates when he died. David hadn't inherited anything from his parents but an old shield and sword and an order to go out and make his way in the world, and while his wife had brought him his lands through the marriage settlement—a more whiny, frightened rabbit of a woman he'd never met. He'd suffered for every acre.

Now he was going to protect another whiny, frightened woman. True, yesterday she hadn't seemed so, but she must be flighty or she'd have not left him chasing after her with a pocketful of her gold. When a man dipped deep into the well of ale, he didn't leap to greet the day. She should understand that.

He remembered the austere, emotionless features she'd displayed the day before.

Then again, she wouldn't understand. Maybe a woman like her was used to being obeyed. Maybe a woman like her . . . by the saints, he didn't want to work for a woman like her. He just wanted to ride through George's Cross and on to Radcliffe Castle, where his daughter and his people waited. He shuddered briefly as he fought the need to see Bert's thin face light up when she saw her daddy. Louis, too, shuddered as if he comprehended, and picked up his pace. "Nay, good fellow," David said aloud. "We've got a bargain to keep, even if we have to chase after the frivolous wimple-wearer to keep it."

Louis sighed, a long, horsey exhalation, then lifted his head and neighed. A neigh answered him, and David realized that over the next hill someone else journeyed—Lady Alisoun and her escort, he hoped. But if he was unlucky, it would be road robbers, and he'd have to smash them to perdition. Loosening his sword from its scabbard, he grinned. He could use a good fight, especially one that he could win.

He placed his basinet helmet on his head, brought his shield forward, and leaned into the saddle. The big horse understood his desire and slipped into a canter. Louis might pretend to be surly, but his curiosity and confidence were as great as his master's. Topping the rise, David saw not robbers but three heavily laden carts laboring along the wooded road. Massive oxen stirred up the summer's dust as they strained to pull their loads. Their drivers walked beside their heads, poles in their hands. But nowhere did David see Lady Alisoun or her men-at-arms.

"Sweet mother of God!" Sure that calamity had found Lady Alisoun, he spurred Louis on and caught up to the carts just as they reached the ford of a brook. "Hey!" he shouted.

"Halt!" he heard from behind.

He twisted in the saddle and stared. In the shadow of the trees, two helmeted knights sat on their horses in battle-ready gear. One held a lance, one held a mace, and David's heart sank. No doubt Lady Alisoun had already been robbed and murdered by these two renegade knights. God help him, he'd lost the moneyed goose before he'd grasped more than a few feathers. He eyed the sharp point of the lance. And if he wasn't careful, he'd lose those feathers, too.

Without warning, he spurred Louis. The great horse leaped from full stop to full speed in the blink of an eye.

David shrieked his war cry as he barreled between the two knights, knocking the lance holder to the ground with his shield and swinging his sword into empty air as the other ducked and yipped.

The expert assault David expected hadn't materialized, and the momentum of his forward rush took him into the dense wood. "Idiots," he growled, struggling to find a place to turn Louis. "They're not knights. Must have stolen it all. Come on, Louis, we've got to—"

"Don't."

The woman's voice stopped him in his tracks. He knew that voice. His ribs ached with the memory. "Lady Alisoun?"

The underbrush rustled and, calm as a nun, the lady stepped forward. "Sir David. I thought you had abandoned us."

She was here. God in heaven, those were her carts, and she'd been in the hands of those villains for who knew how long. "Have they hurt you?" he demanded. Her slender beauty appeared unruffled. Her green velvet riding cloak fell in even folds from her shoulders, her hat curved over her head, and her draped wimple held it in place. Not a strand of hair slipped out of its restraint, and no tears marred the purity of her complexion. Nevertheless, guilt caught at David's throat. If he'd gotten to the inn sooner . . . if he'd skipped the meal . . . if he'd ridden faster . . . God forgive him, he'd failed her. He knew full well what fate awaited her if he failed once more. "I'll save you."

"Save me from what?" She glanced toward the road.

He guided Louis in a tight circle.

"From Ivo and Gunnewate?" she asked.

He'd already prepared himself to charge when her words penetrated. "Ivo and . . . your men-at-arms?"

"The very same." With the deliberation that marked

all her movements, she disappeared again, then returned leading a palfrey. In a tone of censure, she asked, "Who else would guard me? You failed to arrive at dawn."

"I failed to arrive at dawn," he repeated calmly. Too calmly, if she had but known.

"When I give an order, I expect to have it obeyed. If you are going to be my man, David of Radcliffe, you must do as I say."

He removed his gloves and urged Louis toward her at a walk. "So you left the Crowing Cock Inn to teach me a lesson?"

She hesitated, then inclined her head. "You might say I am not unhappy to have accomplished that, too."

He tried to contain himself. He really did. But this . . . this woman had made him feel guilty. For nothing! She'd never been in danger. She'd been in command at all times, and he'd been charging around like a half-wit. "*Me*, a lesson? And if I were a thief and a murderer, my lady, who do you think would have learned that lesson?" She tried to speak, but he leaned far out of the saddle and caught her under the chin. Lifting her face, he glared down at her. "I just proved that a seasoned knight is more than a match for your puny bodyguards, and there *are* knights who prowl the roads. They would have taken your goods, killed your men, raped your body, and strung your intestines across a tree." He let her go and shoved his hand back into his glove in one savage motion.

She touched her chin where the marks of his fingers showed on her fair skin. "I see."

"Those men would make your fear of abduction by a suitor look tame. Next time you hire a mercenary, wait for him."

"Aye, of course."

"What would it have hurt you to wait? Or to send one of your servants for me?"

"It seems my judgment was at fault." She mounted her palfrey, urged it toward him, and stopped at his side. Looking right into his eyes with her cool gray eyes, she said, "Forgive me, David of Radcliffe."

As she moved toward the light of the road, he stared after her. She'd taken his rebuke so well! She'd weighed his complaint, analyzed his logic, and without making excuses, agreed that she'd acted foolishly. Then, just like that, she'd apologized, sincerely and pleasantly. He pursed his lips in a silent whistle. No wonder she hadn't wed again. Every man in England must tremble when confronted with her sensible attitude, for she made it very difficult for a man to feel superior.

"Ivo," she called. "Gunnewate! Pick yourselves up off the ground and let's move along. If we're to make George's Cross in only four days, we'll have to use every moment of sunlight."

David rode out of the woods to see Ivo trying to hoist the armor-clad Gunnewate onto his feet. He guided Louis around the two men. The steel clanked, out-of-tune notes against the harmony of the forest.

"Hurry!" Alisoun clapped her hands lightly, her leather riding gloves muffling the sound. "The carts have gone ahead and as Sir David aptly demonstrated, we're vulnerable to attack."

Smiling, David lingered behind and told them, "Aye, you'd best hurry, my good fellows. The way you're lolling around here, you'd think a knight's armor weighs eight stone." Setting Louis in motion, he called back, "It can't weigh more than five."

He chortled at the cursing he heard, then galloped ahead. Alisoun had reached the creeping carts and now moved along beside them, seeking the open road where the dust would not bother her. Following her, David spoke to her drivers as he passed them. The surly peasants stared as if they'd never heard a nobleman who could converse in their vulgar English language. He spoke again, wanting them to answer, knowing that in this possibly hazardous situation he might have use for their strength and their stout poles. Each tugged on their forelocks and muttered greetings, and he counted that brief communication as a success. Then he rode to join Alisoun and said, "My lady, your men-at-arms are not knights, so why do you let them cavort in knight's armor?"

She cast him a troubled glance. "They do not carry the armor well, I know, but my chief knight, Sir Walter, remained behind at George's Cross as a safeguard against whatever trouble might be brewing. Two of my mercenary knights, John of Beauchamp and Lothair of Hohenstaufen, accompanied me to Lancaster, but they spoke of receiving a better offer while in the town." She lowered her voice. "Apparently, they accepted it, for they failed to return to the inn two days ago, and they took six of my men-at-arms with them."

"That's what you get for hiring a German mercenary. They're an unsavory lot, good for nothing but slitting your throat while you sleep." He ran a finger across his neck as an illustration. "But . . . John of Beauchamp? I've fought alongside John. He's a good man. I can't believe he'd abandon his pledged lady until he'd finished his obligation."

"Yes." She turned in the saddle and examined the carts as if she could protect them with her gaze. "So I thought, also."

"Did you—" He hesitated. Did she search for John? How did a lady search for a mercenary? Visit the alehouses and lift every drunkard's head? She'd done that with him, but—

"I sent Ivo to look for John and my men, but he heard a tale that they had all ridden for Wolston with their new master." She shrugged, an elegant lift of the shoulders. "It's difficult, sometimes, for a mercenary to take orders from a woman."

"Aye." David had sympathy for that, and he scratched the half-grown beard that prickled his skin. "So you dressed Ivo and Gunnewate up in armor. Where did you get the armor?"

"One suit is mine for one of the squires in my household. He'll soon earn his spurs, and I outfit all the boys I have fostered."

Impressed in spite of himself, David said, "That's good of you."

"The other . . . Ivo found it." She watched the road intently. "It's John's."

Pulling Louis in front of Alisoun's horse, David grabbed the reins close to the palfrey's mouth. They halted in the middle of the track, and he said, "There's foul play."

"So I suspect."

"John would never leave his armor. Do you know what a full suit costs?"

"I just said I had purchased one."

"It's too expensive for a landless knight to abandon."

"Much too expensive."

The serenity of her expression never changed. Her demeanor never changed. She had all the vivacity of a stone statue on Ripon Cathedral, and he swore long and eloquently. "Don't you care that a good man in your employ has probably been murdered?"

"'Tis a misdeed I deplore deeply, and I lit candles in his name, praying for his safe return and his soul, should it have departed this earth." She controlled her horse easily, her gloved hands light on the reins. "What else would you have me do?"

He didn't say it, but he thought, *Wail a little. Wipe a tear from your eye. At the least, profess terror for your own safety.* But that was stupid, and he knew it. He abhorred women who behaved so melodramatically, and he didn't want to be saddled with one now.

"The carts will be on us if we don't proceed," Alisoun reminded him.

He released her horse and they moved along the road. It wound upward now, going deeper into the wilds of Northumbria. Englishmen spoke of this area— the looming Cumbrian Mountains, the wild strips of beach along the coast—as barren, frightful, forbidding. While it could be harsh, given to sudden fogs and ocean storms, it also gave great gifts to those who dared to challenge it. Lofty moors fed herds of sheep, the forest provided game and fuel, and the sea gave up its bounty on a regular basis. Until the drought, David had been adding comforts to his tiny castle, bringing new breeding stock in for his peasants. Now his crops were withered, his stock and his peasants dead or dying, his daughter . . . he couldn't think of his daughter and her pinched cheeks.

"Why didn't you hire someone else when your men disappeared?" he demanded.

She flashed him a look of disdain. "I thought I had."

Gaining sympathy for the missing mercenaries, David wished again another post had presented itself. Still, he was lucky to have one at all, so he applied his equanimity with Herculean restraint. "I meant three days ago. True, you hired me, but surely even you can see that one knight is insufficient to defend three carts and a marriageable widow."

"No other knights were available."

He couldn't believe she would use such a lame excuse. "No other knights? Lady, there are always younger sons, men who seek employment to fill their bellies lest they starve." They reached the top of the rise, and he used the height to look both forward and back. "I know. I was one."

"None were interested in coming to George's Cross," she answered steadily.

In a hurry to reclaim their positions as defenders of their mistress, Ivo and Gunnewate galloped up the road after the carts. David grinned, knowing how their defeat, especially to him, must eat at them. Satisfied that this stretch of road, at least, was safe, David turned back to Alisoun. "You must not have asked the right men."

"Perhaps not."

As before, her expression never changed, her voice retained its calm, low vibrancy, but somehow, he thought she was . . . worried? Afraid? Straightening, he studied her again. Why did he think such a thing? What had he seen? She met his gaze confidently, but her eyes . . . didn't they have a sheen? Hadn't the gray color darkened just a little?

And to think he'd longed for a woman who didn't wail with every passing emotion. Comprehending this woman took concentration. He had to try and wiggle through the complex byways of her woman's brain. That was a warrior's nightmare, but she told him nothing, so he had to *think*.

Why would she be apprehensive? She'd lost her men, possibly through foul play. No other knight would hire on with her. Yet she paid well. He knew that from personal experience. He knew, too, that money, freely spread around, eased the sting of working for a woman.

Something wasn't right. Only a very influential man could make it impossible for her to hire other mercenaries. Thoughtfully, he observed while she directed Ivo and Gunnewate to ride behind the carts and protect the rear, then instructed him to continue his surveillance.

She'd never admitted to having a suitor, and no shrewd man who sought a wealthy wife would put her on her guard by stealing and murdering her men one at a time. So perhaps his first surmise had been wrong.

"You must have offended a dread lord." He waited for her to explain, knowing that women loved to talk about their troubles.

She ignored him.

He tried an unjust accusation. "You were probably flirting with him, then refused him. Women like to make men suffer like that."

Glaring, she opened her mouth.

But some of his triumph must have shone through, for she shut it again and sealed her lips firmly.

Finally, he appealed to her good sense. "It would help if I knew how and why you were threatened. Are we likely to be overwhelmed by a large force?"

"Nay." She gave up that information grudgingly. "If anything, there will be a small force, but usually this creature prefers to perform his deeds alone."

"Has he tried to kill you?"

"If he wished to kill me I would be dead. Nay, this beast stalks for pleasure, to invoke fear and loathing."

And she did loathe the man, whoever he was. That slight curl of the lip looked like blatant emotion on Alisoun's still face, and David congratulated himself on reading her so well. "He's doing a good job, in sooth, but I still want to know—"

She interrupted him. "Your job is to keep me safe, not to indulge in ineffectual speculation. If you must know more to properly perform your duties, then return the gold at once and be on your way."

By Saint Michael's arm, she was a cold and ruthless

she-demon! But—he fingered the leather pouch which held the precious coins—for this money he would do as bid. At least for the moment.

Sarcastically, he pulled his forelock. "As you say, my lady. You are always right."

4

Alisoun was awake again. David stared toward the hammock strung between two trees. The hemp creaked as she carefully turned away from him and toward the deeper woods. She'd done the same thing the last two nights, shifting back and forth while taking care not to wake anyone. Unfortunately, as he slipped into his role as guardian, he woke with her every movement. Last night he had blamed her restlessness on discomfort from the saddle or an inability to sleep out-of-doors, but tonight he could no longer deceive himself. She didn't trust him to keep watch.

She lifted her head. He lifted his, too, and scanned the area. Nothing. Just darkness filled with the creak of windblown trees, the growls and squeaks of nocturnal creatures, and the rumble of Ivo's snoring.

Cautiously, she sat up. He sat up, too. No moon lightened the night, the trees' canopy masked the starlight, yet he could still make out the glow of her hair. He had been surprised to discover that she removed her wimple and loosened her braids to sleep. His wife had been most insistent that ladies never revealed their crowning glory. Of course, Mary had quickly discovered that a woman's unfettered locks brought on his lustful desires, and she'd done anything to avoid that.

After they had conceived their daughter, he'd done everything to avoid it, too. Not even the prospect of another baby to cherish could overcome his distaste for bedding a woman who increasingly looked like a molting duck and smelled like its favorite grub.

Alisoun had simply rubbed her bare head with her hands as if she reveled in the freedom, and after all, who could see her in the dark? Only David, and he'd had to strain.

Swinging her legs out of the hammock, she stood, facing away from him. He called softly, "What do you fear, Lady Alisoun?"

She jumped and turned, tangling in her own skirt and stumbling into the hammock.

He rose and walked toward her. "I assure you, I've kept my ear to the ground and heard nothing."

She righted herself, then with a composure he couldn't help but admire, she whispered, "I'm worried about my carts."

He didn't believe that for a moment. Because of their weight, the carts couldn't be moved far from the road, yet she left only Gunnewate to guard them, bringing Ivo and David with her to the site deeper in the forest. She forbade a fire, preferring to eat a cold meal of wheat cakes and cheese. And now she couldn't sleep.

No matter that he'd observed no sign of pursuit. No matter that the only faces he'd seen were those of the people in his party. Alisoun's increasing tension had honed his infirm skills. If only she would trust him to do his job, but already he realized the lady Alisoun of George's Cross perpetually took responsibility for everything and everybody.

"I thought I heard a branch crack," she admitted.

This sign of weakness in her reassured him. She was a woman like any other, then. She imagined threats where none existed and required reassurance when there was no need. He barely realized what he did when he reached out and patted her hair, then smoothed it as he would have a dog's. "My lady, dangerous beasts inhabit this wood, but no men. I've been alert. I'll protect you."

Her fist knocked his hand away, and her voice cracked like a whip over his head. "Do you think this is amusing?"

Bringing his arm close against his chest, he rubbed the sting of her blow. "Nay, my lady, I simply sought to allay your alarm."

"Don't patronize me."

He jerked in reaction. He didn't doubt her animosity. He'd learned, more than once in these last two days, that she could strip a man of pride, of dignity, of sense with a few well-chosen words. Ivo and Gunnewate remained stoic under the lash of her tongue. The oxen drivers seemed to expect insult. But a pox on her! She couldn't talk to him, the king's former champion, that way.

He turned away and walked back toward his mat. "Fretful and nervous," he muttered, loudly enough for her to hear. She didn't reply, and he kicked the mat and ruffled the blankets in a blatant display of annoyance. Shoving the log he used as a pillow into place, he lay down, turned his back to her, and closed his eyes.

The silence assaulted his ears. Their conversation and his noisy displeasure had quelled the sounds of nighttime creatures and woken Ivo, who no longer snored, but breathed long and regularly. Ivo waited, no doubt, to hear any further quarrel between his mistress and the man he clearly considered unworthy to serve her.

They were all waiting. What was Alisoun doing? David didn't hear a sound from her hammock.

He didn't hear her move at all. Did she still stand where he'd left her? Was she still looking, straining to hear the sound of attack? What kind of man would make a woman so afraid? For afraid she was, and as the silence continued, David began to make excuses for her.

So what if she stripped a man of his pride? She was a woman, and a woman's only weapon was words. And in a way, he could understand her displeasure. She'd accused him of patronizing her, and he had. He'd treated her like a child in need of comfort, when she was a woman who sought an honest resolution for her worries. Moreover, he was strong, dignified, made in God's image. A real man didn't flinch when a woman pouted or reproached. A real man reassured a woman, made her feel safe. David was a real man.

Opening his pack, he found the length of rope he kept with him always, then stood and walked back toward the hammock. Kneeling, he tied a knot around one of the smaller trees at about knee height. Then, uncoiling the rope as he walked backward, he circled another one of the trees that surrounded her. Taking a right angle from the first side, he crossed to another tree, then another, forming a square around the hammock where she slept.

"What are you doing?" Alisoun's perfectly modulated voice sounded only distantly curious.

"Any man who tries to reach you will fail to see this rope. He'll trip and wake everyone, and I'll be on him at once. It's an old trick, one I've used to protect myself for years."

"I see. That is clever."

He tied the last knot, then stood up. Straining to see the expression on her face, he said, "So won't you lie down and sleep, my lady? You'll be safe now."

Carefully, she lowered herself onto the hammock.

He watched her and brushed his hands in satisfaction. "Nothing can get you now."

"I feel safe," she acknowledged.

She reached for the rug which had previously covered her. It had fallen to the ground, a dark lump beyond her reach, and the hammock teetered precariously as she strained for it. He reached for it, too, grabbing it before she could topple, and shook it out. "If I may?" He didn't wait for permission, but spread the rug over her legs and tucked it around her feet. Her hand groped for the edge to bring it around her shoulders, and he brushed her fingers aside. Slowly, taking care to respect her person, he carried the fine woven wool up and over. Her skin warmed him when he folded it over her neck. The scars and calluses of his palm snagged her hair and clung when he tried to free himself.

She stayed still, her breath regular and deep. He could see her eyes glistening as he stood over her, and they widened when he gathered the wandering strands of hair into a bunch. He strained to see the color. Blond, he supposed. It had to be blond—pale, washed out, colorless.

But each strand seemed dyed with fire.

He looked back at her. Red? He dropped the hair as if it burned him. Not red, surely. No doubt, the feeble starlight tricked his eye. He cleared his throat. He ought to go back to bed, but he liked this sensation of accomplishment. "It took a real man to make it so safe for you."

"God bless you for your kind thought."

He warmed, wondering if God responded to her

request with the same esteem everyone else showed her. Then he laughed at himself for his nonsense. The woman might have her men-at-arms completely cowed, but she'd had no mystical effect on God—or on him. "Aye." He plucked the rope to make sure the tension would indeed snag a man. "I only use this when I sleep alone or with men I have reason to distrust. The rest of the time I credit my senses, but I can see that a woman would gain comfort from the rope. I'm glad I thought of it."

"I'm glad, too," she said.

"So just go to sleep—"

Ivo snorted, a huge, moist explosion of exasperation. "How can m'lady go t' sleep wi' ye blatherin' on? Stop praisin' yerself an' get back t' yer pallet."

David was insulted. "I'm not answerable to you, my man. Lady Alisoun extends her thanks for my protection and I gratefully accept them."

He'd lifted one foot over the rope to step away when Ivo snapped, "Aye, that rope'll preserve her if she's attacked, but it'll do naught against another arrow aimed at her heart, will it?"

David's foot dipped, caught, and tangled, and he went over with a crash that shook the very earth.

The village of George's Cross looked like heaven to Alisoun. Nestled in a valley not far from the sea, it surrounded a square big enough to hold a market every Lammas Day. Her people cheered as she rode through the streets, and she knew without conceit they cheered more than the contents of the carts which followed far behind. Her people loved her—unlike a certain mercenary who clearly had violence on his mind.

As she entered the square, the people crowded in on them. Ivo and Gunnewate dropped back. The carts appeared to be dots on the road behind them. Only David clung close as a burr on a wool fringe as her people surrounded her. He even tried to block Fenchel when he made his way forward, but she laid her hand on David's arm and shook her head.

"You know him?" David asked.

"He's the village reeve," she answered. David considered the skinny, balding little man and apparently decided he exuded no threat, for he moved aside and allowed Fenchel to approach.

"Fenchel, how goes the shearing?" she asked in English, her tone warm to make up for David's rude challenge.

Fenchel snatched his hat from his head and bowed almost double, replying in English also. "'Tis just over, m'lady. The fleeces are breathin' in the wool rooms all over the village."

"The fleeces are still warm after shearing," she explained to David. "If the night is cold, the fleeces may stir all night long."

"I know, Lady Alisoun. I, also, produce wool on my small estate."

"Of course. I meant no offense," she replied.

David scowled, but he had been scowling for a whole day now, ever since Ivo had opened his big, dumb mouth and plainly told him that an arrow had been shot at her. Lady Alisoun loved Ivo, but he'd created trouble this time, and she'd had to rebuke him. He'd hung his head and not tried to defend himself, and she'd released him after one sharp phrase. How could she not? She understood Ivo's impatience with David much better than she understood David's unexpected nocturnal eloquence. She would have called it moon madness, but there'd been no moon. There'd been no warning that the taciturn man who had taken her to task for leaving herself undefended would suddenly develop such a high opinion of himself. If she didn't know better, she would have thought he had wanted to linger in her vicinity; but why, she couldn't imagine. By Saint Ethelred, he'd even covered her with her rug.

She glanced at his impatient expression. Usually she understood men only too well, and it fretted her to have one who occasionally escaped definition.

Worse, she didn't quite understand herself. There had been a stirring in her when he covered her with the rug. A stirring she'd experienced so seldom in her life, she didn't quite know how to define it. She thought it might be tenderness. Maybe even a tendril of errant affection.

And for a mercenary! For a man she'd hired. Most women wouldn't even have noticed this warmth called affection, but for Alisoun, this revelation almost shook the ground.

Still, she comforted herself it wasn't Sir David who had caused such a reaction. It was only her own solitary heart.

"M'lady?"

Fenchel's wide eyes reminded her of her duty, and she smoothed the expression from her face. "Aye, Fenchel?"

"We'll be packin' the wool when 'tis cold, an' I estimate twelve sacks fer market."

"Another off year." She sighed, then looked curiously at David when she heard him choke. "Are you well, Sir David?"

He nodded, his face ruddy and his eyes bulging.

"Get Sir David a drink from the well," she said to one of the women. Avina hurried to obey, and Alisoun pitched her voice so all could hear. "You've done well, considering the drought."

"Ah, but it rained one day ye were gone." Fenchel's

rheumy eyes shone with suppressed excitement. "'Tis a good sign."

"A very good sign," Alisoun agreed. "Was the weeding finished?"

"The corn's clear," Fenchel assured her as he watched David guzzle the water. "Except fer the bindweed, an' we'll get that when we thresh."

"Has the haying begun?" she asked.

"Fair 'til nightfall."

"Excellent." In her mind, she calculated the profits. The drought had impacted them, but not so much as the lesser landowners, and with the grain she had bought, they should make it through until autumn and the harvest.

Fenchel continued, "The signs point to a good weather year, so we'll fill the barns an' we'll not have t'—"

"Twelve sacks?" David croaked.

Fenchel and Alisoun turned to David.

He took another gulp of water from the ladle that he held and cleared his throat. "Did you say twelve sacks of wool to market?"

Fenchel and Alisoun exchanged comprehending glances. Woolsacks were huge, so big that wool packers stepped into them to skilfully stomp the fleeces into place. Woolsacks bulged under pressure, for as the last layer was thrown in, the wool packers trod it down and stepped out backward along the top, sewing up the sack as they went. They weighed so much and were so cumbersome, they were hauled in wagons, safe from thieves, for they were too cumbersome to steal. A small landowner might produce two woolsacks, so David's bulging eyes and avaricious mouth didn't surprise Fenchel and Alisoun. They'd seen this reaction in other men at other times. Suitors that the king sent, knights and lords who visited as they made their way to another destination: they all struggled to comprehend the wealth encompassed by the estate of George's Cross. Alisoun repeatedly found herself courted by men who suddenly saw her personal attractions enhanced by her ample lands. She and Fenchel had dealt with it before. Indeed, they had become almost practiced in their reactions.

Squaring his scrawny shoulders, Fenchel projected a fierce hostility. "Who's askin'?"

"Forgive me, Fenchel, I have been remiss." Alisoun watched David and saw that greed had replaced his antagonism. That, she understood. That, she expected, and she ignored the tiny disappointment that nagged at her. "As my reeve, you should be acquainted with the legendary mercenary Sir David of Radcliffe."

Fenchel should have replied rudely, making his disrespect clear. That was the method by which he and Lady Alisoun taught the unworthies they could not have the lady of George's Cross.

Instead Fenchel stood silent, silent so long she turned to look. Her man—*her* man—stood looking at David of Radcliffe with admiration and awe. "Fenchel?" she said.

He shook himself as if waking from a dream, and spoke to David in tones of reverence. "Forgive me, sir, but *ye* are the legendary mercenary, David o' Radcliffe?"

"That's me," David agreed.

"Oh, sir." Fenchel pressed forward. "Oh, sir! We've told tales o' yer exploits fer years. How ye killed a boar bare-handed when ye were naught but twelve, an' how the king himself knighted ye on the field o' battle when ye held twenty French knights at bay—"

David corrected him. "Sixteen and fifteen."

Fenchel paid no attention. "How ye won the armor an' saddles an' horses o' all the best knights in the kingdom, then sold 'em back fer a pretty profit."

Holding her hand to her heart, Avina interrupted. "All except one, a young knight seekin' t' better himself. Rather than take that poor lad's only possessions, ye gave 'em back an' taught him t' fight, an' he is yer devoted man t' this day."

"Sir Guy of the Archers."

Alisoun saw that Gunhild finished the tale. All the villagers knew the stories about the legendary mercenary David, and all of them stood, wide-eyed, and stared at him as if visitationed from heaven.

"Look!" Fenchel pointed to the sky. "'Twas clear before, but 'tis cloudin' up now. Mayhap Sir David has brought us luck."

Everyone stared at him, then at Alisoun. "In sooth, I do so pray." Privately, Alisoun admitted that she had experienced that same thrill when she met him. Even facedown in the mud, he had had a prestige about him, but somehow, riding with him to George's Cross had lessened her reverence. Now all she could remember was his pride when he had pissed farther and longer than either Ivo or Gunnewate. Just like any other man, he seemed to think she took his measure by the size of his bladder—and extremities.

So her villagers' worship caught her unaware. Seeing them now, seeing how they pressed toward him and touched his boot with reverent fingers, how the women tightened their bodices to plump their bosoms, both embarrassed and infuriated her. David needed no more fuel to feed the fire of his vanity.

Then she caught his eye. Sheepishly, he grinned, shrugged, and said, "Old legends die hard."

And she realized—that's why she'd hired him. To give her people a feeling of confidence, to ease their fears for her. To frighten off that shadowy, unseen menace. In fact, there had been no incidents on this trip.

She knew that for the first time in months, she'd gone three days without the sense of being watched.

For that she owed him more than money, and as graciously as she could, she said, "I offer my home, Sir David. Make it yours."

Stunned by the riches in her demesne, he accepted, all the time fearing he gaped like a roast pig. True, he was nothing but the son of a baron, and a poor baron at that, but he hated feeling so much like a dairy maid before the king. Yet when he thought about Alisoun's twelve sacks of wool, he was in awe. He didn't even have enough carts to haul twelve sacks of wool, much less enough sheep to grow the fleece. Twelve sacks would support his estate for years!

Lady Alisoun smiled at him, a smooth, practiced movement of her lips that conveyed hospitality. Then she spoke to the peasants crowding around him. "I have returned with grain to keep us until harvest." Slowly the crowd turned to her. "When the carts have reached the castle, it will be counted and distributed, but remember, good people, that this must last until we've brought in our own crops, and if this summer is as dry as the last one and the one before that, it will be a hard winter. So take the burden of extra work with good cheer. Let us be sure that not one of our folk is lost to sloth."

Fenchel had regained his good sense, for he called, "Hear, hear!" and the crowd responded.

Then they broke up. Fenchel and Alisoun moved to one side of the square. The men strode toward the fields, the women walked toward the large barnlike structure which held the wool.

Well, most of the women walked toward the shed. Some of them had found something amiss with their clothing. Gunhild held her skirt up, adjusting the garters that held her stockings . . . except she wore no stockings. The sight of her bare leg almost stopped David's heart, and her flirtatious glance made it clear she appreciated his appreciation.

Pish! He tore his gaze away and found it immediately captured by Avina. Her shift seemed uncomfortably adjusted, and she unlaced her bodice and adjusted her breasts with a hand beneath each. They thrust upward and the dark nipples shone through thin—

He jerked on Louis's rein and, disgruntled, Louis jerked back. "She wants to bed a legend," David told him. "She doesn't care about me."

Louis snorted, and David had to agree. His groin ached from long disuse, and Louis knew that David's mood markedly improved with regular swiving. The damned horse danced in place to give David another chance to stare, and David found himself watching the melons that swayed so enticingly.

Alisoun paid him no attention. She didn't care about him. She wouldn't even notice if his glance lingered on the flaunted . . . "Nay!" More forcefully, David directed Louis to move on, and the horse did. Only a fool would gawk at a servant when the mistress was available— especially when the mistress was single and so wealthy her estate produced twelve sacks of wool for market.

After all, it wasn't as if Alisoun were homely. No, indeed. Her face was very . . . attractive. And her figure was acceptable . . . what he had seen of it beneath her voluminous cotte. And her hair flowed down her back like a glimmering river of . . . molten iron? His gaze lingered on the wimple and gorget she always wore just to thwart him. At least it seemed that way. Red. He'd swear he'd seen red in the dark, but how could such a reserved woman sport such an audacious color?

He shook his head. No, it must be bland blond or reserved brown.

As David rode toward Alisoun, Fenchel backed away, veneration manifested in every line of his slight body. Yet Alisoun watched David, and he would have sworn he saw a flash of cynicism.

Blast the woman! He was observing her again, trying to decipher emotion that another woman would have gladly shared.

"My village women are lovely, are they not?" She stared behind him, where Avina and Gunhild still posed, and he had to fight to keep his eyes focused on where he was going. "They admire you a great deal, and if you wish to linger here, you would still be welcome at the castle when you arrive."

"Me?" He widened his eyes in what he hoped was innocence. "I hadn't noticed any individuals among your village women. I only noticed that everyone seemed plump and happy." Remembering Avina's bounteous breasts, he thought, *overflowingly plump.* "It is a tribute to your husbandry that your people are so well fed."

Solemnly, she considered him, then nodded. "My thanks. Without offense, may I assume that your estate has not fared so well?"

His injured pride blazed fiercely. Through stiff lips he said, "You may assume that."

"Perhaps you would care to send one of my men to Radcliffe with the first month's gold you have earned."

You have earned. Not "that I paid you," but *you have earned.* It was a generous offer sensitively put, and that surprised him. She hadn't been overly sensitive about his previous humors—chiding him for his late arrival, yawning when he won the pissing contest, openly doubting his ability to protect her. But for a woman with twelve bags of wool, he could forgive and forget. "That would be most courteous of you, lady. I thank you for your kind thought. I'd be grateful when a man may be spared."

There. That comely speech surely proved his fitness to be her consort. A most peculiar expression marred her features, as if she smelled something nasty. Quickly, he examined the bottoms of his shoes, then glanced back to review Louis's footsteps. Neither of them had stepped in something malodorous.

Her horse moved on before he could ascertain the reason for her expression. "Is your steward to be trusted with such a sum?" she asked.

"Aye, he is." He grinned at her back. "He is Guy of the Archers."

She swung around in the saddle and stared, wide-eyed, clearly astonished. "There is really such a man?"

Well! That *was* a mask she wore. Emotions seethed beneath it. And he'd just proved that he could strip the mask away. "Did you think the legend all lies?"

"Nay, I . . . nay, it is just so very difficult to realize that the legend lives within such a common . . . that is to say, that you are the repository of such extraordinary . . . "

He would have been offended, but he understood. Being a living fable encompassed a difficulty most people could scarcely comprehend. Women lusted after him, sure that his thistle—undoubtedly the largest in the world—would induce ecstasy. Men clung to his every word, gathering insight where none existed. Everyone expected him to be wise and sincere, and he'd learned one thing well—sincerity was hard to fake.

David knew he was just a man, and when others got acquainted with him, they knew it, too. Disillusionment set in, but he was never less than himself and never asked anyone to believe more than the truth.

Alisoun had gone through all the stages, and right now she looked at him through eyes that saw *him*.

She nodded as if they'd said something important in their silence. "I'll send someone right away."

As he rode beside her up the winding track, he concluded that a decisive woman was not all bad. Above them on a hillock, George's Cross Castle rose like a rocky intrusion on the green, misty mountain. The curtain wall snaked around, mossy green and impenetrable gray. On the highest point, lit by the late afternoon sun, the keep rose, a serpent's fang of smooth black stone. The place frightened David—as it was supposed to.

Alisoun beheld it fondly. "Home," she whispered.

She behaved as if George's Cross Castle would protect her, but she'd hired him for more than the ride from Lancaster to the castle. She'd hired him to protect her, even at her beloved home. Because someone had threatened her? Because . . . "What's this tale of an arrow shot at you?"

"An arrow?"

He had hoped to startle her. He hadn't succeeded. If she'd been cool before, now she was glacial. Icy, unemotional, uninterested.

He didn't believe it for a moment. "Ivo blurted it out last night. He was angry because I wasn't prepared to protect you from murder."

"Murder?" Bringing her palfrey to a halt, she turned to face him with a sincerely amused smile playing around her lips.

It aroused his suspicious.

"I love Ivo, I really do. He's been my personal man-at-arms for years. But I'm sure you realize he's a bit weevil-headed, God bless him. He sees danger where there is none. You'll forgive him."

Louis stood taller than the palfrey. David stood higher than Alisoun. Together, the stallion and the man towered over Alisoun and her mount, and it gave him a feeling of superiority. False superiority, he knew. Alisoun hoarded the truth and dispensed only as much as she believed necessary.

"M'lady." A male voice hailed from the top of the curtain wall. "M'lady, ye're home!"

Alisoun looked up and waved, then waved again. David saw the line of heads bobbing around the crenelations. These were her people, and if she escaped into the welcome of her servants, he would lose his chance to question her in private. He reached for the reins of her palfrey; she pulled them aside and said, "You're our guest. I'll ride ahead and have them prepare your bath."

He almost fell out of his saddle. If Louis hadn't moved to catch him, he would have. "A bath?"

"A knightly bath. The honor which is bestowed on every knight who visits." Her voice deepened with relish. "It is proper."

"Not at my home."

"Of course not. That's obvious." As enthusiastic as he'd ever seen her, she waved at her people. "You have no woman to perform the service."

He couldn't pretend that he didn't know about the custom. He did. He had been a guest in other great homes, been bathed by the wives and daughters of his host—but not for a long time, and never when he'd been celibate for so extended a period. "Your maids are going to give me a bath?"

"Certainly."

"Not you?"

"Nay."

He heaved a sigh of relief.

"I'll supervise."

5

We squires were in the training yard that day, and I'll never forget the look on Sir Walter's face when he heard Lady Alisoun had brought Sir David of Radcliffe back to George's Cross.

Hugh was almost a man grown and as good as any experienced knight. Sir Walter bragged about him, and noblemen came from miles around to watch him spar and to try to woo him from Lady Alisoun's tutelage with promises of an early knighthood and plunder from battle. Hugh bided his time, knowing that Lady Alisoun would treat him generously when the moment came.

Andrew was seventeen and not nearly as impressive to my young eyes. And Jennings . . . well, Jennings was but fourteen, superior only to me, but never letting me forget it. Hugh and Andrew were sparring under Sir Walter's critical gaze while Jennings and I fought with wooden swords, and Jennings was defeating me soundly.

Sir Walter had grabbed my arm and was berating me as a stupid lad when one of his toadies from the village

*came running, yelling that the lady of George's Cross
had arrived. Sir Walter broke off his tirade and shoved
me away. "She made it back, did she?" he said.
"About time, and then some."*

*The toadie leaned against the gate and held his
chest, panting from the run up the steep hill from the
village to the castle, but he didn't let exhaustion defeat
him. "Aye, Sir Walter, but she has a knight with her."*

*Sir Walter couldn't have known, but he must have been
preparing himself for something, for he wheeled on his dirty
little informer and grabbed him by the neck. "Speak."*

*The toadie clawed at his throat, and Sir Walter
released him with the command. "Now."*

"Sir David of Radcliffe—"

*The toadie got no chance to say more. Sir Walter
flung him further than he had flung me, and with considerably more virulence. I would have run from the
expression on his face, but I was already running for
the outer gate. Running to see the legend.*

*I clambered up the great oak smack in the middle of
the bailey, crawled as far out on a limb as I could, and
peered through the leaves. The drawbridge was straight
ahead. I could see all the way down the hill to the village, and I got my first glimpse of Sir David of Radcliffe.*

*From a distance, he was everything an eleven-year-
old boy could desire in a hero. He was tall and broad,
seated on a milk-white charger who I knew to be King
Louis. As he got closer, my awe grew greater, for clearly
he cared nothing about anyone's opinion. He slumped
in the saddle. Dark stubble covered his cheeks, and
beneath that, dirt stained them. His bottom lip stuck
out much like mine when my lady commanded me to
take a bath, and when Sir Walter stepped onto the middle of the drawbridge, my hero's attitude didn't change.*

I relished the coming confrontation.

*   *   *

Looking now at Sir Walter's furious expression, Alisoun wondered if she should have warned him of her intentions. But when she left, she hadn't known if he would be there when she got back, or if she would succeed in finding and hiring Sir David. And if she'd told him, he might have left before she did, and she had needed him to protect the castle during the time she was gone.

Ah, well, now she would pay for her silence. "Sir Walter," she greeted him. "Is all well within the castle?"

"Assuredly," he snapped, his gaze brooding on David. "I always fulfill my duties."

David didn't seem to notice the animosity which clouded the atmosphere. He still sulked, and his destrier—an animal with a mind, if she'd ever seen one—adopted a like attitude. Louis's head drooped, his back swayed, and he clomped onto the drawbridge like a farm horse far gone with age.

What Alisoun wanted to know, of course, was whether any other incidents had occurred, but Sir Walter knew what she wished and refused to acknowledge it. She didn't dare ask. How could she, without alerting David to the circumstances? Her experience with Sir Walter had taught her that men viewed the harassment done to her as justice for a feckless act, and she didn't dare tell David for fear he would turn and leave—and she needed him. Another glance at Sir Walter confirmed it. She needed David *now*.

David didn't respond when Alisoun introduced him, but Sir Walter stood stiffer, straighter, reaching for a height he didn't have. "Sir David. Your reputation has preceded you."

"It always does. Are you going to stand in the middle

of the drawbridge forever, or are you going to move aside for your lady?"

Alisoun sucked in her breath. So David did comprehend the unspoken challenge. Did he not care? Did he dismiss Sir Walter as insignificant? Or did he have a plan?

She looked at the morose man and disconsolate horse again. He *couldn't* have a plan.

Louis moved forward, apparently on his own initiative. Sir Walter came face-to-face with the massive horse. Louis kept moving. Sir Walter stepped aside. It was all very quick, very smooth, very deliberate. She followed in Louis's wake, allowing David to push objections aside and draw her along behind him.

Inside the massive outer bailey, shouts of relief and satisfaction greeted her. Children came running, muddy from the fishpond. Women rose, stiff from weeding the garden, and waved. The milkmaids came to the door of the dairy and her falconer lifted his newest bird to show her. Ah, it was good to be home. Good to know her people rejoiced in her safe return.

Before her, the inner walls rose higher. With a confident swagger, David rode toward the gatehouse. Mingled with the calling of her name, Alisoun heard masculine hails of "David! Sir David of Radcliffe!"

He raised a negligent hand toward the men-at-arms who clustered together on the wall walk. They scattered when Sir Walter shouted, but David didn't flinch. He fell back until Alisoun reached him and they could ride, together, into the inner bailey. Sir Walter hurried to catch them. He had been the castle's warden and Alisoun's right hand; his position had just been changed, and without a word being uttered.

Alisoun wondered if becoming a legend wasn't partly due to an ability to read a situation and assess it immediately.

The four stories of the keep rose sharply in the center of the inner bailey. No windows or doors sliced through the thick stone on the first level, but serving women hung from the tiny window slots above. They clustered on the wooden stairs that led to the second level entrance. Edlyn stood alone on the landing, hands clasped at her waist, waiting calmly to greet her mistress.

Pleased with her ward's dignity, Alisoun sent a special smile of approval toward the girl, and Edlyn beamed. The cook stepped out of the kitchen shed with fork in hand and brandished a plucked goose. Alisoun nodded, and Easter grinned broadly. Easter knew what Alisoun liked. The baker opened the great oven and in a rush of fragrant steam, removed a loaf with his wooden paddle. Kneeling, he offered it, and even from the distance Alisoun could smell the scent of cinnamon she loved. She started toward him, ready to accept the loaf, and behind her she heard the muttered exclamation. "Mercy o' me, but you're rich."

She wanted to ignore him. She meant to ignore him. Instead she turned around gracefully. "You're not the first man to notice that," she said in a low voice with only a hint of an edge.

"I imagine not." David fingered his reins and watched his hands. "At Radcliffe, the only time we kill a goose is if someone's ill—or if the goose is."

She wanted to laugh, but she wasn't sure he jested. The mighty Sir David seemed abashed and in awe. Looking around once more, she saw her home through his eyes. The castle walls contained all the necessities of life. The well sat in the middle of the inner bailey. The storerooms beneath the castle contained supplies enough to repel a siege for six months. She'd grown up with the wealth, but she'd been taught to be kind to those less fortunate. Was Sir David less fortunate? He might not have her resources, but he was a man.

Men were the kings; they held all the land. Men were the fathers; they forced their daughters to do as they were told. Men were the husbands; they beat their wives with rods.

Yet David was one of the small landowners whom the drought had hurt. He looked at her and saw a way to repair his fortunes, and what harm could he do? She understood him completely. She knew he'd charmed her because of her money, and it wasn't as if she were unpracticed in repelling likely suitors. As kindly as she knew how, she said, "After your bath, you can eat the whole goose if you wish."

He looked up at her. He had brown eyes, she realized with a start. Brown eyes, the color of old oak, brown hair so dark that the strands of gray gleamed like pewter, and a tanned face that had witnessed too many battles, too much hunger, too little kindness. For just one moment, he looked at her as if *she* were the hapless goose, ready for the plucking.

Maybe she shouldn't put him in charge of her castle.

Had she said it aloud? She didn't think so, but he must have read her thoughts, for he said, "Nay, my lady, it's too late for second thoughts now." Then his expression changed, becoming mischievous and a bit rueful. "I'll hold you to that promise and eat the whole goose."

She'd been so sure of him, but that one glimpse of his soul left her cold and quaking. Perhaps it would behoove her to remember that he had started with nothing but a knighthood and now possessed both legend and property. That should satisfy any man. She risked another glance at him.

He didn't look satisfied.

But she had a duty. Her role of hostess required the rituals of hospitality. Her people expected it of her. Alisoun expected it of herself, and she had no tangible reason to deny him. She accepted the loaf of bread, wrapped in a cloth, and thanked the baker.

After all, David wanted to gobble up her poultry, not her lands. She broke the loaf open, and he watched with an avid kind of wonder as the soft bread steamed. She took a bite. He observed every movement of her mouth with his own slightly open. Self-conscious, she chewed quickly, then licked a crumb off her lip. She heard his intake of breath. He must be very hungry.

Quickly, she passed it to him. "Share this loaf in welcome," she recited. "Bless my house with your presence forevermore."

"As you command, my lady." David turned the loaf until he reached the place she had eaten. Then he tore the loaf with his teeth like a ravenous wolf with tender flesh.

Did he mean something by his gesture? Or had the fears of the past moons prodded her imagination to new heights of absurdity?

David passed the loaf on to Sir Walter as if unaware of her emotions.

Sir Walter also broke and ate the bread, although from the expression on his face, it might have been baked with bitter horse chestnut. She lost sight of the loaf after that, knowing it would be passed as far as possible and tiny bites taken from it as part of the welcome ceremony.

The keg of ale took longer to arrive, hauled from the keep's cellar on the shoulders of one of her largest men. Again she was given the first cup. "It's my latest," her alewife told her. "And a fine flavor it is."

Alisoun drained it to the bottom. "One of your best," she assured Mabel.

The gray-haired woman winked at her, then refilled the cup and passed it to David. The wink she gave him was considerably more salacious, and he winked back with a smile that would melt iron. The gathering group of servants watched, fascinated, while he drank, observing each bob of his Adam's apple with deference. Alisoun didn't know whether to be amused or exasperated, but Sir Walter knew just what he thought. Taking his own cup from his belt, he filled it with ale and broke the chain rather than drink after David. It was a gesture noted by all, but nullified by the fight which broke out among the men. They all wanted to drink from the same cup as David.

It seemed to Alisoun a good moment to slip away. Dismounting, she found herself face-to-face with Sir Walter. Seldom was she without the skills to diffuse a situation, but today she was speechless. She waited for him to speak. He glared. She turned away toward the keep. He caught her arm.

"Why did you bring him here?" His hands rose toward her shoulders as if he wanted to grasp them and shake her. "What have I done to earn your contempt?"

She kept her fingers relaxed at her side and her face expressionless. "I have great respect for you. Together, we have kept the peace and dispensed justice in George's Cross for years."

"I always said so. I *always* said so." He took deep breaths, his nostrils flaring with each inhalation. "You're the lady. You make judgments and I dispense the justice and direct the punishments. You pay me to be the one the peasants hate. "

He spoke nothing less than the truth. Castle folk knew who directed his actions, but his mediation gave them an outlet for their ire other than their beloved lady.

He went on. "If the folk have been complaining, I

can change my ways. Be less strict with their transgressions."

She knew that in her absence, Sir Walter ran the castle with a stern hand. The exuberant welcome which always greeted her return from her travels told her that. Now she wondered if he disapproved of her tact, discretion, and mercy. His obvious hostility made her wonder a lot of things. "No one has complained about you."

"Then why—"

"Hey!" David appeared beside them, relaxed from his intake of ale and grinning like a dolt. "My lady, you promised me a bath."

Sir Walter began to growl deep in his chest, like a dog who smells a challenge.

"So I did." Alisoun faced Sir Walter. "If you would excuse me?"

"I will not!" He lunged for her arm again and struck David in the back.

Somehow, David had slipped between them, and he seemed unaware of the blow. With his hand on Lady Alisoun's shoulder, he guided her toward the keep. "Your hospitality is faultless, my lady. Even bathing should be a pleasure under your auspices."

"My lady!" Sir Walter called. "I need to speak to you."

"Come along then," David called. "She has a bath to give first." He looked up at the sky and held out his hand. "And I believe we should find shelter, for it's beginning to rain." He could scarcely contain his laughter at the huff of indignation Sir Walter released. David had seen this type of man before. A knight who had held his position for too long, coming to think his place was secure regardless of his actions. It surprised David that Lady Alisoun had allowed it to happen, but undoubtedly the situation had developed gradually, without her realization. At least now she had taken steps to rectify it, and he thought he understood a little better why she'd hired him.

If someone had been shooting arrows, perhaps Sir Walter was the culprit. He glanced back at the puffed-up little grouse of a man. In sooth, Sir Walter didn't act like a probable suspect. David glanced down at Lady Alisoun. And she didn't act like a woman likely to be so wrong in her judgment of her chief knight.

The maids on the stairs greeted their mistress with curtsies and words of welcome. The respect shown her almost amounted to reverence, and she hadn't earned that by being a fool.

The noble girl at the top of the stairs curtsied, too, then flung herself into Alisoun's arms as if she couldn't bear another moment of separation. Alisoun petted her head—for one moment, only, but it was a definite stroke of affection—then pushed her away. "Stand straight, Lady Edlyn, and let me introduce you to Sir David of Radcliffe."

David braced himself for another siege of unwanted adulation, but no recognition lit Edlyn's face at his name. He grinned at his own conceit, and realized that she was too young to recall his mercenary exploits.

She said, "Greetings, good lord, and welcome to George's Cross."

Her pretty manners seemed to satisfy Alisoun, for she patted Edlyn once more, briefly. "Where's Philippa?" she asked.

"Feeding the baby," Edlyn answered.

Turning to him, Alisoun said, "Philippa is my personal maid."

The explanation startled him briefly. Why would she think he cared? Then they stepped inside, moving from warmth to cool and light to dark, and he no longer wondered about anything except the sheer mammoth size of the keep. Stairways spiraled up, rising into the dark. A puff of fresh air told him the stairs extended above three floors to the roof where men-at-arms patrolled. Stairways spiraled down. The scent of damp barrels and bitter herbs rose to tell him of storerooms and wine cellars. A short, crooked passage wound toward the great hall. And once there . . . "A great hall, indeed," David murmured, trying to look everywhere at once.

The upright posts reached from the floor to the angle of the ceiling, then mighty oak beams, carved in fanciful decoration, carried the arch up and over. High, narrow windows let in slivers of light from the setting sun, but already torches smoked in the wall sconces. Chairs and benches clustered around not one, but two gigantic hearths, one on each end of the hall. Their roaring blazes warmed the cold stones, but the whitewashed walls remained white. Where was the smoke going? Stepping up onto the dais, he wandered closer and realized that a stone hood captured the smoke and siphoned it into a channel which took it outside. "Incredible," he muttered, touching the hood with one finger.

Alisoun caught his eye. She watched him without expression, but somehow he thought she read his admiration and amazement.

Well, why shouldn't she? He didn't conceal himself as if he were a miser and each emotion a nugget of gold.

"My lady Alisoun!"

Alisoun swung around, locating the source of the warm voice on the opposite side of the fireplace. "Philippa, I'm back." She walked to the bench tucked into a warm corner where a plump, smiling maid sat nursing a baby.

David stepped to the front of the fireplace and held out his hands as if to warm himself.

"You're not hurt?" the maid asked.

Alisoun shrugged off her cloak. "I am as you see me—well and still single." Leaning over, she embraced the woman. "Although that's a tale for your ears."

"Careful!" Philippa tugged Alisoun onto the bench beside her. "You'll crush Hazel."

Alisoun peeked at the baby, who, old enough to play games, peeked back. Then she pulled away from the nipple and gave a milky grin.

Straining, David stared. Not even Alisoun's impassiveness was proof against a baby's smile.

"Sir David." Taken by surprise, he found himself jerked around to face an irate Sir Walter. "I want to speak to you."

With a fast, efficient twist of the wrist, David freed himself. "By all means." He turned his back. "Later." After he'd seen this one thing, watched this one trial by baby.

Alisoun didn't smile back at the child. She looked vaguely bewildered, unsure for the first time since he'd met her. Tilting her head, she stared into Hazel's big eyes. "What does she want?"

Philippa laughed, indulgent. "She's a baby. She doesn't want anything." Hoisting Hazel into a sitting position on her lap, she elbowed Alisoun. "Smile back at her."

"Sir David." Sir Walter stepped between him and the women, and his voice trembled with rage.

Stupid, David thought, craning his neck to see over him. If they were to be enemies, Sir Walter would do well to disguise his anger with a little more— *Look at her!* His breath caught. Alisoun *was* smiling!

Pish! Hazel knew how to do it better than Alisoun. Alisoun's lips twitched; if she'd been the baby, he'd have wondered if she had colic.

Then, as if she feared detection, she glanced guiltily toward him. Lowering his gaze to Sir Walter, he tried to look as if they were having a discussion. "We'll work together," he said.

"You don't understand," Sir Walter said. "I don't work with anyone. I'm the chief knight and steward here."

David nodded in conciliation and without conviction. "Aye, aye, that's easy to see." Cautiously, he glanced over Sir Walter's shoulder. Alisoun had turned back to Philippa. David edged closer. Sir Walter tried to hold his ground; he gave way when David pushed.

Philippa's hands moved over little Hazel knowingly, straightening her clothes, testing her for wetness. "Wants to eat when she wants to eat, and is done when she's done," she grumbled.

Sir Walter said, "We must talk—away from the women."

But Philippa wasn't really upset. David could see that, even from a distance. Everything about that woman shouted *proud mother*. Handing the baby and a rag to Alisoun, she said, "Burp her. I need to put myself together before I meet *him*." She jerked her head toward David, and David realized the maid had monitored his maneuvers ever since he'd entered the room. "He's the one, isn't he?"

"What?" Alisoun fumbled with the baby, while Philippa watched. After much fidgeting, Alisoun managed to cover her shoulder with the rag and lift the baby. But she held her so stiffly and patted her so uncertainly, Hazel neither burped nor relaxed.

Exasperated by Alisoun's inefficiency, David stepped around Sir Walter. "Here. Let me." He rescued the baby from Alisoun's sweaty grip. Philippa grabbed, but he laid Hazel against his shoulder, patted her efficiently, and challenged the anxious mother with a lift of his chin.

Philippa observed him shrewdly, then relaxed a little. "Aye, you've done this before. Best give him the rag, Alisoun, or she'll spit on him and he'll stink of sour milk."

"It wouldn't be the first time." But David held out his hand anyway, and Alisoun placed the rag in it without hesitation.

Still keeping a watchful eye on him, Philippa said, "Lady Alisoun will have to learn sometime."

Wrestling to put the rag under Hazel's chin, David answered, "She'll learn with her own."

"If she ever has her own, which I'm starting to doubt, she'll have enough maids that she'll never have to touch the child."

"Hm. You probably speak the truth." Amused and a little perplexed that Alisoun allowed her maid such freedom to speak her mind, David rubbed firmly up Hazel's spine until a moist belch sounded in his ear. Turning to face the satisfied little face so close to his own, he said, "Perhaps you'd best go back to Lady Alisoun."

A rumble sounded on the baby's other end, and Alisoun rose from her seat. "Oh, nay. You'll not give her to me now. I have a bath to prepare."

Apparently Sir Walter had given up on David, for he appealed to Alisoun. "We must speak together."

"Of a certainty." Alisoun nodded graciously to him, then called, "Edlyn!"

Her ward came rushing up, her cheeks flushed with pleasure at being called. "My lady?"

"Prepare our guest's bath in the blue bedchamber. We'll need the biggest tub for him." She glanced at David and moved a little away, but he heard her anyway. "Bring the scissors, I'll cut his hair."

He fingered the strands that hung around his shoulders.

She continued, "And I think marjoram and oil of eucalyptus might abate the worst of his stench."

Surprised, he asked Philippa, "Do I smell?"

He thought for a moment she was going to laugh. Her eyes crinkled at the corners, her lips twitched, and even though she would be laughing at him, he looked forward to hearing her. This motherly creature would surely release a big belly laugh, one of those great booms of merriment that invited guffaws in return.

Instead, she controlled herself, quivering with the effort. "My lady has a sensitive nose, and you smell very much like a . . . man."

That hadn't been her first choice of a description, he was sure. Had Alisoun quashed this woman's natural humor? He glanced at Alisoun as she gave instructions to Edlyn. If nothing else, during his stay he'd get Alisoun to laugh aloud and free her servants from this senseless bondage.

With a caution he thought reserved for wild boars, Philippa removed the baby from his grasp. "I'll change her wrapping clothes." But she still looked him over. "You *are* Sir David of Radcliffe, aren't you?"

He stood still and tried to appear unthreatening. "Aye."

"The legendary mercenary?"

Some people, on hearing his name and knowing his reputation, thought he must be constantly savage and brutal. Apparently this woman was one of them. Gently, he said, "I am a mercenary, but the legend is perhaps exaggerated."

"It had better not be," she snapped, then paled and stepped back. She looked as if she wanted to run and her breath came in little gasps. The baby, sensing her mother's agitation, squirmed and squalled, and Philippa patted her rhythmically, her instinct to comfort smothered by wariness. "We need you to be everything the legend claims. We need you to protect my lady Alisoun. If anything should happen to her—"

"Philippa!" Alisoun's voice sliced across her maid's warning. "Go change the baby, then get back to your duties."

Swinging around, Philippa stared at Alisoun with open mouth. Then she said, "Aye, my lady." Hampered by the baby, she bobbed an awkward curtsy. "I was just—"

"I don't care." Alisoun pointed her finger in Philippa's face. "Keep . . . your . . . place. You have no business speaking to Sir David, especially not in such a familiar way."

Alisoun didn't sound angry, but Philippa paled. Tears rushed to her eyes, and she caught Alisoun's outstretched hand. "I know. I'm just stupid, but I fear for you. I should—"

"The only thing you should do is tend to your duties here." Alisoun pushed at Philippa. "Go now."

Philippa rushed away, looking like an abused puppy, and David found himself disliking Alisoun again. Philippa seemed to be all woman, mother to her child first and to the world after, and something had crushed her spirit. He narrowed his gaze on Alisoun. Aye, he wanted to teach Alisoun many lessons.

In a voice as bitter as gall, Sir Walter said, "Philippa proves there's good reason to beat a woman."

Instinctively protesting, David began, "Jesú, man, that's harsh."

Then Alisoun caught his attention. Her face and figure remained absolutely still. She might have been encased in ice. Slowly, her head swung toward Sir

Walter like a door on a rusty hinge, and something about her made Sir Walter step back. In a voice of command, she said, "Do not ever let me hear you say such a thing again."

"If you would just listen to me—"

"I do not choose to follow your advice." Sir Walter tried to speak, but Alisoun lifted her hand. "I do not wish to hear it again."

A pox on all this secrecy! David felt the undercurrents tugging at him. Had Sir Walter beat Philippa? Had he beat his wife? Did he have a wife?

David's gaze narrowed on the disturbed knight. Was Sir Walter the reason Alisoun had not married? Did he occupy her bed, and had they had a lovers' quarrel? David had told her he wouldn't interfere between man and wife, but if she'd taken Sir Walter to her bed, he'd interfere. He'd abandon his half-made plans to court her and abduct her instead. Sir Walter would have no chance against David.

"Did you hear me, Sir Walter?"

Her chilly voice broke David's musings, and he dismissed the daydreams. He believed only what he saw and heard and touched.

"I beg your pardon, my lady." Sir Walter bowed, giving every indication of sincere contrition.

But was he sincerely contrite about saying such an asinine thing, or contrite about infuriating his liege? And why had he advocated such despotism when his liege *was* a woman, and likely to consider it a challenge?

"If you again subject me to such an outburst, you will have no choice. You will be seeking another lord to serve—one more to your liking."

Could she speak to her lover like that? Surely not. Not even Lady Alisoun could sound so disdainful to a man who'd rumpled her mattress.

David looked from the stocky, red-faced, fervently protesting Sir Walter to tall, aloof Lady Alisoun. Nay, Sir Walter hadn't rumpled her mattress.

But she *did* have emotions, he now knew it. Her face didn't show them, her posture remained the same, but behind her gray eyes existed a soul. And he would understand her, if he had to connive, spy, and enlist the assistance of all her people, and even the very heart of the cold and lonely maiden of George's Cross.

6

Under Alisoun's guidance, Sir David stumbled into his chamber. Alisoun quailed at the thought of putting her safety and the security of George's Cross in this man's hands. In this man's *filthy* hands.

He'll look better when he's had a bath, she argued back at herself, and snapped her fingers at the maids. They sprang into action, stripping him of his clothing and tossing it in a basket to be boiled.

"Maybe the poor will take this," one maid said, holding the soiled rags David called his hose between two fingers.

"The poor won't want any of it," Edlyn retorted.

Edlyn's voice roused Alisoun. "Go on, dear," she said. "I don't think it proper for a maiden who is yet unmarried to bathe the guests."

"Will *you* be bathing him?" Sir Walter demanded from the doorway.

Surprised, all the women turned to look at him, then at Alisoun.

"As I always do," she answered.

He placed his fists on his hips. "Are you not a maiden?"

So angry she could barely speak, she said, "I am a widow." By good Saint Ethelred, the man had lost his mind. When had he come to believe he had the right to question her activities? When had he lost so much respect for her that he believed he could insult her without consequence?

Oh, she knew the answer.

When she had confessed she'd risked everything to do what she thought was right. He didn't comprehend that she cared nothing about his disapproval or his opinion. She paid his wages; what she expected from him was his unconditional loyalty. He hadn't given it, yet still she recalled his earlier support and found herself unable to order he find another post.

Mechanically, she reviewed the arrangements for their guest. She spoke to Edlyn about the special evening meal, then sent her on her way. A fire burned in the fireplace. She pressed on the mattress. The bedding smelled clean and dry. Lifting the pitchers which sat on a table beside the bed, she found them empty and frowned. In their excitement over serving the legendary mercenary, the maids had failed to finish preparing the chamber.

At the tub, one of them squealed, and Alisoun glanced impatiently toward the little group around David. So frivolous! Did they think, just because he was a legend, he would be the answer to a maiden's prayer? She glanced at the furious Sir Walter. Is that what he thought, too? Is that why he stood off to the side, watching, bristled up like a mastiff?

The group parted briefly, and Alisoun caught a glimpse of David, naked and dripping. He was certainly *not* a maiden's dream. A cook's dream, because he was so skinny. Or a washerwoman's dream. She'd never seen a man so caked with dirt. It would take hard scrubbing to remove all the grime, but regardless of Sir Walter's opinion, she knew her duty and always did it. Rolling up her sleeves, she picked up the apron the maids had laid out to cover her. If she could have, she would have left him to the maids, but she dared not retreat now or Sir Walter would consider it a victory.

Her level voice cut the chatter. "Where is the wine and water, should our guest have a thirst in the night?"

Heath clapped her hand over her mouth.

She'd been Alisoun's personal maid before; she had been promoted to chief maid when Philippa had come, and when distracted, she occasionally failed in her duties. "Are there other chores left undone?" Alisoun asked.

The group around David melted away. Heath ran from one place to another, assessing each maid's performance. They all remained within the chamber, hoping, Alisoun supposed, to sneak glances at the legend in their midst. She didn't care about that. She feared only that their hospitality might be lacking, not that it would be done too well.

At her approach, David sank into the water as if it might melt him. From the look of him, he hadn't the experience to know otherwise.

Soaping the washing cloth, Alisoun tried to ease David's uneasiness with polite chatter. "Is the chamber to your liking?"

He leaned forward and let her rub his shoulders. "It's lovely," he said politely. "Is it yours?"

Briefly, she considered digging her fingernails into his skin. She had hoped he wouldn't behave like an ass and make offensive comments that insinuated she would warm his bed. So many knights and lords did when she bathed them, assuming that she must hunger for what she did not know and smugly sure they could satisfy that hunger. For them, a few cool words worked much like icicles dropped into the bath water, and she never had the problem again—at least from the same man.

Today she didn't feel so tactful. She, too, was exhausted from travel and this duty seemed onerous beyond belief. Running the washcloth up over David's head, she let strong lye soap drip into his eyes. Jumping to his feet, he yelled, and tried to rub it out. Heath ran forward with a basin of clean water and helped him splash water into his face. When he turned on Alisoun, red-eyed and snarling, she thought to apologize sweetly. Instead she found herself saying, "You'll sleep in here alone, Sir David, unless you choose another partner. I'm sure one of the maids could be persuaded to join you, out of curiosity if nothing else. Now, if you'll sit again, we'll finish with—"

He grabbed her hand in a firm grip, and she wondered if he would soak her. Her training told her she deserved it for allowing her temper to get the better of her, but Sir Walter's growl angered her even more. She didn't need protecting from David; she could handle him.

"This is *my* chamber?" David demanded.

She stood absolutely still. "I have said so."

"I sleep here . . . alone?"

"Aye."

Her soapy hand slipped from his grasp, and he made no move to recapture it. "You have chambers for everyone?"

"For my guests." She began to realize the reason for David's amazement. "It wouldn't be appropriate for you to sleep on the floor of the great hall with the servants. Sir Walter has a private chamber in the gate-house where he can be at the ready in case of attack, but I thought that you should be within the keep."

"Since I'm to guard you."

She felt foolish now. "Aye. I need you to guard me and mine."

Sir Walter stepped forward. "I can do it."

Her hand trembled with frustration, but she answered as she always did. "I need you to preserve the whole castle and the village. There isn't enough time for the special care I have come to require."

She expected David to say something, to step between them somehow, but he didn't. Instead, he sat in the water and looked up at them both as if expecting entertainment. She could have slapped him.

Sir Walter turned away with a grunt.

David didn't try to take the cloth from her, but leaned forward to let her finish his back. A scar snaked out of his scalp and down his back, and when she washed his neck, she discovered the lobe of one ear was missing. She tried to be gentle with it, but he said, "Go ahead and scrub. It doesn't hurt."

Boldly, she inquired, "How did you lose it?"

The work within the room slowed as all the women strained to hear the tale.

"I made a mistake," he said.

"Did the other knight—" Alisoun paused, not knowing how to continue.

"His widow has since remarried."

His flat reply answered more than one question. He didn't brag about his triumphs, but she wanted to know. Not for the same reason as the maids, who simply worshipped without thought, but because she wanted verification of his prowess.

Then he leaned back to give her access to his chest,

and she saw further testament to the suffering he'd endured, both in battle and in his struggle to survive the drought. The wiry muscles across his shoulders lifted the skin in impressive ripples, but she traced the line of his prominent collarbone as she scrubbed. His arms clearly showed the effect of swinging sword and shield. The veins on the back of his big hands rose in massive blue lines, and he'd lost the little finger on his left hand.

Lifting his wrist, she asked, "Sword?"

"Battle ax."

"Did his widow remarry, also?"

Sounding disgusted, he said, "Nay! It was only a melée."

She looked again at the blank place where his finger should be. "You lost it in a play battle?"

"Not play," he answered patiently. "Practice. We hold melées for practice, and to entertain the court." He held up his hand and grinned at it affectionately. "If Sir Richard hadn't pulled back on his swing, I'd have lost the whole hand." Tucking it back in the water, he added, "I was a fledging then, and lucky."

"Lucky."

She looked, and she didn't think he was lucky. A variety of weapons had gashed lines of flesh from his upper chest, leaving a gnarled pattern of black hair and white scars traced over his impressive pectorals. But immediately below, his ribs were delineated with dreadful clarity.

Perhaps he *could* eat the whole goose by himself.

She couldn't wash the parts of him still in the water, and she wanted to, badly. Not because she was curious. She wasn't, although the dirt and soap floating in the water might have frustrated a nosy woman. She'd seen, and washed, many men, and a legend such as Sir David would be no different. But obviously, the man was not enamored of bathing, and she didn't know when she might persuade him to partake again. "Stand up," she commanded.

He didn't answer, but slipped one leg out of the tub and shifted as if the tub were too small.

Well, it was too small for a man of his size and . . . "Fine," she said, and washed his foot. Calluses deformed his toes and snagged the weave of the cloth, but he flexed and grimaced in reflexive action when she stroked the bottom of his foot. Purple scarring rippled the skin from ankle to knee.

"Fire?" she asked.

"Boiling tar poured from the curtain wall during a siege," he answered.

"Did you take the castle?"

He watched as she lifted his leg and washed beneath. "In sooth."

The muscles of his well-formed calf joined a bony knee, and his thigh was thin—too thin for a man of his size.

Holding out her hand, palm up, she silently demanded the other foot. He looked at her hand. She insisted with a wiggle of the fingers, and he deliberately drew his foot from the water and laid it in her hand.

He'd lost a toe on this foot, and the flesh stretched thin to cover the bone.

Before she could ask, he said, "Same siege as the boiling tar. I was running across the drawbridge and the portcullis came down on my foot. Praise God it didn't land on my head."

"Aye. God is good to you." Surprised, she realized she meant it. David had come to the very gates of death and somehow escaped every time.

He raised his voice so all within the chamber could

hear. "That's all being a legend is. Living long enough to brag about your own exploits."

"Might it also be the willingness to be first across the drawbridge?" she asked.

"First one across gets best pickings."

First one across usually gets killed, she thought, but she didn't say that. That was obvious to everyone within the room. Instead she moved to finish the job of washing him so he could eat.

This time he made a funny little grunt when she scrubbed his thighs. She raised an eyebrow at him, but he tucked his lips tightly together and shook his head.

After rinsing out the cloth in clean water, she soaped it up again. "Stand up. I can't wash you if you won't stand up."

He just sat there, gripping the sides of the tub stubbornly, as if the dirt in the tub had affixed him from the rear down.

Then Sir Walter mocked from his corner. "Perhaps more than his fingers and toes have been cut off."

Every eye focused on David. Would he be angry? Would he climb from the tub and tear Sir Walter's gizzard from his bowels? Instead, a slow smile formed on David's face. His lips parted. His chest rose and fell in deep inhalations, and smoky satisfaction practically oozed from him. Like one of the monsters living deep in the mountain lake, he rose out of the water and revealed himself in all his glory.

Laughing out loud, David rolled over in his bed and pounded the feather pillow exuberantly. Never in his life would he forget the look that had transformed Sir Walter's sarcastic face. Even now, he could relive the gratification of seeing the old scoundrel's expression right before he scurried out in abject humiliation. Nay, Sir Walter would never challenge him in such a manner again.

Alisoun . . . David rolled onto his back, wrapped his hands behind his head, and stared at the canopy above him as the misty morning light grew stronger. Alisoun was another story. He didn't know what she thought.

It was that washing that had done it. Alisoun had used a rough cloth, and she'd scrubbed until his skin felt raw, but he'd noticed only the touch of her hands as they grazed him again and again. He hadn't stood up when she commanded him to, for he didn't want to embarrass her by an untimely display.

But when Sir Walter had goaded him and he had finally stood, she didn't seem embarrassed. He didn't know what he'd expected of her. Exclamations of rapture? A beaming smile? A quick grope? He'd gotten none of it, of course. She'd stood without a quiver, a simper or a frown. If she'd been impressed, she hadn't indicated it.

And she should have been impressed. Hell, he'd been impressed, and he'd wielded that weapon all his life.

"Did you sleep well?"

He jumped, flinging the blankets up in surprise. He'd been thinking about her, and here she was, with her arms full of folded material and a pleasant smile on her face.

Again, he looked at her. Perhaps it was an exaggeration to call it a pleasant smile. It was more of a lift of the lips, performed because she'd been taught it was the proper thing to do. But he liked it. He liked her, the way she looked this morning, dressed for work in a faded blue cotte and a sky blue wimple wrapped over her hair and under her chin. A big iron ring of keys hung from her belt, marking her as the chatelaine of George's Cross and a power to be reckoned with.

Rolling onto his stomach, he propped his chin onto his hands and grinned. "Well, it felt odd to have clean sheets, a clean body, and a room to myself, but I suspect I could easily get used to it."

"Aye, it is pleasant to have a clean body." She stacked the material on the bench by the fire hearth. With peculiar emphasis, she said, "It is more pleasant for the people around you, also. The sun is rising. It's time for you to take on your duties."

His grin sagged. "My duties?"

"You'll want to consult with Sir Walter today, and I've told him you're to have the freedom to wander where you will and speak to whom you please."

"That's generous of you, my lady."

Ignoring both the words and the sardonic tone, she shook out a tunic of red linen and a surcoat of berry blue wool. "I thought these would fit you and be appropriate for your coloring."

Dumbfounded, he repeated, "For my coloring?"

"A man as large as yourself with brown eyes, brown hair, and brown skin must take care not to appear to be a tree trunk."

He viewed the colorful array of cloth in her hands with misgiving. "Mayhap being a tree trunk is an advantage when danger stalks."

"I thought of that." With a snap, she shook out a black cloak trimmed in green. "I doubt that you'll be in danger in broad daylight, and in the early morning and late at night, this cloak will keep you warm and protect you from being seen unnecessarily. Get out of bed. I want to cut your hair."

She'd left her scissors on the table last night when she'd left the room, but she obviously hadn't forgotten them. Why was she so insistent on removing his mane? Like bathing, was this some kind of ritual required when one entered the home of Lady Alisoun?

"Let me get dressed first." The door stood open behind her, but she was alone, and for the first time he wondered why. The lady of the house should never have been reduced to carrying his clothing, but mayhap the chief maid had been correct when she giggled and told him that their mistress found him attractive—when clean.

Naked as a newborn, he put his feet on the step stool beside the tall bed, then stepped onto the floor, keeping his gaze fixed on Alisoun for reaction. "Did you bring hose?"

Lifting two black wool tubes, she showed them to him. "Don your braies," she commanded. "Then sit on the bench. You'll not want your clean tunic cluttered with hair clippings."

He did as she told him, watching her carefully for signs of interest or intrigue. There were none. She laid out a towel on the table beside the bench, tested the scissors, then stood and waited, hands folded before her, for him to seat himself.

It occurred to him she was a restful woman. That lack of expression which so frustrated him made her an easy companion. It also made him want to prod her to get a reaction. He sat, and as she wrapped a cloth around his shoulders, he said, "I was wondering . . . why did you leave last night?"

He saw her hand appear from behind him, pick up an ivory comb, then retreat. The comb bit into the hair at his forehead, then slid over the top. A tangle caught it, and it stopped with a jerk at his neckline. "Ow!" He clapped his hand over hers as she tugged to separate the strands. "Ow, ow! Stop that!"

A warm chuckle floated over him, pleasing his ears, and he tried to twist around, to view this miracle of emotion from the lady. That only made the comb bite deeper, and she pushed him back into place. "Do you always whine? If so, I wouldn't want to have been anywhere near when you were actually wounded."

"That's different. This pain is unnecessary." Feeling as if he'd been chided, he folded his arms over his chest and glared at nothing while the comb tugged and maneuvered. Then he realized she'd changed the subject. She'd established herself in control and silenced him all at once. "You vixen," he murmured.

The comb paused in its work. "What?"

He straightened his spine and wished his shoulders had the breadth they'd once had. Too many months of near-starvation had reduced his bulk and made him less awesome than he'd been in his prime. But, he reminded himself, last night she'd still left after he'd stood in the tub. "I did ask why you failed to finish bathing me, didn't I?"

Her hand appeared again, picked up the fine steel scissors, and disappeared behind him. In his ear, he heard the "snick" sound as she tested them, then their cold metal rested against his neck.

She was good, he admitted. Very, very good. Only the most consummate diplomat managed to convey a threat while saying nothing. But, he wondered, why did she feel the need to threaten him? He'd done nothing more than ask a simple question.

She seemed to realize it, for she said, "I do apologize for abandoning you, but on my first night home, I had many duties which required my attention—not the least of which was soothing Sir Walter after your impressive display."

He pounced on that. "So you *did* think it an impressive display?"

The scissors sliced through his hair with that peculiar, irritating sound, and a shiver ran up his spine as wisps of brown swirled down toward his feet. "Every woman in the castle thought it an impressive display, and if they didn't see it themselves, they heard an expanded version."

"But *you* were impressed?"

She blew the hair away from his ear, and he shivered for a reason other than fear. "Very impressed." She clipped off the words as sharply as the scissors clipped off his hair.

Satisfied, he said, "Don't cut it too close."

"Don't you trust me?"

Funny, when he wasn't distracted by looking at her, he deciphered her moods a little more easily. Her voice betrayed her more than she would like, and her hands lost their graceful movement when he aggravated her. "Don't *you* trust *me*?"

The comb and scissors paused. "What do you mean?"

"You haven't yet told me what is threatening you. That's what I'm here for, isn't it? To protect you against some menace."

The comb and scissors moved along. She answered reluctantly, "Someone has conceived a dislike for me."

"Enough of a dislike to shoot arrows at you?"

"Apparently."

"Why?"

"I don't know."

He decided that was a lie. "Who?"

"I don't know."

Another lie. But what she'd told him was almost as interesting as what she didn't tell him, and why she'd told him even more interesting than that. When he wanted information from Alisoun, it seemed, he would have to introduce a subject she wanted to avoid, like her response to his body, then allow her to speak on an alternate subject, like this harassment against her. "Why don't you go to the king and press charges against this lord who so plagues you?"

She combed his bangs into his face. They were long, past his nose, and they tickled. He blew at them, and she scolded, "Stop that. I need to cut these, too." She stepped over the bench and stood in front of him.

Breasts! She had breasts that pressed against the thin blue material. The straight drop of the cotte she wore hid the rest of her shape from him, but her breasts begged him to kiss them. He could almost hear them calling his name, and he wanted to press his ears close to better heed them. Perhaps they were smothered under there. Perhaps they wanted him to free them. Perhaps . . . perhaps he'd better subdue another impressive display. Hoarsely, he prompted, "The king?"

"King Henry already tries to exert more authority over me than law or tradition allows him. I will not involve him in a matter which would leave me indebted to him."

She answered steadily, as if she wasn't aware that her breasts thrust themselves into his face. Maybe breasts were unruly, like penises, and she had no control over their behavior. But he knew what his penis was doing—didn't she know about those impertinent breasts?

"I do comprehend your concern about King Henry, but if you had a man to take care of you—" A wad of hair landed in his open mouth.

She stood back, withdrawing those breasts from his reach, and watched as he spit and sputtered, then sneezed. When he finished, she said, "I don't need a man."

"How would you know?" He pushed back the half-trimmed curtain of hair from his face to watch her. "Your maids call you the oldest virgin widow in England."

Typically, she showed no reaction. "I meant I don't need a husband to protect me. It was easier to hire you."

She didn't deny her maidenhood, he noted. "*I* meant you would do well to take a man into your bed and find out what you're missing."

"And I suppose you have a candidate in mind."

Smiling his guaranteed maiden-melting smile, he twisted the remaining long strand of hair. "Why not me?"

"Because you're a poor, landowning baron. What could you bring me?"

"Pleasure."

She took a startled breath at his bluntness, then reality came to her rescue. "And a babe in nine months. Then we'd have to negotiate a marriage settlement, and you could bring me nothing to match what I have here."

"More important from my point of view—what could you bring me?" He had the satisfaction of seeing her chin drop. "In sooth, you're wealthy beyond my wildest dreams, and that's an advantage to me." He sighed gustily. "The churchmen say that money doesn't buy happiness, but I want a chance to prove it."

"So you admit it. You want me only for my wealth, just like a thousand other knights."

He could have danced with triumph. She hadn't dismissed him with a laugh. His little trout was rising to the bait. "Not at all. Your lands are magnificent, but you're also quite attractive." She opened her mouth to retort, and he added, "When you keep quiet. That just doesn't seem to happen often."

She snapped her mouth shut.

"I'm a gentle man. I've proved myself the better of

every warrior in England." Painfully, he corrected himself. "The better of all but one warrior in England. But I have no need to prove myself stronger than a woman. I don't hit them. I never hit my wife, and if ever a woman . . . well, you can ask any of my people. I don't hit those weaker regardless of the provocation, nor does my dignity suffer when a woman lashes me with her tongue." Placing his hand flat on the table, he leaned toward her. "With me, my lady, you can be right all the time, and I won't mind."

"I *am* right all the time," she said, but her voice faltered.

"You see?" He took the scissors from her hand. "A man could easily murder a woman like you. For your sake, you'd best marry one who answers your sarcasm with wit rather than blows." He chopped the last of his hair off.

"Nay!" She sprang forward. "Oh, nay, now look what you've done."

"What?"

"You've cut it crooked." She combed, parted, separated, then shook her head. "Now I'll have to do the front again until it's even. The castle folk will think I've lost my touch."

"You can't do everything yourself. You can't be chatelaine, chief knight, and barber all in one. That's too much of a burden for any one person to bear. Believe me, I know." He tapped his chest. "I've been trying to do it alone, too. Together we would halve the duties."

"And double the cares."

The new cut her scissors made probably failed to even up the line, but he consoled himself the hair would grow back. "The king wants you married, and married you'll be. You asked for advantage. Well, shouldn't your husband be a man over whom you *have* an advantage?"

Her eyes were round as she observed her handiwork. She combed again, then put her hand over his bangs to hold them down, and leaned close to his face. The scissors touched him again, but her constant handling had warmed them. "When a woman is married, she is her husband's chattel. She can do nothing without his permission." She cut again, then stepped back and looked. A catlike smile curved her lips, then disappeared when she saw how steadily he watched her. "All advantage is lost with the signing of the marriage contract."

"You do yourself an injustice. I give you fair notice, Lady Alisoun, that I intend to demonstrate the advantage you will have, and keep, over me." He laughed out loud. "Come here."

"What?" She actually took a cautious step back, and that for her was a rampant manifestation of wariness.

"I need help donning my clothes and hauberk, and I have no squire."

"I'll assign you one."

He inclined his head. "I would be most grateful."

She hovered for another moment, then came forward to stand beside him. "In the meantime, I will assist you."

By the saints, she was a brave woman!

A stupid woman, but a brave one.

"If your knife is honed, I will shave you before I dress you," she said.

He remembered the implicit threat of her scissors. And she wanted to put a knife at his throat! His eyes narrowed. "Nay. I thank you."

She blessed him briefly with a smile, and he realized how skillfully she put him in his place. But other, greater nobles had tried to keep him in his place. Other, greater circumstances had oppressed him, and he had emerged tough, resilient, superior. His difficult life had taught him much and given him the advantage over this well-bred lady. He had only to remember that.

While he removed the cloth from around his shoulders and wiped off his neck, she laid his tunic and surcoat on the table. As briskly as if he were a dallying child, she ordered, "Raise your arms."

He obeyed, flexing his muscles as he stretched. "Do you think I'm too thin?"

"Aye." Jerking the tunic impatiently over him, she tugged it down to his waist to cover him. "But if you keep eating like you did last night, you'll regain your bulk soon enough." She surveyed him, and he clearly saw a gleam of satisfaction. "Then you'll win your title back. *Then* you'll be the greatest mercenary in England again."

Ripping open his gut would have been more merciful. Since his arrival, he'd pushed his defeat to the back of his mind, ignoring the memories of his defeat. Now she spoke of it casually, as if he would unquestionably regain the title he had held so long. He knew differently. He knew his expertise had been declining even before he'd won Mary and her lands for himself, and in the years since then he'd been more of a farmer and shepherd than warrior. Only his guile and experience in battle had kept him from immediate and humiliating defeat in front of the king.

Was that the price of winning her? Did he have to become the legendary mercenary David again? Because that was impossible. He knew it was impossible.

"What?" she said, as if hearing his thoughts.

She didn't seem to realize how much her shining confidence hurt him. There wasn't a shred of guile on her face. Of course, there wasn't really a shred of emotion either.

He looked deeper. She did have faith in him. He'd better wed her as soon as possible. Before she found out the truth about him—or his damnable honor made him tell her.

"Where is your hauberk?" she asked.

His chain-mail shirt, his pride and joy, had gone to her armorer the night before to be oiled and repaired, but she didn't know that. She just wanted to avoid touching him. "I think I need the surcoat today. No reasonable man would brave this storm to shoot at me."

She lifted her head and heard what he heard. The gray morning light had dissolved into a firm, steady rain. He credited her sense of duty rather than her vindictiveness when she said, "That's true. You'll have to move quickly on your rounds today."

Standing, he pulled on his hose and tied the garters of his left leg. Then he noticed she was watching instead of helping, and he realized his foolishness. While he tied the front strap of his right leg, he said, "Here. The old wound on my hip restricts my movement, and I can't twist around to tie it." He didn't have a wound on his hip, but she didn't know that. Not unless she'd gotten a better look last night than he thought.

Apparently she hadn't. She sank to her knees beside him and groped for the other strap. By the time she found it, tucked inside the back of his braies, and tied it, he had to close his eyes and grit his teeth to keep the groan of lust within him. He'd asked her to help him as a kind of jest, to see if she would perform the duties of a wife without quibble, and now he paid for his presumption with an agonized pleasure.

"There you are, Sir David," she said. "Will there be anything else?"

The tone of her voice made his eyes snap open, and

he looked down at her. It wasn't that she sounded insolent, or openly laughed at him, but he'd been observing
her for days now, and he recognized her amusement.

As she knelt before him, the temptation to show her
what else he would have her do was great, but it was
too soon for that. Instead, he let her stand, and she had
already turned away when he said, "There is one other
thing."

His hands spanned her waist. Her firm flesh warmed
his hands immediately, and he pulled her close.
Women, for him, were normally bits of pleasure, but
the top of Alisoun's head reached almost to his nose
and she spanned almost his whole length. He wanted to
revel in her obvious surprise at his maneuver, but his
training warned him he had best follow up his advantage at once.

Wrapping one arm around her back, he tipped her
off balance. "Alisoun?"

Totally unprepared, she looked up, and he kissed
her.

Her cool, dry lips impressed him with their curiosity.
Whether or not she admitted it, Alisoun wanted experience, but she positively hadn't had it yet.

He broke off the kiss. "Hasn't anyone *ever* kissed
you?"

"Not memorably."

He digested that, then said, "A challenge." He bent
over her again. "The legendary mercenary David always
accepts a challenge."

Apparently she had second thoughts about her cooperation, for she turned her head away. He didn't care.
Her cheek attracted him, as did her forehead and her
lashes. Dark lashes, he noticed, and again he wondered if
her hair was truly red. Everything about her tasted good,
a little like heather. She still withheld her lips, but she

wasn't clawing at his face or kneeing him in the groin, so he knew he didn't personally repulse her, and he could bank on that interest to give him a chance. He touched her lips with his tongue, then withdrew it. Her body tensed against his, and he felt her quick intake of breath.

"Don't be such a coward," he whispered.

Speechless, she glared at him.

"But you're not a coward. You just want to know. I don't tell. I won't tell. Use me." He smiled at her. "I won't charge for *this* service."

Somehow, reminding her that she was in charge freed her from that lingering stiffness. She didn't smile back—she hadn't lost that much propriety—but her lids fluttered, then closed, and she relaxed against him.

Her show of trust almost sent him groping for the bed, but she probably thought he was like this with every woman. Probably she underestimated her own potency, and the power of his knowing she would be his wife. Probably she hadn't even accepted his candidacy, but this cinched her fate. Aye, he wanted her lands, but he wanted *her*.

"Sir David?"

He caught her with her mouth open. His lips molded hers, his tongue thrust inside before she could change her mind. He tasted her shock, and realized she couldn't have changed her mind. She hadn't known what to expect. He wanted to breathe with her lungs, wanted to moan with her voice, but more than that, he wanted to connect with that kiss. That kiss sent her body arcing against his, brought him protectively over her. It was the best kiss of his life. It was . . . she fought him in a spasm, and he let her up for air.

Then he edged his knee between her legs and pressed her against it with his hand on her bottom. "Now *you* kiss *me*."

"What?" Her eyes opened, and she looked at him sleepily.

Immediately he imagined how she would appear after a night in his bed, and he rubbed his knee up and down, up and down. "Kiss *me*."

She understood without further elocution, and wet her lips with distracting resolve.

He was going to die of pleasure, and she hadn't even touched him yet.

Her breath reached him first. He inhaled the scent of mint, felt the first tingle of fever. Then her lips, then her teeth, then . . . oh, blessed day, her tongue met his. For one lucid moment, he remembered the tale his great-grandmother used to tell him. Then the hard slam of desire swept everything before it. He was lost in it, drowning in it, clutching at it, at her.

Probably only one sound could have brought him to the surface.

A giggle. A girl's high-pitched giggle.

He lifted his head, took a breath, opened his eyes, and found himself staring into Alisoun's bewildered gaze. The giggle from the great hall had been abruptly cut off. None of the serving folk or men-at-arms who broke their fasts peered into his chamber, but the damage had been done. Or was it a rescue? Had they been moving toward a cataclysm with no guidance and no forethought? Before he could gather his thoughts, Alisoun's calm facade fell into place. "My thanks, Sir David. It's good to know I have hired a man experienced in every field."

Irritated, he could only stare as she freed herself from his grip. How did she do that? How could she be trembling in his arms one moment, and indifferent the next? He wanted to grab her and shake her until the mask she wore fell away. Instead he watched as she glided away from him with her usual poise. He almost turned away from the sight of her. He almost missed it, but as she walked past the door, she staggered and caught at the frame.

She glanced back at him in embarrassment.

He pretended he hadn't seen it. But he now knew his plan. From now on, he would woo her and win her with kindness and patience. He would oil his tongue and court her, and before she knew it, she would be in the thrall of that fashionable romantic rot.

Perhaps he would have to shave, after all.

7

"What's wrong with Sir Walter?" The spindle slowly spun and dropped as the weight on the end pulled the wool thin and Edlyn's fingers fought to twist thread from the fluffy ball of raw wool.

"Don't get it too thin," Alisoun warned while she wondered how to answer. Everyone within the keep seemed to have a theory about Sir Walter's sudden tantrum this morning. With a calm she didn't feel, Alisoun said, "Sir Walter apparently saw the enthusiasm with which I welcomed Sir David's embrace this morning, and responded poorly. I see now I should not have left the door open."

Edlyn's eyes shone with excitement. "Philippa says if you had shut the door you'd still be in there."

Alisoun's hand jerked. The thread broke and the spindle hit the floor, and everyone in the great hall turned to look. "Did she?" She hid the color that inched up her cheeks by leaning over to pick up the spindle. "And what was the reaction to that?"

Hands freed of labor, Edlyn clasped them to her bosom. "They say it would be so romantic if the fair maiden of George's Cross were wooed and won by the greatest mercenary in England."

Unexpectedly, Alisoun almost laughed. "I thought you weren't aware of Sir David's reputation."

"They told me."

They. Everyone in the castle had been gossiping about David. Alisoun corrected herself. *Sir* David. She'd already learned the danger of thinking of him in a too-familiar way. He responded in a too-familiar way.

Now she'd given them more to gossip about, and from what she'd learned of David, he would nurse that gossip until he'd achieved his objective or she'd thrown him out. And she couldn't throw him out.

Sliding the almost finished skein off the stick, she said, "I'm a widow, and I let a man kiss me. That is surely not so unusual an event."

Edlyn giggled. "Not for anyone but you, my lady."

Poking the unformed ball of wool, Alisoun found a strand and started another thread. The labor of making thread was every woman's constant companion, be she lady or serf. It took twelve spinners to keep up with one weaver, and Edlyn had never developed the dexterity for creating an even thread. So every rainy day, Alisoun took Edlyn into a corner of the great hall and taught her about thread, trying to prepare her for the role of lady of the castle. When she thought today of what she had to tell Edlyn, a sick feeling clogged her throat. Poor child.

Quickly she corrected herself. Lucky woman. Edlyn was a lucky woman, and it was Alisoun's glad duty to tell her so. She would do it . . . soon. Lanolin from the wool made Alisoun's fingers soft, experience made her fingers supple, and again she showed Edlyn how to hook the thread to the spindle. "Twist it evenly," she urged, then sat back to watch and think.

It had been stupid to go to Sir David's room alone, but she'd wanted to prove something to herself. She'd wanted to prove she could be with him, see him, and not become the incompetent of the night before.

Last night, she hadn't shown it, of course. She would never show such weakness. But his display of masculinity had shocked her in a titillating sort of way. She had wanted to stay and stare, and maybe wash him and see if it were possible that such a previously unimpressive appendage could grow yet bigger. That had been what had chased her from the room. Not fear or awe, but temptation.

"Damned curiosity," she whispered.

Edlyn kept her eyes on the thread, but she grinned.

The child was growing up. She was smart enough not to comment on Alisoun's chagrin, but still imprudent enough to think she could ask any question without chastisement. Alisoun had informed Edlyn's parents of her liveliness, accompanied by a suggestion that they chose her husband with an eye to his kindness and not just his wealth. Their reply had been waiting when she returned from Lancaster, and the tone had been ominous. No one wanted advice from the oldest virgin widow in England.

Edlyn reverted to her original subject with the tenacity of a puppy jerking on a meaty sinew. "Sir Walter hasn't been as respectful as he used to be, ever since Philippa . . . "

Alisoun looked up.

The warning in her gaze stopped Edlyn, and she reconsidered. Then she said defiantly, "Well, he hasn't treated you well for a long time now."

Alisoun had hoped nobody had noticed. She

believed that for her people to feel secure, their leaders should be united in purpose. She knew, without doubt, that she, as the lady, should be the highest authority.

In retrospect, she realized she had placed her confidence in the wrong man. She had chosen Sir Walter, raised him from his place as a lowly knight. Then he had not only taken it on himself to reprove her, but he had failed to do the one thing she thought him able to do. When the assaults had begun and she demanded a solution, Sir Walter had suggested that Alisoun remain within the castle walls. For a woman whose responsibilities required that she ride to the village, to the fields, to her other estates, such a remedy proved one thing only—Sir Walter was incompetent. He would have to step aside, at least until the issue had been resolved.

Yet Alisoun didn't know if anything could ever be resolved. Even if Sir David successfully kept her tormentor at bay, she feared—she knew—she would never be sure of her peace. But she'd done what she'd done. Dear God, what choice had she had?

"Edlyn, I've had a letter from your parents." She didn't try to infuse enthusiasm into her voice. She knew that would only frighten the girl more. "They have chosen your husband."

Edlyn's hands faltered. She almost dropped the spindle, and Alisoun heard the audible breath she drew. But she regained her composure with a speed that made Alisoun proud. "Did they tell you his name?"

She'd been practicing, Alisoun thought. She'd been expecting to hear, and practicing her reaction to the news. "It is Lawton, duke of Cleere. It is a very good match for you."

"Cleere?" The spindle began to spin too rapidly. "Where is Cleere?"

"In the south of England."

"How far south?"

"In Wessex."

Edlyn's skin paled to the color of ivory, her lips turned almost blue, but she said nothing.

Heart aching, Alisoun said, "I've met him. He's a good man."

"Does he have land closer to—" Edlyn swallowed, "—here?"

"Not that I know of, but perhaps your family gave him a parcel of land as dowry."

Edlyn stared at Alisoun until Alisoun looked away. "My family has six girls. They cannot afford to give parcels of land away with every marriage. So . . . he's a duke. I'm marrying a duke, and my family has nothing to give with me. Lady Alisoun?"

"Aye?" Alisoun responded as she should, with no emotion whatever. Almost no emotion.

"What's wrong with the duke of Cleere?" Edlyn asked.

"There's nothing *wrong* with him." Alisoun realized she dithered while Edlyn waited in agony. "He's a little older than I would have chosen."

Edlyn's voice rose an octave. "Older than David?"

God shield the child. She thought David old. "Older than two Davids."

"I'm going to go away to a far place, and probably never see you or my family again, to be the wife of a man who . . . does he have any teeth?" Edlyn read the answer in Alisoun's expression. "Or hair?"

"He's got hair," Alisoun said quickly.

Edlyn stared at Alisoun with unnatural calm. "I've been praying every morning at mass for a man who . . . not for a handsome man, or a clever man, or a rich man, but one who . . ." She shuddered. "He'll want to kiss me, like Sir David did with you, and he won't have any teeth. He'll touch me all over, and his hands will be all dry-feeling like a serpent's, and he'll want me to touch him. All saggy and . . . "

Alisoun couldn't stand it anymore. "Edlyn." She laid her hand on the girl's head. "I know Lord Lawton, and I give you my word, he is as kind and generous a man as any woman could want. Nothing can turn the clock back and make him young again. Nothing can move his home closer to mine. But you, of all people, know how important it is to have a husband who will treat you gently. I swear to you, he will do so." Edlyn's head drooped, and Alisoun slid to her knees and looked up into her face. "I've been praying, too, and I'm not dissatisfied with the results."

"He'll die, won't he?"

She should reprimand the girl for ill-wishing such a good man, but such self-righteous nonsense was beyond her now. "Sooner or later."

"I hope he doesn't get me with child." Edlyn seemed to be unaware that she was speaking her thoughts aloud. "I don't want to die before him in childbed."

No cruelty discolored her words, only a plaintive wish for life, and Alisoun found herself without the proper thing to say.

"Lady Alisoun, I think I'll go to the chapel. I need to develop the proper resignation." Edlyn smiled, a poor, pitiful thing, a smile not unlike the one Alisoun saw on so many wives' faces. "Perhaps I can find it there."

Watching Edlyn wander toward the stairwell, Alisoun wondered what had happened to the well-arranged life she'd lived for so long. In her conceit, she thought that if one planned properly, observed clearly, and always shouldered one's responsibilities without reservation, one would escape the clutter and disorganization which ruled the lives of others. It had worked for years. For years, she had been undisputed lady of all she surveyed, unbothered by heartache, sedition, danger, or confusion. It had seemed to her that she had discovered the magic formula others sought, and the ease with which she worked it gave her a faint sensation of superiority.

Although her organization remained firmly in place, the heartache and sedition had found her. Heartache for Edlyn, suddenly an adult, but with a child's vulnerability. Sedition from Sir Walter. Danger from Osbern. And confusion . . . Slowly, she leaned down and picked up the spindle Edlyn had dropped. Confusion. God's shield, David of Radcliffe seemed to sow confusion all around him.

"Lady Alisoun is imagining things." Sir Walter paced along the high walk atop the castle wall.

From here, they could see all the way down the hill to the village and well beyond, and David listened to Sir Walter while observing with a warrior's eyes. "There wasn't an arrow shot at her?"

"An arrow shot, aye. At her?" Sir Walter chuckled and threw his arm around David's shoulders in a man-to-man gesture. "Nay."

David stopped beside a crenellation and leaned out to look across Alisoun's land, soft and green in the falling rain. The movement scraped Sir Walter's arm off on the stone, and he wished he could scrape Sir Walter off as easily. The man had been dogging his footsteps and answering questions in such a munificent spirit he had convinced David of his culpability. Did he think David stupid? Or was he hoping to correct the mistake he'd made—to retain his position, or to diffuse suspicion? "Did you find the archer, then?"

"Nay, but poachers are notorious for being swift in escape, and none of them are likely to admit to shooting an arrow that had hit their lady."

The forest had been cut back on all sides of the castle, leaving no easy cover for attackers, but nothing could remove the giant rocks which thrust themselves up through the flesh of the earth like bones from a compound fracture. "Why would anyone want to shoot at their lady?"

"Lady Alisoun won't listen to . . ." David twisted around and leaned his shoulder against the mossy stone, and Sir Walter pulled a rueful face. "Well, you may have noticed, she has a mind of her own. She's made unpopular decisions at times, but I doubt that anyone shot at her on purpose. I think it was a wild shot."

"Hm." David walked toward the tower nearest the keep. It overlooked the sea, and the scenery beyond changed from soft pastels to vivid stains of color. The purple sea reflected the clouds. Sea creatures rode through the snowy foam on the waves, flipping their browns and grays over and over with no caution for the wet, black rocks. Such a contrast, David mused. The domesticated calm of the village and fields and the ferocity of the water. Lady Alisoun belonged to the domestic side of this castle, just as the domestic side belonged to her.

Yet she'd grown up in the keep, and the keep hugged the ocean, using its rugged backdrop as a natural defense. She'd heard the waves breaking with every storm, smelled the salt and shivered in the untamed wind. Had Alisoun, strong as she was, resisted the might of the sea? Or had the sea formed that part of her that roiled in hidden ecstasy?

"Would you perhaps like to visit the stables?" Sir Walter clapped his hands and rubbed the palms together. "You can see the arrangements we made for King Louis. He's a very famous horse, and we're honored to have him in our care."

"Aye? Has he spit on you yet?" The corner tower rose before them, and David opened the tiny door. Ivo huddled close to the basket of coals that heated the guardroom.

Sir Walter leaped through the door as if one of the coals had fallen in his braies. "Get out to your duty."

Ivo just turned his head and stared. David didn't know whom the big man-at-arms despised more—him or Sir Walter. But if the man despised Sir Walter, that was all to the good. That attitude could be used for David's own purposes, especially since Ivo had shown his unwavering loyalty to Alisoun. Strolling to the basket, he stretched out his hands. "I don't know, Sir Walter. Perhaps we should ask Ivo who fired the shot."

"He doesn't know anything." Sir Walter spoke too quickly. "He's just an ignorant man-at-arms."

David answered. "I've found that if I'm searching for the answer to a puzzle such as the one facing us here, those men who are silent often know the most."

Ivo snorted.

"If he knew anything, he would have told me what he knew," Sir Walter insisted. "Isn't that right, Ivo?"

Rising from his seat, Ivo towered over David and Sir Walter for one moment. Then he gathered his cloak from the hook and walked out into the rain, slamming the door behind him.

Sir Walter seemed torn between relief and embarrassment. "He's half an idiot."

"He doesn't like me," David said, half under his breath.

"Doesn't he?" Sir Walter brightened. "Never mind. I can handle him."

If Sir Walter always handled him as tactfully as he'd done when they walked in, Ivo could come to place his faith in David. And David well knew what a treasure that would be.

He went to open the door, and a young boy fell into the room just as if he'd been listening at the crack. David picked him up by the back of his tunic and held him off the ground as he examined him. A bit of a lad, ten perhaps, all elbows and knees and big blue eyes in a thin face. He kicked heartily while David dusted him off and set him on his feet. "Who are you?" David asked.

"He's one of the pages, and he shouldn't be here."

Sir Walter grabbed the lad by a handful of his blond hair, but David latched onto Sir Walter's wrist before he could give the boy a twist. God, how he hated men who were thoughtlessly cruel. They were worse than the others, the ones who knew what they were doing. Men like Sir Walter never imagined that a blow hurt worse when delivered to a boy trying his best, or that words from an idol could tear a wound that never healed. "He's done no harm."

"He shouldn't be—"

"I should, too." The boy interrupted, clearly lacking any sense of the danger he courted. "The lady sent me."

Glaring, but taken aback, Sir Walter said, "Then give your message and begone."

"I won't. The lady said I should stay."

Sir Walter's hands twitched. "Stay. Here. Why?"

"I am to be Sir David's personal squire."

"Squire? Personal?" Sir Walter stared at the boy. "You?" He looked back at David, then started to laugh. "And I thought she *liked* you."

David's hand tried to form a fist, but he still held Sir Walter's wrist.

Sir Walter's laughter broke and he jerked back.

"Curse you!" He rubbed the marks David had placed on his skin and for one intelligent moment, he saw enough of David to put fear into him. Then he tried to laugh again, not as successfully as before, and said, "I'll leave you with your . . . squire, then."

Wrapping his cloak around his throat with a flourish, he left David and the boy.

Now that the enemy had been removed, the lad lost his cockiness. He bent his head respectfully, then examined David without lifting his chin. David grinned at the boy's idea of subtlety, and asked, "What's your name?"

"I'm Eudo, lord."

"Eudo," David repeated. "And how long have you practiced your duties as squire?"

"Oh . . ." Eudo dropped his gaze to his feet. "A long time."

A lie, but a badly told one. David liked that. He preferred not to deal with an accomplished liar. He also knew Alisoun had sent the lad to him for a reason, and he had faith in her judgment. He just needed to discover that reason. Genially, he said, "That's good." He didn't remove his gaze from the boy.

Eudo began to twist as if he needed to use the garderobe. "I know I'm small, but I'm older than I look."

David judged him. "Eleven, I would have said."

Eudo jumped. "Older . . . than I look."

David still didn't move, standing with his hands lax, waiting for the truth.

Eudo made a bad choice. He decided to expand the falsehood. "I've been squire to lots of men. Dozens!"

Stroking his chin, David pulled a long face. "Too bad."

"What do you mean?"

"I like to train my squires from the beginning. Like most knights, I have my own special ways I want my weapons and armor cared for, the way I want my meat carved, the way I like my—" he rubbed his stubbled chin, "—face shaved. If you've been squire to many men, I suppose you've picked up bad habits." Slowly, he started to turn away and felt the bump as Eudo latched himself onto David's belt.

"Nay!"

"What?"

"I . . ."

David looked down into the big, dismayed blue eyes and managed not to grin at the struggle portrayed therein.

"I wasn't exactly the squire to dozens of men."

"Half a dozen?"

Eudo slid down David's leg just a little as if expecting a rap on the noggin. "A few."

"Too many." David tried to shake him off, but not too hard.

"One!"

Leaning over, David cupped Eudo's chin to keep him from slithering onto the floor. "How many?"

Eudo took a deep breath and tried to speak, then blurted, "I begged so hard, my lady sent me to you with instructions to tell you . . . I'm just a page, and if you want another, more experienced squire, she will gladly oblige."

"That's the truth?"

"Aye, lord."

"All the truth?"

Eudo nodded, and David looked him over. Tears cast a sheen over Eudo's eyes, and his throat muscles clutched as he swallowed sobs. Brushing the hair off Eudo's forehead, David declared, "I like *you*."

Eudo didn't respond for a moment, then he wiped his sleeve across his nose. "You do?"

"You'll do nicely for my squire." David released his chin and Eudo scrambled to his feet. Tugging his belt back up into place, David said, "You're a man who tells the truth, regardless of the consequences."

Eudo straightened his thin shoulders.

"You'll always tell me the truth from now on, won't you?"

"Aye, lord."

"Do you swear?"

"Aye, lord."

David frowned at the easy answer, and knelt beside Eudo so their eyes were level. "A man's word is his most precious possession. When a man breaks his word, no one ever believes him again. So I want you to think, and think hard—do you swear to always tell me the truth, even if it should fetch you a beating, even if it hurts me, even if you fear the consequences?"

This time Eudo hesitated. His long, freckled hand rubbed his arse as he recalled pain. Then he looked again at David's face, and something he saw there convinced him. "I swear, my lord, I will obey you in all things and always, always tell you the truth."

"You're a good man."

Eudo's smile broke forth and David suddenly understood how he had swayed Alisoun to do his bidding. Dimples resided in his cheeks, teeth crowded his mouth, and his grin almost spread from ear to ear. He would be hard to resist.

Standing, David clapped him on the shoulder. "Show me the lay of the castle."

"Oh, thank you, my lord." Eudo jumped in the air.

They stepped out into the rain and Eudo ran ahead along the wall walk, then returned. "Are you going to save our lady from harm?"

"I am."

"Good." He pointed at a jumbled clump of boulders. "The archer hid there when he shot my lady."

His confidence surprised David. "How do you know?"

"I went and looked afterward. I looked in all of them, and found little bits of feather from the fletching and a fresh scratch in that one."

With his gaze, David measured the angle and distance from the stones to the gate. A knave could hide there and shoot, then escape back into the forest easily enough, and none would be the wiser. "Did you tell Sir Walter?"

Eudo made a face. "Sir Walter doesn't listen to me, so I did what I could to protect my lady."

Fascinated, David asked, "What was that?"

"I planted thistles in the dirt in the cracks."

David stared at Eudo incredulously.

Hunching his shoulders, Eudo mumbled, "It was the best I could think of."

With a whoop, David lifted him into air and swung him around. "What a clever man you are." Setting him on his feet, he dusted him off. "If I had ten allies like you, I could conquer France."

"Really?" Eudo tried to subdue his grin, but it broke out. "You liked it?"

David tapped Eudo on the temple. "That's doing the best you can with limited supplies. Every knight-errant learns it, or dies, and you've learned it earlier, and better, than most."

Beaming under the praise, Eudo hurried to the stairs to the inner bailey, moving so quickly he skidded down the last four slick stone steps and landed on his knees. He glanced back quickly, embarrassed, but David plucked him out of the mud and said, "Best take care. I can't use a squire with a broken leg."

"Oh, I never break anything," Eudo said airily. Then

he seemed to recall his vow, for he stammered, "That is, I did once. My finger. But it was only a finger, and my lady set it and it's fine. See?" He held it up and wiggled it. "And once I had to have my lady stitch up my back because I fell on a sword that someone had left laying on the ground." He reconsidered. "Well, it wasn't really a sword. More of a dagger. Or a knife. It was a knife. And it was me who left it on the ground. But I'm careful now. You can ask anyone. Well, don't ask Sir Walter, because he still talks about the time I—"

With a pang, David placed his hand across Eudo's mouth. The long-winded, earnest explanations suddenly reminded him of Bert, and he missed his daughter with an ache that got worse with every passing day.

Did she miss him, too? Would she have forgotten him by the time he got home? He wanted to gather Eudo in his arms, and hug him tight, but he didn't make the mistake of thinking Eudo would welcome such an affront to his dignity. Instead, David said, "I said you had to tell me the truth. I didn't say you had to confess every mistake you'd ever made."

Eudo freed himself. "So I only have to tell you if you ask me?"

"You only have to tell me if you think you should."

"But how will I know what I should tell you?"

"How do you know what to tell the priest in confession?"

"It doesn't matter with our priest," Eudo returned quickly. "He can't hear anyway, and he always gives the same penance, so I confess everything."

Lowering his chin, David stared until Eudo rocked back and forth on his heels uneasily. David said, "You know what I mean."

"I guess . . . I have to tell you the stuff I don't want to."

Only David's masterful control kept his laughter under restraint. "I'll probably hear about it anyway, and I'd prefer to hear it from you."

Envisioning a vast procession of mistakes and corrections, Eudo sighed. "How will I know when I'm ready to take care of myself?"

Rain had soaked David's garments and the wet wool stuck to him, but he answered, "Good judgment comes from experience, and a lot of that comes from bad judgment."

"But bad judgment can be corrected," Alisoun's voice said.

The man and the boy turned to see her standing in the doorway of the kitchen hut.

"Sometimes." Little dribbles of water inched their way down David's flesh, reminding him of the travails of a summer siege when bugs swarmed, crawled, and bit. "Sometimes, a man's reward for bad judgment can be death." He ruffled Eudo's wet hair. "That's why it's best to make your mistakes early, within the safety of my lady's castle."

Alisoun joined them, her face a pale oval beneath the hood of her cape. "Will Eudo be making his mistakes under your guidance?"

"I would have no other," David answered. One cold drop fell out of his hair and slithered down his spine, and he shuddered convulsively.

Alisoun observed Eudo's proudly jutting chin. "Then he is yours to train."

Driven to madness, David began to scratch. First his chest, then stomach, then—

Alisoun made a sound like a wounded puppy, and when he raised his eyebrows in inquiry, she blushed, spun on her heel and marched away. He muttered, "I wonder what's wrong with her?"

"Sir?" Eudo was trying to curb his laughter, and with less luck than David. "I think I know."

"Tell me, lad."

Giggling, Eudo pointed at David as he rubbed his palms over his stockings, hoping to wring a little of the water out. "That. My lady says you're not supposed to scratch when others are watching."

Suspending his scratching excursion, David stared in astonishment. "But I itch!"

"My lady says a noble knight takes care not to wipe his nose while eating."

"Everybody knows that!"

"He never overindulges in drink."

Remembering the first time Alisoun had seen him, David cackled. "How I must have shocked her."

"And he never scratches his body."

Trying to understand, David said, "His crotch, you mean."

"Nay, not any part of his body."

David stared at Eudo. "That's nonsense!"

"My lady is very exacting in her manner."

"Well, she'll just have to learn better!"

Looking troubled, Eudo was about to speak, then visibly stopped himself. Lowering his head, he muttered, "Aye, Sir David."

Defensively, David demanded, "What's wrong with that?"

Glancing at him from the corner of his eyes, Eudo said, "I saw you this morning."

"This morning?"

"Kissing my lady."

"Oh." David started toward the stable. "Is that also something my lady speaks against?"

"Nay. That is, I don't know." Eudo followed closely, anxious to impart his wisdom. "She hasn't discussed kissing with me yet. But it looked as if you liked kissing her."

A glimmer of comprehension broke through David's indignation. "It was enjoyable."

"Philippa said my lady doesn't kiss casually. That if she kissed you, it was a very serious thing."

David relaxed as he strode into the dimness of the open stable door. The rain outside made the hay smell almost moldy, and that, mixed with the odor of curry brushes and manure, combined to produce the odor of heaven. If he couldn't be home, he'd rather be here, lingering to examine the horseflesh of Alisoun's stables. Horses were contrary, rude, and given to senseless fits of jealousy. He understood them much better than he understood women.

He eyed Eudo's skinny back as he skipped ahead. "Kissing my lady was a very serious thing to me. Do you understand, as my squire, that my secrets are sacred and not to be told?"

Eudo nodded.

"I want to court her."

"I *thought* so." Now Eudo turned and, walking backward, looked David over as carefully as David had previously examined him. He might have been Alisoun's father, sitting in judgment of a suitor. After one very long moment, he made his decision and nodded. "If you listen to me, I can help you."

One of the first things a mercenary discovered was that information from a source inside a beleaguered castle could shorten the siege perceptibly. Now David had found such a source, and he could scarcely contain his excitement. "I'm depending on you."

"It's very difficult to court my lady." The lad was solemn, even when he tripped on a rake and fell over backward.

David picked him up and dusted him off, then held him in place. "What does she like?"

"Like?"

"What makes her happy?"

"Happy." Eudo pondered that. "I don't know if my lady is ever *happy*. She likes it when I don't scratch. She likes it when I say my prayers every night without being reminded. She likes it when I write my grandparents without being reminded. She likes it when I bathe in the spring without being reminded."

"What does she like for herself?"

Tilting his head, Eudo stared at David in puzzlement. "She doesn't like anything for herself. She's the lady."

"She never laughs aloud?"

"Nay!"

"Nor ever smiles?"

"Aye, she does that!" Eudo's features softened and took on a distant expression, like that of a man in love. "When she does, she looks all pretty." Then he grew stern. "But men don't make her smile, because she only likes men who work and do their duty without complaining. She says there aren't very many who do that."

David opened his mouth to deny this but found he couldn't. "Perhaps not."

"She says men try to claim more than their rights, and tell her how to order her house and plant her fields and sell her goods, when she knows more than ten of them."

"I wager she does."

Eudo had obviously considered David's tactics well, and with a wisdom beyond his years, he said, "I think she'd like it if some man respected her and washed his face every day and did what he was supposed to without being told."

"I think you're right."

"And maybe—" Eudo sounded shy, "—you could kiss her like you did this morning?"

David thought about that. "I think I might have to hold my kisses in reserve."

"Huh?"

"For an emergency," David explained to the puzzled lad. "For when she really needs it." Turning Eudo, he marched him between the stalls. "But I'll have you trim my hair straight and shave me, and if you see me scratching—"

"Aye, sir?"

"Take the strap to me."

8

"You summoned me, my lady?"

Sir David's broad shoulders blocked out much of the sunlight which came through the open door from her solar. Nevertheless, Alisoun finished tracing the number on her account books before she acknowledged his presence. "I did." She pointed across the narrow table. "Sit there."

His red tunic and berry blue surcoat smelled from the smoke of the great hall's morning fires, and he appeared both warm and well fed as he stepped inside. He looked around the tiny, windowless room with interest. "What do you do here?"

"I settle my accounts," she replied. "And it is for that reason I have summoned you."

"It's chilly and dark as a tomb." He patted the loosely tied leather bag he carried, then swung one leg over the top of the stool and settled on the hard surface. Squeezing himself between the long, sturdy table and the wall, he observed, "Too small, too."

"The chill and the dark encourage me to do my work faithfully and not linger," she answered.

Leaning his back against the stone wall behind him, he stretched his long legs out so they reached the wall beside her and settled the bag on his lap. "I know monks with better cells."

Disgruntled, she ignored his comment. Of course he would think that. He slept in the best guest's chamber, ate her finest meals, instructed her villagers to watch for strangers, and patrolled her estate, looking for . . . for . . . looking for nothing. Since his arrival a month ago, there had been no threat, no danger.

His knee nudged hers, and she looked down. He had placed his legs so they blocked her exit, but that in no way intimidated her. He hadn't mentioned his crazy scheme to wed her since that morning in his bedroom, and she thought he had forgotten—although forgetfulness seemed unlikely. More likely he had taken a taste of her in that kiss and found her repulsive.

He hadn't behaved as if he found her repulsive, though. He'd been polite. Painfully polite. A true chevalier in every manner.

Opening the box of gold before her, she counted the coins and held them out. "Your second month's wages in anticipation of work well done."

The cool gold warmed beneath her touch as she passed it from her hand to his. He fondled the money between his fingers, tracing the moldings on the coins, then looked deep into her eyes and smiled. "I take Eudo and ride your estate every day, looking for possible trouble, but I've found no sign of any malicious activity. Other than that, I've done nothing. Nothing at all."

His pleasant voice revealed no impatience. His well-shaved chin showed a cleft in the middle. He'd just taken another bath—one she had managed to avoid observing, but whose results she appreciated. And with a jolt, she realized he was angry.

Looking closer, she saw the way his jaw flexed when he clenched his teeth, the lines between his brows, the insincere curve of his lips. Aye, he was angry, but why? Evaluating him, she said, "You've done much. You found the place where the archer hid."

"Not I, my lady." He stacked the coins on the table. "A lad of eleven did that. Maybe it would help if I truly knew what kind of threat I faced."

"Nonsense." Inwardly she winced at the heartiness in her voice. "You've done much without knowing. What good would knowing do?"

"It would help me plan for an attack."

"You already strengthened the defense around the castle."

"Aye, that I did, and so successfully that your unnamed intruder has quietly slipped away without a whimper."

Startled, she realized he complained *because* he'd done nothing. She hadn't thought about it, but perhaps inactivity grated on him. Perhaps he wanted to answer Sir Walter's constant little taunts with more than the mockery he usually served. Perhaps he was thinking of leaving—and that she could not allow. Utilizing the tone she reserved to encourage her homesick fosterlings, she said, "That is as I wished. You have kept danger away from George's Cross."

Placing his hands on the table between them, he spread the fingers wide. "With these hands have I done this."

"With your mere presence."

He curled his fingers into fists, and he rapped his knuckles sharply on the wood. "Do you think I'm stupid?"

"Oh, nay!" She placed her hand over his, trying to

encourage him with a brief touch. "You're not stupid at all. I suspect you're feeling used and useless, but in sooth, there *was* a threat and it *has* disappeared, but only for the moment, I fear."

He stared at her hand, resting on his, and his gaze sharpened with something that looked like . . . competition? Hastily she began to withdraw it, but he whipped his hand free and slapped hers flat on the table. He smiled a lopsided smile. "I like to be on top."

She tried to slide her hand out from underneath, but his grip tightened. Not cruelly, but firmly. Her long fingers peeked out from his palm, but his hand swallowed most of hers. His calluses scraped her skin, making the simple act of hand-holding into a sensuous adventure. It had been difficult to linger over the brief contacts when he helped her onto the bench to dine or shared her trencher, but now he held her, and she waited, hanging by her expectations, for him to speak, or . . . whatever.

"Sir Walter proclaimed when I arrived he had no need of my help, and it appears he told the truth." Leaning forward, he turned her hand.

A squeaking noise came from somewhere close. She glanced at the floor, expecting to see a mouse, but nothing skittered over the floor. Then, with his fingers, David traced the length of her palm, and she forgot the noise. While he was touching her in an unusual manner, no one could call it intimate. No one except an aging virgin like her, tantalized by a mere contact. "If Sir Walter told you that, he is not the man I believed him to be."

"Most people are not," he conceded.

Her fingers were so long that she always thought they looked freakish. As he stroked the length of each one, she cloaked her embarrassment with hasty words. "But people are formed by their place in life and their duties, so a wise woman knows what to expect and how to handle it."

The movement of his hand on hers ceased and he searched her face with his gaze. "If that were true, all villains would be the same, all kings would be the same, all knights would be the same."

The amusement and insight in his eyes made her want to squirm. In the turmoil of his life, had he learned something she hadn't? Surely not. She'd lived her life by her beliefs, and a very successful life it had been. He had no reason to undermine her confidence.

He cocked a brow at her silence. "Why do some born to poverty remain there, and others rise above their births to become something greater?"

Was he talking about himself? Had he risen above the circumstances of his birth? And if he had, was it possible for her to sink from the pinnacle of hers? David's babblings seemed to make the chamber close in on her. That, and the way he cupped her hand as he would a sacred vessel.

"What of rebellion?" he asked.

She didn't think he spoke of a political thing. She'd watched him this last month, and every day had been a rebellion against the formality of life as she knew it. Every day he spoke to the common folk. He'd charmed and encouraged them, and in the waning and waxing of one moon, she'd observed the results of his interference.

In sooth, it had been odd to have old Tochi answer her questions about her garden with such confidence, but she hadn't truly minded. Tochi did know more than anyone on her estate about growing herbs, so why shouldn't he beam when he showed her the sprouting seedlings?

"What of laughter?" David asked.

She'd pretended not to notice as he mocked Sir

Walter's pomposity. She blamed Sir Walter for the death of her cat and for Edlyn's abduction almost as much as she blamed herself. Blamed him, because he had been derelict in his duty. Blamed herself because the responsibility for the safety of George's Cross was ultimately hers, and she had failed to notice how complacent, even insolent, Sir Walter had grown.

David's voice deepened, little twinkles lit the darkness of his brown eyes, and a whimsical smile tugged at his lips. "What of dreams?"

"Dreams?"

"Aye, dreams." Lifting her hand, David placed it on his lips and enunciated clearly, as if to communicate through touch as well as sound. "Dreams are the forms in your mind where you dance to the tune of what may be."

She knew that to be nonsense. "Dreams are a waste of time," she said firmly.

"I possessed my dreams ere I possessed truth." He watched her with something that looked like pity. "I was nothing but a younger son, turned out into the world with a shield and sword. I won King Louis in my first French tournament, and I never looked back. I only looked forward, trying to see that place where my dreams would take shape."

If she had ever dreamed a man and hoped to have him, the man she dreamed would be David. It was as if he had somehow ascertained everything she admired in a man and distilled it within himself.

"Radcliffe is that place, and now I dream of the day it will be as prosperous as—" he looked at her hand at rest in his, "—as George's Cross."

Funny thing, though. She rather missed his crude humor and honest reactions, and for that she scolded herself. She wasn't a silly miss who knew nothing of her own needs. She was the lady of George's Cross. "I don't have dreams."

He shook his head sadly and placed the leather bag on the end of the table. "No dreams? But without your dreams, how will you know when you achieve them?"

"I don't know what you're talking about." Truly, she didn't. Dreams wasted precious time. They were wanderings of a mind meant to be snared and trained.

"You don't even allow yourself to imagine?" Somehow he managed to gain possession of her other hand. He might have been talking to himself when he said, "Perhaps I shouldn't have withheld my kisses. I've never seen a woman so in need of kisses."

He stood, seeming massive in the tiny room, and she shrank back as if he threatened her. He didn't, only she had the sensation of hearing something she'd known for a long time and steadfastly ignored.

He encouraged her to think beyond her earliest teachings, and she didn't want to. She wanted to cling to the safety of her prejudices. Yet when he bent over her, she felt the winds of temptation buffeting her.

"Don't be afraid," His lips brushed her forehead, his hands enclosed her arms. "This won't hurt."

How could it not? She could have laughed at his conviction. He was dragging her from safety to peril, and he thought it wouldn't hurt? She ached, she couldn't catch her breath, and all he did was lift her to her feet and wrap his arms around her. The table between them cut into the flesh of her thighs, and probably his, too. She had to lean forward, her spine curved at an awkward angle, and her face pressed against his chest. She couldn't have been more stiff and uncomfortable, but for some reason, she didn't move. One of his hands massaged her neck, the other rubbed circles on her back, in a manner reminiscent of Philippa's comforting of her child. And why did he think she needed comforting? She'd been nothing but sensible this morning. Still, the massage made her want to turn her head and close her eyes, and with a sigh so big it surprised even her, she did so.

"That's better," he crooned. Slowly, rhythmically, he started rocking her sideways, back and forth, back and forth. The keys on her belt rattled against the wood and the motion hurt her thighs where they rested against the table, but she resisted the pain. The motion soothed her, and if she complained he would stop, she knew. After all, that would be the sensible thing to do.

But when she tried to shift her legs, he noticed.

"What's wrong?" Then he recognized her dilemma. "You should have said."

She stepped back against the wall, relinquishing the solace without outward sign. "It was nothing. It's just that the rubbing felt so . . . well, that is, it seemed to . . . what are you doing?"

Stupid question. He vaulted the table. "That's better," he said.

But how he could think so, she didn't know. Between him, the wall, the stool, and the table, they barely had room to stand. He stood so close against her, she had to lift her head straight back to look in his face. "We don't fit," she said.

"But we do. Better than you think, sweetling." He lightly kissed her.

"I'm going to fall."

"You'll have to hold on to me, then." He kissed her again.

Her palms itched to wrap around his waist. "It's not proper."

"Dreams are never proper." In one slow, hot sweep, his mouth slid over her chin and across her throat.

She had to hold him or else totter backward over the

stool, so she held him. For her dignity's sake, of course. And because he warmed like a brazier, giving off heat to toast her very bones.

Cupping her head in his hands, he pressed it sideways and explored under her ear. His breath and the touch of his tongue set off a shudder that rattled her spine.

"You're cold," he whispered.

"Nay." She whispered, too, although she didn't know why. Why did she suddenly wish she'd shut the door? Why did they always kiss in full view of anyone who chose to look in?

"Cold for far too long."

She didn't know what he was talking about. With his lips, he followed the outline of her wimple around her cheek and over her forehead.

Then he tilted her even further and looked at her dazed face. "Do you trust me enough to close your eyes?"

Did she?

"You trust me enough to have me care for your estate," he reminded her. "Have you made a mistake?"

She closed her eyes.

Chuckling, he kissed her lips again. She didn't know why it pleased her to make him smile; he was laughing at her, after all. But it was not in cruelty, and if he laughed at her, she knew without a doubt he laughed at himself just as often. Then he kissed her a little deeper, and she didn't notice when his laughter stopped. She noticed nothing but the care with which he handled her—the slow embrace, the gentle probing of his tongue, the frequent breaks for air and reassurance.

This wasn't like the first kiss, all hunger and fire and sweeping resolution. This kiss gave comfort and reassurance. It frustrated her that she *did* need comfort and reassurance, that she liked this closeness, and the way he delicately tasted her. Yet she was a woman, too, who'd been given a sip of heady passion and wanted another.

Working her arms free, she put her hands on either side of his face and held him until he opened his eyes. "You're not doing it right."

He mocked her gently. "You would know."

"I know more than you think." Her own bravado shocked her. How could she imagine that she knew anything?

But he nodded amiably. "In sooth, you know more of what pleasures you than I."

"Women like—" she thought, then finished, "—different things."

"What do you like?"

Now *that* was an inquiry, asked by the devil for his own purposes. To discover what she liked, she would have to experiment, and no one in George's Cross was available for experiment—except David.

She should be dubious. She should know he did this to further his ridiculous suit of marriage, to gain custody of her twelve sacks of wool and all that went with it. But just moments ago she'd convinced herself he'd forgotten all about that, and the nurturing seemed so real. The comfort she drew from it *was* real, and her need now—that, too, was real.

Too many questions, and no answers she could accept.

Looking at him, his mouth pulled suspiciously straight, his brow set quizzically, she wondered what he thought and wondered why she cared.

Then his arms tightened and he took a short breath. "Too much control isn't good for a man."

Thinking that he meant her, that she suffered from too much control and that he displayed none whatsoever, she tried to correct him. But his hands ranged lower, onto her bottom, and he pulled her tighter against him and rubbed himself against her. She liked being rubbed, and she rubbed him back, undulating against him to increase sensation. From his low groan and the golden flames that lit his brown eyes, she supposed he enjoyed it, too.

He picked her up without respect for her person or status. Knocking her account book off, he deposited her on the table, and when she tried to object, he kissed her—correctly, this time. He took advantage of her open mouth and thrust his tongue inside, then pulled it out. She tried to speak again, and he did it again and again, until she comprehended.

He didn't want her to talk. He did want to kiss her, and possibly he wanted more. Her whole self rested along the length of the table, and he slid her along the smooth finish, then lowered her back until her head rested on the boards. "You can't get away now," he said, and she heard distinct satisfaction in his tone.

She felt sure she still had control. After all, she had only to shout and the serving women in the solar would come running. Still, the hard table chafed her back and David leaned over her, using his arms to trap her between them. And he kissed her with more than his mouth, teeth, and tongue now. Somehow his fervency had brought the weight of desire to bear. Her legs moved restlessly, the keys rattled on her hip, and he noticed. To placate her, he sank onto the table himself and laid his body against hers. One of his legs separated hers, and one of his hands stroked her thigh, creeping close to the place she really wanted stroked, then moving away.

His ignorance angered her—after all, he was the one with experience—and she freed herself from the kiss, grabbed his hand and put it where she wanted it. "There!" She glared into his eyes. "Do I have to do *everything*?"

His lids narrowed. He smiled. Not one of his pleasant, merry smiles, but more like the smile of a big, bad wolf about to eat an innocent girl.

Worse, that smile thrilled her. Thrilled her and frightened her, all at the same time. "David?"

"A man could revel in you."

She wanted to answer in a snap, but he pressed his palm firmly against the fork of her thighs, then released it, then pressed again. She grabbed his shoulders and arched her hips up, seeking more, and he obliged her. Her breasts ached, her stomach jumped, her breath quickened. She closed her eyes, then opened them, then closed them again. He kissed her mouth, not deeply this time, and whispered, "Who's doing this to you?"

Her hands clenched him, echoing his rhythm.

He removed his expert hand. "Who?"

"David!"

"That's right." He kissed her again, caressed her again, and she subdued a moan, fighting to keep it behind clenched lips. "By the saints, you're hot and sweet as honey on a firestone."

His free hand pushed her wimple off, she heard him say, "Saint Michael be praised," but words meant nothing to her. She comprehended only his body as it spoke to hers. The press of his chest against hers, the press of his groin against her hip, the tug of his hand in the hair on her head all promoted this sense of struggle within herself. Something in her fought to get out. Something not proper. Something wild and indiscriminate. It smacked headlong into her propriety and battered at it, using her body as a battleground.

Worse, she was on the wild thing's side. She wanted to allow it freedom, but she just couldn't.

He must have sensed her struggle, for he murmured, "Virgin." Taking his hand from between her legs, he replaced it with his body. He would have crushed her against the wood, but he held himself on his elbows and knees and made contact in only the important parts. The parts which, when placed together, could make a whole. She had to work to force her eyelids to lift so she could look at him, and when she did, she was sorry.

He appeared to be violent. His face was red, mottled where he had shaved it, and drawn into a scowl. But through lips that scarcely moved, he whispered, "You're my dream."

And she didn't believe, not even for a moment, that he was talking about her lands.

Her clothes itched. His clothes covered too much. If she had control of her hands, she would have removed every stitch, but he began to thrust and she forgot everything but the wild thing he'd discovered inside her. As she concentrated on the sensations, she moved restlessly. She tried to lift her legs, but he rested on her skirt and they were caught. She tossed her head and ran her hand through her own hair, clenching it in her fist, trying to find ease.

Her upraised elbow struck his leather bag, and she distinctly heard a mew, followed by a scratching. The two on the table tried to ignore it, but the creature, whatever it was, grew frantic. Both of them lifted their heads and stared at the sack. Irritated enough to scream, she demanded, "What's in there?"

He laid his hand on the bag, and the pressure seemed to placate the inhabitant. With a sigh of what sounded like relief, he asked, "Do you really want to talk about it now?"

"Nay, but I . . . nay." She wrapped her arms around his shoulders again. "Later."

But he didn't kiss her, although she clearly invited him. Instead he lifted his head. "Listen."

Booted footsteps crossed the floor of her solar, and

in a rush she remembered—she'd asked Sir Walter to come and consult with David. She'd thought it appropriate to try and unite the men in their common cause, and then, frivolous as any maiden, she had forgotten.

She had lost control.

"Blessed Mother!" She tried to slide back; David obligingly let her go. Snatching her wimple off the table, she grabbed a handful of flyaway hair. She couldn't subdue it, not easily, anyway, and David tried to help her. But they couldn't move fast enough, and when Sir Walter stepped into the doorway, they remained tangled on the table like guilty lovers.

Which they might have been if not for Sir Walter's interruption.

Taking a deep breath, she decided she could handle this situation. After all, she'd been in worse. Right now, she couldn't remember when, but surely she'd been in worse. Sitting up, she smoothed expression from her face and became the lady of George's Cross, impervious to criticism.

Then David said loudly, "Is the louse out of your hair now?"

Alisoun froze in horror. Was he mad?

He got to his knees on the table and efficiently finished wrapping her hair in the wimple, then nodded judiciously. "You'll have no more trouble, I'm sure." Turning to Sir Walter, he said, "She had a louse in her hair. I removed it." Climbing over her, he slid off the table and onto his stool, angelic expression in place.

The jiggling brought another "mew" from the leather bag on the table, but Alisoun had no attention to spare. A louse? He'd said she had a louse in her hair? She, who had never had vermin on her in her life, supposedly had picked one up in her own castle? She didn't believe it.

Sir Walter didn't believe it, either. He just watched,

stone-faced. No doubt he thought she taunted him, or worse, that she couldn't control her wayward passions.

And could she? She'd forgotten her schedule for David.

She glanced at him and realized it was possible to be peeved at a man and lust for him at the same time. No matter what David had said, she wished she'd ordered Sir Walter chained in the dungeon so she could have finished pursuing that odd, wild pleasure she found in David's arms.

Sir Walter cleared his throat. She still sat on a table in her accounting room with her skirts thrashed and her lips red from the impact of such fine kissing, and both men observed her to avoid looking at each other.

Early in her life, she'd discovered that her imperious lady-face could be undermined by a hint of color in her cheeks, and she'd learned to ignore the emotions that caused her to blush. But this embarrassment was apparently not subject to her authority, and she blushed so brightly she feared to light the room. With a distinct lack of grace, she scrambled off the table. The keys jangled; a bright, cheerful sound that seemed to illumine her mortification. Sitting on the stool, she leaned over to pick up her tumbled account book and found that her fingers trembled. Hastily, she placed the parchments on the table before her and folded her hands to conceal her agitation. In a reasonable voice, she asked, "Sir Walter, would you explain to Sir David what you wish from him?"

Sir Walter bowed, a jerky, graceless obeisance. "You and Sir David should discuss it between yourselves. The two of you obviously have a superior understanding."

His boots thudded, each step louder than the other until he left the solar with a slam of the door. Then she turned on David. "Why did you say that?"

"Say what?"

Mimicking him, she said, *"Is that louse out of your hair now?* Do you think he's a fool? I don't have lice. You condemned us with your playacting."

"Pardon, my lady. I presumed you wanted him to remain in ignorance of our . . . "

He hesitated, and she asked frostily, "Aye?"

"Our growing acquaintance."

His tactful reply infuriated her, and for the first time since she was a child, she spoke without thinking. "I'm the lady. Whatever I do, must be right."

The breath he took expanded his chest. Then it collapsed as he said, "Ah."

She wanted to cover her face. Arrogance. When had she ever shown such arrogance? But the way he sucked in his cheeks, as if he suppressed a smile, made it impossible for her to apologize. She snapped, "Don't ever try to dissemble for me again. You're no good at it."

His concealed amusement vanished, and he snapped back, "A man needs a moment to calm himself, my lady. I've already shown Sir Walter the shape of my passion once. I doubt he wanted to see it again."

When she understood, one of those discerning blushes began again, starting from her toenails and working up. She wanted to ask if he'd calmed himself so rapidly and what it portended if he had not. But she couldn't bear to reveal her ignorance, so she asked, "Well? Will you do it?"

"Do?"

"As Sir Walter desires."

Leaning back against the stone wall, he crossed his arms across his chest and leveled a stare at her. "Where did you learn that trick?"

"I don't know what you mean." But she did.

He explained anyway. "The trick of pretending nothing happened when almost everything that could happen, did."

"On the table, you mean?"

"As delectable a meal as I ever enjoyed."

"We had our clothes on." She'd wanted them off, but that had been a momentary aberration.

"I could have had you, clothes on and all." He pointed at her, interrupting her before she could say anything. "It wasn't my plan, but nothing I did in here was part of my plan. Remember that when you think of our time together, my lady of the frustrations."

How could she reply to him? She knew only the proper forms of address. She didn't know how to quarrel, for no one ever quarreled with her. She'd never learned spontaneous repartee. Most especially, she'd never mastered the art of a lover's frankness, for no one had ever wanted her for a lover. She wanted to think about how David seemed to sincerely desire her, and she needed to understand that wild part of her and what had spawned it.

He waited for her to gather some semblance of order, then asked, "What does the estimable Sir Walter wish from me?"

"Ah." She fiddled with the book of accounts to avoid any eye-to-eye contact. "He suggested that since you have little to occupy your time, you might take over the training of our squires. They respect you a great deal and would receive instruction gratefully."

Now she waited, and when he didn't reply, she looked up. His mouth had dropped open, and he just stared.

"Will you train the squires?"

"Nay!"

His explosion startled her. She knocked the book off the table again and it landed with a thud.

He didn't care. Pointing his thumb to his chest, he

said, "I'm Sir David of Radcliffe. I'm a legendary knight. I don't train mere squires."

She pursed her lips. No one challenged her arrogance, for in her prideful heart, she knew she was better than anyone around her. But Sir David didn't think like she did. The greatest warrior England had ever produced shrugged off the worship lesser men offered. In some ways, he was a humble man, and a humble man didn't refuse to train a pack of worshipping youths who followed his every move with eager gazes and knelt at his feet to hear pearls of wisdom. "You like to train Eudo."

"He's just a lad." Deep in thought, David scratched his stomach. "He doesn't know much."

"If they know much, you don't wish to train them?"

"Hugh's a man grown. He's a better fighter than . . . well." His braies must have grown looser, for he adjusted himself. "He'll be a knight, soon."

"'Twas Hugh's armor I purchased while in Lancaster. I would like to sponsor his knighthood with a whole heart, but . . ." She dangled the bait, hoping he would take it.

He sneered at her obvious gambit, then he took the bait anyway. "What's the problem with Hugh?"

"His swordwork is exemplary, he handles every horse in the stable with ease, he is a terror with a lance and mace, but he refuses to work with a knife."

"Why?"

"He says an honorable knight has no reason to fight with a knife."

"I suppose you'd want me to teach Andrew and Jennings, too."

"I had hoped—"

"What's Sir Walter going to do while I take over all his duties?"

Her voice sharpened at his petulance. "I had hoped he would assist you."

"What makes you think he'll settle for assisting me?"

"It was his idea."

That drew him up short. Slowly, he drew the word out. "Why?"

"He said you had not exercised your skills since you arrived, and thought perhaps it would be a pleasant way to practice while performing an added duty."

David snorted, and for the first time she wondered at Sir Walter's sudden spirit of cooperation. She had thought he simply detested David's inactivity and sought to remedy it. Did he have another motive? And what was it? She didn't like dancing to Sir Walter's tune all unknowing. "Perhaps this is not such a good idea."

David pinched the bridge of his nose. "Why not? At least you'll get something for your money. That's the idea, isn't it?"

Grateful for his surliness, she forgot the warm, soft sensation he'd given her and remembered only her earlier resentment of him. Of the luxurious life he'd lived at her expense, and how every one of her people worked for less than Sir David. It made her remember, too, that earlier he had seemed to resent his inactivity, and she again confronted the puzzle of a man. "It would give me much pleasure if you would at least—" The leather bag wiggled and released a definite "meow." She snapped, "What *is* in that bag?"

"That? Oh." She could read the fury in him, but he subdued it to loosen the strings and lay the bag open.

A blinking black kitten lifted its head and looked around.

Alisoun jumped back.

"It's only a kitten," he said.

"I can see that," she answered irritably.

"You're acting as if it were a wolf, prepared to eat you." Gathering up the tiny creature, he scratched it under the chin, then waved it in her face. "Isn't it cute?"

She flinched. "What are *you* doing with it?"

"Giving it to you. Eudo said your cat had been killed, and—"

"Oh, nay." She waved her hands. "I don't want another cat."

Placing the creature on the tabletop, he said, "I thought you liked cats."

"I do." She watched as the little thing scampered over to the edge and looked down. "In their proper place."

"In the stable?"

Sure that it would break something if it tried to jump, she nudged it back. "Aye."

"I barely rescued it from under Louis's hooves."

The kitten tried again to look over the edge, and again she pushed it away. "I can see why."

"Why I rescued it? Aye, it's a darling thing."

"Nay, why it was under Louis's hooves. It's stupid."

He sighed. "If you don't want it, you can just put it down on the floor. It'll *probably* survive among the dogs and the other cats, and its life will still be better than it would be in the stable."

She stared as the kitten sauntered toward one of the lit candles, then realized that David, too, sauntered— but he was heading out the door. "Wait! You take it." Then, belatedly, "Where are you going?"

"To train your squires." He stuck his head back in. "May I depend on your messenger to again take the gold to Radcliffe?"

"In sooth, but the cat—"

"Bless you, my lady." He disappeared, and both the gold and the kitten remained on the table.

9

Sir David erupted out of my lady's solar. He didn't notice me or anything else. His lips were tucked tight and his face was red, but I didn't read the signs of interrupted pleasure on his face. Usually I knew, for to speak to one of the men when they were nursing blue ballocks could bring on a cuffing or worse. But I didn't think Sir David would bother with something so trivial as mounting a woman. Of course, I badly wanted the man I so idolized to marry Lady Alisoun, my lady and my liege, but I never considered that their union would end with two bodies wrestling on a bed.

As Sir David strode toward the outer door, I shoved a large chunk of bread in my mouth and scampered after him. I had to know whether my ploy had succeeded, for in my eleven-year-old mind the only thing standing in the way of Lady Alisoun's love for Sir David had been Sir David's own behavior. By dint of coaxing and instruction, I had turned him from a crude, common knight to a prieux chevalier, and now I *expected my reward to be the happy news of their betrothal.*

Instead Sir David snarled like a grumpy old tomcat. "Put on your boots. We're going out."

And when I tried to tell him I didn't need boots in the summer, he looked at me and I found myself scrambling to obey. While I tried to squeeze my rapidly growing feet into the boots that pinched, he loitered in the great hall, teasing Heath in quite a normal manner and playing peek-and-squeal with baby Hazel.

Philippa allowed it now. She no longer treated Sir David as if he were a fork-tongued viper. Neither did she leave her baby alone with him.

When I finally had my boots on I rushed at Sir David. Gently, he wiped the drool off the baby's chin and waved bye-bye, and I demanded, "Did Lady Alisoun like the kitten?"

"You gave her a kitten?" Philippa sounded scandalized.

Standing up straight, Sir David glared at her. "Why shouldn't I?"

His stare might have been a fist. Philippa snatched her baby, holding her so tight Hazel howled, and shrank back against the wall.

Sir David muttered an oath and stomped from the great hall, and I followed. Slamming the outside door open, he stepped out on the landing before he said, "You don't have to tell everyone everything we planned."

Well, he hurt my feelings. I was young, but I wasn't stupid. I hadn't told anyone what we planned, and I couldn't see what harm it did that Philippa knew he'd given Lady Alisoun a kitten. She was only a maid. By her speech I knew she was probably an obscure cousin of Lady Alisoun, and fostered in a noble household. But

I was being fostered in a noble household, too, and if I failed to become a knight, I'd be nothing. Less than nothing. A mere servant like Philippa.

I guess some of my thoughts showed on my face, because all of a sudden Sir David ruffled my hair. "Lady Alisoun will come to love it as she loved her other cat."

David knew he ought to tell Eudo the truth. It would be bracing, like this fresh breeze. He ought to explain that Eudo's mistress was a cold woman who wanted labor for her money and feared affection because of the loss it eventually brought. It would save the lad from later disappointment. But he didn't. Instead he ruffled Eudo's hair and lied.

Eudo grinned as he led the way down the stairs and into the bailey. "I knew it. I knew it! That was the best idea I've had yet. You stick with me, Sir David, and I'll turn you into the perfect mate for the lady. Why, right now I bet she's cradling the kitty just as she'll later cradle your babes."

Eudo's confidence amazed David, and he was already overwhelmed from an excess of unrequited passion. After that tiny, dark chamber, the summer sunshine seemed a tonic and he soaked it up as he strode toward the stables. "You may be anticipating a little too much."

"Why?" Eudo demanded, quick as a squirrel to pick up acorns.

"The lady doesn't seem to like me."

Sometimes young Eudo displayed a frighteningly adult comprehension. "She's been kissing you again, hasn't she? I'd say she likes you a lot."

Abruptly, David's sense of humor returned. "Mayhap, but she shows it too infrequently."

"You're the one who decided that restraint would

win her." Eudo was still young enough to sulk. "I saw no reason to wait."

"You're impatient, lad." But not as impatient as David. He badly wanted to go home to Radcliffe. Last month, Guy of the Archers had sent a message back with Alisoun's servant. The drought seemed to be broken and everything was growing with the summer. His daughter grew, too, and Sir David ached because he missed her.

He wanted to find that which threatened Alisoun and rid her of it at once so he could go home. She still didn't trust him with the information he needed, and that both infuriated and relieved him. After all, he needed this time to court Alisoun. He wanted to learn her preferences and cater to them. If he *could* leave, he would forget all about those twelve sacks of wool and rush away. Then Alisoun would never allow him to take a permanent place at her side.

Still, the sense of urgency propelled him, and he wished to woo Alisoun rapidly, rush her into bed, circumvent her clever mind with more of his kisses. But he had become a legend by being a tactical genius, and it didn't take half his genius to know that wouldn't work with Alisoun. With Alisoun, he had to be crafty and reserved. He had to let her make her own decision about him while tipping the scales in his favor.

Eudo had apparently decided he'd been quiet long enough, for he piped up, "What are we going to do?"

"Train squires." David bit off the words, and Eudo retreated back into silence.

So David had been trapped in her tiny accounting chamber for an hour, talking about hopes and dreams like some castrated monk while she said nothing. He might have been talking to himself for as little as she understood. The only smart thing he'd done was hug her, for that proved that she'd been thinking about him more than he'd realized, and certainly more than she would like.

Unfortunately for him, he'd been thinking about her, too. Thinking with a particularly active organ, and wondering if she could possibly be as good as she appeared to be.

Not good with estate management or good to her people, but good in bed. It had gotten to the point where he feared to touch her for any reason, or he'd never stop. He could have sneaked into the village and swived one of the very available women, and Alisoun wouldn't have known, but he didn't want to. He dreamed about her long, cool hands on his body and her tall, warm body moving under him on the bed . . . or on a table.

He'd built a fire on that table with the two of them as kindling. A youth of seventeen would have shown more restraint. If he knew anything about women—and his knowledge was dated, but surely they hadn't changed—she would bolster her defenses when next they met.

"But her hair *is* red," he said aloud.

Eudo cocked his head. "Sir David?"

"Lady Alisoun's hair is red."

"It's not so bad," Eudo said defensively.

"Bad?" David grabbed Eudo's shoulder and stopped him. "Who says it's bad?"

"The priest says red hair is a sign the fires of hell reign. I think she should replace him, but he's old and he's been here forever, so she won't turn him out."

The pinch-faced priest who said Mass every morning should indeed be replaced. He was stone-deaf and half-blind, with a sour disposition that showed itself at random times as he hobbled through the castle. His disapproval, especially if he was Alisoun's childhood confessor, explained why she kept the flame of her hair guarded by such stern coverings. It made David all the more intrigued with the way she relished its freedom when she loosened it.

Eudo leaped ahead of David and held the stable door open. When David had passed, he carefully shut the door. David realized the lad foresaw trouble. He was right, of course, but it wouldn't be Eudo's trouble. It was all David's, and Louis, by God, was going to share it.

As he neared Louis's stall, he heard a loud, rude snort and a banging noise, and saw a stableboy come flying over the top rail of one of the stalls. Louis stuck his head over the top and bared his yellow teeth at the youth, and the lad glared back as he painfully stood up.

"There you are," David said, walking up to his horse and letting him smell his arm. "Have they been taking good care of you?"

Louis grumbled, making sounds from his belly that kept Eudo and the lad well back.

"Stop stomping the stableboys every time they come in to feed or groom you," David advised, "and you'll have no more complaints."

Belligerently, the lad said, "He's nasty."

Eudo turned on him, fists doubled. "He's Louis, the legendary destrier. You can't say he's nasty, Siwate."

Siwate took a fighting stance. "Can, too."

"Cannot."

"I can say anything I want to you." Siwate sneered. "You're just a little bastard my lady took in out of pity."

David caught Eudo when he lunged. Holding his struggling squire, David pointed at the stableboy. "You can, of course, say what you wish about Louis, but Louis understands every word you say, and he's not partial to insults about his disposition."

Siwate blanched and stepped back, and Eudo said, "Ha!"

David continued, "Lest you worry, however, let me inform you that Louis is no longer your responsibility. Eudo will now care for him."

Eudo froze, and Siwate retorted, "Ha!"

"Eudo is my squire, and he is not afraid of Louis."

From beside him, David heard Eudo's squeaky voice murmur, "Sir David, you made me swear to tell the truth . . ."

Lifting Eudo, David seated him on the high boards around Louis's stall. "Louis is a reasonable horse. He loves to terrorize those he doesn't know, but he'll accept *you*." David held his hand through the gate to offer the strong yellow cheese he'd saved. Observing the cheese, Louis stretched out his neck and with great care, nipped David's fingers. Cursing, David dropped the cheese, and Louis scooped it off the floor, then with teeth bared, showed it to David.

Siwate ran. Eudo shrank back so far he fell over backward onto a pile of hay. After baring his teeth back at the destrier, David said, "Louis *is* a reasonable horse."

Louis ate the cheese and exhaled the odor into David's face.

"When he's been exercised." David lifted the reins off the wall and stepped into the stall. Eudo peeked up over the wall, saw the horse accepting the restraints David placed on him, and clambered back into place. Louis reached out with his head and sniffed Eudo's foot. Eudo gripped the boards until his knuckles turned white, but he didn't stir as Louis worked his way up his leg. "That's your lad," David advised him. "Take care of him, and he'll take care of you."

Louis rolled his eyes at David.

"You can't nip him. That wouldn't be fair. And be careful not to step on him, his bones are still young and thin." David smiled at Louis and in a confidential tone said, "He's already broken his finger."

Louis nudged Eudo's hand, and Eudo hesitantly petted his head. "He's nice," the lad said in astonishment.

"He's the meanest piece of horseflesh you'll ever have the misfortune to meet." David opened the gate, then led the horse toward the door. "But he thinks he owns you now, and he protects those he owns."

Eudo hopped down and followed, staying well back from Louis's hooves. "Even bastard boys?"

David and Louis eyed each other with understanding, then David said, "Especially bastard boys. Do you think Louis's parents were wed?"

One shocked moment of silence. Then a boyish giggle.

David beckoned. "Come here, Eudo." When the boy stepped forward, David lifted him high enough to scramble into the saddle. Louis stood still for it, although it was early for him to have such tolerance, then he paced forward, letting Eudo get the rhythm of his gait. Eudo managed to let go of the mane long enough to wave at Siwate in a superior manner, and as they left the stable, Louis released from his hind end an opinion of its inhabitant that made the stableboy scramble away.

Eudo was still giggling when David led the destrier into the training yard, but he straightened when the other squires froze. Sir Walter froze, too, hand outstretched as he prepared to gut Andrew with a wooden sword.

Feeling foolish, David nodded amiably. "I've come to train the squires."

"I'll finish the accounts on the morrow," Lady Alisoun said as she knelt in between the fanatically neat rows of parsley and rue. "After all, it's not as if I'm actually shirking my duties. The herb garden needs to be weeded, also." Her long fingers grasped a weed firmly at its base and she jerked it up. "Damn," she muttered. She'd left the root in place, and before Tochi had withdrawn, he'd specifically forbidden such sloppy work.

Philippa grabbed Hazel's shirt and held her in place long enough to allow the kitten to escape the baby's grasping fingers. "The sunshine will do you good."

From the bailey that surrounded Tochi's pride and joy, the two women could hear willow branches rustling like satin hangings. Inside, the tall stone wall created a private world. Alisoun had carried the kitten in and it had promptly made a nest in her skirt and gone to sleep. But her constant slow progress down the row disturbed it, and at last it stretched and scampered away, exploring with a child's sense of adventure. Hazel crawled after, eyes intent, nappies in motion.

With a digger, Alisoun set to work freeing the root from the clinging dirt. The scent of damp earth rose to her nostrils, tantalizing her with the delectation of summer and the promise of harvest. "I've never weeded before, but my parents instructed me to learn all aspects of my demesne, so I'm grateful for Tochi's instruction."

Philippa laughed, although whether at her child or her lady, Alisoun did not know. "He certainly enjoyed giving it."

"He did, didn't he?" The root came out, and Alisoun sat back on her heels and waved it. Bits of dirt flew, but she didn't care; she was triumphant.

Philippa laughed again, and this time Alisoun knew she was laughing at her. "It's not often anyone can tell you anything."

Throwing the root into the slowly growing pile of weeds, Alisoun bent to her task again. "Am I so intimidating, then?"

"Not to me. *Don't* eat the dirt."

Surprised at the command, Alisoun looked up in time to see Philippa lunge after her daughter and pry her little fist open until the earth she clutched fell back on the ground. "Uck!" Philippa made a dreadful face at Hazel. "Don't eat that. Nasty."

Fascinated, Hazel stared at her mother. Then her bottom lip came out and quivered, her big eyes filled with tears, and she sat up and bawled like a calf.

Alisoun couldn't help it; she laughed aloud. It had been a long time since she'd done so, and she laughed again when Philippa gave her a sour look.

Searching through her bag for something to distract Hazel, Philippa said, "Wait until you're a mother."

"A fearsome thought." Still grinning, Alisoun bent back to her task.

"I think you've waited almost too long as it is."

Alisoun looked up sharply. "What do you mean by that?"

Philippa handed Hazel a dried gourd. Hazel rattled it once, then threw it away so vigorously it dug into the loose soil. "You're turning into an old maid with a cat."

"That's not my cat!" She tried to see the scrap of black fur that had so firmly attached itself to her, but it had disappeared, and she was glad.

Besides, it could scarcely come to harm in a garden surrounded by stone walls.

"Very well," Philippa said. "You're turning into an old maid."

Dumbfounded, Alisoun tried to joke. "I *am* the oldest widowed virgin in existence."

Apparently not even Philippa thought her amusing, for she dangled a string of colorful beads before Hazel's eyes and continued as if Alisoun hadn't spoken. "You're set in your ways. I don't think there's a man who could change you. I had great hopes for Sir David, but he's failed, so what's left but to hope for a child?"

Straightening, Alisoun rubbed the aching place on her lower spine. "What *are* you talking about?"

"You need to have a child."

Staring at Philippa, Alisoun tried to decide if this was some kind of new humor—the kind she didn't understand. The saints knew, that was likely. But Philippa stared directly back, as earnest as Alisoun had ever seen her. With impeccable logic, Alisoun prepared her answer. "I'm not married."

"Marriage isn't what brings the children," Philippa advised. "Bedding is."

"I know that." When Philippa grinned, Alisoun realized that *that* had been humor. "I mean, I'm the lady of George's Cross. I can't just take a lover and—"

"Why not?" Philippa demanded. "What's the use of being the lady of George's Cross if you can't do one wicked thing?" Bored with the beads, Hazel threw them after the gourd and grabbed another handful of dirt. As Philippa wrestled with her, she said, "I suppose I should say—one *more* wicked thing."

"My conscience is at rest. I confess my sin to the priest every day, and do the penance he assigns."

"He's deaf," Philippa said in exasperation. "If he wasn't, the whole village would be excommunicated."

Alisoun subdued the smile that threatened to break out, and said primly, "God works in mysterious ways."

"Aye, He sent you Sir David!" Philippa lifted her voice above Hazel's new and loudly expressed indignation. "Give me your keys."

Alisoun touched the big iron ring of keys at her belt. "Why?"

"Because she's not supposed to have keys, and if she has something forbidden, she'll be happy."

Alisoun wanted to point out that this was a dangerous precedent to start, that if they rewarded the child for crying by giving her what she should not have, it would become a habit. But it occurred to Alisoun that Philippa had more than she could handle. Without a husband, Philippa had to love the baby, discipline the baby, worry about the baby all alone. Most of all, worry about the baby. Philippa hadn't lost weight as Alisoun did when she worried. She had actually become plumper, but nothing could erase the lines etched on her forehead.

Alisoun tossed the keys. They landed with a thunk among the lemon balm, uprooting one tall plant. The tart scent only accented Alisoun's horror, and Philippa hastily plucked the broad, broken leaves and replaced the herb. "Maybe Tochi won't notice," she said, and rattled the keys before Hazel's face. Hazel's eyes grew big and astonished; she reached for the keys eagerly, and Philippa placed the heavy ring in her lap. Satisfied that her child was entertained, she turned back to Alisoun. "Sir David would give you fine, plump babies for you to cradle."

"Then he'd be on his way."

"Perhaps. If you sent him. But I doubt he'd refuse you should you propose marriage."

"Why would I want a man like that? We're nothing alike."

"I don't know." A smile played around Philippa's face, and she plucked a weed or two from the ground. "Why *do* you want him?"

"What makes you think I want him?"

"I'm the one who chased the curious from the door of your accounting room."

Alisoun framed a tart response, then discarded it. This was Philippa, after all. She could tell her the truth.

"He's awful. He laughs at customs, and at protocol that is right and proper."

"You're still angry because he went out to the kitchen and cajoled the cook into putting those live frogs in the pie shell so when you opened it they all jumped out and you screamed."

"Nay, that's not the bad thing." Alisoun wiped her hand on her apron. "I wanted to *laugh*."

Philippa did laugh. "There's hope for you, Alisoun."

"He's an evil influence on me." Philippa just grinned and shook her head, and Alisoun tried to impress the dire results of his personality on her. "One evening I sat and spoke with him for the pleasure of his company, and I didn't even busy myself with needlework."

"*One* evening," Philippa mocked.

"But once a person starts the slide down the winding road of sloth, she'll find it hard to claw her way back to the straight and narrow way."

"Do you have to quote Lady Frances to me always?" Philippa complained.

"She was the lady who fostered us!"

"She was a mean old woman who sucked the joy from life."

"I didn't know you felt that way. I am shocked."

Philippa flung her little pile of weeds at Alisoun, scattering them across the herbs. "Nay, you're not. You always thought that, too. You just never dared to admit it."

Alisoun withered like the uprooted lemon balm. "I *am* wicked. Do you know that when Sir David makes fun of the king for being so pompous, it's as if he saw into my mind and plucked my own thoughts before I had given them birth?"

"It's when he does that imitation of Sir Walter that I can scarcely contain myself."

"And Sir Walter doesn't even realize it's him."

The women looked at each other and burst out laughing.

Alisoun grew ashamed, sobered, and bent to her work again. "Do you realize that when he kisses me, I forget my duties?"

Philippa gurgled with what sounded like laughter, but when Alisoun looked at her she bent her head to the ground.

"My organization has suffered since he came, and when he—" The heel of his hand had brought her such strange feelings, but she couldn't bring herself to say that. "When Sir David applied physical manipulations to my skin, I almost lost control."

"Almost?"

"I did lose control."

"No wonder he's a legend," Philippa said reverently.

Shocked, Alisoun said, "Sir David is just as bad an influence on you as he is on me. You've never spoken this way before, and you certainly never suggested I should give birth without benefit of marriage."

"It's not Sir David who makes me say these things. It's living and thinking and doing everything that was proper and godly all my life, and then finding that my reward is exile and a life of fear." Philippa crushed some of the marjoram leaves in her hand and lifted them to her nose. "Marjoram for happiness. I want you to be happy."

In an odd sort of way, Philippa's suggestion began to make sense, and Alisoun feared it was because she, too, had considered bedding Sir David. Still she argued aloud. "He's not as noble as I am, and he's certainly not as rich."

"All the men who are noble and rich enough for you are old, disgusting creatures." Philippa plucked a few weeds from amongst the balm.

"Marriage is not for enjoyment."

"*I* know."

Alisoun wished she hadn't said that. Now Philippa pulled weeds with a vengeance, and a frown puckered her brow. But the words couldn't be called back, so Alisoun added, "And the king would be angry."

"Once the deed is done, he'd resign himself, wouldn't he? It wouldn't be the first time. Anyway, if it's not marriage you want, then fine. I understand that. But you need a babe."

"Why?" The kitten stalked through the row of parsley to pounce on one sprig which apparently taunted it.

"To inherit your lands."

Alisoun lifted the kitten free of the green forest before it ruined Tochi's best plants. "That's why *you* think I need a babe?"

A ghost smile touched Philippa's lips. "I think you just need a babe to love."

"I have this stupid, skinny, sharp-toothed kitten." Who clung like a burr as it climbed her bosom to stand on her shoulder, and who purred in her ear and rubbed its face against her cheek.

"That cat's not going to do it. Nothing makes you a real person like your own infant to care for, plan for. All the thinking in the world doesn't replace the excitement of holding your child for the first time, and when I look at Hazel—" Philippa stroked the baby's bald head, then wiped at the dirty streaks with her sleeve, "—it makes my insides squeeze all funny."

"That's attractive."

"I don't know how to describe it. You were always the clever one. All I know is if someone hurt Hazel—" Philippa's face lost expression and her eyes grew cold, "—I would kill him."

Startled, Alisoun stared at her gentle friend. She

didn't know Philippa as well as she thought. Or else what Philippa said was true. Having a child changed a woman in some basic way. "Do you think I'd be a good mother?"

"If you're going to embark on this course, I would advise planning on more than one child. You'd be obsessive about a single babe, I think, and smother it with care. Two children would distract you and you'd not ruin the one."

"You know this, do you? You with the one?"

"I'd have ten if I could. You know that."

Alisoun laughed lightly, trying to pretend she'd been joking, when in fact the plan sounded more and more reasonable. "This is a ridiculous conversation. Advising me to have a bastard is a stupid idea. I don't know why I listen to you."

"Why did you?" Philippa said shrewdly.

Something lit inside Alisoun, something she didn't recognize until it spilled out as a flash of anger and spite. "You've got no father for that child, and you're frightened and miserable. Do you want me to be like you?"

Philippa snatched Hazel up and hugged her against her chest while the baby struggled to get down.

Aghast at herself at once, Alisoun stammered, "I don't know why I said that. It's just—I always thought if I lived my life logically and organized well, I would have the life that I wanted. But I couldn't have planned for what happened to you, and it's made me examine myself and realize—" she plucked the cat off her shoulder and hugged it much as Philippa hugged her daughter, "—what I have are just things, and there's no reason to care for them when there's no one to enjoy the fruits."

"Don't cry!"

Alisoun hadn't realized she was, but tears were dropping onto Tochi's plants.

"Oh, Alisoun." Holding Hazel, Philippa walked over on her knees and embraced her lady. "I wasn't trying to upset you. It's just that—"

"Well, I can't. I can't have a child. That's unacceptable. But when I think about it, it just seems that . . . "

"I know." Philippa wiped her nose on her sleeve. "I feel like that, too."

Hazel squirmed between them and Alisoun gave her a tentative peck. The baby didn't cry, so she gave her another one, then laid her head against the child's sparse hair. The thin strands felt like silk beneath her cheek as Hazel leaned into her, and just for a moment she conjured up seditious thoughts. Thoughts of holding her own child and having it love her.

So foolish. So seductive. She mourned. "All our bright plans, all of our youth, gone already, wasted—"

The gate swung open and the women sprang apart. Sir Walter walked in, a definite swagger to his step, and stopped at the sight of their tearstained faces. "Lady Alisoun?"

"We're just helping Tochi with the weeding," Alisoun said.

He surveyed the damage and politely said, "Of course."

Alisoun looked around her and saw what he saw, but she made no apology. "Was there something you wanted?"

He didn't smile, but something about the way he stood indicated his smug superiority. "I think there is something you should see."

10

As Alisoun approached the training area, she asked, "Why are all these people lingering here, hanging on the fence, when they have work to do?"

With relish, Sir Walter said, "They're having their eyes opened."

Alisoun didn't like that. She didn't like Sir Walter's attitude or the way he held her elbow as if she would try to escape. Stopping, she disengaged his fingers from her arm. "I can walk alone, I thank you, Sir Walter."

"We'll see, my lady."

Then he strode on ahead and held the gate for her.

An open fence surrounded the training yard, built to retain the destriers in case a knight was unhorsed during an exercise. Alisoun entered with caution and looked around. Lady Edlyn and the house servants, the stableboys, and the washerwomen hung over the rails, all watching the scene unfolding before them with the same dazed, horrified expressions. Ivo stood with his arms crossed over his massive chest, disgust tying his forehead into a knot. Gunnewate leaned against the fence, picking at his few teeth and staring as if he couldn't credit his eyes.

Alisoun followed their gazes and saw Hugh, her oldest, most talented squire, on his warhorse, facing Sir David and King Louis across the tilting run. Both men wore hauberks that glinted in the sun, and open-faced tilting helmets, and they held ash lances and great curved shields. They were waiting for the signal from Andrew, who seemed to be waiting for Sir Walter. When Sir Walter nodded, Andrew shouted and the men charged at each other.

Hooves pounded the beaten ground as their lances reached out. Alisoun held her breath as each made contact with the opposing shield. They squealed as they scraped, then David's lance shattered in three places, and he lurched in the saddle. Hugh's lance slid off David's shield and caught him across the chest, knocking him off Louis. The spectators gasped as he landed on the ground with a clatter of armor.

He didn't move.

Hugh leaped from his horse, handed the reins to Andrew, and ran toward David's prone body. Louis skidded to a halt and trotted over to examine his master. Alisoun, too, started toward him.

No one else moved. Everyone just stared with vacant, disbelieving expressions, and she realized what had happened.

This wasn't David's first defeat by Hugh.

"He's been here all the morning—on the ground, most of the time. His swordwork isn't the equal of Hugh's. He almost lost his head when Hugh swung a mace. And now he's proved that his jousting is pathetic." Sir Walter kept pace with her as she walked, and he didn't bother to disguise the triumph in his tone.

"The legend is dead. Sir David of Radcliffe is nothing but a washed-up, has-been failure."

She wanted to hit Sir Walter. She wanted to take a lance herself and knock him heels over helm. *Didn't he realize what he had done?*

Louis reached David first and sniffed him, then released a moist snort that made him flinch. Hugh arrived next and gently pushed the destrier away, then turned David over. David released a heartfelt groan, and Hugh muttered, "Praise the saints."

Finally Alisoun knelt beside them and assisted Hugh in removing David's headgear. His helmet had gashed the bare part of his cheek, and only the padded arming cap he wore had saved him from further cuts. His eyelids fluttered open and the black of his pupil had expanded to cover the brown. Then they reacted to the light and shrank, and Alisoun sighed with relief. "Is anything broken?" she asked him.

"Nothing of importance," Sir Walter said.

Again she wondered—*Didn't he realize what he had done?*

David took a few quick breaths before he replied. "Nay." He closed his eyes as if the light hurt, then opened them again. "Maybe a rib. Bruising." His gaze slid to Hugh. "Your patron saint . . . should be George."

Hugh's hands trembled as he helped Alisoun remove David's gauntlets. "I beg your forgiveness, my lord. I never thought—"

"Say no more. You're the best I've ever faced."

David's gasps between each word warned Alisoun of extensive and painful bruising on his chest. She stood and snapped her fingers.

Like stone figures brought to life, the spectators moved. The stablemaster sent his underlings for a plank on which to lift David. Mabel, Alisoun's alewife, was also her best healer, and she hobbled into the training yard and knelt on the other side of David, asking him questions about his pains. Heath climbed the fence and ran toward Alisoun, begging for instruction, and Alisoun sent her into the keep to boil water for the poultices they would make. Lady Edlyn walked briskly toward the keep also, and Alisoun knew she had remembered her duties.

But no one spoke unnecessarily. No one teased David about his defeat. They could scarcely stand to look at him, and Alisoun could scarcely stand to look at Sir Walter.

Instead she looked at Philippa. Covered with the dirt of the garden, holding the baby, she presented a placid facade as she stood outside the fence, but Alisoun sensed the renewed fear that curled through her. Sensed it, because she felt it herself.

"'Tis as I suspected all along." Sir Walter sought her attention. "'Tis the reason I requested your 'legend' assist me. No knight retains his abilities without constant diligence, and yon legend has not set foot in the training yard since his arrival. I surmised his command of his art—if ever, in truth, there was such command—had faded, and I could no longer bear to have you so deceived."

Still Alisoun refused to meet his gaze. "Deceived? You no longer wished me to be deceived?"

Sir Walter spoke loudly enough for those around them to hear, and he even had the gall to rest a paternal hand on her shoulder. "I know it is painful, my lady, to find you've been made a fool of, but—"

At last she allowed herself to say the words which haunted her. "Don't you realize what you have done?" She controlled her features, she controlled the volume of her voice, but nothing could stop the whiplash in her tone. "My people had thought themselves safe, protected by Sir David of Radcliffe. Now they'll live in dread again, and rightly, for my enemy would hear of David's failure, and reap the reward."

Sir Walter's hand fell away.

"Sir Walter, if you wish to remain at George's Cross, stay out of my sight. I will do my duty. I always do my duty." She looked up at him, this stupid knight with his jaw clamped tight and his eyes bulging. "And in the future, have faith that I will know what that duty may be."

She turned her back on him, joining Mabel as she scolded David for trying to stand when he was clearly unfit. By the time they had placed David on the plank and lifted him, Sir Walter had disappeared.

David could have walked into the keep on his own two legs, but one look at Alisoun dissuaded him. She was going to throw him out as soon as he could leave, and humiliation already burned like a hot coal in his gut.

He'd been defeated. Again. The last time had been bad enough. It had been in front of the king and the court, and that pompous ass who proved himself David's superior had ground every last, bitter admission of surrender from him. No one who had seen that combat came away thinking he had been anything but soundly scourged.

But this time! He'd been defeated by a snot-nosed youth who hadn't even been knighted. Probably hadn't been blooded. Who hadn't even been born when David started his career. Defeated in front of every person in this castle. The shame made him want to curl up, to run away, to never again look on their faces.

If it had been up to him, he'd stand, take Louis and leave, never looking back. But he couldn't. His people, his daughter especially, depended on the coins his employment brought.

And he'd come to think, this last month, that Alisoun depended on him, too. Not just for defense, although his reputation—or his former reputation—had probably served her well. But because she was the loneliest woman he'd ever met, and she didn't even know it. She kept so busy with her schedule that she'd never learned to laugh, to show affection, to have fun. The seasons defined her existence by the duties they imposed, not by the rhythm of life they sang, and he feared one day she would wake and realize that her youth had fled and she had nothing. Why he felt he should be the one to change that, he didn't even understand. Maybe his old granny could have told him. All he knew was that he courted Alisoun for her lands, for her wealth, and for the rare jewel of her smile.

So he allowed the men to carry him on a plank up to his chamber and dump him, none too gently, on the bed. He didn't restrain his groan at such rough handling, and he admired the scolding Alisoun gave them, but he didn't imagine for a moment the crisis was past. He would have to think, and think fast. He had to do more than mourn the loss of his legendary status—a status he had scorned when he had it and missed bitterly now that it had vanished—to retain his advantage.

So he shut his eyes as they stripped him and listened for Alisoun to exclaim sympathetically about his bruises.

She didn't. She didn't say a word.

The alewife commanded that the men drag the table to the side of the bed so she would have somewhere to place her medicines, her bandages and warm water. She handled him rather briskly as she washed him, for she was a wise woman and knew he wasn't hurt so badly.

But the pain with each breath told him he had broken a rib, and she wrapped his chest tightly in linen strips.

Then she flung a light wool rug over him and left, and he was alone—so he thought.

Opening his eyes, he jumped. Alisoun stood close to the bed, staring at him. He couldn't believe she had gotten so close and stood so quietly. Too quietly.

His instinct told him to be cautious, and he always obeyed his instinct. In a low, gentle tone, he said, "My lady."

She didn't answer. She still just stared, and it struck him as odd. If he didn't know better, he would have thought her unconscious of the ramifications of his defeat. She wasn't; he'd heard her chide Sir Walter. So why did she look at him—at his body outlined beneath the cover—with such a curious intensity? She might have been a butcher considering a lamb for slaughter.

Quite an odd experience, to feel like a lamb. "My lady, I never lied to you. When you came to the tavern to hire me, I told you I was no longer the greatest warrior in England."

She still didn't speak. She simply laid a hand on the thigh of his leg and pinched it as though testing it for meat.

He raised his voice a little. "And your Hugh is magnificent. I doubt that anyone here realizes how magnificent."

His hands lay on top of the rug across his stomach, and she stared at them.

His fingers twitched. "But that's no excuse. Some skills are lost to me forever. The speed of youth is gone. But with practice, I can become a warrior to be feared once more." The warmth of her palm began to work on his flesh. The strength of her gaze began to work on his mind. If she had been another woman, any other woman, he would have wondered if this clinical survey meant she was considering him for a bed partner. But not Alisoun. She had over and over again demonstrated that her mind worked in a logical manner. Although—his own logic floundered—why she was looking at his body when it had proved inadequate for her combat purposes, he did not know. "Let me stay. I can teach Hugh many things, and he is ideal to bring me back to prime condition."

She didn't answer, and he jiggled his leg. "Lady Alisoun?"

She jerked her hand back, then stared at the palm as if it belonged to someone else.

"Shall I stay longer and establish that I am worthy of your trust?"

She looked at him and wet her lips. He could see the word forming. *Nay.* She was going to say *nay.*

But she didn't. She said, "Aye," then looked as surprised as he felt. But she repeated it firmly. "Aye. You can stay. If you practice every day with Hugh. But only until after the market on Lammas Day. 'Tis less than a month away, and if you haven't improved by then, then you must go and I . . ." Her lips trembled, then firmed. "I'll have to organize the defense of George's Cross myself. I suppose that's what I should have done to begin with. It would have been more efficient."

His reaction was instinctive and immediate. "Defense is a man's job!"

"I've had two men to do it, and both failed me."

He flushed and turned his head away.

"I beg your pardon." She placed her hand on him again, but this time on his shoulder. "You have done as I hoped and kept trouble away with your mere presence, but we can no longer depend on that. Everyone in the village knows that Hugh defeated you by now. They'll gossip to any chance-met merchant, and soon all of Northumbria will have heard. I'll not don armor, of course, but my safety depends on organization, and my organization has proved superior to any man's."

Taking her hand from his shoulder, he shoved it back at her. "And if you succeed, my lady, what use will you have for a man?"

He saw it this time, he knew he did. A flare of interest, of hot intent, then with her hand she stroked his ribs. "Are you in a lot of pain?"

That wasn't an answer, and he replied curtly, "I can perform my duties."

"Good." Her fingers fluttered down his hip and away. "Good."

As she left the room, he watched the sway of her hips thoughtfully.

There would always be one reason a woman would need a man, and from Lady Alisoun's expression, David could have sworn she'd decided to investigate the possibilities.

"My lady sent me in here with a tray."

David stopped contemplating the darkness captured by the bed canopy above and turned to contemplate Eudo. The lad stood in the open doorway holding a laden dinner tray. He stepped into the room, set the tray on the table beside the bed and, using the candle off the tray, lit the candles Heath had placed earlier.

Eudo, David now saw, wore the kind of expression David associated with a rebellious serf. He didn't want to be here. He didn't want to serve a fallen hero, and he didn't care if David knew it.

What was worse, David didn't want him to have to serve him. What a blow to the boy's already damaged pride to be the one who waited on the man all considered to be a craven. But if Lady Alisoun had told Eudo to serve him, then both man and boy must uphold her authority, so David plumped the pillows under his back and said, "Bring it here."

Eudo dragged his feet through the rushes as he made his way toward the bed. He watched the contents of the tray intently, and stepped up on the stool beside the tall bed to present the tray.

The array of delicacies astonished David. Fish stew steamed in a pewter bowl, redolent with parsley from the herb garden. The bread was tinted yellow with kingly saffron, the herb of happiness. Fresh pressed wine had been mixed with cinnamon, and spring lamb dressed with sprigs of mint had been cut thin and placed on a silver plate alternately with a creamy white cheese. "Good God!" David said. "Is it a saint's day I've forgotten?"

"My lady said you'd need your strength," Eudo answered.

"For fighting, you mean."

Eudo snickered.

Reaching across the tray, David took Eudo's tunic in his hand and slowly brought him forward. "Why did you laugh?"

"I didn't laugh."

"A lie, Eudo." Letting him go, David took the tray. "Because you're disappointed in me, you think your vow to tell the truth invalid?"

"Nay." Eudo's voice rose and cracked. "But I don't need you hitting me because of what I think."

"How often have I done that?"

Eudo squirmed. "Never." He jumped off the stool and stepped back a safe distance. "So I did laugh at you. Everyone's laughing at you."

David placed the tray across his lap, shook out the massive napkin and spread it on his chest. "Because I failed today?"

Eudo tucked his hands into his armpits and hunched his shoulders.

Humiliation began to gnaw at David again, and picking up the spoon, he gripped the handle tightly. "If you don't want to be in here with me, why don't you go?"

"They're laughing at *me*, too."

David glanced toward the door. Of course. The disappointed servants of George's Cross would have to take their ire out on someone. David wasn't available, so even better was his squire, a small, bastard-born lad who couldn't defend himself against the jeers.

Now David really despised himself as a craven, leaving the boy to suffer his punishment, and he offered himself to Eudo. "Do you have anything you want to say to me?"

"Nay," Eudo muttered.

"Another lie," David chided.

Eudo's eyes flashed. "Well, why not? You lied to me."

"When?"

"When you let me think you were a legend."

Getting a grip on his composure, David said, "I didn't create the legend, nor did I encourage it. If I let you think anything, it was that I was still the greatest fighter in Christendom."

"Fine."

Eudo almost spat the word, and David realized that facing the rest of the castle would have been easier. After all, adults knew how to pretend respect with their faces and their voices. Eudo displayed all the fierce honesty of an eleven-year-old, and David found himself scrambling to assuage the boy's disappointment. "Once I was the greatest fighter."

"Should I believe *that*?"

David grappled with his suddenly unsteady temper. "Keep a civil tongue in your head," he warned.

Eudo flinched and huddled farther into himself. "Don't tell my lady."

"Have I ever?" David tore off a piece of bread and spread it with cheese. "Do you want some?" He offered it in Eudo's direction. "It's good."

"I'm not hungry." Eudo shot him a rebellious glare and said hatefully, "Nay, wait, that's a lie."

David waited, but Eudo didn't continue. Prodding him, David asked, "What's the truth?"

"I can't tell you the truth."

"Why not?"

"Because you told me to keep a civil tongue."

The lad was so angry and so clever at tormenting David with it. He reminded David of his own daughter, and for the first time since his backside left that horse, David's mood lightened. "It's a tough balance, isn't it? Very well, never mind the civil tongue."

Eudo answered now with glee. "I don't *want* to eat with you."

"Hm." David spread another piece of bread with cheese. "That is tough. It's hard to remain hostile when you share a tray. That's why when two enemies share a table, it cancels all animosity. But only for the evening. Come and eat now, and you can hate me again tomorrow." Dunking the bread in the soup, David slurped it noisily. "This tastes good!" He did it again, then speared a slice of lamb and waved it so the scent wafted across to Eudo. In a singsong voice, he said, "I wager this tastes good, too."

Eudo glared and weighed the situation, but he didn't have a chance. He was a page, the last to eat, and a growing boy. When David folded lamb into the bread and took a bite, he gave up the struggle. Climbing on the bed, he sat facing David as David carved the loaf into a bowl and served him. Wisely, David kept his silence until the two of them had demolished almost everything on the tray.

Eudo's motions slowed, and David waited for the first question. But Eudo didn't seem to be able to ask, so David broke the silence. "Did you take care of Louis after my fall?"

Relieved, Eudo nodded vigorously. "Aye, and he was good for me. The other stableboys couldn't believe it, and Siwate tried to make him buck while I was inside the stall, and Louis bit him."

"I told you Louis would care for you," David said.

"Then Siwate said—" Eudo took a breath, "—that it probably wasn't King Louis at all."

"Who is it, then?"

"Siwate said it probably isn't even . . . are you *really* the legendary mercenary Sir David of Radcliffe?" Eudo asked.

David thought himself braced, but nothing could have prepared him for the hurt the lad inflicted with that simple, honest query. "Who else would I be?"

"I don't know." Eudo shrugged. "Siwate said you killed him on the road and took his things so everyone'd think you're him."

"Siwate had better hope that's not true, or they'll find his little body buried beneath the floorboards," David snapped. Then Eudo shrank back, and he was sorry. "I'm really Sir David of Radcliffe. I'm just a little older than the legend you speak of."

"You can't protect our lady if you fly off a horse like that whenever you face another . . . knight."

David read Eudo's mind. "And Hugh's not even a knight." Hiding his face with the napkin, David wiped his mouth until he could speak without showing his grief. "I know how to be the best. I just need to practice. In the morning, I'll be in the training yard."

"But when will we ride the estate to see if there's mischief afoot?"

"Do you want to go with me as you always have?"

Eudo thought first, then answered, "Aye."

"Then we'll go in the afternoon tomorrow, but we'll have to ride at different times every day. If there's someone watching who wishes to harm Lady Alisoun, then we shouldn't lull him with consistency, especially not now. Not after my . . . defeat." David said the word steadily, and that accomplishment encouraged him to think he might survive this humiliation. Handing Eudo the napkin, he said, "Wipe your face."

Eudo did as instructed, then wadded it and placed it on the tray. "But that person seems to know what goes on inside the castle. Some of the servants think he is inside the castle. And now he'll know that you're not so wonderful as we thought."

David's suspicions of Sir Walter flared again, but he said only, "If he's in the castle, then it will be easy to apprehend him when he strikes again. I need someone to keep watch for me out in the great hall. Would you watch for anyone suspicious?"

"Aye!" Realizing he might have sounded too eager, Eudo slid off the bed and took the tray. In a more moderate tone, he said, "This sounds like a good plan. Is there anything else I can do for you before you sleep?"

"Douse the candles." David watched as Eudo did as instructed. "All except this one by the bed. And shut the door behind you. I don't need to hear the talk from the great hall." He saw Eudo's face fall, and he realized how difficult Eudo's evening would be. "You don't need to hear it either, lad. Hurry through your chores and come back to your mat in here."

"Aye, Sir David." Eudo threw him one valiant grin and plunged into the great hall, pulling the door tight and shutting himself out of the safety which David's chamber represented.

David relaxed, replete and at ease with himself now that he had a plan. He would spar with Hugh, practice until he reached his former fighting form, and not worry about those whose pride and safety rode on his success. Not about Eudo. Not about Alisoun. Not even about . . . himself.

Sudden tears stung, and he pressed his thumb and forefinger to his eyes to cut off the unwelcome flow. How could he be concerned about himself when so many people depended on him? But he was. Defeat tasted bitter in his mouth, and he would have done anything to wipe this afternoon from his mind. Younger men, better fighters, had been nipping at his heels for years, but always he'd floated within the bubble of that legend. Now the bubble had burst and he'd fallen to earth with a crash. All those years of fighting in tournaments and battles, and his goals had been ever foremost in his mind. Land, a home, a family. He didn't realize when he got them they'd consume him, lull him, so thoroughly he'd neglect the very skills by which he'd earned his way.

Now he was older, slower. Being a fighter was a young man's game. Yet . . .

If his skills had disintegrated, his wit had sharpened. Surely he could protect Alisoun and reclaim Eudo's respect with a combination of skill and guile. Surely he could earn his way and support his child, and most important, face himself in the basin of still water where he washed his face.

On that resolution, he dozed, waking only a little when the door creaked open. He thought it was Eudo, come to sleep away from the teasing of the other boys, so he allowed himself to drift, still caught in the current of sleep.

Light footsteps crept close to the bed, and he almost spoke, wishing Eudo a good night.

Then a scent enticed him. His nostrils twitched; he had to be dreaming, but he'd never dreamed a fragrance before. It smelled like marjoram and rue and lemon balm—an odd combination, and one he'd smelled earlier today. But where?

The step stool scraped closer. The sheet lifted. Opening his eyes he saw her—Lady Alisoun, clad in a white linen shift, climbing into bed beside him.

Not even surprise could make him hesitate. Placing his hands on her waist, he helped her in beside him.

11

David had had dreams like this before. A woman came to his bed, leaned over and said, "I want you," with husky passion in her tone. This must just be another satisfying, ultimately frustrating dream.

But this dream girl behaved differently than she should. She was distressingly silent. She didn't smile seductively. And she didn't utilize the expertise his usual dream-women exhibited.

"Alisoun?" he asked, the sound of his own voice whimsical and distracted. "Are you really here?"

"Lie back," she directed. "You're hurt. I'll do all the work."

That snapped him out of his reverie. Only Alisoun would use that tone of voice when visiting a man's bed dressed in a gauzy shift. "What are you doing here?" he demanded.

"Learning how to swive." She appeared astonished, then abashed. "That is, if you are willing to oblige me."

Aye, it was really Alisoun. Only Alisoun would wear

a wimple to hide her hair and keep the sheet draped over his hips. Only Alisoun would order a man to be still while she used his body to debauch herself. Only Alisoun would want to retain supremacy.

Only Alisoun lacked the experience to bring her desire to fruition.

This situation required much thought. He needed to understand why she was here now, after the day he'd had, but more important, she needed immediate reassurance. Placing his hand against her neck as she sat beside him on the mattress, he said, "I am yours to do with as you will."

That apparently was all she needed to hear. She briskly arranged the pillows under his head, as he tried to comprehend what had brought him this sudden blessing. She seemed to have no concept of her body and how it would work on him, for as she bobbed around him, he could see her breasts moving through the thin linen of her shift. The nipple of one rubbed his shoulder, and his hand rose to cup it in an involuntary reaction.

Oblivious, she moved back before he made contact. "You're very bruised." She checked his bandage to assure herself of his comfort. "Are you able to proceed with this?"

For a moment, he wondered if she were jesting. Then she peered at him, all earnest inquiry, and he managed a simple, "Aye."

"That's what Philippa said you would say. She said a man could be halfway to heaven and be called back by the promise of a nature romp." She sighed as if his irresponsibility weighed on her. "I don't want you to feel you must swive me, for there is always the morrow."

How many tomorrows? he wanted to ask. Somehow, he didn't think this was about his suit of marriage.

Something told him she wouldn't have changed her mind about her requirements or his inadequacies. But she'd decided he was good enough to bed, and if he performed successfully, those tomorrows could stretch through the rest of their lives. The lady was ripe and willing, and the strategy and skill of a legendary mercenary resided within his breast. A smile curved his lips. He would succeed.

She sat on her heels before him like a supplicant before her lord, and she stared at his body as if deciding how to best achieve her goal. "Philippa knew you were coming in to me?" he asked.

"She advised it."

He nodded slowly. "Did Philippa advise you on your attire?"

Alisoun glanced down at herself. "She was wrong, wasn't she? I wanted to wear something a little grander. Something made of velvet and trimmed in lace. But she insisted that simple was best—" Alisoun came to her knees and spread her arms wide, "—and look at me. I'm not attractive at all."

The worn linen clung to her hips, and he saw the shape of her thighs and the triangle of color between muted by the gauze above it. A simple bow gathered the material at the neck and held it closed and he could have sworn he saw one end of the ribbon waving to him, begging him to grasp it and pull it free.

He had to clear his throat before he spoke. "Philippa is a wise woman."

Slowly she lowered her arms to her sides. "You like this?"

He corrected her. "I like what's under it."

She almost smiled. Then, rather briskly, she said, "Well, let's get on with it. What would you like me to do first?"

If she'd been more certain of herself, he would have burst out laughing. But beneath that superficial confidence, he sensed a virgin's self-doubt. "I always like to start with just some cuddling."

"Cuddling?"

He patted his chest. "Lay your head here and rest."

"I didn't come in here to sleep!"

He could be stubborn, too. "*That's* the way I like it."

"As you wish." She hovered over him. "But I wasn't expecting this."

She didn't seem to be settling. Like a bird sneaking up on a meal, she almost touched him with her hand, then snatched it back. She sat down beside him, then skittered away. She'd been able to make contact to adjust his bandage, but not in an affectionate display. Finally, he had to ask. "What were you expecting?"

"Philippa said men were always in a hurry."

He snapped, "Then I suppose Philippa never bedded *me*."

"Actually, I suppose Philippa doesn't know too much."

She wanted to do this, he realized, but she lacked the nerve.

She chatted on. "She's only had the one, although I think she's talked to quite a few women."

Taking her hand, he laid it on his chest near his neck, where the bandage did not cover. "Then Philippa probably knows that men who are in a hurry leave their women wanting."

Her fingers flexed. "Wanting what?"

He slid her hand to his far shoulder, so she leaned across him and had only to make minor adjustment to lie on her side and rest her head on his chest. She didn't; she remained stiff and uncomfortably upright, leaning on her other elbow. "Cuddle with me and I'll show you."

"Philippa said satisfaction is a myth." Her elbow skidded along the sheet until her shoulder fit in his armpit and her head hovered above his shoulder. "Philippa said most of the women just snorted when she asked if they enjoyed it."

"Then they've not been in my bed, either." He placed his palm on her ear and gently pushed her down the rest of the way. Her arm against the mattress moved restlessly as she sought a comfortable spot for it, and she kept a discreet distance between the length of their bodies. For now, that satisfied him. Tucking the sheet around her, he said, "You need not worry, my lady. I will satisfy you."

Sounding surprised, she said, "I never doubted that."

Her flattery, for such he considered it, could go to a man's head. Reaching up, he popped her wimple off and flung it away. "Lie back down."

He must have put enough authority into his tone, for she obeyed him. But she hadn't answered his question, and he would ask again later . . . when she wasn't so skittish. "Now we just lie here."

And they did. Her head rested on his shoulder, he wrapped his arm around her back and rested his hand against her hip, and at irregular intervals, he'd pat her. At first, she was so stiff she couldn't stiffen further. Then involuntarily she began to relax, and when he moved his hand, she stiffened again. Then when nothing happened, even when he moved his hand, she relaxed and stayed relaxed, but when he started to rub her with a slow and steady pressure, she asked, "Is this it?"

"For now." His hand slid down to the base of her spine and he massaged the muscles there. "If we do no more tonight, there is always the morrow."

She started to speak, then no doubt realized that he

quoted her, and she settled beside him. But she must have been thinking, wanting to finish this in one efficient event, for on his far shoulder, her fingers curled. As he held his breath, she cupped the joint and pressed it gently, using her palm to stroke the muscles. Slowly she worked her way down his arm, then back up again and across his chest to his neck. There she touched her fingertips lightly to his ear, down his jaw, and along his throat.

His own hand hung suspended above her back. For a novice, she had very good instincts, and it would not do for him to underestimate her intelligence. Nor would it do for him to allow her to take the initiative. In this matter, at least, he was determined to retain control.

He moved enough to shift the feathers beneath them and she rolled into him.

Her fingers stopped their stroking. He thought she'd stopped breathing. The length of her rested against his side, and while she still wore her full-length shift, he wore nothing but a bandage.

It was the kind of intimacy she most needed to learn. It was the kind of intimacy that made him forget, just for a moment, that he was dominant.

Then he felt her muscles gather and strain as if she were preparing for some great effort, and she scooted closer. She put her knee over his thigh and moved it up and down a little too briskly. Catching her thigh in his hand, he slowed her down, eased the pressure, made it more of a sensuous dance and less of an activity, and closed his eyes beneath the onslaught of unexpected pleasure.

"Are we going to finish, now?"

Her matter-of-fact voice in his ear rallied him. She might know enough body language to arouse him, but her tone needed work.

Making a special effort to keep his own voice low and seductive, he said, "We've barely started."

She took her knee away.

Bit and starts of courage, he diagnosed, followed by fragments of embarrassment and uncertainty.

"You've used some kind of rinse in your hair." Turning his head, he gathered a handful and sniffed it. "Kind of flowery."

"It's probably marjoram and lemon balm and . . . "

She sounded so prim and informative, he wanted to see her face. Gently, he lifted her head and slid out from underneath it, then rolled onto his side and faced her. The sheet stretched taut between them, forming a tent, and she watched him without expression. If he had succeeded in easing her inevitable apprehension, she cloaked that. She still concealed everything from him, all emotion, and he lost inhibitions in one blast of impatience.

Too good a strategist to let his aggravation show, he allowed himself one brief grin. "It's delicious."

Her eyes widened and she moved back an inch. "You seem distracted tonight."

So she had spied something in his face that made her wary. "Why is that?"

"Discussing the scent in my hair when you could be performing other, more pleasurable duties is not something I had supposed would happen. If you're too tired—"

"Why would I be tired?" He scooted down so the top of his head matched her collarbone and the sheet protected his expression from her gaze. "I've dozed half the day. Why, this could take all night and I'd have no problem."

She took a big breath. He saw it as her bosom jutted out. Then she said, "I have to get up in the morning. It's already taken longer than—"

He kissed her breast through the veil of linen.

"—Than I'd planned. If we miss—"

Wetting the cloth with his tongue, he sucked the nipple into his mouth.

"—Mass." She took another breath. "If we miss Mass, we'll have extra penance and I'll already have more than I—"

"Keep talking." With his lips moving against the damp material, he encouraged her. "I can listen."

"I have only so much time scheduled."

He rubbed the stubble of his beard on the shift, and it snagged the weave of the material. It must have scratched her skin, too, but softly, for she jumped and her hands flexed. The urge to have her out of the shift grew in him, and he reveled in it. Aye, he could prevail without forfeiting passion. But he wanted to see Alisoun, just once, forfeit everything to passion. It should be easy, for she was so unaware. Gravely, he promised, "I will do everything in my power to maintain your schedule, but of course you *were* planning to sleep here with me."

"I was?"

He kissed lower, finding her navel, skirting the curve of her hip. "Although it would be amusing to see you leave after you have spent so much time in here. I wager every conversation in the great hall would cease."

"Everyone who beds in the great hall is asleep!"

"Have you never slept in a great hall?" He lifted the sheet off his head and looked up at her. She shook her head, and he smiled. "One sleeps lightly, especially when there's intrigue afoot, and when the lady of George's Cross visits her defeated mercenary for a night, that's intrigue of the best kind."

"They would gossip about me?"

"And me, lady. Have you no thought of my reputation?"

"What will this do to your reputation?"

"Enhance it, I would suppose." He dropped the sheet and slid his hands around her hips, turning her onto her back. "So in this battle, I had best provide evidence of expertise for all to see."

"What do you mean?"

"I will love you so well none will doubt your pleasure." She jerked the sheet around her neck and he grinned in the dim light beneath it. That maidenly gesture of dismay only trapped him more tightly with her long slender body. Like a starving man before a feast, he intended to savor each nibble and taste.

Pressing the shift into the indent of her navel, he watched it spring away as she sucked in her stomach. She was wary again, and if he proposed cuddling once more, she would rise from the bed and never return. Nay, he had to get on with it now—show some efficiency, dazzle her with his skill, make her think he was doing as she wished when actually, he was stealing that vaulted authority away from her.

He scarcely felt the pain in his ribs.

Resting his head on her thigh, he blew softly into that sensitive junction where he wished to be.

"What are you doing?" she asked sharply. But she didn't lift the sheet.

"I'm waiting for you to relax your legs. I can't do what you request without your cooperation, as you no doubt comprehend."

She did comprehend, but her cool mind did not have total sway over the impulses of her body. No matter how much she wished it otherwise, she was still an untutored virgin with her first man, and she couldn't command her knees to part.

He felt the quiver as she tried, and said, "Let me help." He inserted his thumb in the space between her thighs and nudged up until he touched the place he knew she would like. "There." He rubbed her. "More relaxed now?"

She tensed so much he feared she would splinter. It was going to be tougher than he'd first realized. Lifting his head, he pressed his hand to her diaphragm. "Breathe," he instructed.

She inhaled with a deep gasp that told him she'd been holding her breath. When she'd absorbed enough air, she demanded, "What are you doing?"

"Pleasuring you." He rubbed her again. "Is it working?"

"I know not. I only know it makes me want to . . . "

She moved her legs restlessly, and he consolidated his position with his knee. "To do what?"

"To jump up and run or fly or . . . I can't think when you're doing that."

"Good." His free hand rode the shift up from her calf to her hip. He kissed a mole which appeared to the right of her pelvis, then kissed it again because he enjoyed it.

The movement of his lips on her skin brought her to a half-sitting position. "I wish you'd get out from under that sheet!" she said in her most annoyed tone, but her voice trembled.

"Why?" He poked his head free of the cover and grinned at her indignant, too-flushed face. "It's where I've dreamed of being since the day I met you. Lift your hips."

She opened her lips to argue, then shut them and did as he ordered. Free of her weight, the shift billowed up around her waist, leaving her bare below, and she snatched at the edge of the sheet again.

"Beautiful." Ducking his head, he tried to submerge again.

She caught his hair. "This is not what I'd planned."

"If you'll lie back on the pillows and kiss me, I'll do whatever you tell me," he promised.

"Do you so vow?"

"Whatever you tell me," he repeated.

He could see her examining his statement, trying to see a trick, but she couldn't conceive of herself so far gone with passion that she couldn't speak or even think, and so she slid back on the pillows and crossed her hands over her bosom. With a crooked smile, he took her hands and placed them on his shoulders. "It just makes it seem as if we're doing this together."

She didn't comprehend the jest, and when she tried to ask for an explanation, he kissed her.

Kissing she comprehended. Kissing they'd done before, and from her response, she enjoyed the touch of the lips, the slow penetration to the mouth, the first taste. . . . He groaned when she thrust her tongue into his mouth, and he wanted very badly to lever himself over the top of her. But first . . . his hand tangled in the laces of her shift. They had enticed him long enough, and he slipped the knot free and spread it with his hand. He didn't like this shift. He didn't know why he'd told her he did. It was too long, too revealing, and horribly in the way. He wanted it off, and when he placed his palm in the middle of her chest, the thud of her heart encouraged him. She tore her lips free when he cupped her, but he chased and captured them again. She didn't fight, but caught fire easily, and he began to hope.

Familiarity warmed her, obviously, and whatever he did, he had to do twice. Once to show her, once to incite her. Inching closer, he stroked the shift all the way open. Her shoulder slipped free, then her arm, then her hand. Lifting her with his arm around her shoulders, he removed the linen and flung it away.

She struggled to semi-awareness. "David."

But he didn't want to hear her behest, so he touched her as he'd touched her when he'd been beneath the covers. She bucked and moaned, her head falling back on the pillow, her red hair spread across it like writhing flames.

He was right. He was right. All he had to do was accustom her to each movement, and she followed his lead. He could do that. He could do everything twice.

Everything except . . . well, by then he'd have her so far gone with passion she wouldn't notice. Assuredly, she was a virgin, but men exchanged stories on the night before battle, and he'd heard that a virgin of advanced age softened. He'd been told muscles relaxed and barriers broke with activity.

With his finger, he entered her, testing the truth of it. She seemed tight, and he frowned. Then she shuddered, and he saw her face. She struggled to regain control so she could evaluate this initial contact. Quickly he withdrew and caressed her as he'd done before, and he vanquished her restraint. Her hands grasped his shoulders and her close-cut nails sank into his flesh. She began the rhythmic motions that invited him inside, and he praised her with a kiss so intimate, it brought tears to his eyes.

His body hummed with triumph, with gratification, with pure carnal energy. She was his. He knew how to manipulate her now. She was his, and he wanted inside her so badly . . . of their own accord, his fingers sank deep within her.

He watched, but while her eyes opened, she didn't focus. All of her attention centered on her own body, on her own reactions.

A selfish loving, this first time, but he never doubted she'd return the favor another time, and what he felt now could scarcely be repeated.

Was she ready? He was. He was so ready he feared to trust the damp evidence on his hand. But the men around the campfire had said something else, something he'd not understood at the time. The difference between an old virgin and a young virgin, they said, was that an old virgin followed with caution while a young virgin leaped after new adventures.

That he had confirmed. Now he could only hope their other wisdom proved as true.

Rising up and over her, he spread her legs and rocked against her.

This time she focused, saw him, and she stilled as she adjusted to the dominance of his position. He rested on his elbows, holding his weight back, not wanting to frighten her, and he remained still while she thought about how it felt and what would happen.

Then he rocked against her again, and again, and her already sensitive flesh began to respond. He moved into position slowly, holding himself in suspense as each moment he waited and feared to hear her logical voice instructing him. But although she remained silent, not giving vent to her pleasure, her body reacted to each of his thrusts with first timid, then sure thrusts of her own.

"That's it." He crooned in her ear. "When I'm inside you, do just that."

He shouldn't have said anything, he guessed. He wanted nothing to distract her now, but he was too close and it was going to be so good, and so easy . . .

He entered her, but she fit him almost too tightly, if such a thing were possible. He trembled as he held himself in check, moving slowly, slowly. Then he found her maidenhead, and it in no way responded to his gentle movements.

The men had said older virgins were easy. But the men didn't know Alisoun. Alisoun was now and would always be contrary.

With an effort, he held himself still. Reluctantly, he opened his eyes and looked down into her face.

Passion no longer held her in its grip. She laid beneath him, perfectly composed, waiting for more pain.

"Alisoun . . ." He groaned.

"Don't worry. You haven't hurt me badly, and I was prepared for this." Her hands slid off his shoulders. She folded them across her bosom and closed her eyes. "Go ahead and finish."

He wanted to scream, to pound his fists on the pillow, to kick like a three-year-old throwing a tantrum. But he didn't want to frighten her, and the second time . . . he moved forcefully, and she cried out in one uncensored feeling . . . the second time she would be accustomed, and she'd be everything he ever dreamed.

12

The little cocoon of warmth around Alisoun made her want to stretch, but when she moved her legs, every muscle skidded along the bones and she moaned.

"Sore?" David's voice sounded warm and sure, and his hand—the hand that had been resting on her ribs—moved to her thigh. "Let me . . ." His fingers moved across the skin, kneading first with gentle strokes, then deeply. "That better?"

For one cowardly moment, she didn't want to face him. But that was stupid. She'd made the decision to pleasure herself with him yesterday after her discussion with Philippa, and she couldn't hide from him now. Not after the intimacies of the previous night. Cautiously, she opened her eyes and found him face-to-face with her. She was warm because his body draped over her left side and one of his legs wrapped around both of hers.

Maybe she should have pretended to sleep until he'd left the bed—even if he rested all through to the next morrow.

"Good morning." His brown eyes were almost golden when he smiled, but his gaze was watchful and his smile studied rather than exuberant.

In the early morning light, she could see the chip of an ear that testified to his legendary status, but the hair on his chin and jaws had sprouted black and stubbly, just like any other man's. Yet she'd never seen another man from so close. She ought to say something, to show him she was the same Lady Alisoun she'd been the day before, but she didn't feel the same. She felt almost frightened, as if she'd dangled over a precipice and saved herself at the last minute.

He'd dangled with her, too, and gone over by himself. It was dark down there. She couldn't see what waited below, but she imagined thorns and jagged boulders would tear her to pieces, and what if David didn't catch her when she fell?

And what if he did?

He gathered a handful of long red hair and moved it behind her back. "Alisoun?"

Shaking herself, she abandoned her silly fantasy and said, "Good morning. Aye, that rubbing does make me feel better. My muscles aren't used to such activity, I suppose, and that's why . . ." He was still smiling, still massaging her, and she began to lose track of her thoughts. "I'm better now, so probably you can stop."

Still smiling. Still smiling.

"Really, probably you should stop, or we'll miss Mass and the priest will be irritated."

Still smiling.

"Even more irritated than normal." She couldn't think of another thing to say.

He waited, and when she was done babbling—she, Alisoun, countess of George's Cross, had been babbling!—he unwrapped himself from around her and kicked the rugs aside. Stretching, he groaned loudly. It didn't really sound like the noises he'd made last night—last night had been quieter and more intense—but she shivered under the impact, and she glanced down the length of him. Yesterday, when the men had carried him in and dumped him on the bed, she'd sized him up as a potential mate and father of her child. She'd been pleased to note that her regimen of regular meals had given him a bit more flesh; his muscles no longer stretched like wires under his skin. Yet now the fresh bruises had darkened to purple except where the old scars shone shiny white.

Any man who had survived and prospered as a mercenary knight had proved himself wily and tough. Any man who became a legend might be her match.

Had she swallowed the whale, or been swallowed by him?

"I'm sore, too," he said. "Probably more from tumbling off Louis than from tumbling you, but I lost my virginity years ago, so for me, last night was pure pleasure."

How was she supposed to respond? *I enjoyed myself, too? Summon me anytime you have need of hospitality?* She knew the niceties of etiquette, but no one told her how to return a compliment like that one.

He studied her, then sat up in all his naked glory. She scrambled to cover herself while he fished around among the bedclothes, and when he came up holding her shift, she just stared at it.

"Sit up." He urged her with a hand under her back. "You'll want your clothes."

She did want them, but she didn't want him to dress her. He bunched up the hem of the shift just like Philippa bunched up Hazel's gowns. Then he dropped it over her head and helped her thrust her arms through the sleeves. "This is ridiculous," Alisoun said. "I know how to dress myself."

"Aye, but I doubt if you get as much gratification out of it as I do." David tied the ribbon at her neck, then dropped a kiss on her forehead. With his fingers, he brushed the tangled mass of her hair. "I still can't believe this is red."

"Nor can I," Alisoun said sarcastically.

"It's glorious."

"It's sinful."

"If the sunrise be sinful, then this may be. If the daisies be sinful, then this may be. If God's creations bring pleasure to the eye, who dares complain?" He twisted the end of one lock around his finger. "I will pluck the beard from any man who says my wife's hair is sinful."

She fell back. His clasp in her hair caught and jerked her head around, and she exclaimed, "Ouch!"

"Careful." He untangled his hand and rubbed the painful place on her scalp in a manner that staked a claim. "You're mine now, and I don't want you hurt."

"Yours? I'm not yours."

He smiled with every evidence of happiness, but that mindful cast still shadowed his features. "I can see that a woman like you might take exception to that, so let's just say . . . that I'm yours. Is that better?"

"You're not mine, either. We don't belong to each other. We're not going to—"

Although his lips still smiled, his eyes narrowed.

"—Not going to . . . get . . . "

"Married?"

"Not . . . nay, not . . . married."

"How will you avoid marriage with me if this night bears fruit?"

Comprehension came slowly this morning, but when

she understood, she asked bravely, "You mean, if I am with child?" Yesterday when she had decided that Philippa was right, that it was time to lose her bothersome virginity and learn the secrets of the sheets, she had faced the odds of pregnancy with a mature equanimity. This morning, when she imagined that a babe might already be nestled in her womb, she didn't feel so confident.

But she had to stick with her scheme. She'd considered it deeply, after all.

Well, perhaps not too deeply. She feared there might have been a physical part of herself that blocked a paltry bit of her good sense. When she examined her logic today, she might even wonder what she'd thought the day before.

But nothing *David* could say would change her plan. In a reasonable tone, she said, "If I'm with child, I'll not point a finger at you or hold you responsible. I know it's unusual, but legitimate or not, my child would be the heir to my lands."

"Not if you marry again."

She was regaining control, and she rejoiced. Coolly, she said, "I've begun to believe that's not likely to happen."

He sat up. "Is that why I was granted the honor of your bed? Because Simon of Goodney refused you?"

He might have struck her across the face, so brutal were his words. Her burgeoning control fled, and she stammered, "Nay, 'tis not so."

"I was used as a sop to your pride?"

But wait. He hadn't said anything, really. Accusing her of using him because she'd been humiliated in front of the court should bring nothing but scorn to her lips. Valiantly, she straightened. "Simon of Goodney could never damage my—" She took a breath and fought these conflicting currents of anger, hurt, and embarrassment which threatened to tear her authority from her.

"And you think you can bear my child and I'll gladly leave it in your incompetent hands?"

"Incompetent?" Amazed by his accusation, she scrambled up and sat on her heels. "I'm not incompetent."

"You have no idea what a child needs." She tried to interrupt, but he swept on. "Water, food, clothing—aye, I know you'll supply those. But what of affection? Will you hold the babe when it cries? Will you nurse it through illness? Will you do more than teach it its duties? I doubt you will, my lady. I doubt you even comprehend a word I'm saying."

"Why should you care? I would think you'd be glad to be rid of any consequences of this night. I know that men beat their babes for doing no more than crying."

He jerked back. "What kind of men do you know?"

That had been the wrong thing to say. That had been a betrayal, and Alisoun scrambled off the bed. "Just . . . men," she said, in what she hoped was an offhand tone.

"No wonder you've found fault in every bridegroom, if that is your experience."

"I didn't find fault because I feared them, but because they were unsuitable to my station, my wealth, or because they failed to take their responsibilities seriously."

"Which am I?" He stood and stripped the sheet off the bed.

"Well, station and wealth, of course."

"Ah, aye, my lady." His brown eyes gleamed with some obscure emotion. "Doesn't it strike you as ironic that twelve sacks of wool separate us?"

And a title. But she didn't say that. When one looked at the matter, one could call a title just a word spoken by the king which segregated his friends from his enemies. Doggedly, she pushed on. "Although you've been negligent in your knightly practice, I understand your reluctance to show yourself incompetent against Hugh." He turned his back and walked away from her, dragging the sheet. She wasn't used to such treatment. Irritated, she demanded. "What are you doing?"

"Announcing our marriage."

For a moment she didn't understand. Then her gaze fell on the bloody stain that marked the center of the white linen and she realized he moved toward the window. "Nay!" She lunged for him.

Nimbly, he sidestepped her and flung open the sash. Leaning out, he shook the sheet and let it flap in the breeze. "Look!" he yelled.

She ran up behind him.

"I took your lady's—"

Without thought or sense, she hit him in the back. If God were in His heaven, David would have tumbled to his death below. But the Lord obviously favored the miscreant, because David caught the sides of the window and saved himself—but not the sheet. It went flying, flapping, whirling to the ground into the middle of the vegetable garden while the castle folk watched. White and red on a background of lush green, it landed beside Tochi, who rose from his weeding and lifted it in his grubby hands. Everyone who stood below in the bailey—and today everyone in the castle seemed to be working outside—witnessed the evidence of her sin.

As Alisoun stared in dismay, Tochi grinned and flapped the sheet like a tournament flag. The others nudged each other. One by one, they pointed up at Alisoun where she stood framed in the window with David. A few of them bowed, a few waved, a few pulled their forelocks in respect. And who did they respect? Not her, she wagered, but David.

David, who stood naked and unashamed. David, the man they thought had seized control of her with the simple, animal act of taking her maidenhead.

"That was—" she sputtered, "—despicable."

"Why?" David leaned out and waved back. "Everyone's happy."

"I'm not."

He pulled himself inside and turned to her. "You were."

"Nay, I—"

"For a time."

She blushed. How could she help it? His brown eyes gleamed with a sure knowledge of her pleasure, brief though it had been. He knew so much more than she did. He knew more about *her* than she did.

"You do us an injustice, lady, when you place so little value on the passions of the night." He grasped the ribbon that tied her shift and gave it determined little jerks. "I put you in your shift, now I would have you out of it."

"There's not time for that! I have things to do, and we—"

"Occasionally, Alisoun, you show incredible stupidity."

He untied the bow and loosened the neck of her shift. She grabbed at his hand, but he was too strong and she was too surprised. What did he think he was doing? He was a rational man; she'd seen the results of his thoughts. So why was he taking off her clothes when she needed to be donning them in preparation for the day? Especially a day such as this one promised to be.

"Sir David, you must know that this is unacceptable

behavior from the lady of George's Cross and her mercenary."

"And what we did last night was *acceptable* behavior?" He slid the shift down over her arms and trapped them there against her sides.

"Would you stop that?" First she tried to push her arms down into the sleeves, then she tried to pull them out. Anything to free herself.

But he wrapped his arms around her, rendering her struggles ineffectual, and lifted her against his body. Her feet dangled, but she commanded, "Put me down at once."

He looked at her and grinned. "Aye, my lady."

She found herself deposited on the table beside the bed. Picking up the medicines and bandages, he flung them on the bed. Then with a sweep of the arm, he cleared the pewter pitcher and cup off the surface. The pitcher struck the floor and wine mixed with water splashed everywhere.

"Sir David, this is not amusing. Now stop—"

Catching her lip in his teeth, he bit her.

Not hard, but she shrieked. "How dare you?"

"How dare you plot to keep my child from me?" His voice rumbled from deep inside his chest.

She pushed at him as hard as she could. "There is no child!"

"Yet." Shoving her shift up to her waist, he stepped between her legs and promised, "But soon."

"I am the lady of George's Cross, and I command—"

His laughter stopped her. She looked at him, at the way he grinned and his gleam of determination, and she fathomed he was going to have her. He had something to prove, she didn't know what, and this day which she had organized would suffer for . . . for what?

"Schedule this." He put one hand behind her hips to

hold her still and used the other to touch her low and deep.

She jumped and winced.

"Too much, Alisoun?"

His touch lightened at once, easing the irritation and replacing it with a soothing sensation. She still strained for a moment, thinking she should fight him, but her eyelids slid shut, then her spine relaxed onto the wooden boards.

Just for a moment, she promised herself. She'd let him do this just until he was appeased. Inevitably, the illusion of her compliance would calm his ire.

She let him do what he would. His callused fingers proved surprisingly supple as they caressed her stomach, her thighs, and everything between. Last night the sensations had been too new for her to fully analyze their effect, but now she realized that when he stroked her skin, it first lulled her, then brought a tightening, almost a stimulation. What he did made her want him to do more, and she rolled her head on the boards in instinctive denial.

She couldn't want more. Surely madness didn't sweep one away at unsuitable times, but it was almost as if it were easier for him to arouse her this morning.

Opening her eyes, she braced her arms against the table to push herself upright. "This proves it."

"What?"

"If one loses control once, one starts the long slide down into dissipation."

His brown face appeared sinister—surely a trick of the light—and he said, "Slide faster, my lady. Slide faster."

Most men would be looking at what she so unwarily displayed.

David looked at her face. She thought she had

schooled herself to hide her emotions well, but he seemed to be judging his assault by her expressions.

"We need to halt now." Her voice sounded weak even to herself.

"Not ever."

She tried to recoil. He slid a finger inside of her.

"Don't. I'm not . . . ready."

"Believe me, you are."

How did he know she was lying? He'd learned too much about her in one night. She closed her eyes against the sensation, then opened them when he took her arms and put them around his shoulders.

"Hold *me*," he said. "I'll support you."

She needed no man's support, but she liked it as his arms cradled her.

His arms . . . She jerked to the realization he still touched her intimately, but no longer with his hands. She shuddered with passionate demand, then looked up to see if he had noticed.

He was watching her as carefully as a mother watched her child, waiting for knowledge and skill to take the place of ignorance. She looked into his eyes, wanting to please him, wanting . . .

"We are so close, my lady." His voice crooned to her as he slid inside her. "Feel me. Take me into your body and let me into your soul."

She whimpered when he moved. This was all sweet and hot. She tried to brace her heels on the tabletop, but they slipped off. She wrapped them around his waist, and his smile blossomed.

"All mine," he whispered.

And she realized she shouldn't have opened herself to him so freely. But he rewarded her by thrusting, by moving faster. This wasn't the gentle, considerate loving of the previous night. It was sunshine and speed and fragments of breath. Discipline spun away and she fought to get closer while he fought to move away.

Or was it the other way around?

"David." She wanted his flesh, and she bit his shoulder. It tasted salty.

He jerked, laughed under his breath, thrust harder.

She wanted everything about him in the selfish, greedy way of a child. She wanted because she wanted, because he made her move and clench and feel . . . and shudder and cry out and . . . she fell backward and he caught her, lowering her to the table. The cool surface arched her back up toward him. She tried to grasp something, to make sense of sensation, but there was only David and, ultimately, herself. She cried out his name. She came up off the table in one giant convulsion that rattled her world.

She lost control.

He leaned over her, urging more.

But she couldn't do more. She didn't understand what she'd just done.

Then he said it. "More." And the rusty sound of his voice in her ear, the caress of his breath and the touch of his lips made it happen again. "Please." She whimpered, trying to escape the ecstasy and find more at the same time.

He climbed on the table with her, and up on his knees he rose above her. He held her hips as he thrust harder, then gave an exultant roar when he finished.

She didn't understand it. Not any of it. But she didn't have time to think. He pulled her close against him. His chest rose and fell as he gasped, and hers did the same. His heart galloped beneath her ear, an echo of her own.

In her life, she had come to believe men and women

were nothing alike, yet it seemed they reacted in a similar manner to this one act.

Mayhap that was why the Church sanctified marriage. To celebrate this one time men and women found accord.

Then slowly, he released her and rose on his knees again. She looked at him above her, felt him inside her, and knew somehow power had shifted.

"Did you think I could fail in everything and never move to regain my losses?" Determination bit hard lines beside his mouth and anger brought fire to his gaze.

"I don't understand," she stammered.

Thrusting his hands into her hair from her neck, he turned her face up to his. "Don't think you can resist me again. When you come to my bed, be prepared to surrender control—or I will wrest it from you."

"I don't have to come to your bed!"

He laughed with a touch of maniacal amusement. "Then I will come to yours, my lady." He let her go so suddenly she slid backward. The table rocked as he climbed down. Grabbing an armful of his clothing, he opened the chamber door, turned and promised, "And you will welcome me."

13

The night before, I'd fallen asleep a miserable, unhappy boy. In a brutal demonstration of his ineptitude, my hero had failed to defeat Hugh. Lady Alisoun had gone into Sir David's chamber, and no one had let me retreat there to sleep. The great hall—indeed, the whole castle—was quiet, waiting for the outcome of some momentous event, and I feared my lady planned to discharge Sir David.

Then when I rose in the morning, every servant in the great hall was laughing! I didn't understand, so I asked Hugh. He hugged my shoulder and told me everything was fine. I asked Andrew. He grinned and ignored me. At last I asked Jennings. He turned his fourteen-year-old, superior face on me and said, "Stupid cur! Your precious Sir David bedded Lady Alisoun last night, and he just tossed the bloody sheet out the window to prove it." His wide eyes narrowed. "And you're his squire." Cuffing me on the ear, he muttered, "It should have been me."

I was stunned. Sir David had bedded Lady Alisoun? I had schemed for Sir David, aiding and abetting his suit, but this seemed all wrong. I had thought it would be like one of the stories the minstrels sang of. I thought Sir David would woo Lady Alisoun, save her from danger, and they'd be the living celebration of a pure love. Stained sheets and sweaty bodies never existed in my mind. But before I could stumble back and hide in a corner, Sir David stormed out of his chamber and slammed the door shut behind him.

Everyone cheered. The previous day's defeat might never have happened. In their eyes, he'd done the impossible; he'd conquered Lady Alisoun.

The hurrahs stopped him in his tracks. His gaze swept over the smiling assemblage, and he glared with enough fury to halt the demonstration. The servants ducked their heads and hurried to their tasks. He pointed his thumb at Philippa, then at his chamber. "She'll want you," he said.

Philippa handed her baby to one of the other maids and with head bent and shoulders slumped, she hurried to obey.

Then he saw my horrified stare, and he seemed to comprehend just how I felt. "Well," he asked, "are you still my squire?"

Did I have a choice? Clearly, I did, and I knew better than to abandon my knight for any reason. I answered, "Aye, Sir David."

Snatching a loaf of bread off the sideboard, he tore it and tossed me half. "Then let's break our fast and go to work."

He strode from the great hall with me on his heels, and behind I heard the footsteps of Hugh, Andrew, and Jennings.

Hell was about to begin.

"Where did he hurt you?"

Philippa's voice intruded on Alisoun's daze, and she turned her head slowly to stare at her friend. "What?"

Philippa rushed toward her as she rested on the table. "Where did he hurt you? He was so angry, and I'm sorry I suggested . . . but he never even slapped Susan when she poured boiling stew in his lap while she was trying to entice him."

The hard table hurt Alisoun's tailbone, so she sat all the way up. "That's not a very clever way to do it."

"She wasn't pouring it into his lap to entice him, she was leaning over the table and showing off her udders and accidentally—good Saint Ethelred, that's not important!" Philippa took Alisoun's hands and chafed them. "Did he put you on the table to beat you?"

Alisoun dragged her drooping shift up over her shoulders. "Nay!"

"Then, did he use you roughly?"

"Not exactly." Gripping the edge of the table, Alisoun slid off and stood on wobbly legs. "He was just rather . . . forceful. He was angry about something."

"What?"

"I just told him that we'd spent too much time in bed and he'd ruined my schedule."

Several expressions crossed Philippa's face, and in a tone of voice Alisoun couldn't comprehend, Philippa said, "I don't know why that would bother him."

"I don't, either." Philippa "tsked" in disgust and this time Alisoun recognized exasperation. "*Why* would that bother him?"

"Men are funny that way." Philippa turned Alisoun around and spread the shift's gaping neck yet wider.

"What are you doing?" Alisoun demanded.

"You have no bruises."

Craning her neck to look at Philippa, Alisoun said, "I told you I did not. Why would I lie?"

"Because sometimes it's embarrassing to admit that the man you picked is so . . . careless."

"The word is brutal."

Philippa flinched. "Perhaps. Would you like a clean shift?"

"And my work clothes. I am determined to continue the day as if this never happened." Alisoun's mind had returned to its orderly functioning. As Philippa hurried back to Alisoun's chamber to retrieve her costume, Alisoun resolved to shove Sir David's odd behavior into the background of her thoughts. She couldn't allow him to disrupt her schedule both day and night. But when Philippa returned, arms full of clothes, Alisoun immediately spoiled her resolve by blurting, "He's angry about the child."

"I was afraid of that." Philippa laid the clothes on the bed and poured water in a basin for Alisoun to wash. "Men don't like having you distracted from their needs by a child."

"Nay, I mean he says I wouldn't know how to raise his child." Alisoun leaned over the basin, waiting in suspense to hear Philippa's verdict.

"That's nonsense," Philippa said stoutly. "You love as deeply as any other."

Encouraged, Alisoun splashed in the cold water.

"You simply aren't demonstrative."

Alisoun stopped and waited in dread.

"And of course children do thrive with holding and kissing."

Alisoun accepted the towel Philippa handed her. "Do you mean you encouraged me to bed Sir David with the intent of getting myself an heir and you don't believe me capable of acquiring the skills to raise a child?"

"I didn't say that. I just remembered how Sir David entertained Hazel and didn't complain when she drooled all over the front of his shift."

"Why did she drool on him?"

"Because she's teething," Philippa said patiently.

"How long has she been doing that?"

"Since before he got here."

"All that time for one tooth?"

Philippa stepped back and looked Alisoun over as if she were none too bright. "Hazel has four teeth now. I'm weaning her to a cup."

"But she's just a baby!"

"That seems to be the best time for people to acquire teeth."

Alisoun couldn't comprehend such a rush. It seemed only yesterday when Hazel had been born. She'd been helpless, unable to sleep all night or eat without a belly-ache. Now she was sitting up and rolling around and getting teeth. While Alisoun wasn't looking, Hazel had become more than an infant. She had become a babe, and for the first time Alisoun realized David's concern. She was ignorant of children, and what if she made a mistake? What if she was too busy for the baby, or disciplined it at the wrong time, or rewarded the wrong behavior? All adults started out as babies, innocent and sweet as Hazel, and look what a mixed bag of villains and saints they became. Undertaking child rearing was a chore of unspeakable magnitude, with results that echoed far into the future.

Alisoun sank onto a stool.

And she had thought to raise a child alone. It couldn't be done. She pressed her hand to her womb. Who knew what horrors might result?

"Don't look so stricken," Philippa said. "If nothing else, *I'll* help you raise your child."

"Aye." Alisoun released her breath in relief. "You'd know what to do."

Alisoun knew herself to be a woman of good sense. She could learn how to raise a child if given enough guidance. Only . . . how did one become proficient? It seemed to Alisoun that if she practiced on her own babe, she'd not realize her mistakes until the child was grown. But on what babe did one practice? Without a doubt, Philippa wouldn't allow experimentation on Hazel, and did Alisoun really wish to possibly ruin her dearest friend's child with her own ineptitude?

"Look, Alisoun, we must face facts. I may be forced to leave here some day."

"Nay, you won't," Alisoun said automatically.

Philippa smiled, but her lips trembled. "Sometimes I wish I could go back."

Alisoun surged to her feet. "But why?"

"Not for lack of hospitality in you," Philippa assured her. "But because . . . oh, sometimes I think it was all my fault, and if I went back, I could—"

"Die," Alisoun interrupted flatly. "And leave your baby alone for as long as she survived."

Now Philippa sank onto a seat, her complexion several shades paler. "In sooth, you're right. But I may be forced, and neither one of us will be able to do anything about it."

"I know." Of course Alisoun knew. She had nightmares about being helpless in that situation. Walking over, she put her hand on Philippa's shoulder.

Philippa patted it, then looked up. "So. Sir David has many good qualities and he's right about a lot of things. Did he say anything about marriage?"

Alisoun didn't want to discuss that, not even with Philippa, so she stared at the clothing laid across the bed. "Why did you bring the yellow cotte? That's not my work dress."

"Because your people believe you simply celebrated the wedding night before the ceremony. It's common among the villeins, and quite a few of the noble people I've known have done it as well. I think they expect to see you in something besides that gloomy old brown work dress."

Alisoun stuck out her lip and removed her old shift.

"Did he mention marriage?" Philippa snatched the clean shift away before Alisoun could don it. "And you're not getting dressed until you tell me."

"Very well! I'll tell you."

Philippa handed her the shift.

"He mentioned it." Alisoun dressed as quickly as she could and headed for the door with Philippa on her heels.

Philippa didn't say another word, and Alisoun thought she had escaped easily until she stepped into the great hall. Then the impact of a dozen pair of eager eyes hit her, and she almost staggered from the weight of expectation that descended on her shoulders. She glanced back at Philippa and saw that her shoulders shook as she suppressed her amusement. Alisoun whispered, "This isn't funny!"

The outer door blew open and slammed against the wall. Sir Walter stomped into the great hall and glowered around him, and Philippa abruptly straightened. "You're right. This isn't."

So much confused Alisoun now, but she knew one thing. She'd told Sir Walter to stay away from her, and now he stalked toward her, totally ignoring her command.

She didn't care what had happened in the night. She didn't care that David had tossed her sheet into the vegetable garden. She only cared that Sir Walter disobeyed her. She marched to meet him, calling across the gap, "Why are you here when I told you—"

"Did he hurt you?" Sir Walter wrapped his arm around her shoulders as if he thought she couldn't stand alone. "Did that mercenary force you? For I vow, my lady, if he did, I don't care who he is, I'll kill him."

Alisoun staggered, off balance both mentally and physically. "Of course he didn't force me."

"You can tell me, my lady. After all, you have no brothers and no father to protect you."

"I don't need protecting," Alisoun said firmly. "At least, not from Sir David."

"How did it happen? Did he hold you down, or did he—" he choked with what looked like embarrassment, "—seduce you?"

"I think I . . . seduced him."

His arm dropped away from her. They glanced at each other, eyes wide, but for the first time in months, no hostility existed between them. Both were uncertain; both struggled to comprehend the sweep of changes in George's Cross.

Alisoun couldn't conceive of a George's Cross without Sir Walter, not even after their disagreements. He had been a valuable servant; it would behoove her to try and understand his discontent rather than go through the trouble of training a new steward. She said, "If it would please you, we could talk."

"There." He pointed to a bench in the corner.

Together, they went and sat down. They looked out at the great hall, and the servants who stared so curiously turned away as if to give them privacy. In actuality, of course, they wanted to hear, and all lingered as close as they dared.

Sir Walter didn't seem to notice them. He sat stiffly, could hardly speak. "Sir David was . . . your choice?"

She found herself similarly afflicted. "I have to have someone to . . . ah . . ." How to tell him what she thought when she didn't know for sure what she thought herself? She tried to think how to present this in a manner he could comprehend. "I want an heir. Or . . . I wanted an heir, but Sir David demands that I marry him if I conceive, so . . . "

Sir Walter leaned back and sighed in relief. "At least someone is thinking clearly."

Surprise moved her beyond embarrassment. "You *wish* me to marry Sir David?"

"My lady, you have no choice! The deed is done. You've mated with him, and the news has by now no doubt reached London."

"You exaggerate."

"Do I?" He leaned toward her, his fists on his knees. "Do you know what they're saying in the village? That *you're* the reason for the drought for the last two years, because your womanhood was drying up and the saints disapproved of the waste."

Stunned, she stammered, "They . . . they've blamed me for the drought?"

"Not before. Not until now. That wretched reeve Fenchel started it, I trow. He's the one who always watches the signs, and he says that it started raining the day Sir David arrived and has rained just the right amount since. No heavy downpours have broken the crops or washed away the soil. No dry spells where the plants struggle and show yellow."

"So it's Sir David who broke the drought."

"Nay, he says 'tis you. You're the lady, the one they worship as the spirit of George's Cross. They say that Sir David's coming has renewed your youthfulness and turned you once again from a withering crone to a fruitful goddess."

"That's pagan."

"Aye, they are half-pagan, you know that." He

harumphed and looked out at the busily working servants. "The virgin has been sacrificed, the blood sacrifice has been made, and now prosperity is guaranteed to George's Cross."

"Saint Ethelred save us," she said faintly.

"If Fenchel is right, then the child is conceived and my lady, you must marry Sir David!"

"I thought you disapproved of Sir David. You've certainly done all you can to ravage his good standing."

"I fear my dislike had little to do with Sir David. I couldn't sleep last night, and during the dark time I thought long and deeply." Sir Walter hung his head. "I apologize for showing his incompetence to George's Cross. I was so blinded with fury that you'd brought him to replace me, I never thought you would have a plan, and that that plan depended on something as simple as his reputation as a legend. It was a stroke of genius, my lady, and I should have known you better than to think you would hire a mercenary without testing him."

"Look at me," she commanded. Searching his face, she looked for proof of sincerity and found it in the worried lines of his brow and the clench of his chin. "I accept your apology, but I must tell you—I, too, have been angry." She spoke slowly, trying to negotiate through this unfamiliar maze of misunderstanding and old allegiances. "You have known me for many years. Have I ever given you reason to think me volatile or emotional?"

"Just in the matter of—"

"Sh!" She cut a glance toward the servants, and he lowered his voice.

"Just the one thing, my lady, and it is so overwhelming in its lack of intelligent consideration . . ." He sighed like a man sorely tried.

She placed her hand on his shoulder and stared into his face. "Everything I did before, all the years of good sense and duty, are washed away by one matter on which we disagree. I thought you would understand that I had weighed the consequences of this one act of recklessness in an efficient manner, but you did not." She usually tried to properly consider what she said before she said it, but for once prudence failed her. Sir Walter had been her most faithful advisor for years, and his lack of faith infuriated her. "I went from being your wise and sworn lady to being only a silly woman, and you made your opinion clear, not only to me, but to my servants, my villeins, my men-at-arms."

"I beg your pardon, my lady. 'Twas I who was foolish, I confess."

"I told you what I had done because I believed that to do otherwise was unfair to you—not because I sought your approval."

"I never thought I should give approval to anything that you did, but, I confess, I treasured the times you consulted my opinion." He answered her now with respect, but with the familiarity of an old friend. "I think it perturbed me that you presented me with such a momentous decision and cared nothing for my thoughts." He gave a bark of laughter. "I suppose I've grown complacent in your employ, and thought myself above my station. You have no family, and you so willingly placed me at your side, I thought myself more than a steward and imagined myself a brother instead." Slowly he slid off the bench and knelt at her side. "I am only a rough knight, my lady, and I pledge myself to you. I beg you, excuse my presumption and trust me once more."

Looking at the top of Sir Walter's bent head, she realized he hadn't renewed his fealty in years. That had been her mistake, and possibly not her first mistake. "I, too, have treasured your advice and come to consider you more than steward and more than a friend."

Lifting his head, he smiled, clearly pleased by her disclosure. He looked at her with the direct gaze she recognized from the years of their companionship. "I still can't approve of your actions, but regardless, you are my lady and I would do nothing to harm you."

"I know you wouldn't."

"And that's why I have to beg you to marry Sir David. I grant you, you have always been a lady of infinite good sense—excepting the matter on which we disagree—and I believe that marriage to Sir David would go far in eliminating the danger which threatens you."

"Why do you say that?"

"That knave who shoots arrows at you, my lady, would hesitate if threatened by a man whose sole interest is in keeping you alive."

"Sir David has no money. He has no breeding."

"*Exactly* why he would fight to the death to keep you alive. He'll not want to battle any other claims on your wealth."

Startled, she laughed. "Are you saying the reasons Sir David is ideal are the same reasons I rejected my other suitors?"

"And he is the father of your child."

"Do you believe this crazed tale of drought and my fertility?" He shrugged sheepishly but did not reply. "You do!"

"Not really, my lady, but you asked me if I trusted your good sense, and I do. If you took Sir David to your bed after so many have failed—"

"None ever tried," she snapped.

"They have, I assure you. You simply never noticed them." He took a breath and repeated, "If Sir David succeeded where so many have fallen, then I believe you have made your decision and I urge you to embrace it."

She just stared. What had she started with her impulsive behavior?

"Ask young Eudo, and he'll tell you. Every child should have a father."

A telling blow, and one that reached its mark. She said, "I'll take your advice under consideration." Leaning over, she gave him a kiss on the cheek to signify peace between them.

Neither one of them saw David, watching from the dark hallway near the entrance of the great hall.

14

"You're thinking of him again, aren't you?"

Alisoun jumped at the sound of Edlyn's voice and dropped her spindle on the floor of the great hall with a clatter. "What?"

"You have that look on your face, as if you've bitten into some new dish and are uncertain whether you like the flavor." Edlyn crossed her hands over her wrists. "Are we going to go out and watch him practice again today?"

Alisoun almost pretended not to know to whom Edlyn was referring. But only the new Alisoun would even contemplate such cowardice, and she shunned the new Alisoun. Leaning over, she picked up the spindle and straightened, hoping the bending would account for the rush of color to her face. "I should go to see if Sir David has fulfilled his promise to improve."

"Well, he has. He improves every day. Even Sir Walter says he's better now, and in only a month."

Alisoun viewed Edlyn's uptilted chin and wanted to sigh. "But Sir David is not better than Hugh."

Now Edlyn's color matched Alisoun's. "Hugh is younger and bigger, and Sir David said he's never seen a man so skilled."

Placing the spindle on the bench, Alisoun tucked her arm through Edlyn's. "He would say so, though, since he can't defeat him."

"Hugh de Florisoun is special," Edlyn said.

The worship in her voice made Alisoun want to weep. The preparations for Edlyn's wedding proceeded apace while the bride sighed for another man—a man who never noticed her except to chuck her under the chin and grin. Even if Hugh *had* noticed Edlyn, it would do them no good. They were both poor; should an attachment develop, they would be unable to wed. It was just as well Edlyn went off to Wessex soon, Alisoun thought grimly, as she collected all the wool and put it in her basket.

Edlyn pulled Alisoun to her feet. "Sir David and Hugh are providing much entertainment to all who have come to market."

"I don't like to expose you to so many strangers," Alisoun said. "The Lammas Market attracts less than savory characters, I fear."

"I don't go down to the market," Edlyn protested.

"You don't have to. They're coming up to us. I've never seen such traffic between the castle and the village."

As they stepped outside, Alisoun saw that a crowd once again lined the fence around the practice area—her people and many strangers. Alisoun never knew who or what she would see when she stepped out of her door. Greasy sheep farmers mingled with her serving maids, who used their spindles to keep the men at bay when they became too bold. Fenchel stuck close to his friends from the village. Avina strutted among the merchants, trying to attact one of the wealthy ones. Ivo stood just as he always did, arms crossed over his chest with an attitude that rejected David's efforts as feeble. Gunnewate had his eyes closed as if the activities bored him. Both men came to the alert as Alisoun neared the training yard.

Normally, she would reprove her people all for sloth, but not this time. The summer work seemed to be getting done, and this time watching the combats was time they would have spent loitering at the market instead. And they needed reassurance that Sir David of Radcliffe would indeed protect them.

They were getting it. David had justified her faith. He worked with every weapon all day, every day, ignoring the pain of his broken ribs and the bruises that mottled every surface of his skin. His transformation proved awe-inspiring, and if not for Hugh, his reputation would be almost as good as new.

The men would fight with swords until both fell panting on the ground. They fought on horseback with mace, lance, and shield. They wore their armor on the hottest days to accustom themselves to the weight.

But Hugh consistently defeated Sir David.

Andrew and Jennings imitated them while young Eudo performed the onerous duties of squire to them all. Alisoun was pleased to see that David's constant courtesy to the lad inspired the others to a like courtesy, and she never once heard the epithet of "bastard" thrown at him. Even Sir Walter found it prudent to keep his lips sealed about Eudo's parentage.

Seeing him now inside the training yard, Alisoun sighed. "Sir Walter has tried to be a most gentle knight."

"He has tried," Edlyn said sharply. "I would that he always succeeded."

"Perhaps if Sir David rode him less harshly, those

small fits of temper would abate," Alisoun said. "I don't understand the reason for Sir David's displeasure."

"He doesn't like that Sir Walter has wormed his way into your affections once more."

"We but spoke and came to a new understanding. I would think that Sir David wished for such an accord between me and my steward."

Edlyn spoke matter-of-factly. "New lovers want all attention for themselves."

"And how do you know that?"

"Philippa told me."

"Philippa discussed Sir David and me with you?"

"Philippa tells me much, trying to prepare me for marriage," Edlyn answered.

Feeling irked and strangely hurt, Alisoun said, "If you have questions, you should come to me."

"I thank you, my lady, but although your experience in most issues I hold in the utmost respect, in this one issue I would prefer Philippa's council."

Edlyn spoke pleasantly, giving the rebuke in a manner Alisoun recognized—it was much like her own.

Walking toward the training yard, Alisoun kept her spine stiff and her shoulders squared, and everyone moved well back, bowing and tugging at their forelocks.

"My lady." Sir Walter bowed before her and Lady Edlyn. He kept a constant eye on the proceedings in the training yard and scowled at any bold souls who came too near to Alisoun. "Have you once again come to watch your expensive apprentice?"

Alisoun's gaze lingered on the two men who engaged in throwing light lances at a straw target, and she didn't make the mistake of thinking Sir Walter spoke of Hugh. From the irritation in his voice, she guessed that David had been antagonizing him again.

Before she could try and ease his offense, he held out his hand, palm up. "Never mind me, my lady. I try not to be offended by his hostility, for I fear I deeply offended him when I opened him to the ridicule of your folk."

"That could be the reason for his rude and unnecessary animosity, of course, but I expect more from my . . ." she hesitated.

"Consort," Sir Walter promptly finished.

Edlyn giggled.

Alisoun glared.

Holding out the flat of his hand, Sir Walter looked toward the sky. "We're due for another rain soon, I suspect."

Alisoun couldn't take teasing. Not about that. Not about a legend it seemed all of her people believed.

Sir Walter realized it, because his expression changed from teasing to compassion, and he said, "I beg you, my lady, pardon me. I thought to ease your discomfort about that legend, but I will mention it no more."

She nodded gratefully, then with none too much grace, she changed the subject. "What do Ivo and Gunnewate think of Sir David's improving skill?"

Sir Walter's face changed at once. Harshly, he said, "I don't ask men-at-arms their opinions."

Sir Walter might have sought reconciliation by humbling himself to her, Alisoun realized, but he still thought well of himself. A crab didn't file his claws, but waved them to display his strength. Sir Walter was a crab.

Unaware of her amusement, he continued, "*I* seldom have seen a man blessed with a combination of such natural skill and dogged determination as Sir David." He stroked the dangling strands of his beard. "I'm not saying you got what you paid for, understand. If it were me, I'd be demanding he account for his failures. But you're a woman, easily led astray, and at least he's willing to better himself." He leaned against the fence and muttered loudly enough for her to hear, "He'd be a fool not to, with the gold you're paying him."

A yell from the field distracted her before she could chide Sir Walter. Glancing up, she saw Hugh go down under an unexpected attack from David. In only a moment, David had Hugh pinned, a knife at his throat. "Wha— what happened?" she stammered, climbing up on the bottom rail of the fence to catch a better view.

"I like that." Sir Walter grinned. "He's knocking the arrogance right out of Hugh. *I* can't tell the youth anything anymore. My woman says I'm like a father to him, and since he's grown beyond my skills, he doesn't listen to a word I say. That David has taught him a thing or two."

"I don't understand."

"David heard Hugh say a true knight doesn't use a paltry weapon like a knife for any reason but to spear his meat. But David's teaching him differently. Told him that a mercenary knight spent more time in dark streets and isolated inns than in tournaments and sieges. Said Hugh had best learn to defend himself from others, poorer even than a mercenary, who would seek his armor and his horse with the point of a dagger." Sir Walter nodded as David took the point of the knife away from Hugh's throat and offered a hand. "In this area, at least, David is by far Hugh's superior."

Hugh took David's hand in every evidence of gratitude, then jerked his mentor down and over his head. While David floundered, Hugh jumped on his back and began pounding his face into the grass. Alisoun didn't see what happened next, but she thought it had to do with David's elbow, for Hugh doubled up and rolled off, groaning.

David levered himself up, leaned over Hugh, and said something. From the smirk he cast on the writhing youth, it obviously wasn't a compliment.

"My lady, may I go to him?" Edlyn asked.

For one wild, jealous moment, Alisoun thought Edlyn wanted to help David. Good sense returned, and she realized Edlyn spoke of Hugh. Curtly, she said, "Nay. Go inside and ask Philippa to help you with your spinning." Edlyn didn't move, and Alisoun turned on her sharply. "Now!"

Edlyn gave a little sob as she fled, and Alisoun saw the horror on Sir Walter's features as he realized Edlyn's infatuation. She could see the words hovering on the tip of his tongue—*You're setting a bad example for the girl*—but he restrained himself.

She *was* setting a bad example, she knew, but she had no choice. At various times, her conscience smote her, and she tried to barricade the door of her bed-chamber or refuse to have commerce with her lover, but David would not accept *nay* for an answer.

In an undertone, Sir Walter asked, "Have you told your hero yet why you hired him to protect you?"

"'Tis not necessary that he know," she answered as quietly. "Only that he do it."

"He's a hard man." Sir Walter watched as David strolled toward them. "What makes you think he will see it any differently than I do?"

She wanted to say that he would. In sooth, life had made David hard, but he showed compassion every day—to Eudo, to the servants, to all who had not his strength. But he *was* a man, and what man would ever support her in her course?

The doubt Sir Walter saw in her face satisfied him, for he smiled without humor. "Aye, and he could lose everything for assisting you. Everything he's labored for all his life. Have you thought on how he will extract his vengeance on you for that?"

David loomed over Sir Walter's shoulder. Dirt and blood stained his face, and he clearly didn't like the whispered conversation he'd interrupted, but with every evidence of respect, he bowed before her. "My lady."

"Sir David." She nodded graciously, playing the game as it should be played. It was absurd, she supposed, to be so formal when Sir David disappeared into her solar every night and never left until the morning, but he seemed to want everyone to know he still respected her person and her station.

He nodded as well to Sir Walter, and Sir Walter nodded back. "Good work," he said gruffly, jerking his thumb toward the still-groveling Hugh. "Out there."

"Aye. The practice goes well. Hugh improves every day." David turned to Alisoun. "As do I."

"Both Hugh's progress and your own are pleasing to me." Her answer came automatically even as she confronted again the effort he made every day to bring his body back to its former condition. She admired his persistence with every fiber of her being, as well as his unfailing sense of humor in the face of his occasional humiliating failure.

If only he acted more like other men in every way, she would have better luck dismissing his pretensions. If only he had strutted and crowed the morning after she yielded to him, rather than acting irritated. With her! As if she had denied him something that was his right.

"The other squires are performing well, too." David spoke as Eudo came across the field, dragging a full bucket. Accepting a dipper of water from the lad, he drank deeply, then took a white rag from Eudo's hand

and smeared it across his own face in a halfhearted effort at cleanliness. Alisoun winced as the cloth scraped across old scabs and new wounds. "And Eudo is a constant companion." David smiled down at Eudo, opening the cut on his lip where fresh blood now oozed.

She couldn't stand it anymore. She climbed through the fence rails, took the rag from his hand, and dipped it in the bucket. "Sit down," she told David, and while Eudo dragged over a stool for his master, she said, "Eudo exceeds all expectations in performance both on the field and in the keep. Now sit down, Sir David."

David bowed in ready deference. "As you command, my lady." Sinking onto the stool, he turned his face up to hers, closed his eyes and awaited her ministrations.

She glanced around. Everyone, especially her own people, leaned over the fence, waiting with avid attention for her to touch him. It wasn't as if she had never tended another's wound. She was the lady, required by tradition to care for the injured. But her folk seemed to see this as something special, a sign of her emotions.

It wasn't. She couldn't stand to see dirt. They knew that. And no woman with a shred of compassion would leave a man to bleed.

Then Avina from the village said, "She's going t' wash him wi' the water from the sky."

Alisoun set her teeth in annoyance, but Sir Walter said, "Of course it's from the sky, you slop-brain. Where else would it be from?"

"That's rainwater." Fenchel made the distinction precisely. "Not from the well, an' not from the stream. It'll heal him more quickly because their mating called it from the sky."

David's eyes popped open. "What are they talking about?"

He hadn't heard that absurd tale, and Alisoun didn't want him to. She looked to Sir Walter in appeal.

In a loud and companionable voice, Sir Walter said, "Have you noticed, Ivo, how there is none of the normal jesting with my lady and Sir David that accompanies a newly formed union?"

In his rough way, he was trying to help her by changing the subject, but David scowled. Everyone in the castle and the village had been stricken with delicacy. No one mentioned David's nightly visits to her solar, because David refused to allow anyone to bandy her name about. He both demolished her reputation and protected it.

"I think it's because of that frown." Sir Walter pointed out easily, as if he expected David to be displeased. At the same time, he inched away. "When Sir David wishes, he can look ferocious, like a dangerous beast loose in our midst."

Sir Walter wasn't making things better. He was making them worse. Still he bumbled on. "We're throwing our lady to him as tribute, fearing to stand in his way."

David bunched his fists. "Sew your yap shut," he ordered.

Fenchel didn't seem to hear David. Instead he gently corrected Sir Walter. "It's that together, they make the rains come. M'lady yields t' him because she must, t' help her people."

With a compelling stare at Alisoun, David inquired, "You yield to me because you must? What nonsense is this?"

It was nonsense, of course. He'd made her a vow when he'd left her sitting on the table, almost naked and almost defenseless. He'd sworn to come to her bed and make her welcome him.

Every night since, he'd kept his word without an

invitation, without caring for her mood or her desires. But always, somehow, he made her mood and desires his. She could have told herself she yielded because she had to, but she didn't lie. She yielded because he excited her, because what he taught her she could never learn from another man. Sometimes the hours drifted, one into the other, while he caressed her, kissed her, gifted her with pleasure. Other times he treated her as if he were a conqueror taking her as his right. Always, she fell asleep satisfied, knowing herself treasured above all women.

"Come, come, old man," Sir Walter said in a jocular tone. "Lady Alisoun hardly considers taking Sir David to her bed a sacrifice. From the sounds issuing from the room, I'd say it was quite the opposite."

Alisoun winced, and David leaped to his feet. Striding toward Sir Walter, he said, "You don't talk about my lady Alisoun in such a familiar manner. She's not yours. She'll never be yours. And I'll kill if you if you ever disparage her again."

"David!" Alisoun grabbed his arm, but he shook her off.

Sir Walter backed away from David, waving his hands. "Nay. I meant no harm! I only tried to distract you from that which my lady didn't wish you to know."

With a growl of animal rage, David grabbed Sir Walter by the chest, then pushed him backward into a puddle.

"Into th' sky water," Avina commented with approval.

Sir Walter came off the ground in a flurry, ready to attack David. Then he hesitated. David could beat him. He knew it, David knew it, and he had no wish to prove it to everyone in George's Cross. Yet David's blow had stripped him of prestige and authority. Taking one step back, he spat at David's feet, then stalked away.

This wasn't what Alisoun had intended. Lately, nothing made sense. Not Sir Walter and his bumbling attempts to ingratiate himself. Not David, angry that she dared try to keep any possible child from him. Angry about something else, too, and not just that she wouldn't marry him. Although she couldn't comprehend the workings of his mind, she knew that without a doubt.

David looked at her with his blazing eyes and dared her to complain.

She shuddered beneath the impact of his gaze.

Sometimes she imagined she was a gemstone swept along by a relentless river, formed and shaped by the current. It tumbled her along into ever deeper waters, and sometimes she feared to drown. Other times . . . well, other times she welcomed the turbulence.

She didn't understand it. During the day, her mind controlled her actions. But at night, it was as if another being ruled. A being with urges blatantly opposed to the Alisoun she thought she was. She couldn't help but wonder if it wasn't the same being David called forth when he laughed at authority. Being with David exposed a whole new part of herself, and she had to wonder—and worry—what else he would reveal.

Without a word, she handed him the rag and walked away.

15

David watched Alisoun leave and didn't know whether to worry or shout for joy. Over and over again, he would think she had grown used to him. Then she would skitter away like a wild bird, and he realized he was no closer to understanding her than before. She was a constant enigma, but lately he'd begun to suspect that God and all the saints were on his side, and he'd win this battle as he had any other—with a combination of skill, intelligence, and luck.

Standing, he leaned over the bucket and washed until Eudo told him he'd eliminated the worst of his grime. Then, taking the wet rag, he followed Alisoun's trail. He followed her easily. Everyone he encountered indicated where she'd gone. Only after he left the castle walls did he have to use his tracking skills, searching for the bent grasses into the woods, then seeking the leaves and branches that showed the signs of her passing. He caught sight of her as she broke into the woodland meadow, and he watched from the shadows as she spread her arms wide to the sunshine. Then she whirled in circles like some Crusader's heathen bride. He crept closer, fascinated by the open elation she displayed, and when she dropped to the ground, he waited in suspense to see what else she would do.

She did nothing, only covering her eyes with both hands as if worry had overcome her or she'd been drained by the burst of emotion.

She *was* behaving uncharacteristically, he thought, as he walked to her side. But that was to be expected of a woman in her condition.

She didn't move. It seemed to him she was thinking too hard to notice anything outside of herself, but when he moved to block the sun from her face she came off the ground with her fist up.

"Whoa!" He waved the white rag above his head in mock surrender. "Don't hurt me, my lady. I'm a peaceful man."

She let out her breath in a half-laugh and dropped her fist. "Of course you are." She sounded as if she didn't believe it, and she sank back to the ground. "It's those who aren't so peaceful who concern me." Plucking the grass, she asked, "Why did you follow me?"

The truth would not do, at least not yet, so he offered the rag. "I need my face washed."

She looked at the rag, then at his face. "Do you?"

"According to you, my lady, I always need my face washed. Here." He shoved the rag into her hand. "Take it."

She held it gingerly as if she didn't want to touch it, or him, then spread it over her hand and sat up on her heels. He stretched out on the ground and wiggled around until his head rested in her lap, then squinted up at her. "I like this."

"You would."

She stroked the rag over the oozing scrapes and David flinched. "Hey! Be gentle!"

"Being gentle won't get the dirt out of these scrapes." With unusual enthusiasm, she scrubbed at the sore place on his forehead. "Hugh showed quite a bit of innovation with his use of the ground as a weapon."

"Everything he knows he learned from me," David mumbled as she pressed the rag against his split lip.

"You've worked miracles," she said.

"Enough miracles to justify another month's wages?"

The rag, and her hand beneath it, smacked against his already sore nose, and when he yelped, she apologized in her careful, measured tones. If he hadn't been in pain, he would have laughed—who would have thought, two months ago, that the correct Lady Alisoun would descend to such a petty revenge?

But she said, "You'll be paid on the day of the accounting, no sooner."

"I'm glad." Sitting up, he took the rag away from her and flung it away. "I want to keep protecting you from whatever makes you bring up your fist when you think you're alone." She folded her hands in her lap and looked down at them. "Don't you want to tell me about it yet?" he coaxed.

She shook her head.

Disappointment made his voice sharp. "Isn't it my duty to see that you are safe at all times? I think that a walk such as you've just taken could scarcely be considered prudent."

"Even foolish." She glanced around the open meadow. "Still, he hides himself. I almost wish he would return so we could end this."

Her intensity surprised David. He'd chided her, true, but he'd almost forgotten why he beat his body into submission day after day. The reward he received every night pushed danger far from his thoughts. Now he, too, glanced around the meadow. They sat in the open, exposed to any predator's gaze, and a frisson of warning went up his spine. "Mayhap we should sit in the shade of a tree."

"Mayhap we should go back."

They should, of course, but he wanted to talk to her, and when they returned to the castle she'd be inundated with duties and he'd need to go make his peace with Sir Walter. "A few more minutes alone," he begged. "I have a question to ask you."

Warily, she agreed. He helped her up and then put his arm around her waist. He liked the easy intimacy of that, the knowledge that he could have her out here and she would yield. It had been a significant victory for him that one morning on the table, and he'd often wondered why his burst of fury and impatience had worked when all his careful preparation the previous night had failed. He'd been too angry and disappointed to think about it at first, and that night he'd shouldered his way into her bedroom and let his emotions drive them. Later, he'd experimented, trying to see what evoked her passion, and he'd discovered she sought, recognized, and responded only to genuine ardor.

If he tried to seduce her, she resisted him with all her fiber. She sought his genuine affection, and she was an expert at detecting the sincerity of others' feelings. What excited her most were the times he concentrated on the two of them to the exclusion of all else. Luckily for him, that proved easy, for when he allowed desire to sweep through him, her response rewarded him beyond his wildest dreams. She acted like a woman in love, and he liked her that way.

Choosing a place in the shade where she could rest

her back against a tree, he swept her a bow and said, "Sit here."

Solemnly, she obeyed him, arranging her skirts carefully and tucking her feet beneath her. She sat with her spine straight and her face composed. Without a word spoken, he understood. She was the lady; he was the mercenary. She would speak to him, but she took care that he saw no glimpse of skin or any part which might excite him, for today she wanted to forget their intimacies of the night before.

Too bad he couldn't allow her such privacy.

"Why did you run away back there?"

She hesitated, and he could see her wanting to pretend she didn't remember how abruptly she had left. But unlike most people he'd ever met, she faced trouble when it came.

"Everything we've done previously, we've done in the privacy of our chambers, and although everyone knew what was occurring, they hadn't actually seen."

"Except for the sheet," he reminded her.

"Aye. Except for that." Her nostrils flared with disapproval, just as they always did when he reminded her of the sheet. "But when I wished to do something as simple as tending your hurt, my people watched as if it were an event, an indication of . . . something."

"Like affection?"

He'd struck a nerve somehow, for she sat up on her heels and her hands twisted in her lap. "I have affection for you! I couldn't have let you come to my bed if I did not. Just because I don't show every passing emotion, it doesn't mean I'm cold or unfeeling. It simply means I've learned that women are better obeyed when they restrain their emotions."

Startled by her vehemence, he agreed.

She went on. "From the moment of my birth, my

parents explained to me the difficulties I would face as an heiress with no close male kin. My godparents helped me realize my position and how others would try to take advantage of it. All of them trained me in appropriate behavior, and tempered me by maintaining a proper distance. Just because I keep to myself, it does not mean I have no feelings."

"I know that." He kept his voice low, half-afraid she would flee again when she realized what she'd revealed. "I've always known there's more to you than meets the eye."

She collapsed back onto the ground. "Aye. Like wealth."

Her cold suggestion left him shocked and indignant until he remembered why he'd courted her in the first place. He did want her money, her land, her influence. He needed it, all of it, but that wasn't the only reason he courted her now, and he wanted to tell her in the eloquent language of the troubadours. Instead he gulped and said, "There's more than that."

"More. Aye, more. More time, mostly."

"Time?"

"Time between my birth and now. I'm old."

He laughed. He shouldn't have, but compared to him, she was a child, an innocent babe inexperienced with anguish or struggle.

Then he glanced at her and saw the way her lips tightened and the glare she bent on him. Hastily, he said, "I beg your pardon, my lady. Your experience in diplomacy and management is far beyond the reach of mine, yet your beauty has never been touched by frost." His flattery failed to mollify her, and he sighed. "My lady—Alisoun—have you thought that lately, in the last fortnight, you have occasionally lost your serenity on more than one occasion?"

Incredulous, she said, "That's your fault! You'll take nothing less than my complete participation."

"Aye, in bed." He took her hand and petted it. "Have I told you how happy you make me in bed?"

She stiffened yet further. "You've mentioned it, although I scarcely believe we should have such a discussion outside in the sunlight."

Leaning forward, he whispered, "Do I make you happy in bed?" She glanced around as if expecting the stern monitors of her behavior to materialize and chide her, and he raised his voice to recapture her attention. "Do I make you happy in—"

"Aye." She clamped her teeth together hard, as if that one-word admission pained her.

He kissed her hand, then put it back in her lap. His hands lingered, rubbing her thighs through the material of her skirt. The friction warmed her even as she batted ineffectually at him, and she relaxed a little. He said, "I've observed that you occasionally laugh out loud."

"Not frequently."

"Not frequently," he agreed. "But it's startling. Pleasant, but startling."

"I won't do it anymore."

"Don't stop. It's made everyone quite cheerful. Haven't you noticed?"

"Maybe." She begrudged him even so small an acknowledgment.

"I've seen you blinking tears from your eyes, too."

She pushed back so quickly her head hit the tree trunk, but she didn't seem to notice the pain. He heard panic when she demanded, "When?"

"The musicians made you cry last night with their ballad about the brothers who were rival pirates and sank each other's ships."

"I have no sympathy for pirates."

"That's why it surprised me when you wept."

Tears filled her eyes now—not that she would admit it—and he ached for her. She was experiencing a full range of emotions for the first time, and she was as susceptible to the pangs as any adolescent. But he couldn't coddle her. Not now. It was far too late for that. She had to face this sensibly, like the lady Alisoun, and slowly she would grow into this other, newer role. "I've also noted that you observe Hazel when she's close to you."

"Hazel?"

"The baby. Hazel. You offer to hold her, too." She didn't say anything, and he probed. "Is there any reason why she interests you now?"

"Babies are just interesting."

"Aye, I always thought so." Since the first time he'd held his daughter in his arms. "Your emotions are easily touched, babies fascinate you . . . Do you have something you want to tell me?"

"Why?" She was beginning to sound defensive.

This was proving every bit as difficult as he had feared. "Because you haven't had your monthly flux in the time we've been together."

She just stared at him as if he were speaking some foreign language.

"I just thought that since you're laughing and crying easily, and I've noticed when I touch you here—" he caressed one breast slowly, trying to calm her, "—you're sensitive, and you haven't had—"

"Are you trying to suggest I am with child?"

She understood! He almost wiped his brow in relief. "That had occurred to me. Do you think that you might be?"

"How should I know? I've never been concerned with such trivial matters." She must have realized how odd that sounded, for she explained, "As lady, my task has never been to deal with the early signs of conception. My task has been to assist in delivering the babes into the world while the man responsible drinks himself into oblivion."

"I wondered if that might not be the case," he answered mildly.

Ignoring him, she swept on. "And how do you know so much about a woman's body, anyway?" Her eyes narrowed as she looked at him. "Oh, I suppose you have a hundred bastards loitering around your estate. Well, if you know so much about it, why didn't you just say, 'My lady, you're with child,' and be done with it?"

She resented admitting her ignorance. He understood that. She was more than a little frightened, and he understood that, too. That explained why she lashed out at him, and he maintained his composure. "I don't know for sure that you carry a babe, and to the best of my knowledge, I have no bastards on my estate. But with our nightly activities and the symptoms you're displaying, it seems likely you'll bear me a child before the first planting."

"Some women don't bear children for years after they begin mating."

He grinned, he couldn't help it. "A lusty planting in a fallow field, my lady."

"It's not funny!"

"I smile for joy, not because I'm amused. Making a child is a moment to celebrate."

"For *you*. Your job is done. Mine's just begun."

He began to lose patience, although he'd had dealings with pregnant women before and well knew their uneasy temperaments. "It's true that in these next few months you will indeed bear the burden, but a father's duties do not end with conception."

"Yours do."

Her cruelty struck at him like a well-aimed blow. He took a quick breath and let it out slowly. "I know you had originally thought to raise my babe alone, but surely you've seen the error of your plan."

"What error? There is no error."

"Do you deny the pleasure we find in each other's company? Not just in the bed, but in the evening when we speak together?"

"Do you think I should take a husband based on the pleasure of his conversation? I've lived alone for a long time, and no one treats me like an equal except you. No one dares argue with me because I'm the lady and have a sharp tongue. Now a crude mercenary sits at my table and tells me what he thinks of me, my management, and of our world without constantly bowing to my superior status."

Her tongue lashed him, and he fought his resentment. "I didn't realize I offended you."

"You don't offend me." She rose to her feet slowly, walking her hands up the tree trunk behind her. "I enjoy it. It's a powerful enchantment, this companionship, and you've used it to destroy the efficient functioning of my mind."

She'd as good as labeled him a wizard. Incredulously, he said, "It's called honesty, my lady, and if you've been so seldom exposed to it you call it enchantment, I pity you."

"Pity me? You envy me. You want to marry me. You want to use this child to control my . . . my twelve sacks of wool. To control my life!"

"Your money? Your life?" She confused him. She infuriated him. Didn't she know what was important? "This is a babe we're talking about. I do want to marry you, and I know you said—"

"I said I wouldn't, and I never change my mind."

Her eyes were gray as flint, and just as hard and cold, and he lost control of his temper. After all, he'd failed in the greatest gamble of his life. "You said you wouldn't, but when I covered you at night, I thought I'd found a woman, the true woman that you were. I was mistaken. You used me just as I use Louis to cover a mare, and now my duties are accomplished."

"You don't have to wait for accounting day." She scrambled for her keys and shook the one which opened her strongbox at him. "I'll give you the gold at once."

"Double the gold." He could hurt her, too. "Gold for being your mercenary, and gold for being your stud."

"I'll send Eudo with it and you can be gone."

"Send Eudo with half of it. Keep the other half for my son, and tell him it is his patrimony, to be used anytime he wishes, to travel to Radcliffe and be with me, his father." Tapping his finger on his chest, he said, "You might be able to keep my child from me, but you can't take that. I am his father and always will be."

"Be gone with you, then."

"I wouldn't stay if you begged me."

They stood facing each other, panting, as if they'd run a race and exhausted all their energy. Alisoun's wimple sat cocked on her head, her cheeks flamed, and she smelled of brimstone. He didn't look much better, he supposed, and he knew one brief moment of chagrin, one moment of wanting her last glimpse of him to be Sir David of Radcliffe, the legendary mercenary.

Instead, anger and hurt had stripped him of all pretense. She tossed her head and strode away, putting as much distance between them as quickly as she could. He whirled and stormed in the opposite direction.

He'd gone only a short distance before conscience brought him to a halt.

He couldn't leave her to navigate the woods alone. His month of stewardship hadn't ended yet. Quietly, so she wouldn't notice and draw false conclusions, he followed her through the woods, where he halted in the shadow of the trees. From there he watched her walk across the clearing and into the stream of people moving from the village to the castle.

She never looked back.

And he didn't care. With a curse, he punched both fists into a tree trunk, then grabbed his scraped and aching knuckles and swore ever louder. Damn the woman! She had him doing stupid things for stupid reasons. He stomped back into the woods, sucking his bleeding wounds. He hadn't meant to lose his temper, but by Saint Michael's arms, he'd not return and beg her pardon when she'd been the one who insisted on following her asinine plans. He circled through the trees. Aye, she'd warned him, but he'd thought she'd see the good sense of marrying him. He'd thought she was an intelligent woman. He should have realized those two terms were mutually exclusive. When a man—

"God . . . "

David stopped and cocked his head. That sounded like an animal in pain.

"Saint . . . John help . . . "

An animal who groaned. An animal with a vocabulary. His senses suddenly went on the alert. He scanned the area, noting broken branches on the underbrush and a dribble of some dark substance marking the leaves. He leaned closer.

Blood. His earlier itch returned, the sense of being watched, and he glanced around at the green enclave. He could see no one, but that broken voice called again.

"Help . . . please."

Determined, wary, he followed the dark speckled trail. The sound of labored breathing grew louder. Then he saw him. Sir Walter. A bloody wound where his mouth should be. Eyes swollen shut. Leg bones cocked at an ungainly angle.

"By Goddes corpus!" David leaped over the barrier of bushes and knelt at the battered man's side. "What happened?"

Sir Walter lisped, "David?"

"Aye, it's me." David grimly ran his hands over Sir Walter, seeking more injuries and finding them. "I need to get help."

"Nay!" Sir Walter clawed at David's arm. "Help."

David glanced around.

"Help," Sir Walter insisted.

David understood. If he left Sir Walter, what would be left when he returned with assistance? Carefully he reached around the stocky man and hoisted him onto his shoulders. Sir Walter didn't make a sound, making David respect him for his fortitude. Standing up slowly, David adjusted Sir Walter's weight to ease his suffering.

Then Sir Walter moaned in a burst of pain. Or David thought it was pain until he caught the name.

"Alisoun."

And David grasped the fact that someone had attacked Sir Walter and beat him brutally. If that someone would do that to a seasoned warrior, what could he do to a woman alone?

"Alisoun," he whispered. Where was Alisoun? She'd been headed into the castle when last he'd seen her, but had she continued on her way? He started jogging.

Sir Walter gasped for breath as if he were dying, but when David slowed, he urged, "Go . . . on."

They broke free of the forest and into the cleared

area around the castle. Villeins from George's Cross
and strangers visiting the market walked the road from
the village to the castle. They gaped at the mercenary
and his gory burden, swerving aside to avoid him, but
David paid them no heed. Heading straight across the
drawbridge, he bellowed, "Lady Alisoun. Where's Lady
Alisoun?"

No one answered at first. The servants stood trans-
fixed as he hurried on into the inner bailey and toward
the keep. "Did she come back? Where's Lady Alisoun?"

Two women stood on the landing of the steps, and
he shouted, "You stupid cows! Where's your mistress?"

"I'm here." Alisoun spoke from the door of the dairy,
and David swerved that direction. She looked as cool as
the first time he'd met her, and her gaze was as cold as
a winter's breeze. In a voice that should have frozen the
marrow in his bones, she began, "How dare you return
after . . . ?" Then her eyes widened, and she gasped in
horror. "God his soul bless, 'tis Sir Walter." Without
pause, she ran for the keep, calling, "Get out my medi-
cal supplies! Warm water and blankets. Prepare the
solar, we'll put him there." She returned to David and
reached out a gentle hand to Sir Walter. She touched
his head lightly and spoke to him with a caress in her
very tone. "Good Sir Walter, who did this to you?"

Sir Walter didn't answer. Only David felt the sigh of
relief that shuddered through the grizzled warrior and
turned his body from an anguished sack to an comatose
burden.

When Sir Walter didn't answer, Alisoun took her
hand away and smeared the blood between her fingers.
"Carry him upstairs," she told David. "Let me work on
him before he regains consciousness."

His burden dragged at him as he climbed the stairs
to the keep. The women had disappeared, and the corri-

dor inside seemed miraculously clear of obstacles. A few moments ago he'd thought never to see this great hall again, now he barely glanced around as he headed for the solar. Someone held the door open, and hands assisted him as he lowered the unconscious man onto the mattress. Then Alisoun pushed him back, and he moved to the far corner of the bed where he could be out of the way, yet watch the proceedings.

He didn't enjoy them, especially not when Alisoun set first the bone in one leg, then the bone in the other. Menservants had to hold the now-conscious Sir Walter, and the screams drove mighty Hugh from the chamber to empty his gut outside. Alisoun's face was the color of parchment, but she tugged, cleaned and splinted before she stepped away from the bed.

If David had any doubts about Alisoun's strength, her courage in the face of blood and pain reassured him. Life in all its vicissitudes would never defeat this woman.

As she stepped off the dais, she staggered and he sprang forward, ready to assist her.

Something hit him from behind, knocking him aside. He spun around, fists up, and found himself face to face with Lady Edlyn.

"Don't touch her!" the girl shouted. "Everyone knows what you did."

Everyone knew of their quarrel in the woods? He glanced at Alisoun, but she looked as amazed as he felt. "What did I do?"

"*You* did this to Sir Walter." Lady Edlyn skittered back as if he were an animal about to attack. "You quarreled with him, followed him into the woods and you—"

"Wait!" Lady Alisoun stepped into the fray. "Sir David didn't hurt Sir Walter. To say so is absurd."

Philippa stood in the doorway, clutching her baby. "He's a dangerous, angry man."

"He spent his time with *me*," Alisoun said.

"The whole time you were gone?" Philippa asked.

"Nay, but—"

"Who else has the skills to beat Sir Walter?"

In the moment of silence that followed, David glanced around the room. Alisoun's servants stood in a sullen circle watching him. Some simply looked confused, but some held knives and pokers in their hands.

Alisoun saw them and declared, "This is ridiculous."

"I've done nothing," David said.

Dismissing his objection with a gesture, Philippa said, "He quarreled with Sir Walter, and when you returned to the castle, you made it clear he quarreled with you. You're not safe, Alisoun, and you know what men are like."

David swallowed his instinctive protest. He would never forget this scene. Like the climax of a passion play, it stood alone as the apex of an eventful day. In his mind, this moment remained fixed, highlighted by powerful emotions. Somehow, somewhere in this morass of fear and accusation rested the kernel of fact which would explain his presence here and the danger which threatened his lady.

Alisoun stood still, letting the heated emotions swirl around her while soothing her people with her very tranquillity. "I have every faith in Sir David. He was angry, true, but he has an impeccable reputation, and he has always treated me with honor."

Lady Edlyn gestured toward him. "Look at him, my lady! His hands are scabbed and bleeding. How else could he have done such a thing except by beating Sir Walter?"

Holding up his hands, David flexed them in chagrin.

Everyone saw, and the servants stepped forward with a growl.

"David!" Stepping close to him, Alisoun gathered his hands in hers. "You didn't do *this* in the practice yard."

Fearing the prick of a knife against his neck, David trailed behind her as she tugged him closer to the light. "It's nothing."

In a voice clogged with fear, Lady Edlyn said, "Lady Alisoun, please move away from him."

"They need to be bandaged," Alisoun said.

"They're fine." He tried to wrench them free. Again the servants stepped closer, their weapons raised, and he hastily ceased resistance. He was going to have to tell her what he'd done, admit his stupidity, and he slumped in embarrassment. "I hit a tree."

Her hands tightened on his. "What?"

"I *hit* a *tree*."

Everyone heard that time. Alisoun stared at him as if he'd run mad. "You mean you . . . walked into a tree with your fists?"

Philippa said, "My lady, surely you don't believe *that*."

"Why would you hit a tree?" Alisoun asked.

"To avoid striking you or Sir Walter or one of the serving maids or kicking a dog or any of the other lovely ways a man picks to display his anger." He swept an accusing glance around at the men, and one or two coughed and shuffled backward. "I didn't beat Sir Walter."

Then Alisoun did it. The thing he'd dreamed of all his life.

"I know that." She laid one hand on his chest and looked up into his eyes, her own calm, sure and trusting. "I was never in doubt."

And Sir David Radcliffe fell in love.

16

The solar filled with a silence that lapped up and over everyone, and they were silent, David knew, because of the awe and reverence he displayed . Only now, when Alisoun showed her trust, did he realize—he was living the legend his crazy old great-grandmother had told him.

"David?" Alisoun raised her hand to touch his face. "Have you hit your head?"

Hit his head? He almost laughed. Aye, Alisoun would think something like that. The truth was, he had all the symptoms his granny described—unusual strength, a sense of rightness, a glow from within. He didn't even have to be around Alisoun to feel the effects. Granny had called them signs of a great love.

"David, no one's going to hurt you. You don't need to look so—" Alisoun cocked her head, at a loss for a description, "—preoccupied."

Granny had entertained him and the other children in the long winter nights, and the best story, the one they always asked for, was the one about their grandmother and grandfather, and how they'd come through trial and sorrow to a special place, a special feeling, just for each other. Not everyone had it, Granny said. Most people never witnessed such a phenomenon in their whole lives, but it had shone through his grandmother and grandfather's everyday activities. It had warmed the whole family and every servant and serf. It had been precious, inviolate, and it had worked miracles. Even after Grandfather died, Grandmother carried the glow with her to her grave.

"I think it would be best if you sat down." Alisoun tried to steer him toward a stool, but he took her hand off his arm and just held it.

Aye, it had been his favorite story, but he'd grown up. By the time he reached the great age of eight, he'd realized what nonsense Granny spouted. After all, she wasn't his grandmother, she was his great-grandmother, so old he had believed his mother when she said Granny had lived through four kings. Granny didn't remember what she'd eaten two hours before. She didn't remember his name, or his mother's, or even her own maid's. She was nothing but a crazy old lady who told crazy old stories, and he'd scarcely thought of her since the day she died.

Now he couldn't forget her, because he was living that story she told. His union with Alisoun was almost mystical, as if they had been separated long ago, lost to each other across time and space, and now reunited to form one being, one self.

"I wish my Granny were alive to see this." David brought Alisoun's hand to his lips and kissed it respectfully, then turned it over and kissed her palm with the passion of a lover.

Her puzzled frown faded; she must have seen something in his demeanor that hinted of his thoughts, for she stepped closer and placed her hand on his chest once more. "David?"

His heart pounded from the contact, and the glow from him reflected in her eyes. They drew closer and closer still, caught in the precious moment of recognition and dedication—until Sir Walter coughed.

Alisoun turned away from David at once, and he let her go without a qualm. There would be time and place for this later. Now Sir Walter needed tending, and Alisoun took that responsibility seriously. She went to his side and took his hand, then leaned close to his battered, swollen face. "It's Lady Alisoun. Did you want me?"

The sounds Sir Walter formed weren't words, not really, but he spoke urgently, as if he needed to make himself heard.

Alisoun winced and reached for an icy cloth to place over his puffy eyes. "Pray you, Sir Walter, don't speak if it gives you pain."

"Must!"

Moved by the urgency in that one word, David came closer.

"Grave."

Puzzled, David shared a glance with Alisoun.

"I don't know what you mean. Grave trouble?" she suggested. "Grave wounds?"

The breath Sir Walter took came up through a windpipe so battered it scarcely functioned, but he lisped, "*The* grave."

Suddenly alert, Alisoun bent so close her lips almost touched the injured man's ear. "The grave? In the churchyard?"

"Open."

David observed the appearance of bluish veins in Alisoun's forehead as the color washed out of her face.

"Is that where he found you?" she demanded.

A tear squeezed out between Sir Walter's swollen lids and trickled down his cheek. "Stupid."

Some great shock held Alisoun in its grip, then she started as if she woke. "Nay, you're not stupid. We weren't expecting that he would be suspicious. Sleep now, and heal. I'll have need of your services when you are better." After giving his hand a light pat, she placed it on the covers. Then she turned and surveyed the room. No one except she and David had heard Sir Walter's words. They'd been spoken in a low tone and his injuries had rendered him almost inarticulate. Nevertheless, she examined each servant and maid, requesting their discretion without saying a word. Clearly, she held their complete loyalty.

Near the door, Philippa and Edlyn huddled together, victims of the fear this violence had brought. To them, Alisoun said, "Warm sand in the sandbags and brace it against Sir Walter on both sides. Bring blankets and keep him covered. Don't let him get chilled this night, and if his condition worsens, call me."

"Where are you going?" Philippa questioned her sharply, as if she had every right.

"I'm going to order added patrols and find some way to return security to George's Cross."

"What did Sir Walter say?"

Alisoun wrapped her arm around Philippa's shoulder. "I'll take care of it. You take care of Sir Walter."

She walked toward the door and Philippa followed her, but David grabbed her before she could jerk Alisoun around. Gruffly, he said, "*I'll* take care of her."

Philippa stared at him and gulped audibly, then nodded.

"Alisoun." He caught up with her when she was

halfway across the great hall. "Lady Alisoun, we need to talk."

She kept walking with a serenity that belied her intentions. "I have to go instruct the men-at-arms to watch for strangers, to be more careful."

"That's for me to do."

Without looking at him, she asked, "You'll stay?"

His hand shot out and grabbed her elbow. Spinning on his heel, he used her forward motion to turn her toward his bedchamber. "You couldn't drive me away."

Trying to jerk out of his grasp, she said, "I need to set watches."

"And have them beat, too? Anyone who tries to protect you is in danger." The horror on her face proved everything he could have desired. "Every person in George's Cross knows what happened to Sir Walter by now. They'll be cautious, I have no doubt, and I wouldn't want to be a new merchant come to visit the market this night. He'll find himself without a place to stay."

"Aye." The door of his chamber loomed before them and she grabbed the sill and tried to hang on. "This will be bad for our prosperity, but what can I do?"

He stuffed her through the entry and shut the door behind them. Leaning against it, he said, "Come with me to Radcliffe."

She whirled on him. "What?"

"Radcliffe," he repeated. "It's small, there's no market, and any stranger who visits is noted and marked and treated with suspicion."

"I can't come to Radcliffe with you."

"You could if you married me."

She turned away. "We've already had this conversation."

"It wasn't a conversation, it was a shouting match."

She moved her shoulders uncomfortably. "Nothing's changed since this afternoon."

He chuckled. "Oh, Alisoun."

"Except Sir Walter!"

"I can't keep you safe here. I can't keep your people safe here. You have a market, and a busy town center. Peddlers come through, and country people and farmers who've heard about your prosperity and seek some for themselves. I can't keep track of every stranger every moment he's here. Neither can your men, and this vicious attack on Sir Walter is going to put your villagers at odds with the very people who come to trade with them."

"I know that." She placed one hand on her stomach and one on her head. "I don't know what to do."

He moved closer and pressed her hard for a decision. "Can you take a chance with them?"

She didn't move.

"I've seen robberies and beatings on the road less vicious than the one inflicted on Sir Walter." Laying his hand over the one she pressed to her belly, he asked, "Can you take a chance with the babe?"

She looked up at him, and for the first time, her every emotion showed on her face—fear, distress, anguish. And he wished he had his old Alisoun back. He wanted that serenity for her. He wanted her to have the time to relish her accomplishments, her skills, her pregnancy. But he wanted her to do it with him, and she had to understand their marriage was no longer just an option. It was a necessity.

He hadn't intended to comfort her until she'd given in, but he couldn't bear to see her so upset. Wrapping her in his arms, he rocked her against him.

Turning her head into his chest, she wailed, "I'm so embarrassed."

"Embarrassed?" He moved her back a little. "Why embarrassed?"

"I failed in my responsibility to care for Sir Walter."

"Corpus Christi." He picked her up and carried her to the bed. Setting her down in the middle, he leaned close and told her, "If there's something keeping Sir Walter awake tonight, it's that he failed in his responsibility to you."

"Nay, I—"

"Alisoun." He kissed her.

"I should have—"

He kissed her again.

"I didn't—"

He kissed her again. And again. Soft, gentle kisses that cradled her senses and finally brought her relief from the endless round of self-recriminations. Then he tasted her tears and used his sleeve to wipe them from her cheeks. "You're the best lady any demesne could have. You know you are."

She pressed her lips together and sniffed.

"Admit it." He kissed her. "Admit it."

"I am."

He wanted to grin at her reluctant confirmation, but more than that he wanted to kiss her. She needed his kisses now, needed solace and security. With his tongue, he outlined her lips. When they parted, he ran his tongue along the bumpy ridge of her teeth. She lay there, limp, and he thought she was doing nothing more than absorbing peace of mind from his embrace and affection, but when he thrust his tongue into her mouth she met him.

He pressed harder, sealing their lips. She wrapped her arms around his neck. He climbed onto the mattress next to her.

The pillows lay above them, and the blankets lay

below. Their feet banged the footboard. He'd done this all wrong, but he hadn't planned to do more than console her. He hadn't planned on his rush of desire or her ready response. He still wanted to console her, but with his touch on her cheek, his kiss on her breast . . . and when she pushed her wimple off, he perceived she wanted it, too.

He lifted each individual lock of hair to his lips, then arranged it around her face like rays of the sun. Quiescent, her eyes half-closed, she let him do what he would. Some men might have been offended. He himself might have remembered his long-dead wife and the way she had lain like a limp fish when he touched her. But with Alisoun, her very lack of motion was a confession. She'd ceded her power to him and trusted him to not abuse that power.

"So you like to talk to me." With his finger, he curled the short wisps of hair in front of her ears. "You think I enchant you when I tell you what I think."

She stretched, adjusting her shoulders. "You don't say the things other men say."

"Like?"

"The other noblemen always talk about themselves and how strong they are and how they killed a boar with their bare hands." She blew a puff of air out and rolled her eyes. "Like I'd believe that."

Putting his fingers under her neck, he massaged the taut muscles. "They just want to impress you."

"Why? What makes a man think he can impress a woman by telling lies?"

"Some women aren't as discerning as you are."

"Some women pretend to believe."

He grinned and imagined the scene. A respected warrior, fabricating his strengths to impress the cool woman beside him. And the cool woman questioning him until he stumbled in his tale. No wonder she'd remained unmarried.

He looked down to see her staring at him. "You don't tell tales," she said.

He shrugged. "I haven't killed any boars with my bare hands lately." He trailed those hands down the front of her and loosened the laces that held her gown together.

As he widened the gap in her gown, his hands brushed against her breasts, still covered by her shift. She shivered, and goosebumps tightened her skin. "I doubt you've wasted time on something so trivial. You were too busy—"

He cupped her and she took a big breath.

"You were too busy becoming the legendary Sir David."

Rubbing his thumbs over her nipples, he said, "Not much of a legend anymore."

She smiled. "Your lance strikes ever true."

He froze and searched her face for an explanation.

"What?" she asked. "What?"

"You made a jest."

"So?"

"A bawdy jest."

A spark of indignation made her stiffen. "I am not without humor!"

"Aye, it's been there all along." He slipped the gown over her shoulders and down, stripping it from her completely, and as he worked on divesting her of the rest of her clothing, he said, "But you do make me think I'm a wizard."

Sir David's face loomed above me where I slept on my pallet in the great hall, and his hand shook my shoulder. "Get up, Eudo. I need you."

It never crossed my mind to question his command. I stumbled to my feet, rubbing my eyes, and pulled my short cape over my clothes. I think he had to help me— no one wakes an eleven-year-old boy after a strenuous day without having to fight the lingering consequences of sleep.

The others in the great hall rolled away from us, but no one grumbled. Sir David had reestablished himself as a legend once again, and we all knew our safety depended on his experience.

The rush lights on the wall flickered eerily as he led me by the hand to the outer door, then we stepped outside into the darkest night I'd ever beheld. The cool air slapped me awake and Sir David asked, "Can you walk now?"

I nodded and stifled a yawn, and we moved toward the drawbridge. The men-at-arms challenged us before we even knocked, and Sir David mumbled, "Good. They're nervous."

His whispered instructions took only a moment, then two of the men-at-arms disappeared and the chains that held the drawbridge rattled. The sound carried through the still night like the clatter of a corpse's bones, and my skinny knees knocked in sudden alarm.

The drawbridge was never lowered at night, certainly not after an attack like the one that had occurred that day. But without hesitation, Sir David strode across the planks and I followed. I had no desire to leave the castle, but if I had to go, I wanted to keep nigh to my lord.

"Not so close, lad." Sir David craned his neck and looked at the starry sky. "Don't you want to know our destination?"

I did, but I didn't think I would like the reply.

"We're going to the churchyard." Sir David looked down at me and I thought I saw him grin, although his

mouth was nothing more than a black hole in the dim glow of his face. "What do you think of that?"

I thought he was mad, but wisely kept my own council. Instead I tentatively suggested, "If you have need to pray, Sir David, there's a chapel in the keep."

"I don't want to pray. I want to visit the graves in the village church."

I crossed myself and with a boy's hysteria wondered why Sir David's eye sockets appeared empty.

Set on a rise above the village, the church stood apart from the other buildings, and the graveyard sloped off to the side toward the forest. I hoped in my deepest heart Sir David jested, and he would lead me somewhere, anywhere but there.

But nay, the damp grass beneath our feet made squeaking noises as we cut a straight line across the meadow.

Sir David seemed utterly at ease in the darkness, moving with the poise of a cat and speaking in a cheerful tone that eased a little of my paralyzing fear. "Are all of Lady Alisoun's family buried there?" he asked.

"Some of them. The older graves are there. The more recently dead were laid to rest within the church under the altar."

"Are the villagers still buried there?"

"Aye, sir, although not close to Lady Alisoun's family."

"The countess's family is set apart?"

I nodded, although I knew he couldn't see me. "By a fence, aye."

"So no one has been buried in the family plot for years?"

"No family has been buried there for years, but if a visitor is taken sick and dies, we bury them with honor in that place."

"Ahh." Sir David's exhale sounded like he'd had a

revelation. "*Has anyone died and been buried there recently?*"

"*Oh, nay. The last time anyone was buried there was clear last winter.*"

"*That is a very long time ago,*" *Sir David agreed.* "*Who was it?*"

"*My lady's friend and her babe came to visit, but they sickened and died within two days.*"

"*Who was this lady?*"

"*The duchess of Framlingford.*"

Sir David stumbled and almost went down.

I grabbed for him. "*Are you ill, sir?*"

His hand found my shoulder, and he pressed it. "*Afraid you'll be left alone out here?*"

I saw no reason to lie. "*Aye, sir.*"

"*The moon is rising. See?*" *Sir David pointed toward the eastern horizon, and indeed, I saw a white glow on the mountain tops.* "*You could find your way back, even by yourself, but to tell you the truth, I doubt anyone is mad enough to come out so late.*"

"*Except maybe the man who hurt Sir Walter and tried to hurt my lady.*" *My low voice wavered abominably, but Sir David heard.*

"*So you think he's mad, too?*"

"*I hope so, sir,*" *I said fervently.* "*I hope he's obviously raving mad, for I don't want to think he's someone who walks among us undetected.*"

"*Well said.*" *Sir David didn't offer any reassurance, however.*

I noted that, and started walking close on his heels again.

"*Tell me what happened with the duchess of Framlingford.*"

I searched my memory. I hadn't really paid much attention, and at that time in my life, the previous win-

ter seemed eons ago. "The duchess was a friend of my lady's, I recollect, and apparently had come for a visit to Beckon. That's one of my lady's other castles."

"Why?"

"I don't know, sir."

"I thought you might have heard gossip."

"There's not much gossip about my lady. Never before has she given us anything to gossip about."

"Before me, you mean."

I knew better than to answer that, but Sir David didn't seem to require a reply.

He pondered, then asked, "Why did Lady Alisoun and the duchess come here? Were you expecting Lady Alisoun?"

"Nay, sir, we were surprised that she would travel so deep into the winter, and the duchess and her babe arrived already ill."

"A babe?"

"So they said. I never saw either one of them. My lady feared they had brought contagion to the castle, and she tended them alone, putting only herself at risk. When they died, she prepared the bodies and placed them together in the coffin."

"Completely alone? No one helped her in any way?"

"No one."

Sir David walked now in silence until we reached the churchyard. A short wooden fence surrounded all the graves, and the gate creaked when Sir David opened it. At the heart of the cemetery, a smaller rock wall surrounded the family of my lady. I lingered outside the wooden fence until Sir David called, "This ground is consecrated in the name of our Lord. Suicides and heretics only are buried outside the fence."

I found myself standing at his side before he'd finished the sentence.

The rising moon caught in the tops of the trees from the nearby forest. The white light it delivered showed an assortment of gargoyles and saints atop the stones that marked the family's individual graves. In the stark shades of night and moon, the saints leered and the gargoyles hunkered, waiting for unwary prey to pass. I clung to Sir David's surcoat as he trod the narrow path through the older graves to the place where the visitors were buried.

One of the graves stood open.

If I could have moved, I would have run. When my long legs started pumping, no one could have caught me.

If I could have moved.

As it was, I stood there and stared with mouth gaping wide as Sir David dropped to his knees and peered down into the ground. He grunted. "Nothing here." Dusting his hands, he stood and looked around.

I knew what he sought. I even spotted it before he did, but I shut my eyes tight to avoid my duty to inform him. It didn't help. He marched toward the coffin with sure strides and I scampered in his wake, wanting to stay close to him even while I longed to be away from that half-open wooden box.

I thought my prayers had been answered when he halted partway there, but he only handed me his knife and said, "That madman we discussed might be out there now, so I want you to watch my back."

My teeth chattered too much to reply.

Sir David moved closer to the coffin, and as he did the moonlight sneaked down the trunks of the trees, creeping ever closer, as if it wanted to illuminate the body within the box. I heard the scrape of wood on wood as he moved the lid completely to the side. The odor of decay wafted to my nostrils. I fixed my gaze on the trees and the area around the churchyard, staring so hard my eyeballs ached while I wondered if I would disgrace myself and puke from fear and horror.

Sir David was silent for so long I finally glanced at him.

He stood, hands on hips, staring in that coffin as if he'd never seen a decomposing body before, when I knew he'd seen them hanging at every crossroads. Working up my fortitude, I called, "Sir David? Will we be done soon?"

He didn't answer, and I crept closer. "Sir David?" He still didn't answer, and I turned to look at him fully. "Sir David!"

At that moment, the moon lifted above the trees and the full light of it illuminated that thing inside. A rotting pelt of short black hair that covered the whole corpse. A long snout with a mouthful of canine-looking teeth. Four legs that ended with curved claws. And a smaller version of the beast tucked beside its belly.

I dropped the knife, abandoned Sir David and ran as fast as my legs could carry me back to the castle where I huddled by the raised drawbridge until Sir David came and rescued me.

17

Someone was sneaking through her bedchamber. Someone who wished her ill. Alisoun tried to open her eyes, but could only listen to the whisper of footsteps as they padded along the floor. She tried to move, to call out, but the nightmare gripped her tightly. Somewhere close, something scratched, sounding like a thin blade on a whetstone.

That thing had returned from the grave. She'd meant to go out at first light and cover it with dirt once more, but it was too late. The wolf she'd placed in that coffin even now crept toward her, reanimated by the holy ground in which she'd placed it. She wanted David, but he had abandoned her. She wanted Sir Walter, but he was horribly hurt. She was alone, weak, helpless—and something jumped for her throat.

Sitting up, she screamed and struck out at the intruder, and that misbegotten kitten went flying off the mattress and landed on the floor with an indignant squall.

"Oh, nay!" Alisoun tumbled out of bed and picked up the cat, cradling it close. "Did I hurt you?"

The kitten sunk its sharp claws into her skin and clung to her. Alisoun petted it, crooning, seeking any injury, and the kitten settled down and purred.

Alisoun wanted to laugh. She wanted to cry. She wanted everything to be as it was before, when she had control of her life and her destiny. She wanted, for the first time in her life, to deny the consequences of her actions. Stupid actions, when viewed in retrospect, but even now she saw no other course. She had to help her friend, she had to hire Sir David, she had to welcome him into her bed. . . . She sighed. Well, nay, she hadn't had to welcome him into her bed, but she knew without a doubt that when she was old, she would remember his intrusion into her safe world as the best thing that had ever happened to her.

The scratching noise started again.

Alisoun froze, then lifted her head and peered around.

David sat at the table, candle at his elbow, writing. She readily identified the scratching noise now; it was the sound of a sharpened point on parchment. But what was this all about? And why was he ignoring her?

"David?"

He lifted his head and fixed her in his gaze. "Alisoun."

Her father used to look at her almost that way when he was trying to make her cry about her shortcomings. But David's demeanor shouted genuine disappointment in her. Self-consciously, she rose and slid back in bed, holding the kitten as if it were her one true friend. Subsiding under the covers, she asked, "What are you writing?"

"I'm drafting our marriage contract." He flicked bits

of dirt off his sleeve with the feather. "How often must I agree to bathe before you will sign it?"

She couldn't think of an answer. She couldn't think of anything. "I . . . had never considered that matter something to be included within the solemn document of a marriage contract."

"I would have no more surprises in our alliance." Without a smile to lighten his manner, he suggested, "I have always thought once a year to be sufficient in the normal scheme of life. However, I suspect that will not be sufficient for you."

"Ah . . . nay."

"Twice a year."

Why were they talking about bathing? "Once a month?"

Picking up his knife, he scraped at the parchment. "Once a month it is."

Silence settled on them, the kind of silence that stifles speech at its source. He bent his full concentration to the writing and she bent her full concentration to the kitten.

It frolicked on top of the covers, and when Alisoun moved her foot, it jumped as if the movements of the wayward foot challenged its supremacy. Alisoun moved again; the kitten growled and leaped. Alisoun couldn't help laughing, then she glanced guiltily at David. He watched the kitten's antics with a half-smile, and she relaxed. If he could smile at the kitten, she could speak to him without fear of retribution, although he'd never in any way threatened her. She didn't know why she worried now. Looking at him more closely, she announced, "You'll need to bathe sooner than I anticipated. You're dirty."

He looked at his grubby fingernails. "I went out."

"At this time of the night? Where did you—" Then it

struck her. She knew why he looked so grim. She knew where he'd gone.

"I've been paying my respects to the dead."

Gooseflesh covered her at his cold tones and flat gaze. "Did you see it?"

"I reburied it."

Relief rode hard on the heels of her horror. "Was the coffin . . . ?"

He lifted a brow inquiringly.

"Open?"

"That thing scared young Eudo into a gibbering jelly."

She hadn't thought it could get worse, but she now lived the nightmare she feared. "Eudo saw?"

"He won't tell anyone."

Perspiration formed a sheen all over her body and she dabbed the blanket on her upper lip. The kitten hunkered down and watched, its hindquarters twitching. "How do you know that?"

"I instructed him to keep his silence, and anyway, he's ashamed."

"Ashamed?"

"That body frightened him so badly he abandoned me and ran away. I told him that every knight I knew would run from such a thing, and I tried to ease his torment." He looked grim. "I wouldn't have that brave lad fret about such a trick."

She wanted to cover her eyes and wail at the failure of her plot. A lifetime of sensibility, destroyed by one act of mercy. But she had to assure herself that no one else would suffer. Only Alisoun would pay for her charity. Desperate, she asked, "Will *you* tell?"

"That you buried a wolf and her pup in your family plot?" No muscle moved in David's face. His hands remained still. He gave nothing away with his stony

blankness. "Never. I would not have the Church author-
ities arrest my wife."

So that was the price. Marriage to Sir David.

It would not be so dreadful. Not dreadful at all.
Except that this hard stranger facing her across the
room expressed no empathy. He was like a merchant,
bargaining his silence for her hand and knowing she
had no choice but to agree.

Bowing her head, she gave herself into his keeping. "I'll instruct the priest to announce the banns
tomorrow."

"That's today." He indicated the growing light which
shone through the window. "He'll call them every day
after that, also. I would not have anyone cry foul about
our marriage later."

"I wouldn't do that!"

Solemnly, he said, "That hadn't occurred to me.
However, you are a considerable heiress and the king
wished to dispose of you as he would. As it is, we'll
have to pay for a wedding without his permission."

She winced as she thought of the gold which would
leave her coffers.

"It's for a good cause," he said. "How soon can you
be ready to move to Radcliffe?"

In a normal year, she spent time in each of her castles and moved her household accordingly. Moving to
Radcliffe would require extra preparation, for she had
no idea what circumstances she would face when she
got there. She combed the fur on the cover with her fingers and considered. "Four days."

"How efficient." His lips quirked and he looked a little more like the candidly demonstrative man she knew.
"I should have expected nothing less. So three days calling the banns and negotiating the marriage contract.
We'll be wed on the fourth day and leave immediately

after the ceremony." He stood and placed the quill and parchment in one corner. "And Alisoun?"

She tensed, anxiously awaiting his new demand.

"That cat's stalking you."

She glanced down just as the kitten pounced on her restless fingers. She gasped. David laughed. The kitten hung onto her hand and licked her until Alisoun could disengage herself and climb from the bed.

"Have you named the kitten, yet?" David asked with more than casual interest.

Alisoun automatically demurred. "Nay, I do not care to give it a name." Then she stared at the little creature and saw how its feisty nature camouflaged, but could not conceal, its vulnerability. "But perhaps we could take it with us to Radcliffe."

"Let me come with you."

Alisoun paused in the act of packing her finest plate and lifted her head to look upon Edlyn. Illuminated by the great hall's rush lights, the girl looked pinched and miserable, and Alisoun's store of compassion welled within her. But she knew her duty, and answered, "Dear, I can't do that. You must go to your parents' home and prepare for your coming marriage."

"My mother is even now preparing for my nuptials. She's putting a pair of sheets in the trunk, a new gown atop that, a new wimple atop that, some packages of herbs for physicking. My father is picking out his best horse from the stable and tightening the cart against the long journey. They're contacting the monastery for a monk to accompany me. They don't need me for that. When I arrive, I'll be given a welcome-and-farewell dinner and be hastened on my way—they need the money the duke of Cleere will settle on me, so there's no need for delay." Edlyn leaned forward and placed her cold hands on Alisoun's. "But I want to delay, just a little longer. I want to know that all is right with you before I leave. Let me come."

Alisoun longed to grant Edlyn's wish, and her own hesitation in doing the proper thing horrified her. Mayhap her pregnancy had loosened the bonds she placed on her emotions. Mayhap, as all her doubts about her marriage rushed at her, she wanted the support of all who loved her. Mayhap she wanted to give Edlyn the gift of one more month of maidenhood. Whatever the reason, she said, "Sir David says the plight of his hungry people is very bad, and I do need someone to coordinate the packing of foodstuffs for Radcliffe."

Edlyn's hands tightened. "I can do that!"

"And someone to distribute the foodstuffs when we arrive."

"You know I can. You taught me how to look for those who need help the most."

"Aye. I taught you." She'd taught Edlyn the practical things and she could only hope that the girl had absorbed enough of Alisoun's stoicism to ease her way in her new home. But not yet. Slowly, Alisoun nodded. "If you would come with us—"

"Aye. Aye!"

"—I could easily leave Heath here. I would feel better if she remained to care for Sir Walter, and having you with me would remove a burden from Philippa." Taking that as permission and not wanting to hear more, Edlyn tried to jump away. Alisoun caught her before she could flee. "For a month, only. Then, regardless of my situation, you must go to your parents." Sighing, she added, "When this shortcoming of mine becomes known, no parent will send me their child for fostering."

"I will." Edlyn's eyes glowed. "If I ever have a daughter, I'll have her fostered by no one else."

On that promise, Edlyn fled as if fearing Alisoun would change her mind, and Alisoun watched her with a heavy heart. Resuming her packing, she said to the furs, "After all, it's not as if I am leaving her here within temptation's reach." She glanced toward the solar where Sir Walter lay. He had survived these two days, and with the saints' help he would live a long life. Yet for now George's Cross needed another chief man-at-arms, and David had named Hugh.

Hugh, who swore on bended knee he would protect Alisoun's demesne. Hugh, who had celebrated by sleeping with half the maids. Hugh, who broke Edlyn's heart without even knowing she existed.

"Besides—" Alisoun wrapped her largest silver platter in one of her softest rugs, "—what will the passing of another moon matter to Edlyn's duke?"

"Radcliffe is not what you're used to. It's small and it's dark."

David had scarcely left Alisoun's side during the five days they'd been on the road. They'd ridden at the front of the column which included Lady Edlyn, Alisoun's maids headed by Philippa, Alisoun's carts, and of course, Ivo and Gunnewate and her men-at-arms. During that time, David tried to brace her for the great disaster of his home. She didn't know whether it was truly as bad as he said or whether he simply sought reassurance, but she knew how to be gracious. "Many of my other holdings are less genteelly appointed than George's Cross."

"Actually, it probably won't offend your senses. Of course, it's not nearly as clean as you like, I'm sure."

The morning sun shifted through the leaves and dappled David's face, and she liked the way the shadows lessened the toughness of his brown skin and the stubble which covered his unshaven chin. He looked younger, with a raffish distinction.

"Not as clean as you like," he repeated. "But what is?"

Taking his comment as permission, she allowed her gaze to wander down his form. She thought him the finest figure of a man she'd ever seen. Oh, he hadn't grown the lobe of his ear back or a finger to replace the one he'd lost, but he had big feet to plant on the ground and a height that lifted him to the clouds. A pleasant mixture of earthiness and whimsy was her husband.

"But it has a very nice solar with a glass window."

"Glass?" Surprised, she tore her attention away from his body. "I would not have expected that, when you've been so ill-served by the drought."

"Oh, we had a few good years when I first got the keep, and—" his voice dropped to a growl, "—my wife insisted."

The northwest coast was easily the least civilized corner of England, with forests that overhung the narrow tracks and transmuted the sunshine to a deep green. The sides of her carts brushed branches on each side and more than once the men-at-arms had had to join with the ox drivers and chop the wood away to allow their passing. David had been unhappy when he'd seen the chests she packed for their move and he'd grown more unhappy with each day on the road.

She could hardly blame him for that. Not even robbers frequented this road. Yesterday a pack of wolves had run parallel through the brush and eyed them in a considering manner. At the sight, young Eudo had broken down and sobbed with fear. That night, after they'd made camp,

Alisoun had taken him a decoction of wine and herbs to calm him and she sat with him until he slept.

All for naught. Deep in the night when only a slip of a moon showed through the trees, she'd woken to find David and her men taking flaming brands from the fire and waving them at the edges of the narrow clearing. Lady Edlyn, Philippa, and the other maids huddled close to Alisoun as if she would protect them, while Philippa's baby had woken and laughed at the fiery display.

Yet Alisoun experienced no anxiety. David no longer vanquished every foe on the tournament grounds, but his experience more than made up for that. He combined the craftiness of a seasoned fighter with the predatory instincts of a pillaging wolf. And although David didn't realize it, the wilderness protected them as nothing else could.

That miserable coward who stalked her worked alone. He wanted no other *man* to know the depths of his depravity, and he wouldn't follow them to play his pranks here. Not when he could be eaten by wolves for his trouble.

So the decision to go to Radcliffe had been a wise one, and Alisoun could think of nothing that would make her unhappy there—if she could only reassure David. "I'm sure I'll be grateful for the comforts your wife added to Radcliffe."

David squirmed in the saddle until King Louis twisted his great head and made his displeasure known with a reproving neigh. Removing his hat, David slapped Louis between the ears, saying, "Don't you complain! We're going home, aren't we?" Louis exhaled with great force, then turned his face forward and moved back into place beside Alisoun's palfrey.

"Does he understand everything you say?" Alisoun asked.

"Most of it." David glared at the white horse while Louis royally ignored him. "The rest, I suspect, he only pretends to misconstrue."

His lugubrious expression brought laughter bubbling to Alisoun's lips. As always, the unexpected gladness caught her by surprise. She hadn't thought she would enjoy marriage. She'd thought she would only remember the ties that bound her. Instead she found herself secure in the knowledge that David would never harm her. He would always treat her with respect, a respect that had not been bought by her title, but earned by Alisoun herself.

In the same tone he used when discussing Louis, David said, "There *are* certain things that happen when one is married."

It took Alisoun a moment to realize they'd returned to their original subject, then she said tartly, "Aye. You get glass windows."

"I mean there are people who might make a new wife feel . . . "

"Unwelcome?'

"I wouldn't go that far."

David had said they would arrive today, and Alisoun now noted that the trees seemed to be thinning. "Are you trying to warn me of something?"

"Nay, nay. It's just that—"

"Your wife had a maid as loyal to her as Philippa is to me, mayhap?"

"Nay!" He made a face. "Nobody ever liked her."

A sudden thought brought her to a halt, and she faced him. "You have a jealous mistress?"

Slouched in his saddle, David smiled at her. Only a smile, but a thrill shot up her back. In a slow, teasing drawl, he said, "The only jealous mistress I have is Louis, and he cares not who shares my bed."

"I don't care either."

Surprised, his brows shot up. "Nay?"

"After all, I am a practical woman. I can't expect that you would have gone without release before we met."

"Practical, indeed." Leaning out of the saddle, he took her hand and worked it free of the leather riding glove which protected it. Slowly, he lifted her fingers to his mouth. He kissed each one, then turned her hand over and pressed his lips to the center of her palm. His whiskers tickled, his tongue caressed, and she closed her eyes to better absorb the sensation.

"If we'd had a private moment on this journey, my lady, I promise you would not be bothered by such musings."

Practical, she repeated to herself. *I'm practical.*

"'Twas a damned poor wedding night."

His thumb circled the pads beneath her fingers until her skin tingled. The sensation worked its way up her arm and caused a flutter in her heart.

"When we get to Radcliffe, I promise to prove myself as devoted a husband as I was a lover." Easing her glove back on her hand, he muttered, "Although I wish I had the opportunity to bind you to me ere we arrive."

Her eyes popped open. "What *is* wrong at Radcliffe?"

"We'd best move on," he said. "The carts will catch up with us and we don't want them to have to halt so close to our destination."

"We're close?"

"Very close. Ride to the top of that rise and you'll catch your first glimpse of Radcliffe. Although the keep is not up to your standards, I think you'll find the valley a sight fit for royal eyes."

Seeing his fond, proud smile, she thought perhaps she comprehended all he'd tried to say. David's mistress was not any woman, but this land which he had won with such difficulty and cherished with his every breath. That she would allow. That she would encourage. Spurring her mount, she rode forward. The trees thinned rapidly now, and at the top of the rise a vista opened up.

The forest cupped the valley in its palm. Dark green fingers of pine reached out and separated the golden fields and emerald pastures. Here the air, scented with wild thyme and domestic flowers, smoothed her face with a gentle touch. A giant stone stood balanced on the side of the hill and around it tumbled a stream laden with its bounty. Birds escaped the safety of the forest and dove toward the valley to work the fields behind the plowmen. The track dove straight down from Alisoun's feet, through the brown thatched village and to the small castle perched on a rocky outcrop.

David turned Louis sideways and stared as intently as any man returning from a long absence. In a voice filled with awe, he said, "The crops are growing. God be praised, the drought is broken." A grin broke across his face. "We'll survive this winter!"

Alisoun watched in stupefaction as he whooped and rode Louis in a circle. Then she realized her surmise had been correct. It was this he feared she would find unsatisfactory, for it was this he loved. Pulling up beside her, he leaned out of the saddle and with one arm around her neck, hugged and bussed her in one lightning-fast strike. Before she could reprove him, he skittered away.

"Come on." He started down the hill at a canter. Looking back, he saw her following at a sedate pace, and he rode back and slapped her mount on the rump. "Come *on*!"

She didn't want to gallop into her future home, her wimple loose and her clothes rumpled, but David gave her no choice. He harried her down the track, laughing maniacally and singing nonsense songs. She tried to reprove him, but he ignored her and at last she decided she would look more foolish if she struggled than if she joined in. Or perhaps he infected her with his delight. He had a way of doing that.

She didn't sing, of course, or laugh out loud, but she smiled and leaned into the ride, relishing the wind on her face and the sunshine which shone unfettered by the trees. And after all, she told herself, this was a small price to reassure David that she found his home acceptable.

The villagers spotted them and ran in from the fields, and when they reached the little square, men, women, and children were waiting for them.

Alisoun stopped, sure the villagers would wait respectfully while David spoke some formal greeting. Instead David stared at her as if she were the embodiment of beauty while the villagers shouted in a tumult of welcome.

"Glad ye could come back, m'lord."

"Pretty lady, m'lord."

"No wonder he didn't return sooner."

"I wouldn't either, if that were me company."

The people seemed respectful enough, but Alisoun stiffened. Surely they didn't always treat their lord and his visitors with such impudence. To David, she said, "Aren't you going to reprimand them?"

David stopped staring at her and glanced around at the smiling faces below. "Reprimand them? They seem to have the right of it." Waving his arms, he commanded their silence and they gave it willingly enough. "Good people of Radcliffe, I bring you Lady Alisoun of George's Cross to be your new mistress and the guiding light of our village."

Mouths dropped in unison.

Dismayed by their reaction, Alisoun greeted them. "How do you do, good people?"

Someone—one of the unkempt men who'd run in from the fields—said, "Ye're jestin', m'lord. Ye married Lady Alisoun o' George's Cross?"

David took her hand. "I have her here."

Every eye examined her from head to toe.

One of the women said, "Are ye sure ye have th' right one? We've heard o' Lady Alisoun, an' she's all stiff an' mannerly an' crotchety."

Alisoun tried to tuck hairs back under her wimple.

David grinned. "So she was—before she met me."

The villagers, Alisoun noted, laughed with unnecessary vigor at David's poor jest.

He pointed a finger at them. "She'll have every one of you behaving in a proper manner before the summer's over."

Someone groaned.

"You especially, Alnod." David didn't even need to look to know the groaner. "And you'll all cooperate with your new lady."

"What if we don't want t' be proper?" the man called Alnod asked.

"Her villagers do as they're told, and she's brought them great wealth. They didn't starve, not even last winter."

The villagers glanced at each other. Every one of them was too thin, and none wore much more than rags.

No longer laughing, David stated solemnly, "She is the lady of my heart."

Alnod nodded, as did the others. "Then we'll treat her as if she were one of our own."

"I can ask no more," David replied.

"I will do my best to be the lady you deserve," Alisoun said, and if her phrase carried an undertone of anger, no one seemed to notice.

Beaming at her, David started toward the castle. This time she ignored his urgings and rode with dignity and grace. Her experience in Radcliffe Village proved that, should the nobles abandon their pride, the common folk would fail in their proper homage.

To her surprise, David respected her wishes and led her horse while she made the necessary repairs to her appearance. Yet he glanced constantly at the castle. His chatter died away; he rode like a man restrained, yet in a hurry.

Someone must have been watching from the castle walls. As they neared, the drawbridge began to drop. It didn't creak, the chains didn't squeal. It slid down easily, cleanly, like a gate in perfect repair. This was the home of a mercenary, and it gave Alisoun the first indication of the kind of repairs David had deemed important. Whatever conditions she found in the keep, the outer walls would be invulnerable to siege or attack.

Maybe that explained why the villagers, despite their hungry appearance, displayed an almost cocky confidence. It certainly explained why David insisted that they come to Radcliffe for her safety.

"There." David let go of her bridle. "Look."

Alisoun saw a little boy running down the lowered drawbridge. A man ran after him.

Alisoun shaded her eyes. "Who is it?"

King Louis danced in what looked like equine excitement.

"That's not Guy of the Archers, surely. No man of his mastery would run after a child in so undignified a manner."

David vaulted from the saddle.

"Unless the child was . . ."

David began to run in a manner equally as undignified.

". . . yours."

18

David ran toward Bert, and the thump of her small body against his brought tears of joy to his eyes. He lifted her high, then brought her close, absorbing love and warmth, feeling her squirm and knowing the ecstasy of holding his healthy, active, stubborn daughter once more.

"Daddy." She used her hand to push his head away. "I wanna *see* you."

He leaned back so she could see him, and he could see her, and for the first time he absorbed her amazing transformation. The gold he had sent had obviously gone to feed the child, for she looked healthy and far from starvation. But her brown hair had been cut to a stubble all around her skinny face. She had a scab above her eyebrow and one on her chin. "What have you done to yourself?" he demanded.

"I'm going to be a warrior like you."

Lifting her away from him again, he stared at her while her feet kicked uselessly. "What are you wearing?"

"A page's uniform." Her brown eyes sparkled. "I can practice my swordwork in it."

"That's your sword?" He nodded at the wooden stick hung from a belt at her waist.

"I made it myself." She whipped her head around and glared at Guy, who stood off to the side. "Uncle Guy wouldn't do it. He said I had no business being a warrior, but I'm going to be a mercenary like my Daddy."

Guy met David's gaze with a rueful shake of the head. "I beg your pardon, David. She cut her hair with a kitchen knife. I heard the cook squalling and—"

"'Tis I who am sorry, Guy." David brought Bert close once more. She wrapped her skinny arms around his neck and her skinny legs around his waist, and beheld the rest of the world with the air of a princess. "I should have known better than to think anyone could control this terror."

"I'm not a terror!" Bert exclaimed.

"You're no warrior, either," Guy said.

"Am too!"

Before David had to interfere, Alisoun brought her horse closer and distracted the child. "Who is that?" Bert demanded.

"Let me introduce you." Proud of them both, foreseeing trouble yet facing it head-on, David walked up to Alisoun's stirrup and said to Bert, "This is Alisoun, countess of George's Cross and the lady who graciously became my wife four days ago." To Alisoun, he said, "This is Bert."

"So I see." Alisoun nodded gracefully in acknowledgment of the introduction. "You never told me you had a son."

David could have groaned, and his pugnacious child stuck her chin forward and her lip out. "I'm a *girl*."

"Her name is Bertrade," David told Alisoun.

If she had been a lesser woman, she would have gasped and exclaimed. As it was, her eyes narrowed as she inspected the child. "A girl. You're a girl?"

Bert wiggled out of David's arms and stood close to him. Sticking out her skinny chest, she placed her scabbed fists on her hips and spread her feet in an imitation of manly confidence. She examined her new stepmother as critically as Alisoun examined her. "A countess? You're a countess?"

Alisoun said nothing, but to David her still expression expressed much. She was shocked by such blatant impudence, shocked by Bert's appearance, shocked that he hadn't informed her of her role as stepmother earlier. And he really should have. But Alisoun had been so stunned by her own pregnancy that he had feared to give her more reason to doubt their union. In his mind, he'd imagined Alisoun meeting a clean, well-behaved Bert and being charmed out of her distress.

Instead, Bert couldn't look worse or sound more sassy. When had she grown so spoiled?

Stepping firmly into the breach, Guy suggested, "Perhaps this would be better continued inside." With a gallantry he had learned on the tournament circle, he introduced himself to Alisoun, took her bridle, and led her across the drawbridge.

She went easily, chatting with him, putting him at ease as she had been trained to do. David watched, torn between jealousy that Guy performed the duty he should perform and discomfiture that his child had so embarrassed him.

He had wanted to show Alisoun the castle himself. He had wanted to point out to her how the smaller perimeter of his walls made defense easier, that his men were constantly on alert and every weapon always at the ready. He wanted to show her that although he'd spent most of his time and his insignificant income on fortification, the castle still boasted a few amenities. Although his stable could use whitewashing, the roof structure remained sound and her horses would be well housed. A stone wall surrounded his herb garden, and the woman who tended it mixed ointments and elixirs, and when necessary she worked a bit of healing magic.

His keep . . . David squinted as he considered the difference between her keep and his. The chapel in his keep was small and dark. The great hall, the undercroft, and the gallery in his keep were equally dismal. Only the solar came close to Alisoun's standards, and there, he hoped, he would charm her out of the consternation he feared she must be experiencing.

As he gazed after Alisoun, a small, repentant voice spoke from below. "Daddy?"

He waited.

"Are you mad at me?"

"Shouldn't I be?"

Bert scuffled her feet in the dirt. "She thought I was a *boy*."

"I don't blame her. You've got no hair, you're dressed all wrong." Pinching the edge of her short tunic between two fingers, he shook it and dust flew. "By Saint Michael's arms, you're unclean."

"So?"

Smothering a sudden smile, he realized how like Alisoun he had become. Before, he would not even have noticed Bert's filth. "So you can't become a warrior!"

"I want to. I want to." Tears hovered close now, and she flung her arms around his leg. "I want to go with you next time you go away."

"Ahh." Now he understood. Peeling her off his leg, he knelt before her. "You don't want me to go away anymore?"

"Nay." She sniffed.

"Didn't Guy take good care of you?"

"Aye. I like Guy. " She wiped her nose on her sleeve. "Most of the time. But he's not you."

"That's why you must be polite to Lady Alisoun," David said. "I've married her so I won't ever have to go away."

The tears that swam in Bert's eyes dried at once. "Why not?"

"She's rich and no one in Radcliffe will ever go hungry again."

"You married an heiress." A gaminlike grin spread across his daughter's face as she immediately grasped his unspoken reason. "You married her for her money!"

"Not just for her money, dear. Alisoun is warm, kind, giving—"

Bert snorted and punched his shoulder. "I saw her, and *you're* not supposed to lie."

"I'm not lying." He stood and held out his hand. "You'll see. You'll like her a lot."

"I hate you." Bert faced off with Alisoun over a steaming tub of water while David's serving folk watched with avid interest. "I'm sorry my Daddy married you!"

"And I'm sorry to hear that." Alisoun rolled up her sleeves while Philippa and her other maids set up screens around the open fire in Radcliffe's great hall. "But you still have to have a bath."

Torn between explaining his daughter and supporting his wife, David took a step off the dais, then back up again, then back down.

Seated on a bench at the trestle table where they had eaten their afternoon meal, Guy warned, "Leave them alone."

"But I've got to intervene before they come to blows."

"I'd say your Lady Alisoun has the matter well in hand," Guy said.

Bert shrieked at Alisoun, as if in defiance of Guy's assurance. "My daddy doesn't want you here."

"Well in hand," David muttered. He stepped down again and walked toward the fire. In the stern voice he so seldom used on his daughter, he said, "Bert, Lady Alisoun is correct. I told you—"

"David." Without looking at him, Alisoun spoke in a clear, cold voice. "You'll not interfere with me."

David's mouth dropped and he halted.

"Bertrade and I will deal with each other well when we have taken each other's measure, I am sure." This time her gray eyes flicked in his direction. "For that, you should leave us alone. Set the last shield, Philippa. We don't want a draft to chill young Bertrade."

David was left staring at a tall screen. Retreating, he sat once more at the trestle table on the dais. Guy poured him a mug of ale and pushed it in his direction, and he sipped it in what he hoped was a casual manner—but he kept himself free of any entanglements in case he had reason to rise.

His servants moved closer to the screens, raking the rushes off the floor, and in a desultory manner swabbing it with a mixture of urine and vinegar, all the while listening to the quarrel.

The keep had not been the disaster of filth David feared—after all, he'd been gone less than three months—but Alisoun had set to work at once to destroy the fleas that hopped everywhere. She'd given the orders and when David's servants proved slow in responding, she'd set her own people over them.

Lady Edlyn had proved herself capable as she harried his servants and ordered the cooks, all at the same time. Philippa acted as an enforcer, making sure her lady's orders, once given, were followed.

Now it irritated David to see his staff awaiting the results of this altercation as if it would have any effect on whether they would have to obey their new mistress. He wanted to say something, to order them on their way, but Lady Edlyn put her finger to her lips and nodded with a smile. She seemed certain her mistress would triumph. He just wished he were as certain.

From behind the screen, he heard a splashing, then a bawl of what sounded like agony. "You got me wet!" Bert cried.

"It works so much better that way." Alisoun sounded as calm as ever, and that seemed to infuriate Bert once more.

"You're ugly!" she yelled. "You're stupid!"

"Damn." Once more, David started to his feet and moved toward the screens.

Guy followed and grabbed his arm. "Alisoun said not to interfere."

David wavered.

Then Bertrade's voice rose to a high-pitched scream. "My daddy only married you for your money."

Tearing himself away from Guy, David bounded forward. "I never said that." He didn't know to whom he spoke, but he clearly heard Alisoun's answer.

"I know that. I married him for protection. You needn't worry that I'll entice your daddy away from you. I don't even care to try."

David skidded on a wet place on the floor and went down heavily. Bruised in body and spirit, he scarcely noticed when Guy helped him up from the floor.

"Did you bring some new horses?" Guy asked. When David nodded morosely, Guy said, "You can show them to me."

Guy led him outside into the small bailey, now bustling with activity. David's servants greeted him with varying levels of enthusiasm, and as they neared the stable, Guy broke the silence. "The reaction to Lady Alisoun amazes me."

Instantly hostile, David asked, "What do you mean?"

"Yesterday everyone of these villeins moaned about the hunger in their bellies and how they would do anything to ease it. Now Lady Edlyn and Lady Philippa have distributed meals from Lady Alisoun's stores—"

"She's not a lady," David said.

"Lady Edlyn?" Guy stared in wonder.

"Philippa."

"Isn't she? I would have said she was, and a very attractive lady, too." David shook his head, but Guy seemed unconvinced. "Lady Alisoun has made it clear the duties everyone will perform if they expect to continue to eat so well. Reasonable expectations, I might add, yet your servants seem to be struggling between relief and resentment."

"They'll do as she says, or I'll tack their ears to a stock."

Guy eyed the open stable door, then looked at the indignant David. "Let's walk around one time before we go in to see the horses."

David nodded, knowing his restless vigor wouldn't sit well with the animals, who even now were adjusting to their new stalls.

As they started around the saggy wooden building, Guy returned to the subject. "Tacking their ears won't work. She has to win them over herself, and I don't know whether this lazy bunch of knaves and sluts will respond to the woman when they know you married her for her wealth."

Grabbing Guy by the throat, David snapped, "I didn't!"

Guy jabbed David's unprotected stomach with his fist, and when David released him and reeled backward, he asked, "Why did you tell the child that, then?"

"I didn't. She just assumed . . . and where did she even get the idea, I'd like to know?" David glared insinuatingly at the man who'd raised his daughter these months.

"She was lost when you left, and she ran from one person to another, trying to garner suggestions of how you could come home soon. A couple of the men told her you'd be wise to marry an heiress. A couple of the women suggested you'd be better off to have a squire at your side. She couldn't do anything about the heiress, so she decided to become a lad and be your squire." Guy rubbed his head as if it ached. "She's a very smart little lass."

David found himself fighting a headache. "How am I going to explain?"

"Bert's not going to believe you wed Lady Alisoun for any reason other than greed."

"I meant to explain to Alisoun." Narrowing his eyes, David asked, "Why won't Bert believe?"

They had reached the stable door once more, and Guy looked at it, then at David. "Let's go around again."

It never occurred to David to disagree.

As they began the wide circle again, Guy said, "Because she's had you all to herself these years, and she won't easily give you up to another woman. She adores you, you know that."

"I adore her, and I'll not adore her any less because I'm wed."

"Bert and Alisoun will fight—are already fighting—and you'll have to make your choices. Who will you side with? The woman you've wed who, by all appearances, is stiff-necked and conventional, or your wild child, who needs to be taught proper behavior without breaking her spirit?"

"Alisoun, of course."

"Of course." Guy mocked him. "You've raised Bert, but not like any other child I've seen. Most especially, not like any girl I've seen. You've given her her head more often than not."

"Why not?" David asked indignantly. "She's learned by trying and failing, or trying and succeeding. I've made sure she didn't hurt herself, and it's worked well."

"Aye, it's worked. She's tried anything she chose, and you and I, we're old warriors. We just watched and made sure she didn't get hurt. What do you think Lady Alisoun will think of such a way of raising a child?"

David remembered his early impressions of Alisoun. He'd thought her humorless, unemotional, frigid. That was how Guy now saw her, but it wasn't the truth, and David clapped his friend on the shoulder. "You'll see. She'll defer to my greater knowledge."

"Will she?" It never occurred to either one of them to enter the open stable door this time. They just passed it and kept walking. "So when Bert tells Lady Alisoun she wants to train as a squire, she's going to encourage Bert?"

David didn't answer.

"Because you know Bert. Once she decides to learn something, nothing will stop her until she's mastered it. She's going to be after you every day to teach her swordplay and jousting and every other manly pursuit. It's your contention that Lady Alisoun will allow such behavior without saying a word?"

"Damn!" David smacked his hand into the stable wall, then wished he hadn't. The horses needed serenity to settle, and even the stablemaster would be moving as quietly as possible. He listened, but heard nothing but a few startled neighs. Softly, he spoke again. "Alisoun has a strong sense of duty, and she'll consider training Bert to be a lady her duty, and nothing will keep her from it."

"There's nothing wrong with that."

"But what's the harm in Bert learning a squire's duty if she wishes?"

Guy pounced. "So you are going to support Bert against Lady Alisoun?"

"Nay, I . . ." David took a breath. "Why does it have to be so complicated? When I met Lady Alisoun, I thought she was mean-spirited and bloodless. Then I saw her demesne and thought, 'Ooh, all this beautiful wealth waiting for me.' So I courted her and talked to her, and she's . . . she's . . ." Turning to Guy, he grasped his shoulders. "You know how it is when you look in one of those clear, polished crystals and it just looks like a hard, cold stone? Then as you stare, you notice the rainbows that dance on the surface, and when you hold it up to your eye and look through it, it makes all the colors brighter and all the hard, horrible things look like they're touched by an angel's wing?"

Bewildered, Guy stared at his old friend. "Nay."

David swept on. "That's what she's like. You think she's hard and cold and easily seen through, and then she transforms your whole world."

Guy laid his hand on David's forehead. "Are you ill?"

Laughing, David knocked him away and entered the dim stable, hushed except for the restlessness of the old horses and the uneasy snuffling of the new. "Did I ever tell you about my granny?"

Trailing after him, Guy said cautiously, "Your granny?"

"She used to talk about how some couples share a great love."

"You and Lady Alisoun share a great love?"

Guy could have sounded less incredulous, but David ignored that. "Well, she doesn't know yet."

"You share a great love, but she doesn't know yet?"

David stopped to pet one of the horses from George's Cross. "She didn't want to marry me."

"So why did she?" Guy asked suspiciously.

"For the same reason she hired me. For protection." David frowned. "In fact, we need to spread the word that if anyone sees a stranger lurking about, I should be informed at once."

"What does she need protection from?"

"I don't know." David could see little in the fading light, but he did catch sight of Guy's blatant stupefaction and said, "That is, I have a good idea, but I don't know everything yet. She'll tell me soon."

"Probably when she realizes you share a great love."

"Probably." Entering one of the stalls, David checked the gelding's hooves and hocks. "This one stepped into a hole on that wretched road and has limped ever since. I'll get the stablemaster to heat a poultice and put it on him."

Guy watched with intense interest. "May I ask a question?"

"As you wish."

"Why did Lady Alisoun marry you for protection when she had hired you for protection?"

David didn't want to think about that. He didn't want to talk about that. But Guy wanted an answer, and they'd been friends too long for David to evade or lie. "I rather forced her to wed me."

Guy straightened so quickly David wondered if he'd gotten a sliver. "Forced her? You mean at swordpoint, or by kidnapping? One of the king's heiresses? Are you mad?"

Irked that Guy would think such a thing, David snapped, "I didn't force her with any violent means. I simply came into some knowledge that she would prefer remain hidden. And there is the babe, of course."

Guy staggered backward and sat down on a stack of hay. "She's with child?"

David grinned proudly. "Aye."

"With *your* child?"

His grin disappeared. "Aye!"

Guy seemed overwhelmed, unable to speak another word.

David waited, and when Guy did nothing but shake his head, David stepped out of the stall, closed the gate behind him, and hefted Guy to his feet. "So you see we have to blend these families and these estates."

"It's going to be a difficult task," Guy warned.

"With your help, my friend, we'll do it. My granny always used to say that with a great love, it casts a glow of warmth all around it and makes everyone content." David moved toward Louis's stall. "You'll see."

Ahead of them, something flew over the door of one of the stalls and landed in the aisle. Something else followed and landed on top of it, and in an awesome silence the two things tumbled and rolled. Unable to make out details in the dim light, David hurried toward the creatures.

Lads, fighting just outside Louis's stall. The great horse watched stoically, but David grabbed one and Guy grabbed the other, and they dragged them along the aisle and out the door.

"Eudo!" David shook the boy in his grip, then looked at the one Guy held and recognized his own Radcliffe page. "And Marlow! What are you two doing?"

Eudo extended a shaking finger. "He started it!"

"He tried to tend Louis." Marlow kicked dust at Eudo. "It's my task to tend Louis. Tell him, Sir David."

"Aye, tell him, Sir David." Eudo pointed his thumb at his chest. "It's me you want to tend Louis."

Dumbfounded, David stared at the two boys until Guy said sarcastically, "Oh, aye. A great love. Warmth of glow. Everyone content." David met Guy's gaze, and Guy wagged his great head. "Better sooner than later."

That night at the meal, no one spoke much. Worn out by the fight which she had lost, the child Bertrade had fallen asleep on her bench and been carried away. David's servants maintained a watchful vigil, and Edlyn and the maids showed obvious signs of fatigue.

Alisoun was grateful. She hated to acknowledge her own lack of courtesy, but she would have been hard pressed to carry on a civil conversation.

The trip had been tiring, settling into a new castle proved difficult, the child Bertrade expressed a defiant spirit, and Alisoun had finally been forced to face facts. The one thing she'd always feared had happened.

She'd been married for her wealth.

"Could I cut you a slice of bread?" David scooted as close to her as he could get. The bench they shared allowed him to press against her, knee, hip and arm, and his knife hovered over the loaf placed before them on the long table.

Alisoun nodded graciously. "I would be beholden."

The blade began sawing back and forth, back and forth, and Alisoun realized how hard the bread would be. But Edlyn had taken one look into the baker's ovens and demanded he clean them before he bake another thing, so they'd dine on stale bread and be grateful this night.

She had been stupid to hope that David had married her for any other reason than her money. She could dream he did it out of affection for his unborn babe, or because of the pleasure she'd offered him in bed. She could pray that he valued her for herself.

But the truth was always and forever that he wanted her twelve sacks of wool, and all the assets that went with them.

Oh, she couldn't even blame him. He had a child he adored. She'd helped give Bertrade that bath, and the child, while healthy, was far from plump. She could comprehend his decision to wed and provide for his daughter.

"The bread is stale, so I had your maid warm it." Pushing the heated slice into her hand, David said, "I've had an egg yolk whipped in white wine for you to dip it in. 'Twill be good for our child, also."

"My thanks again." She touched her still flat belly. "You are ever thoughtful."

If she were a less honest woman, she could claim she'd married David to give her child a name. Instead, she'd wed an inappropriate man for no better reasons than companionship and desire. She was no less a fool than another woman she knew who had wed her dream of love and found nothing but a belt to blister her skin and a rod to break her bones.

"My cook took dried strawberries from this very spring and steamed them to plumpness and made a compote." David waved the fragrant bowl slowly before her nose. "For you, my lady. Won't you eat?"

If it weren't for the danger which threatened, she'd go back to George's Cross and take her chances, but that open grave proved that her enemy knew the truth, and she feared he would do anything now to take his revenge.

So she had a choice. She could fret and complain and be like David's first wife, a weight to drag him down. Or she could do as she had always done. She could do her duty.

Armed with a new resolve, she looked at David. He, too, seemed tired, and lines of concern marked his dark tanned skin. She smiled at him graciously and picked up her spoon. "This all smells quite delicious. I look forward to the end of our first day at Radcliffe."

David sat back with a sigh that sounded like relief. From his hungry expression, she expected that he would gobble his food in the manner of a barbarian. But he ate politely and drank his fill, always attentive to her needs and chatting like a host making his new guest at home. When at last he pressed the goblet to her lips and let her drink, then turned it to the same spot and drank while gazing at her, she realized the reason for his desirous aspect—and all her pretense of serenity almost went for naught. She rose so quickly he knocked their bench over trying to get to his feet, and she moved toward the solar with a firm stride. She heard him scrambling to catch up, but she refused to look back or in any way acknowledge his presence. But when he trod on her skirt, it jerked her to a halt, and when he took her arm, it brought her around to face him at the very door of the solar.

"I wish to sleep now," she said.

"So we will," he answered.

"Alone."

"We're married."

"I am aware."

"So I'll be in the marriage bed with you."

He looked so firm, so calm, so determined. She wanted to retort, but she couldn't breathe. She felt as if bands were tightening around her throat. Only now did she realize what a facade she'd erected around her emotions. She wasn't tranquil. She wasn't serene. She was absolutely livid.

She meant only to lay her hand on his chest. She really did.

But she hit him so hard she knocked him backward. She didn't yell, but only because she couldn't. In a low tone, she said, "I will be the mother to your child. I will be the mistress of your people. I will be the money chest which provides prosperity, and I will give it gladly." She slapped her hand on his chest again and this time she heard his grunt of pain. "But I will not be an expedient body in your bed. Go and find yourself a mistress."

David's people couldn't hear, but they watched the scene avidly and the humiliation struck at his pride, just as she knew it would. Exploding in a display of exasperation, he said, "Fine! I know where ten mistresses are, and willing ones too."

With a tight smile, she shut the door in his face.

Ruefully, he looked at his hands, especially noting the one missing a finger. "Well, nine mistresses anyway."

19

"*God's teeth, man,* you've got to do something about Lady Alisoun." Guy shoved his way through the crowd that surrounded David in the castle bailey. "If you don't, she's going to drive me mad."

David raised his weary head and stared at his steward through bloodshot eyes. "Why should you be any different?"

Glancing around, Guy observed the angry expression on the face of every servant who worked in the castle, but he clearly had no sympathy. "She's supposed to be supervising *them.*"

The servants murmured angrily.

Guy ignored them. "But the guard is none of her affair. 'Tis mine, and I resent her sending her two trained apes in to teach me what I already know."

With a sigh, David agreed. "She should not. I will speak to her." He looked around at the household staff. "I will speak to her about all of you, too."

"Do it, m'lord," one of the women said. "We did well enough without her before."

David frowned and pointed a finger right under the

woman's nose. "Well enough isn't good enough, and with Lady Alisoun I find that she's always right. If she says there's more to be done, then you'll work until you do it. I'll do nothing more than suggest she weed out the troublemakers and promote the more ambitious among you."

The woman drew back, clearly frightened.

"That way, you'll be working for one of your own, and not for a stranger from George's Cross. But you'll still be working for the food which Lady Alisoun has provided, I promise you. You'll still be working."

As David stepped away from his servants, he heard no sound at all. He'd given them ideas to ponder, and thought it best if they pondered them on their own. Guy apparently thought so, too, for David heard footsteps as Guy hurried to join him.

"You told the lazy knaves well enough that time," Guy said. "They've been slacking on purpose."

"I know." David rolled his shoulders, trying to get the kinks out that came from sleeping on the floor of the great hall. "I've been waiting for the chance to warn them what would happen. But I'm warning you, too. If my lady comes to you with suggestion to improve your defenses, listen with an open mind."

"You've got eels for brains! What would a woman know about defense?"

"She knew enough to hire me." Guy laughed and David jostled him. "You know the best defenses, and if you listen to her, you'll hear her respect for that. But she's so organized there's no operation she can't make better."

"If you say so, but she certainly has a way of getting my back up."

This time David laughed. "Aye, she's good at that, and here she has had so many new people unused to her effectiveness she's alienated them all at once."

"The servants. Me. My men. If it weren't for Philippa calming me after Lady Alisoun had left the guardhouse, I would be angrier yet." Guy half-smiled. "She's a lovely lady."

"Alisoun?"

"Philippa."

"She's not—" David gave up. If Guy wanted to call Philippa a lady, David didn't care. "Unfortunately Philippa isn't following Alisoun everywhere, for half the village has been complaining."

Guy waited, and when David didn't continue, Guy said, "And Bert?"

"Bert hides from her. She only comes out for her lessons as a warrior, and that, I suspect, only so she can learn to use a real sword—on Alisoun."

"You're training her with your squire, aren't you?"

"Eudo? Aye, I'm training them together."

Guy stopped at the base of the keep stairs. "What does he think?"

"I haven't asked him."

"You should. He's a bright lad, and sees much."

David smothered a grin.

"And what's so funny?"

"I don't have to ask what he thinks of training with Bert. His manliness is greatly offended."

"But he doesn't dare complain because she's your daughter?" Guy's eyes lit with answering glee. "Poor lad."

"Aye. He's offended that he must train with a girl, and he's offended that Louis allows Marlow the stable-boy to care for him."

"Did you not explain that Marlow had that duty first?"

"I also told him that normally, stable work is beneath a squire's dignity, but he well knows Louis's worth, and none of it appeased him."

"And I imagine Bert torments him."

"Worse." David succumbed to laughter. "She worships him."

"Poor, poor lad," Guy repeated. Leaning against the stairpost, he said, "Eudo, in turn, worships Lady Alisoun."

"So Bert says nothing aloud to her detriment. But she thinks it very loudly."

"A muffled Bert could be dangerous," Guy warned. "She could explode at any moment."

"I live in fear," David said.

"Does the lady know any of this?"

"I didn't think any situation existed which Alisoun had not dealt with. But she's proved me wrong, and if she doesn't know, I have the unenviable task of telling her."

"You'll do it alone, then. I'm not so brave as that."

With a resigned wave, David sent Guy on his way. Inside the great hall, a seeming peace reigned—but then, his serving women stood outside in the bailey. Alisoun's maids sat in a clump, like colorful spiders producing wool thread from their spindles as they laughed and talked. Seeing him searching, one called, "Lady Alisoun is in the solar, my lord."

Alone? David's heart leapt at the thought. Would he at last catch her without the group that constantly surrounded her? He hadn't spoken to her without an audience since she'd shut the bedroom door in his face a fortnight ago.

And his nine mistresses had proved inadequate. He wanted his wife. He wanted her badly.

At first, he'd been furious, vowing that he would not speak to her until she spoke first. Then she'd circumvented his pledge by greeting him in the morning with a civil word and a polite smile, and he realized she would always do what was proper.

But sleeping with her husband was proper, and she seemed never to think of it.

His anger had faded. He'd indicated a willingness to kiss and reconcile. She'd indicated a willingness only to reconcile. Kisses were strictly forbidden, and kisses were what he longed for. Kisses were what he would steal—if she were alone in the solar.

He dusted his clothing with slaps of his hand. Making a detour to the washbasin, he rinsed his face and hands. Wetting his hair, he raked it with his fingers and wished he had time to take an entire bath. No torture was too great to get in Alisoun's good graces once more.

Nervous, he stared at the open door of the solar until a giggle from the maids urged him forward. He raised his hand to knock on the sill, then changed his mind at the last moment. After all, it was *his* solar.

He swaggered in with his most charming smile in place, and he realized he was in luck. She sat on the bed, her back to him, leaning against the footboard. Not wanting to give her a chance to escape, desperate to see some real emotion from her, he snuck up behind her and wrapped his arm around her shoulders.

She screamed. Not a little scream, but a full-bodied scream of horror.

He leaped away. She leaped away. She turned to face him.

It was Philippa.

Her baby woke where she slept on the bed and screamed, too, frightened from sleep by her mother's terror.

"Philippa!"

"My lord!"

"I thought you were Lady Alisoun."

"I thought you were . . ." Philippa put her hand on

her chest for one moment, then gathered her child close and tried to comfort her. "Forgive me, my lord, you startled me."

Startled *her*? His heart still raced.

"My lord." Alisoun spoke from behind him. "Why did you sneak up on her?"

Turning, he saw Alisoun. She sat in the alcove, needle clasped in her long fingers. The sun from the window lit the garment spread on the table and left her face in shadow, but even so he could see her offended astonishment. "I thought she was you," he tried to explain.

"Why would you sneak up on Lady Alisoun?" Lady Edlyn sat across from her patron, stabbing the cloth with her needle as she waited for an answer.

Philippa gave him no time to get angry or defensive. As Hazel's shrieks died to whimpers, she said briskly, "No harm done. 'Twas my fault for being jumpy as a spotted hare."

"I do beg pardon." David moved close once more and caressed the baby's soft head. "I never meant to frighten you or the child."

"Of course you didn't. Get up, Edlyn, and give my lord your seat. I doubt he came to speak to you or me."

Sullenly, Edlyn rose as if Philippa had every right to command her. Giving him a wide berth, she moved away, but didn't leave the room.

David looked first at her bench, then at Alisoun's. Both had been built to hold two women, sitting side by side and sewing. Alisoun naturally sat in the middle of hers. That left just enough room for him if he pressed against her tightly, and he slid in beside her before she realized his plan.

"My lord!" Then she saw his challenging grin and abandoned that fight before battle was fairly joined.

Instead she moved to the far side of the bench to free herself from contact, taking her hemming with her.

He gladly followed. This should have felt no more intimate than sharing the day's meals in the great hall, except that he was alone with her in their bedchamber for the first time.

Well, not quite alone. Lady Edlyn rummaged through a chest and glared at them and Philippa coaxed Hazel to drink from a cup. The kitten who had slept in Alisoun's lap woke, disgruntled by the activity, and jumped to the floor. But compared with the crowd of servants and comrades who attended the meals with them, this was a small audience.

Alisoun wore proper clothing, of course. Even in her own bedchamber, even in the company of her maid and her fosterling, she would don nothing less. Yet the blue wool cotte was worn and soft, with lacing at the front from her waist to beneath her breasts. The linen shift she wore beneath the cotte had a tie at her throat, but it gaped open down to the point where the cotte covered it—just at the place where the swells of her breasts began.

No other woman, he was sure, could show as little flesh and still be so provocative.

His thigh rubbed against hers and he turned sideways to face her, wrapping his arm around her like a parent supporting his child's first attempts to sit up.

Alisoun was not amused.

He didn't care. She had nowhere to go except farther into the corner, and she refused to damage her dignity with such a worthless evasion. He had her fairly trapped.

In her most civil tone, she asked, "Was there something I could help you with, my lord and husband?"

"Aye, there is, but you won't do *that*."

One look from her gray eyes should have given him frostbite.

Instead he warmed himself against the fire of her body. With his fingers he started at her waist and explored her spine, one vertebra at a time. He marveled at the tension that kept her so erect, and as he neared the nape of her neck, the tautness grew ever greater. He pushed the weight of her laden hair crispinette aside and bared the fine fair skin. Leaning close as if to kiss it, he let her flex in anticipation, then said, "I want to talk to you about our servants."

She jumped, although whether from his words or the movement of air across her flesh, he did not know. Her fingers faltered, then she resumed her sewing. "Our servants?"

"Yours and mine." He breathed in the scent of lemon balm that clung to her. "Surely you've noticed we have a problem."

"Not one I understand."

"Nay?" From this angle, he could see down her shift. Leaning back a little, he fixed the angle until he had a view of one entire breast. "Guy complained to me, too."

"Guy? He seems so pleasant!"

"Oh, he likes you. He simply thinks you should mind your needle. It's a prejudice you've faced before, I know."

"Aye, with Sir Walter, but it wasn't Guy's abilities about which I inquired." When she faced him their faces were inches apart. She looked earnestly into his eyes and her lips moved close to his as she protested, "It was the preparation of the foodstuffs for the men-at-arms and—" her gaze dropped to her own shoulder as if looking at him rattled her, "—the times they should eat."

They sat so close he could almost taste her. "Why do you care?"

She realized it, too. Her color rose in her face, and she cast him one quick glance, then again spoke to her shoulder. "I thought perhaps we could manage to get them their food from the kitchen so they wouldn't have to prepare their own on those braziers."

"You didn't explain that to him."

"I'm the lady. I don't have to give explanations."

He could only see the top of her head and the gape in her shift, and the top of her head couldn't compete for his attention. "Yet when a new lady comes and changes the way things have been done for generations, some might feel resentment and fail to cooperate as they should."

Her chest rose and fell as she considered, and he longed to weigh her breasts in his hand, to see if they had grown.

Then she looked up at him, and he forgot about her body in his pleasure at seeing her face. "What do you suggest?"

"Do you know who among my servants should be in command?"

"Aye, of course."

"Will your maids work for them?"

"My maids will do as they're told."

"Unlike their mistress."

She faced front again and picked up the sewing she'd dropped.

"Appoint my servants to their tasks and place your maids within their ranks. Tell them they now know how you would have your household kept, and that Lady Edlyn and Philippa will watch to ensure they continue as you have instructed."

"Why should they listen to Lady Edlyn and Philippa if they balk at taking orders from me?"

"They know you're their lady, and they know you've rescued us from at least another month of starvation until we can get the crops in. But they don't relish having all of their number stripped of authority and replaced with your people." He shrugged. "It's the way of all folk, I think."

She sewed until she reached the end of her seam. Then she bit off the thread and said, "You're an intelligent man. I should have seen it myself."

Modestly, he kept silent.

"However, you should apply your intelligence to the way you're raising your daughter. It is inappropriate."

He stiffened. "How so?"

"She's a girl, and you're teaching her manly ways."

"What's wrong with manly ways?"

"She's seven years old. She knows not how to clean, nor sew, nor spin, nor cook."

"There's time for her to learn."

"Why would she want to? She's told me frankly that men's work is much more interesting then women's." She stared ruefully at the garment in her hand. "Of course she's right. Cleaning a pot is not nearly as exciting as breaking a wild horse."

He watched as she licked the brilliant yellow thread, then ran it through the needle's eye and began to embroider a pattern at the neck. "Do you like to sew?"

She glanced at him sideways. "Why do you ask?"

"You're always doing it. All the women are always doing it. I just thought—"

"That we enjoyed it?" She laughed, a bright waterfall of amusement, and Philippa and Lady Edlyn joined her. "Keeping a household in clothing takes every available moment, and will for the rest of my life. For the rest of my servants' lives, also."

He looked at them in awe. "So you have to do something you hate forever."

"I don't hate it." Holding the baby, Philippa drew closer to the table. "Not most of it."

"I hate spinning." With her arms crossed over her chest, Lady Edlyn exuded hostility.

David drew a little away from Alisoun. Their moment of privacy had passed, but he didn't mind so very much. Contact had been reestablished, and that was enough for now.

"What about you, Alisoun?" He held his arms out to Hazel, and the baby came into them willingly. "Do you hate sewing?"

"I try not to think about it." She put her needle down with an air of decision. "But you're evading the question. Bertrade is an heiress. She'll have Radcliffe, at the very least, for dowry."

He stood Hazel on the table and she laughed as she tested her new upright stance. When had Bert grown beyond this simple stage of life? When had she become a headstrong girl rather than a dimpled babe?

Unaware of his paternal concerns, Alisoun continued speaking, forcing him to face facts. "She'll have fathers courting you on their sons' behalf, and they'll want her to wed at twelve. Do you want her to go ignorant to their homes, to never take her proper position as lady?"

"Nay, of course I don't want that." He clenched his jaw. Guy had warned him that his loyalties would be torn. He hadn't warned him he would be called upon to conspire against his own child. "But twelve's too young to wed."

"And seven's too old to be untrained in women's ways."

He gave up. He had no choice. "Train her then." A suspicious wetness darkened Hazel's diapers, and he told Philippa, "Get me the cloths and I'll change her." Philippa tried to refuse, but he wouldn't give up the baby to her care. He wanted to hold this child, to touch her soft skin, to reminisce about Bertrade's babyhood.

"I've done it before." He looked meaningfully at Alisoun. "And I'll do it again."

Alisoun watched his suddenly possessive clutch on the babe without comment, but she wouldn't leave the subject of Bert alone. "I can't train her. She runs away from me."

Folding her hands, she waited for him to offer a solution, but he busied himself with Hazel. He laid her on the table and unwound the cloth, making faces to keep her entertained. He said, "Right from the beginning, Bert kicked and fought every time I changed her. This babe laughs and coos. Hazel behaves like I thought a girl child would behave. But Bert wants to be moving and doing, and she was like that from birth." Hazel stuck her foot in her mouth and chewed on it while watching him thoughtfully. He could have sworn she understood every word. "I can't imagine Bert sitting and sewing, but she's good with swordwork. As good as any seven-year-old, lad or lass, could be."

"What good will such knightly arts do her?" Alisoun asked. "It's not as if *I* have ever had use for them."

"I don't know," he replied. "If you knew how to stick a knife in a man's ribs, I wouldn't have to interrogate every stranger who wanders through my village." He bared the babe's rump and passed the wet cloth to the hovering Philippa, then took the dry one and slipped it under Hazel. "If you knew how to stick a man with a knife . . ." he repeated. An idea sprang full-blown into his brain. Placing one hand on Hazel's belly to keep her from rolling off the table, he turned to Alisoun. "That's it!"

"What?"

"That's what you can do with Bert. Take a lesson with her."

"What?"

"On the morrow, come and take a lesson in fighting with Bert."

"Are you mad?"

"On the contrary, I'm brilliant. If she could see you learning something she already knows, it'll make her realize you have to go through the same process everyone does to achieve competence. She'll no longer think you're a . . . well!" He leaned over the babe once more. "Still, I suppose a woman in your condition should not attempt something so new."

"There's nothing wrong with my condition." She spoke through her teeth. "But I am not a young girl trying to escape my fate. I am a woman who uses already learned skills and I refuse—"

He turned the baby's behind into the light.

"—to put myself on display simply to make contact with a lass who should have more respect—"

"What's this on Hazel's rear?" He touched the red mark with his finger. "She looks as if she's been burned."

Silence filled the room. No one said a word. He looked up into Alisoun's face as he stroked the rippled skin, and she stared at his finger with a fascination akin to horror. He glanced at Philippa. She had paled. Only Lady Edlyn seemed able to move, and she walked rapidly to his side. Cranking her head around, she observed the spot and in a casual, too-loud tone said, "Oh, that. It's a birthmark."

"A birthmark? It looks like a brand." He rubbed the red spot again. "Feels like one, too."

He looked again at Alisoun, but she was staring at Lady Edlyn with something akin to awe.

Meanwhile, Philippa jerked into motion. "Just a birthmark."

He could scarcely believe *that.* "It's a perfect shape."

"I have one, too." Philippa touched the back of her shoulder.

"A birthmark that looks like a—" he stared at the baby's behind, "—ram?" Incredulous, he lifted his eyebrows at Alisoun. "Have you seen this?"

"I'll do it," she said.

He didn't understand. "What?"

"I'll learn to handle a sword, or whatever it is you want me to do." Alisoun pushed at him until he moved aside, to finish diapering Hazel.

He watched as Alisoun quickly wound the baby in her dry cloth. But he could see that it drooped, and would fall right off as soon as someone picked Hazel up. This was, he would wager, the first diaper Alisoun had ever replaced. But she wanted to distract him, and he supposed he would allow her to do so. After all, he was getting his way. That mark would be there on the morrow, should he want to question it again. "You'll come and train with Bert?" he asked.

"So I said." She lifted the baby and handed her to Philippa.

As David thought, the wrapping clothes slipped and Philippa caught them before they could slide off entirely. "Thank you, my lady." Her gratitude seemed excessive for one badly done diaper.

But Alisoun caught his arm before he could wonder more. Decisively, she said, "I'll be there in the morning."

20

Bert scuffled her feet in the dirt of the training ground and wailed, "Daddy, I don't want her here."

"She has to learn how to protect herself, just like you have. You don't want her to be hurt because she doesn't know how to use a sword, do you?" David observed his daughter as she struggled with her answer. She didn't care whether Alisoun learned to use a sword; as he'd told Guy, he believed his daughter dreamed of using her own prowess against Alisoun. But Bert's fierce heart hid wells of tenderness, and David thought he could plumb those wells. "Your new mama has been threatened by someone."

"By who?" Bert demanded.

"I don't know, but that's how we met. She hired me because someone tried to shoot an arrow at her."

"She tried to give someone a bath," Bert muttered.

David ignored that. "Someone took her cat and hurt it until it died."

"Nay, they didn't!" Bert rolled up her sleeves as if

something—her anger, David guessed—made her hot. "That lady has a kitty. See?" She pointed to some long red marks on her arm. "It scratches."

"I gave her the new kitty because she was crying over her old one."

"Did you see her tears?" Bert asked suspiciously.

"Nay, it was worse than that." Glancing at the sky, David observed the solid gray overcast of clouds that hid the sun. A good day to train squires; not hot, not bright, not likely to rain. "See those clouds?" He pointed, and his daughter nodded. "They have rain in them, but they won't let it go. They hold it in, aching, wanting to cry out all their water, but they can't. For some reason, they hold it in. Your new mama's like that. Her tears are the kind of tears she keeps inside, and you know how much those hurt."

"Like when you left me here and I knew I had to be brave but I wanted you really, really bad?"

"Like that."

Scratching her chin, Bert thought, then said, "She doesn't like the kitty you gave her. She never pets it or anything. She never talks to it." Her mouth drooped. "She never gives it a good-night kiss."

Bert didn't speak of the kitten, David realized. She didn't care whether that cat got a good-night kiss, but the child's fragile ego couldn't comprehend Alisoun's hesitant affection. Bert's bold emotions demanded a mother who would hug her and kiss her and tuck her into bed, not speak to her of propriety and spinning and baths. Kneeling beside his daughter, David framed his words carefully. "She's afraid to like the kitty. She liked her other one so much, and she's afraid if she likes this one it'll die, too."

"That's stupid. You're not going to let someone take her kitty and hurt it again."

No one matched Bert's implicit faith in him—especially not Alisoun. "But she doesn't trust me."

She wrapped her grubby arms around his neck. "But you're my daddy!"

Hugging her against him, David explained, "She doesn't understand what that means. She doesn't understand that I would do anything to protect you and her. You're my daughter. She's my wife. We're a family, and our family is the most important thing in the world to me."

"You gotta tell her!"

"I'm showing her. I'm letting her come and learn with you and Eudo how to be a warrior."

He'd left Bert with nothing to say, and that unusual experience heartened him. Perhaps he was doing the right thing. "Come," he said. "Help me get the weapons out of the storage shed."

As they laid out the shields, the knives, the swords, and the bows and arrows on the trestle table set up for his purpose, David's mind returned to that scene in the solar. If anything proved Alisoun didn't yet trust him, it was that.

That spot on Hazel's behind was no birthmark. He'd wager Radcliffe on that. The child had been burned somehow, and her mother didn't want to confess. But why did Alisoun lie, also? And Lady Edlyn—Alisoun had been startled when Lady Edlyn stepped in and fibbed so easily. It all meant trouble, and he feared he would have to do what he told Bert. He feared he would have to protect his family against a very great challenge. He'd learned a lot in these last years of famine, and he only hoped that this time he would make the right choices.

"Here they come."

Bert's gloomy voice pierced his reverie. Alisoun and

Eudo walked toward them, and he grinned when he saw Alisoun's idea of proper warrior wear. She wore an old cotte with tight sleeves, a sturdy pair of over-boots and a wimple tied at the base of her neck. Two long braids of hair hung down her back, and grim determination stiffened her spine.

David recognized her expression. Eudo sported the same one every time he had to train with Bert. She was going to do this. She wouldn't like it, but she would do it.

"Welcome, my lady, to our squire instruction." David bowed with mocking delight. "Are you prepared to obey my every instruction and learn to use your weapons as every squire should?"

"I am, my lord." She stood still as he circled her. "Although I still do not understand what use this will be to me."

"It's so no one will kill your kitty again," Bert piped up.

David cringed. He knew Alisoun didn't want her distress announced to anyone. The woman hoarded her emotions and valued her privacy, and he wondered if she would take her unhappiness with him out on Bert.

He gave her too little credit. Alisoun stared at Bert in astonishment, then in a small voice said, "That is indeed a reason."

David jumped into the fray before any other indiscretions could be aired. "*First* we're going to learn how to shoot a bow and arrow."

"Aye!" Eudo grinned. Guy taught archery, and he assured David that in Eudo they had found a natural talent. Still too small to have any advantage in a close fight, Eudo found the singing flight of an arrow evened his chances for victory, and he relished every moment spent with a bow in his hand.

"Aye!" Bert imitated Eudo. She had her own miniature bow, and she practiced for hours trying to match her hero's skill.

"Set up the targets, squires." David picked up a training bow and a quiver of arrows. "I will instruct Lady Alisoun."

Bert set her heels in the dirt and glared. "I want you to instruct *me*!"

Eudo pushed her from behind. "My lord told us to set up the targets."

"He's *my* father."

"A good squire doesn't argue with his lord." Eudo started toward the shed that housed the training weapons. Over his shoulder, he yelled, "Lasses can't follow directions."

"I can, too." Bert scampered after him. "I can, too."

"Does Eudo resent you training me?" Alisoun asked.

David handed her the bow. "Hold this while I put the wrist and finger guards on you." She ought to learn to do it herself, he knew, but he wanted the chance to touch her, to stroke her skin with his fingers. "Nay, it's not you he resents. It's Bert." He glanced at the children as they dragged out the targets and argued about their location. "You'll be pleased to know Eudo also disapproves of my daughter's combat training."

"Why would I be pleased to know that?" She kept her gaze on his hands as they worked the leather over her wrist. "I taught Eudo to have respect for his lord and obey his every command."

"He obeys me."

"Cheerfully?"

"Not that," David admitted as he set the bowstring. "But Bert does make that difficult sometimes. Mayhap if you . . . nay, never mind, that's a stupid idea."

"What?"

"Really." Standing behind her, he placed the bow in her hand. "It's nothing."

"I do not think, my lord, that your ideas are nothing." She took a deep breath as he wrapped his arms around her.

Taking her hand, he showed her how to wrap her fingers around the string. "It just seems that if you show Bert affection and respect while we work here, mayhap Eudo would behave in a like manner."

"I always show every one of God's creatures respect."

He said nothing.

Grudgingly, she asked, "What kind of affection?"

"I've seen you place a hand on Eudo's shoulder when you praise him."

"Bert doesn't like me to touch her."

"That's because you only touch her to clean her. I'm talking about a gesture of regard."

She stood relaxed within the circle of his arms as she considered. Then she nodded decisively. "I could do that."

"And inquire about her progress with her studies."

"As far as I can see, she has no studies. She neither picks up a book nor learns womanly arts."

"Right now, she is learning to be a warrior."

"I don't approve of that. Why would I ask after her progress?"

He managed to keep the triumph from his tone, but only barely. "You're doing it, too."

"Only because—"

He could almost hear her thinking. *Only because I wanted to distract you from that diaper on the baby.* But she didn't say that.

"Only because you are right. If I am to be threatened, I need to be able to defend myself in some small degree."

He wanted to pull her against him and kiss her until he'd ruffled some of her dignity. He wanted to reward her for saying those so difficult words—*you are right*. He wanted to pledge himself to her again and again until she believed he would always protect her and hers.

Instead he shouted at a few of his servants who were loitering to watch him and Alisoun. "If you have nothing to do, I'm sure I can find you something." They wheeled away, and he told Alisoun, "Pull back the string with gentle yet firm tension. Back further. Back further. Pull it almost to your cheek and hold it higher. That's it. Now let it go."

She released the empty string and it struck her wrist guard with a sharp thump.

"Ouch." She dropped the bow and rubbed her arm. "That hurt!"

"Let's try it with an arrow." Pulling an arrow from the quiver, he set the nock in the string and showed her how to rest it on her fingers. The children hastily finished setting up the targets and ran back to their sides.

"Go ahead and practice, children," Alisoun called.

They paid no attention to her words. They focused totally on the point of the arrow as she pulled the string back once more.

"Hold it up! Use a finer tension! Hold it up!" David squinted as the bow quivered in her grasp. "Now, let it fly!"

Plowing a furrow along the dirt, the arrow came to rest against a clump of grass not five feet in front of her. The children stared at it in confounded silence.

David told Alisoun, "You can open your eyes now."

Her eyes popped open. "I didn't realize I'd closed them." She looked eagerly at the targets.

Bert's laughter exploded in a snort and Eudo smothered it with his hand. Bewildered, Alisoun looked at them, then looked again at the targets. Taking her head, David moved it down until she could see the abused and dirty arrow.

"You didn't point high enough," he said.

"Oh." She looked at the children again, but they had their merriment firmly under control. "I'll do it again."

One thing David had to say about Alisoun, she didn't give up easily. More arrow points ate dirt than in his entire history of teaching squires. At last he said, "That's enough for now. Your wrist will be swollen if you don't stop."

"I've almost got it." She set her chin with determination. "Just one more." Notching the arrow, she lifted the bow high, and let it fly . . . over the training ground, over the weapons shed, and out of sight.

David, Alisoun, and the children stood frozen, waiting, wondering.

They heard a squawk. One squawk, then nothing.

"What have I done?" Alisoun whispered.

One of the goose girls came flying around the shed, holding a dead gander by its feet. "Who did that?" she shouted. "Me best stud, killed by an arrow!" She turned the bird and showed the shaft embedded in the gander's head.

"I'm sorry," David shouted back. "It's my fault."

"Likely story." The girl shook her finger toward Eudo. "'Twas probably this one, wi' his fancy aimin' an' his foreign ways."

Bert shouldered her way to the front. "Nay, Nancy, 'twas me." She took the bow out of Alisoun's limp grip and waved it. "I'm getting good, aren't I?"

Nancy squinted at the bow, then at the child holding it. She wanted to call Bert a liar, but she didn't dare.

"Take the gander to the kitchen," David instructed. "We'll have him for dinner and my lady will get us a

new gander." He put his hand on her shoulder. "Won't
you?"

"Aye, and gladly, too." Alisoun tried to smile, but it
was nothing more than a lift of the lips to show her
teeth.

Nancy nodded resentfully, and when she disappeared again Alisoun turned to David. "I am so sorry."

"'Tis nothing." He rubbed her back.

"Your best gander!"

Bert patted her hip. "Nancy thinks all of the ganders
are her best gander."

Alisoun seemed to suddenly realize David and Bert
were touching her, while she herself had not complied
with David's request to give his child affection.
Awkwardly, she patted Bert on the head. The girl
looked up in astonishment. David waited, cringing, but
Bert just shrugged and moved away.

"Can we do the swords now?" Bert loved the swords
best. Laid out on a trestle table, the gray practice blades
shone in the sun. No rust speckled their surface; even
worn swords such as these merited good treatment. The
wooden swords, too, had been carefully formed and
kept for the younger boys' practice.

With reverent hands, Bert reached out and stroked
one of the iron blades.

Catching her wrist, David said, "Swords would be a
good idea." He thrust a wooden sword into her hand.
"With this."

She pouted, sure she wouldn't get her way but
resolved to try. "I'm big enough for a real sword."

"You're not."

"Let me try."

Hefting his own short sword, Eudo said, "A real
squire wouldn't beg like a girl."

Even Bert's ears turned red. David could see the tips

where they stuck out from her butchered hair. But she shut her mouth with a snap.

David turned to Alisoun. "We'll start you on a wooden sword, also."

Bert saw her chance to take her pique out on someone else. "Aren't you going to have her lift the broadsword?"

"Not this day." David spoke to Alisoun. "You hold the hilt in both your hands—"

"You made me pick up the broadsword first." Bert spoke in a singsong voice. "You always make the new swordsman pick up the broadsword first."

Annoyed, David said, "Nay, Bert."

"What's so entertaining about picking up the broadsword?" Alisoun fondled the handle of the biggest blade.

Bert smirked. "Have you ever picked one up?"

"You're such a baby," Eudo said in obvious disgust.

"She's not going to pick up a broadsword," David insisted.

"I think I would like to, now." Alisoun asked for permission with an appealing glance.

David glared at his daughter, then answered, "As you wish, my lady. However, they're very heavy and if you're not careful—"

She withdrew it from its sheath. It slid it off the table and the tip of the blade slapped to the ground.

"—you'll drop it." He tweaked Bert's hair hard enough to stop her from giggling, then moved to Alisoun's side. Again he took the opportunity to wrap his arms around her. Putting his hands over hers, he helped her lift it. "It's a good blade still," he told her. "Can you feel the balance? The weight?" Swaying back and forth, they swung it until it whistled. "In a fight, it's not necessarily the man with the most skill who wins. Often, it's the man with the most endurance."

"I understand. Let me hold it now."

"Don't make any sudden moves," he warned.

Never taking their gazes from the sword, the children moved away.

"Aye."

"I'm letting go now." He loosened his grip, and when she didn't immediately drop it, he stepped away.

She continued to move it, staring at the tip in amazement.

Then Bert said, "Lift it over your head."

David yelled, "Nay!"

He was too late. Alisoun brought the blade up. It hesitated just over her head, then tilted backward. She didn't have the strength to control it, but she didn't drop it. Instead she followed it as it tilted farther and farther, and at last she toppled backward.

She hit the ground as hard as one of her arrows.

David reached her side even as dust ruffled up. "Alisoun? Alisoun!"

She blinked her eyes open.

"Are you hurt?"

"It didn't feel good."

He slid his arm around her and helped her slowly sit up. Her wimple slid off the back of her head. She grabbed at it, but her braids dangled free and she grimaced. "Do you think—" David glanced at the children and lowered his voice, "—the babe is injured?"

"I think the babe is better cushioned than I am." She answered as quietly, then rubbed at her tailbone.

A small voice broke into their conversation. "I'm sorry."

David didn't turn his head, but Alisoun did.

"Daddy, I'm really, really sorry. I didn't know she'd hit so hard."

For the first time ever, David found himself thoroughly angry at his daughter. He could scarcely maintain a civil tone when he said, "Don't ask my forgiveness, Bert. Ask your stepmother's. She's the one who suffered."

"I beg your pardon, my lady." Bert fought tears now. "I didn't mean for you to get hurt."

"I am only bruised, Bertrade, and of course I forgive you." She reached over David's shoulder and patted the girl's head, and this time she did it comfortably. "After all, it's mostly your daddy's fault."

"My fault?" David reared back. "Why my fault?"

"Isn't that jest one you play on all your squires?"

Trying to be righteous, David proclaimed, "It gives them an idea of the work they need to do before they can be dubbed a knight."

"I think it's mean."

David found himself wanting to squirm.

"So why wouldn't your daughter want me to supply the same entertainment the other squires have provided?" She shook her head reprovingly. "I'm afraid you're going to have to take credit for this, David. Now help me up and we'll go to work."

When had he become the one who needed to be taught? Trying to regain control of the practice, David said, "We'll do the knifework now." Bert began to protest, but he stared at her until she shut her mouth, and he added, "'Twill be your most likely source of defense anyway, my lady."

Eudo put away the swords while Bert removed the wooden knives and put them on the table, never touching or asking to touch the real blades with their sharp edges. The children both showed off their best behavior, realizing, no doubt, that David had quickly reached his limit.

Too quickly, he admitted ruefully. If he had been sleeping regularly in Alisoun's bed, he might have felt secure enough to listen to Alisoun's reproval without becoming defensive.

Bert tugged at the hem of his gown. "I'll use the wooden blade, Daddy."

"Good." David nodded.

Eudo's hand hovered over the hilts. "Which blade would you like Lady Alisoun to use, my lord?"

"The light one," David answered.

Eudo handed it to Alisoun hilt first, and she accepted it with a gracious smile. "You have been good to allow me to interrupt your true instruction."

Bert wiggled in between them. "It's my true instruction, too."

Eudo rolled his eyes.

Without even seeing him, Bert said, "Well, it is!"

"It's harder than I expected." Alisoun cradled the knife between her two palms. "You must be very proud of your skills."

Inveterately honest, Bert was forced to admit, "I'm not good yet, but I'm a lot better than I used to be. You'll see. You'll get better, too."

Something loosened in David. The training session might have gone poorly, but his intuition had been correct. Bert was talking to Alisoun now. She saw her as someone who had to learn, to grow, someone whose apparent perfection had been hard won, and who was willing to study under those who knew more than she— possibly even from Bert.

David tugged on one of Alisoun's loose braids until she turned and looked at him. "Bert is one of my best pupils, and with Eudo's ingenuity he'll be the new legendary mercenary of England."

Eudo flushed and Bert grinned, and Alisoun

swung the knife enthusiastically. "Long live Bert and Eudo!"

Suddenly the end of the braid was dangling from David's hand.

He stared at it. He stared at her braid, shorter by five inches. He stared at an open-mouthed Bert, at round-eyed Eudo, and finally at Alisoun. Alisoun, too stunned to speak or move.

The moment seemed frozen in time.

Then a tiny sound broke their paralysis.

Alisoun choked.

"Don't cry," David begged, removing the dagger from her hand.

She choked again.

Bert wrapped one of her own mutilated locks around her finger. "It'll grow back."

"It's not so bad, my lady," Eudo said. "You've still got lots of hair left."

Alisoun laughed. Not too loudly, but she laughed.

After a moment, Bert joined her, and then Eudo.

Smiling, David shook his head at his three warriors. "I've never failed with a squire yet."

Alisoun laughed again. Giggling, Bert leaned against her for support, and Eudo straightened his face only to have his grave expression crumple beneath a new onslaught of amusement.

When Alisoun had gained control, she held out her other braid. "You might as well cut this off, too." David took it while she lifted the shortened hair on the other side. The string that held it was gone, cut off by her knife, and the braid unraveled in great, heavy waves.

He measured one side against the other, then evened them up with a clean slice.

She lifted her face to his. The smile still quivered on her lips. "I apologize for being so difficult a pupil."

The exertion, the laughter, the companionship had washed the stiffness from her face and left it open to him to read. Or had he just grown skilled at deciphering her thoughts? "A difficult pupil, aye. And just so you come away with a lesson you can use, let me tell you about the dagger."

Taking one of the wooden knives—he would take no chance with real steel—he pointed at each part of her body as he spoke. "If you have need to defend yourself or to attack another, aim for the eyes, the throat, or the gut."

"Not the heart?"

"The heart is the best place, but you're likely to hit the ribs and I think in your case the less difficulty, the better."

This time Eudo giggled out loud, and when David looked around he realized the children stood watching them, heads cocked, eyes bright with interest.

"Mama, will you come back tomorrow and practice with us again?"

Bert spoke without a shred of self-consciousness, but David wanted to clutch his heart and cheer at the same time. Alisoun has won his daughter over. She hadn't even tried, and he doubted she knew how she'd done it.

But Alisoun did know enough not to show surprise at her new title. "There's much in the keep which requires my attention, and I fear I'll not have the time to practice these skills as much as I obviously require." She sighed. "If only I had more help . . . "

Eudo stepped up. "A squire should know all manner of things around the keep, and so I would be honored to have you teach me all you know."

Bert stuck her skinny elbow into Eudo's ribs. "Hey! I was going to tell her to teach me!"

"You never wanted to work in the keep, and you're just a girl. No girl could learn knightly skills and a lady's skills at the same time. You'd collapse from brain fever."

"I would not!"

"Would, too." Eudo carefully inserted the daggers into their sheaths.

"Would not." She collected the wooden blades.

With his hand on her arm, David moved Alisoun away from the training ground. In a low voice, he explained, "That's how we got her to read. Bert always faces a challenge head-on."

"I'll remember." Alisoun tried to work the guard off of her hand, but her fingers shook and she finally extended her arm in appeal. "Would you help me with this? I did very little, yet I'm exhausted."

"Doing it badly is much more difficult than doing it well," he assured her, and they stopped before the gate of the herb garden while he worked the leather off her wrist.

"Yet *you* do it very well, and you must have started out as badly as I did."

He glanced up at her quizzically.

"Fine. Insinuate I performed more poorly than you." She tossed her half-braided hair over her shoulders. "But you must have started out with a little less skill than you have now."

"A little less." He freed her from the wrist guard and rubbed the bruised flesh there. "Your skin's too tender for this."

She ignored him. "And you became the best mercenary in England and France. You became the legendary mercenary David of Radcliffe."

With a wry twist to his mouth, he stripped off her finger guard and stuffed the leather into his pouch. "Aye, that's who I am. The legendary mercenary who fought a dragon and won."

"I think you have yourself confused with Saint George," she answered seriously. "But truly, with the practice you have performed at George's Cross and your experience, I would wager you are the best mercenary in England this day."

"Have you seen the herb garden?" He opened the gate and waved his arm inside.

"Aye." She stepped inside. "'Tis very well kept."

He hesitated. He didn't want to go inside with her. Not when her hair hung loose down her back. Not when amusement softened the curve of her mouth. But she kept talking, and he dared not cut off this communication. Not after so many days and nights of only polite conversation.

"Don't *you* think you're the best mercenary?"

He walked in and left the gate gaping behind him. "I'm not. Not anymore." She opened her mouth to protest, but he shook his head. "There's more to it than just skill, strength, and experience. I'll never fight like I did before, because I've lost my taste for killing."

She had leaned over to break off a sprig of mint, but she looked up at his words. "Really?"

Leaning against the wall, he watched her pluck the leaves and sniff them. "Battle is a young man's game, and only men who have no respect for death can face it with equanimity."

She tasted the mint and he could almost taste it with her. "Now you have respect for death?"

"I've seen the grief it can cause. I've lost dear comrades for no better reason than another knight on the circuit wanted his armor and got too enthusiastic in the melée."

Her soft whimper of sympathy soothed him, and he moved toward her. "I have something to lose now. I have a wife and a child—two children!" He corrected himself and she stroked her belly. "I think there are better ways to retain what I've earned than by battering myself bloody."

"Is that why you wed me?" She moved away as she asked the question, using a careless tone as if she cared nothing for the answer.

He suspected—he hoped—that she did. He should have chosen his words, taking care not to frighten her with undue emotion or anything less than good sense.

Instead he spoke from his heart. "I felt I owed you protection, but what I owed you and what I wanted to give you were two different things. I owed you security."

She stopped. He stopped. When he didn't finished, she asked, "What did you want to give me?"

"Love."

"Love?" She whirled and stared. "Love? That's nothing but stupid, romantic nonsense. Love doesn't exist!"

"I never thought so, either." He took one huge step and stood before her. "But I never thought someone like you existed, either."

"First you tell me you chose to be the kind of warrior whose thoughtful good sense makes you a welcome mate and I think I can tell you all and you will understand. Then you say something as crack-pated as—"

He gripped her arms. "Tell me."

"I can't."

"Tell me."

"It's not my secret to tell."

"But you're the one in danger."

Her eyes filled with tears. Her lips moved, but no sound came out.

"Have I ever betrayed your trust?"

"Nay."

"Then let me start you. Your dearest friend was married to Osbern, duke of Framlingford."

All expression left her face. She became Alisoun, countess of George's Cross, just as he had first met her. But now he knew how to read her.

Calmly, she replied, "Everyone knows that."

"She lost her affection for him." The tension around her mouth relaxed, and he realized he had guessed wrong. "Or maybe she loved him, but he beat her half to death."

Her jaw tightened.

So Osbern did beat his wife. This was no surprise to David. Most men did. "So she wanted to leave him, and you helped her."

"Why do you think that?"

"There's a wolf and a wolf cub in her coffin, my lady. Do you think I'm a fool who believes she turned into a wolf when she died? That's what you wanted, wasn't it? That if the coffin were ever opened, superstition would overwhelm suspicion and the wolf would be reburied as furtively as it was dug up."

Alisoun fixed her gaze over his shoulder, trying still to defeat him as he guessed at the chain of events which had brought them together.

David wouldn't allow it. Not anymore. Not when he was so close. Taking her chin, he made her look toward him and bent down so he filled her gaze. "You staged Lady Framlingford's death, then whisked her away . . . somewhere."

Alisoun's breath escaped her harshly now, and she trembled under his hands.

"Tell me where. Has she gone to a lover? Is she in one of your other castles? Have you sent her to France?"

Alisoun tried to shake her head.

"Ignorance is dangerous, Alisoun, at least in this case. Framlingford is dangerous. At least tell me where she is so I can—"

"Send her back?"

"You do think ill of me, don't you?" He didn't give her a chance to reply. "I have my friends, and believe me, Framlingford knows them not. If I could send her to them, he'd never find her and you would be innocent of any knowledge of her whereabouts."

"How would that stop him from stalking me?" She blasted him with the pyre of her frustration. "He won't be happy until he makes me hurt as he hurt . . . my friend."

"I won't let him hurt you."

"How will you stop him? You say you don't relish killing anymore. Well, Osbern does. He especially likes to do it slowly." Pale with disgust, Alisoun asked, "Do you know that he killed one of the pages in his care?"

"I had heard that." David didn't allow his compassion for one dead boy to divert him from his purpose. He needed to protect Alisoun and all connected with her, and so he said, "The lad had no connections— Osbern manages his cruelty as a cold-blooded sport."

"A sport." She nodded. "Aye."

"You are well connected. We can go to the king and—"

"Philippa is an heiress. The king married her to Osbern. If the king knew that I had helped her escape her husband, he would—"

"Philippa?"

Alisoun's hand flew to cover her mouth.

"Did you say Philippa?" Rage blew like a cold wind through his body, chilling his blood and bringing his terror to a new level. "By Goddes corpus, she's here in this castle now?"

Grasping his arm, she said, "I had to keep her with me. The babe was just born, and I dared not send her on a long trip."

Still he could scarcely comprehend the expanse of Alisoun's betrayal. "She's here? You never sent her anywhere away from you?"

"No one suspected she was anything but an impoverished cousin with an illegitimate child."

"In my own castle. I'm harboring Osbern's wife in my own castle." He closed his eyes against the immensity of the disaster.

"Osbern watched George's Cross. I feared to send her anywhere because I feared he would take her."

"Obviously he suspected, for he dug up that grave."

"He knew how I despised him. Once he broke both her legs." She shook him hard. "That's when he got her with child."

Pain twisted in David's gut. Aye, he knew Osbern. He despised Osbern. But David had a daughter, and a wife who carried their child. Osbern knew that somewhere his wife lived, and Osbern would never give up until he had her in his hands again. A measure of calm had returned to Alisoun. She knew what should be done but she seemed unable to comprehend the danger. "I promised I would keep Philippa and the baby safe, and with your help I can do it."

"You've given me no choice."

She enveloped him in an embrace. "You'll see the right of it soon enough. I know you will."

But she was wrong. He would never see the right of it. Not when they stepped out of the herb garden and heard the hail from the visitors beyond the drawbridge.

"Osbern, duke of Framlingford to visit his dear friend Sir David of Radcliffe."

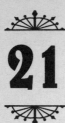

21

I have lived in castles all my life, and I've never known how it happens. Yet I've seen it time and again—rumors about the lord and lady travel at the speed of a spring tide. That day was no exception.

Within moments of Sir David and Lady Alisoun's disappearance into the herb garden, everyone knew that something of importance had occurred in the training yard. Somehow the lord and lady had come to an accord. The rains would again nourish the crops, the servants would quarrel no more—and the newlyweds would once again share a bed.

I admit I might have had something to do with that rumor, not by anything I said, but by my actions. It was a small thing, but I picked an apple off one of the fruit trees and gave it to Bert. Watching Sir David with Lady Alisoun had mellowed a bit of my adolescent intolerance of bratty tagalong girls, and the half of the castle folk who had found reason to linger in view of the herb garden gate noticed.

So when the call came from outside the gate that the duke of Framlingford waited for permission to enter, everyone scowled. It wasn't so much that he was considered an unsavory character. Everyone knew he was; his reputation resounded throughout England. But he was too lofty a man to be bothered with Lady Alisoun's servants, and Radcliffe had never been important enough to visit before. Yet he had come now, just when we wanted our lord and lady to have a chance to secure their peace.

Instead, Sir David marched Lady Alisoun out of the herb garden like an infuriated parent with a misbehaving child. She tried to shake him off, but he just walked her faster, and when she called to me, I had to run to catch up.

She grabbed me and dragged me with them. "Go into the keep," she said. "Tell my maids that Osbern, duke of Framlingford, has arrived. Make sure all of them know, and tell them to prepare a feast worthy of our honored guest."

She sounded urgent. Sir David looked grim. I nodded and ran.

Bert ran with me.

Why now? Alisoun wondered desperately. She needed time to accustom David to the fact of who Philippa really was, but time she did not have. The open gate and lowered drawbridge left the way open to any who chose to enter Radcliffe in the daylight hours, but with a courteous flourish, Osbern waited outside for permission. And what could they do? They had to let him in, treat him hospitably, and pretend nothing had ever happened.

The subterfuge made her feel ill. Asking David to share in it seemed unfair, and from the scowl on his face, he felt the same way. In a low, apologetic tone, she said, "David?"

David moved toward the gate. He didn't look at her. In no way did he acknowledge the plea in her tone. "We must welcome our guest."

"I beg you, David . . . "

He stopped and turned her to face him. He clutched her arm tightly. The black of his pupils had swallowed all the tenderness in his eyes. When he spoke, his deep voice grated like flesh over gravel. "I will do nothing. You took responsibility when you brought Philippa with you into my castle, and so I will simply hope no disaster overtakes us." Moving forward again, he dragged her behind him. "But when Osbern leaves, you and I will talk."

She had only a moment to realize that she'd underestimated the strength of his fury, then their heels clomped in hollow bursts on the wooden drawbridge.

"My lord!" David waved at the small party of horsemen waiting on the road. "Welcome to Radcliffe."

Osbern's face lit up at the sight of his host and hostess, and Alisoun had to close her eyes against the surge of anger and dismay.

With his sleek black hair and his flashing eyes, he appeared the embodiment of masculine beauty. His steed matched his hair and the background of his coat-of-arms matched his steed. He moved with an oiled grace, and kept himself in the best of fighting condition. He looked, in fact, the perfect knight.

He and his squire moved away from his knights to come before Alisoun and David. Osbern dismounted and strode forward to grasp their hands. "Is the rumor then true?" he asked. "Are you wed?"

"Lady Alisoun graciously consented to become my wife," David answered smoothly.

Osbern's fingers tightened uncomfortably on Alisoun's. "You are a lucky man," he said to David.

"Luck had nothing to do with it." David smiled with practiced ease. "I'm simply the better suitor."

Throwing back his head, Osbern boomed with laughter. "No false modesty from you, eh?"

"None at all." David freed himself from Osbern's grip and indicated the gate behind them. "But come inside and take refreshment. It's not often Radcliffe hosts so honored a guest as the duke of Framlingford."

"Best get used to it, Sir David." Now Osbern's fingers squeezed Alisoun's to the point of pain. "With Lady Alisoun as your wife, the king himself will lead the way."

David picked up her free hand and kissed it. "Aye, I've married a national treasure."

"That you have." Osbern kissed the hand he held, then in a voice meant just for her, he said, "But feel how cold her fingers are—and on such a summer's day."

Releasing her, he stepped up to David and they walked shoulder-to-shoulder into the bailey, leaving Alisoun staring at their backs.

So that was how the men would play it. Deceitful courtesy, smiling falsehoods, manly fellowship, and beneath it all, the knowledge that tormented them all. The knowledge of Philippa's existence.

Had Eudo told Philippa of Osbern's appearance? Alisoun stepped out, making a wide circle around David, Osbern, and the stable which seemed to have captured their attention. She hoped viewing the horses would keep them busy while she got to the keep and took the precaution of hiding Philippa.

Behind her, she heard the clomp of horses' hooves as Osbern's knights crossed the drawbridge, then the jingle of tack as they entered the bailey. It sounded as if they were getting closer to her. Even pursuing her. She glanced back.

The horses seemed about to ride her down. Astonished, she stopped and stared. The horses kept moving. The fully armored knights grinned beneath their helmets.

Then Osbern shouted, "Roger!"

The knights came to a halt, and the lead knight dismounted. He walked toward Alisoun, his hand on his sword. David started toward them at a run.

"Roger!" Osbern shouted again.

Lifting his hands, the knight removed his helmet and grinned, his one tooth winking in the light. "Do you remember me, my lady?"

Of course she remembered him. Roger of Bissonet, Osbern's steward and faithful servant—and another man who could recognize Philippa if he happened to see her.

David grabbed her arm and faced Roger. Without a smile, he said, "We greet you, Sir Knight, and offer our hospitality for you and your fine animal." He looked at all the knights. "For all of your fine steeds. If you'll go to the stable, my servants will show your squires where to place your horses. After you've ascertained they will have good care, please come to the great hall and wash down the dust of the road with our newly brewed ale."

Osbern loomed on her other side. Jerking his head toward the stable, he commanded, "Go on."

Roger bowed and signaled to the other knights, and they moved away.

Osbern took Alisoun's hand again and bowed over it with every evidence of contrition. "My pardon, Lady Alisoun. Roger is a mighty fighter, but he's not a deep thinker. He just wanted to greet you and didn't realize how his actions might alarm you."

Alisoun knew Osbern too well to believe his protestations. His charm scarcely covered his wretched soul, and that he bothered to use that charm at all spoke highly of his respect for David.

She must have paused too long before answering, for David answered for her. "It would never have occurred to Lady Alisoun to be alarmed by your knight, Your Grace. Her courage knows no bounds, and for that reason I have sworn always to protect her."

"Even from her own foolishness?" Osbern asked.

She found her tongue quickly enough this time. "I am the lady of George's Cross. I am never foolish." She moved toward the keep and to her dismay, both men walked behind her, an unshakable escort.

"Don't listen to her, Sir David." Osbern sighed in gusty melancholy. "I thought my dear wife above foolishness, also."

"What happened to change your mind?" David sounded no more than politely interested, but Alisoun detected the thread of steel in his tone.

"She was in such a hurry to show our child to her dear friend Lady Alisoun, she rose from childbed and rode to Beckon Castle. That's another of Lady Alisoun's holdings, if she hasn't told you. Philippa sickened there, so the ladies took to the road—I told you they were foolish—and went to George's Cross where my dear wife died of . . ." Osbern paused as if confused. "What was it she died of, Lady Alisoun?"

Alisoun climbed the stairs to the top, placed her hand on the door latch, and looked back down at Osbern. "To my enduring sorrow, Philippa and the babe died of a contagious fever."

"I have so few clear memories of that dreadful time." Osbern's sharp gaze remained at odds with his words. "What kind of fever was it?"

"A dreadful one."

"Ah, I remember now." Leaning against the wall, Osbern said to David, "That dread disease that swept away the life of my beloved wife was so severe, Lady Alisoun could not wait until I arrived to bury her. Lady Alisoun so feared an outbreak among her people she placed Philippa in the ground at George's Cross—the first duchess of Framlingford not buried in Framlingford's graveyard in the family plot."

Opening the door, Alisoun said, "There are a great many duchesses in your family plot, Osbern. Every duke in your family seems to have had an extraordinary number of wives. One less hardly matters."

"But it does." A smile played around Osbern's lips. "My father and my grandfather accounted for every one of their wives. I would hate to be less of a man than they were."

Alisoun meant to step inside. She knew she shouldn't answer, but the words popped out of her mouth unbidden. "Osbern, you are exactly the man they were."

"My thanks, lady." Osbern bowed with a flourish.

David pushed Alisoun inside and spoke to Osbern. "Come inside, my lord, and sample our humble hospitality."

With a light step, Osbern ran up and followed Alisoun closely. Too closely. "Ouch!" He had stepped on her heel, and he apologized while she slipped her boot back into place. She took two steps. He did it again. She turned on him this time and commanded, "Stay back."

"I thought you would want to know where I was," he answered. "And what I was doing."

The whoreson knew Philippa wasn't buried in that grave. He'd as good as said so. He knew she lived, and lived somewhere under Alisoun's protection. He acted as if he knew her to be here, at Radcliffe. Yet how was that possible? She had hoped that hiding Philippa so close at hand would distract him, should he ever discover the empty grave.

David spoke to Osbern as she fitted her boot to her foot again. "As long as I know where you are and what you're doing, my lady Alisoun need have no more than her normal prudence."

She should be grateful. David seemed to be dedicated to caring for her. But it was Philippa she worried about. Philippa, who had been married for her wealth. Philippa, who had no relatives to ensure her husband would treat her well.

Pausing beneath the arch that led into the great hall, Alisoun scanned it bitterly. But she had been wed for her wealth, too. She had no relatives to guarantee her safety. Women like her and Philippa were as vulnerable as that kitten David had given her—just as likely to be kicked as petted.

In the great hall, manservants assembled the trestle tables. The serving maids, both hers and David's, placed white cloths upon the head table. The pages polished the silver plate. Eudo placed the great salt before the noble guest's chair.

Nowhere did she see Philippa. God be praised, Philippa had vanished. Abruptly, Alisoun asked, "My lord, what brings you to Radcliffe and so far from the king?"

It was rude to demand his business before he'd had refreshment, but she had a reputation for coldness. Let it serve her now.

Predictably, Osbern only chuckled and shoved his way past her and to the fire. Looking freely around the hall, he dropped his cloak and gloves to the floor and paid no attention to the serving maids as they scurried to pick them up. His voice boomed out. "I detect Lady Alisoun's fine hand in your home, Sir David."

David, too, shoved his way past her. "You do indeed, Osbern. She hung the tapestries the first morning she arrived, and she's been busy ever since."

The great hall did look more impressive, Alisoun admitted. Just that morning, she'd set one of David's craftsmen to work on the wall behind the dais. Under Philippa's direction, he had painted the whitewash with red lines to represent masonry blocks, and within each block, he'd drawn a flower.

Philippa had supervised him. Where had she vanished?

"A fine woman, but better now that she has a man to guide her." Osbern watched Alisoun as she wandered farther into the huge chamber.

She heard him clearly. How could she not? He projected his voice so all could hear.

He asked, "Sir David, you will guide her, won't you?"

"I find Lady Alisoun needs little guidance," David answered. "Her wisdom is renowned throughout the land."

"Her wisdom, like all women's, is tainted with emotion."

David's eyes widened. "Are you saying my lady is emotional?"

Accepting the cup of ale Eudo poured him, Osbern drank before he replied. "Lady Alisoun does not show emotions as other women do, but I believe she has them, and I believe they run deep."

A shudder ran up Alisoun's spine.

Osbern stared into his cup as if he could read the truth in its depths. "Nothing could change the course of her emotions. Not the dictates of a mere man, not the dictates of the king, not even the dictates of God. She would make a dread enemy, for if she hated she would hate until she had harried you from the face of the earth." He looked up at her, his eyes gleaming. "Or for a good friend, she would sacrifice everything."

Controlling her expression, she said, "You see something that is not there, my lord."

"Do I? Perhaps." He traced the lip of the cup with his long finger, and his stacked rings glistened in the firelight. "Still, I think a husband will do well for you. After all, any husband who married you worked for his position through stealth and boldness, through bravery and cunning. He'll not want to lose the fruit of his labors for any reason."

Osbern always knew where to strike the telling blow. For her, he mocked her with the fact she'd been tricked by a master into marriage, and for her fortune only. For David, he suggested that her scheme to protect Philippa would result in the loss of that fortune.

Philippa. Alisoun had to maintain control of herself for Philippa. "You never told us why you are here."

"Ah. Lad, help me remove my armor." Eudo came at once to Osbern's aid while the man continued, "I had a fancy to travel about the countryside and found myself at George's Cross with my troop. There I found a most interesting arrangement. Sir Walter lay in bed, beaten mindless, advising that young man . . . what's his name?"

"Hugh," David said.

"Hugh," Osbern repeated. "Sir Walter was instructing Hugh in how to direct the operation of the castle. I found it fascinating that Lady Alisoun would leave her most valuable stronghold in the hands of a youth and someone so damaged."

"That was my decision," David said. "I've sent four messengers and received as many from them, and all seems to be well. Is that not the truth?"

"Your decision! Of course. I admired the wisdom of

the arrangement, especially since it gave you the freedom to come back to your stronghold at Radcliffe."

"So all is well at George's Cross?" David insisted.

"Very well. They served me an admirable meal." Osbern glanced at the table the servants had prepared for them. Although they had been unprepared for guests, Alisoun always assured herself a proper table had been set.

Osbern continued, "Sir Walter was not yet able to sit up and eat, but young Hugh kept me company, and entertained me highly, too."

Alisoun warmed to his praise. "Hugh is a youth of which any foster parent would be proud."

"Aye. It was he who told me you'd been married, and of all the wild rumors surrounding the ceremony's hurried occurrence." He looked pointedly at Alisoun's waist. "Have we a reason to congratulate you, Sir David?"

"Would you not always congratulate a bridegroom?" David parried.

Osbern took the rebuke with smiling good humor. "True, true."

His knights and his squire strode in with Guy on their heels. David's steward walked stiffly, annoyed about something, and he came at once to David's side. He spoke quietly, but Alisoun heard him. "Cheeky whoresons. They act as if they own Radcliffe."

Osbern must have heard, too, but he took no obvious offense. "Guy of the Archers, is it not?"

"My lord, the duke of Framlingford." Guy bent his head in reluctant homage. "I'm honored that you remember me."

"I never forget a good fighter, nor one who refused service with me."

Alisoun's respect for Guy rose.

"I could never leave Sir David's service." A commotion attracted Guy's attention, and he yelled, "Hey there. No fighting!" Roger and Ivo had dropped into an attack crouch. Guy swore and started into the circle which formed around them, but before he could reach them, Ivo dropped Roger with a single blow to the face.

Osbern cackled. "Stupid sot." Following Guy, he reached Roger and gave him a casual kick in the ribs, then told his other knights, "Two of you! Take him out and leave him in the stable. Let him sleep with the horses. The rest of you—we're guests here, and you'll make conversation with the lord's people, and show some deference for your hosts."

His knights obeyed without question, and as they mingled Alisoun realized Osbern might have a plan. Radcliffe's people were decent folk who saw no reason for subterfuge. If Osbern's knights spoke courteously, the men-at-arms and the maids would speak freely to their new comrades, and might they not tell of their special instructions to watch for strangers? Alisoun had done her best to keep her secrets, but too many others knew at least parts of them. How could she expect others to remain silent, especially when they didn't comprehend the hell of Philippa's experience?

"Come and sit in the place of honor, my lord." Alisoun indicated the place before the salt, and Osbern took it with an ease that showed how seldom anyone else took the place of honor before him.

"Daddy?"

At the sound of Bertrade's voice, Alisoun almost lost her fragile hold on her composure. What would Osbern say when he saw her stepdaughter's bizarre outfit and bearing? How would he mock her?

Sir David smiled. "Bertrade. How lovely you look."

The child stepped up beside him and tucked her hand into her father's, and Alisoun glanced at her quickly. Then she looked again, a lingering gaze, and her head buzzed with relief.

Bertrade had washed. She had brushed her hair. She had dressed in a gown. She looked like a girl, and she grinned at Alisoun in a manner that reminded her of David at his most mischievous.

Alisoun smiled back feebly, then noticed Lady Edlyn as she hovered in the background. She had helped the child, Alisoun guessed, and she smiled gravely when Alisoun mouthed her thanks.

Then Osbern spoke. "You have a daughter! Sir David, a daughter. How charming."

Something about his tone, his obvious pleasure, made Alisoun's stomach roil and David's smile disappear. Bertrade observed Osbern with her sharp gaze, then she bobbed a curtsy and moved to her place between Lady Edlyn and Guy.

Osbern ignored Bertrade thereafter, but Alisoun knew he hadn't forgotten her existence—and David had been reminded of his daughter's vulnerability.

The serving folk brought food, seated themselves, and dinner began in an atmosphere of conviviality.

False conviviality. Alisoun watched for Philippa. Osbern watched Alisoun. And David ate with every appearance of self-possession.

When had David learned her strategy?

Once their hunger had been sated, Osbern made random conversation—but with Osbern, nothing was unplanned. "Hugh told me a great deal about the people who accompanied you here. He spoke highly of your men-at-arms, Lady Alisoun. Also of your squire. What's his name?"

"Eudo," David said. "His name is Eudo."

"Is he the lad who helped me disrobe?" He indicated Eudo as the boy carried a large platter covered with sliced meat. "That boy? A good lad, indeed." When his own squire stuck out his foot and tripped Eudo, Osbern smothered a grin. "But he is clumsy."

Alisoun had seen it time and again. Osbern forgot, sometimes, that he played the part of benevolent duke. He never really thought anyone could stand in the way of what he desired.

Eudo picked himself up, stacked the meat back on the plate, and turning, knocked the heavy platter hard against the strange squire's leg. The platter rang with the chime of silver against bone, and the meat slices splattered into the squire's lap.

"What Eudo lacks in grace he makes up in guile." David answered Osbern as the two adolescents rolled on the floor in sudden, furious combat. "It is a trait which I require in my squires."

"An admirable quality."

Osbern seemed sincere, even when his squire groaned and curled up into a miserable ball. This man who had power, who had wealth, and who should have no need of guile, did admire it. He enjoyed watching others use their guile on him, and enjoyed more crushing any feeble schemes to influence him. Osbern wanted those around him to be nothing more than scurrying bedbugs, coming to him for sustenance yet fearing the swat of his hand.

Alisoun signaled to the manservants, and they hurried to the scene of the spill and helped Eudo clean the mess.

"Why don't your dogs eat it?" Osbern asked.

In her piping voice, Bertrade said, "My new mama doesn't allow us to feed the dogs during the meal. She says it's uncivilized."

"Really?" Osbern drawled. "And do you like your new mama's rules?"

Bertrade inspected him in the confident manner of a well-loved child. "Not all of them, but my daddy says we'll indulge her until she doesn't remember anymore."

A ripple of laughter swept the hall as Alisoun glared briefly at David.

Smiling that pleasant, toothy smile, Osbern said, "Sir David, I see you have the knack of handling Lady Alisoun."

"There's little hope of that—" he stared at his daughter, "—now."

"It seems I did know Lady Alisoun forbade the feeding of the dogs during the meal." Osbern wiped his knife clean and tucked it into his belt, signifying he had finished his meal. "Young Hugh told me when I visited George's Cross."

The page who collected the gravy-soaked trenchers for the poor came with his large container and held it for Osbern's offering.

"Your wife has made this place a home." Osbern lifted the trencher of bread which had held his stew. It hung, heavy with gravy, and he tossed it to one of the huge mastiffs at the rear of the hall.

Alisoun flinched as the other dogs pounced, trying to get a share. Their snarling disrupted the even tenor of conversation, and Osbern's contempt for his hostess and her rules brought an awkward silence.

"I don't like that man." Bertrade's voice echoed clearly through the hall, and Lady Edlyn shushed her.

Osbern seemed oblivious as he said, "Hugh told me so much about you, Lady Alisoun. He should probably be warned that not all visitors have benevolent intentions before he reveals some secret which you would prefer to remain unknown."

Hugh. Of course. He knew a great deal about fighting and almost nothing about people, and Osbern could have led the conversation until he learned just what he wished. Had Hugh mentioned Philippa by name? Alisoun wondered.

"Aye, Sir David, how I envy you your clever daughter, your perfect wife, your many homes, your people who love you."

Hugh had. Aye, that explained Osbern's sudden visit, and the threats that grew ever more bold. He planted the arrows of doubt and fear successfully, striking at David's heart.

Even as he spoke, the servants and squires who belonged to David and Alisoun glanced at each other, at their plates, or at the floor. That threatening tone projected well, and everyone understood too well how Osbern's power could be turned against them.

"So many people who depend on you, Sir David." Osbern smoothed Alisoun's hand before she snatched it out of reach. "What would happen to them if you were challenged to combat and you died? What would happen to them if someone discovered that you harbored a fugitive against the rules of God and king? I shudder to think—"

A dim, solitary figure appeared in the shadowed doorway of the solar, and before Alisoun could move, Philippa spoke. "I'm here, Osbern."

22

Alisoun jumped to her feet, but Osbern moved more quickly. He shoved his chair back and cried, "Dearest!"

She moved to intercept him, but he jumped the table.

David grasped her arm. "Let him go."

"He'll hurt her."

Osbern reached Philippa and gathered her into his arms.

"He isn't hurting her."

"Not now."

After a brief hesitation, Philippa embraced Osbern and buried her face in his chest.

Guy hurried from his place to their sides. "What's happening?"

"Can't you see?" David asked. "Osbern found his long-lost wife."

"Philippa?" Guy paled. "Philippa is married to that lout?"

David nodded. "So it would appear."

Someone might have been strangling him, so garbled was Guy's voice. "We must rescue her."

"She came out on her own," David said.

"My wife!" Osbern turned Philippa toward the great hall and wiped a tear from his eye. "The wife I thought dead has returned to me. 'Tis a miracle. A miracle!"

Osbern's men cheered and a smile quivered on Philippa's lips.

"That's why he's been talking so loud," Alisoun said. "He knew she was hiding here somewhere."

"Probably." She tried to move toward them again, but David jerked her so hard he bruised her. "But she made her decision."

"Of course she came out." Alisoun could scarcely speak for fear and indignation. "She's my friend, and he threatened us."

"I'm not deaf."

Anguished, Alisoun said, "We can't let him take her."

"She made her decision," David repeated, and he lost patience with her at last. "Do you think we can keep a man from his wife?"

With a groan of defeat, Guy backed away toward the shadows by the stairwell.

David continued relentlessly. "And Osbern's not just any man. He is the king's cousin. He's a great knight."

"He almost killed her."

With gestures and smiles, Osbern indicated his delight in recovering his wife. If Alisoun hadn't known him as a slippery worm, she might have even been convinced.

"If what you told me in the herb garden is true, Philippa is one of the king's heiresses. Osbern wouldn't risk the king's anger by *killing* her."

"Oh? He'll only beat her senseless, and that's acceptable?" Furious with his stupid, unfeeling logic, Alisoun cried, "And who's going to know if he kills her? Who's going to care? The women all know the truth about Osbern, but the men are too stupid or too unsympathetic to notice."

"Daddy?" Sensitive to the anger and pain in the hall, Bertrade had crept close. "What's wrong? Why are you fighting?"

"We're not fighting, sweetling." David hugged her to his side, but still he kept his grip on Alisoun's arm. "Your new mama is just going to miss her maid, that's all."

"Lady Alisoun . . ." Edlyn whispered the name as if it were a talisman. No girl who had been betrothed had any business witnessing such a scene, but Alisoun had no tenderness left over with which to comfort her. All Alisoun's emotions bubbled in a brew of anguish for her dear friend Philippa. For the friend she would never see again.

Philippa and Osbern stood before the table, and Philippa said, "Alisoun? I'm going back with him."

Turning to David, Alisoun demanded, "Challenge him."

David flushed ruddy red. "I can't challenge him."

"This is what I hired you for. The time has come to earn your wages. Challenge him."

"It would do no good."

Osbern chuckled, a sound that slipped and congealed and clogged Alisoun's desperation. "Don't you know, my dear? *I* am the king's new champion."

"What do you mean?" Such a stupid question, but Alisoun couldn't have understood him correctly.

"I mean that your Sir David and I fought before the king, and I defeated Sir David in combat."

It wasn't possible. It simply wasn't possible.

But David shook her arm. "I told you I was defeated. You didn't care. You insisted on hiring me."

"You never told me."

"You didn't identify *your* enemy. You wouldn't tell me who tormented you. If you had, my lady, I would have spoken at once. My defeat at the hands of the duke of Framlingford is not easily forgotten."

So her clever plan had been doomed from the very beginning, and all because she hadn't investigated properly. She'd fixed her mind on the legendary mercenary Sir David, and now Osbern would take his wife and baby away and no one would fight for her. Helpless rage swelled in Alisoun, and she said to Philippa, "Forgive me."

"There's nothing to forgive," Philippa said. "You sheltered me, but I'm going back with him now."

Osbern gloated. "She loves me, Alisoun."

"I'll be a better wife to him this time," Philippa said hastily.

"You were always a good wife." Alisoun's voice rasped in her throat.

Osbern continued as if the women had never spoken. "I hold no grudge against you, Sir David. I recognize your wife's hand in this, and I'll not bring siege or have the king strip you of the lands for which you labored so desperately—as long as nothing else like this ever happens again."

"That means much to me." David acknowledged Osbern's words as if they were a boon.

"You gilled freak." Alisoun didn't even know who she insulted. Then she did. "You worthless traitor." She'd always known Osbern to be the lowest form of scum, but David . . . David she had believed in. David she had thought to be truly a legend, and now he sent a woman to her death to hold his land and her wealth.

"I'm doing the right thing," David said. "Probably for the first time in my life."

"Let me go." Alisoun jerked at his grip. "Let me go!" Freeing herself, she ran around the table and knelt at Philippa's feet. "I promised to keep you safe . . . I promised, and I failed."

Lady Edlyn released a stifled sob, and as if that signaled the end of restraint, the other maids began to sniffle.

"Nay." Philippa touched the top of Alisoun's head. "Never think so. You are my dearest friend."

One by one the women in the hall broke down, and Osbern snorted in disgust and called his men. "Come on, we're going while there's still daylight to get away from here. Philippa, we're leaving *now*."

He dragged her toward the outer door while Philippa called back, "You didn't break your promise. Always remember your promise."

And Alisoun's eyes, shut tightly against the tears, popped open. The babe. She'd promised to keep the babe from harm, too, and Philippa was now leaving— without Hazel. Osbern must have forgotten about her in his triumph.

But David didn't remember the babe, either. He just couldn't bear the sobbing. He couldn't believe the phalanx of female eyes that glared at him so disdainfully. Even his dear friend Guy of the Archers, the comrade who knew David's trials, stared at David with a most peculiar distaste.

Mostly, he couldn't sit there and look at Alisoun, a dazed and battered expression on her face, kneeling on the floor before the place where her friend had stood.

"And I sure as hell don't trust that bastard to leave without trouble," he muttered to himself as he jumped to his feet and followed Osbern, his men, and his wife out the door.

The afternoon sun had burned its way through the clouds and David squinted at the tangle of men around his stable. Roger swayed in the saddle, the lump on his head closing one eye, while the rest of them mocked him. The growl of their voices reached David clearly, as did Osbern's command. "Just do as I tell you and ride. I have what I came for."

He mounted his charger and pulled Philippa up before him, settling her without cruelty. Indeed, he played the role of loving husband well, for Philippa smiled tremulously when he circled her waist with his arm.

David found relief in the display. After all, Alisoun could be wrong. Mayhap Osbern had been a little rough with Philippa and the woman had run crying to Alisoun. Mayhap Philippa was like David's first wife, given to exaggeration, and Alisoun had taken a whisper of pain and turned it into a shout. His first wife had been like that. So all women must be like that.

Osbern's voice rang out over the jangle of tack and his men's shouting. "Philippa? Where's the babe?"

The babe. David staggered back against the wall. Where was Philippa's babe?

The sounds of their leave-taking died, and everyone stared at Osbern and Philippa.

"She died, Osbern." Philippa's eyes glistened with tears, but her voice sounded strong and true. "I was weaning her and she got the fever and . . . she died."

"A real fever this time?" Osbern caught sight of David and prodded his stallion to a brief gallop, then jerked him to an abrupt halt in front of the stairs. "My long-lost wife says our child has died. Tell me, Sir David, is this true?"

Sunshine seemed to dim as David stared at Osbern, so smug and triumphant, and at his wife, pleading and contrite. Firmly, without a hint of indecision, he lied. "Your daughter died but two weeks ago. We all mourn her death."

Nothing about Philippa changed, but David felt her gratitude like a reproach.

"'Tis a shame, indeed." Osbern's eyes gleamed. "But that babe was young and only a girl child. We can always make another child."

Philippa winced.

Shaking her shoulder, Osbern asked, "Can't we, Philippa?"

Obediently, she replied. "Indeed, my lord, we can."

"You did what was right, Sir David, never doubt it." Osbern lifted his hand in farewell, and at that moment, David saw it.

A gold ring, a long oval, with the crest of Osbern's family etched into the metal.

A ram. The duke of Framlingford's crest, David knew, was a ram.

He stared at that ring. The bright yellow burned into his brain.

Osbern rode away. His men followed him. The bailey quieted once more.

And still David saw that ring.

Fingering the latch, he opened the door and stumbled inside the keep. The passage to the great hall seemed darker than usual. The noises the servants made clearing away dinner seemed far away and alien.

That ring. That damned ring.

Not even Osbern could have done that to a baby. To an *infant*. Hazel had not been even a month old when Philippa had fled from Osbern. But Philippa, that adoring mother, had abandoned her child to go with her husband. What other reason could she have than to protect her babe?

The stones rasped his fingers as he groped along the wall. Agony rasped his mind as he groped toward the truth.

Had Osbern taken his signet ring, heated it, and branded the babe on the tender skin of Hazel's rump? Would he be so perverted, so twisted, so cruel?

The opening to the great hall yawned before David. He wanted to be with Alisoun. He needed to comfort her, to wipe that lost expression from her face. He needed to talk to her, to discover the truth and deal with it as he could. He needed guidance, and Alisoun would be the one to give it to him.

But first one manservant hurried past him holding a pile of unwashed dishes, and he spoke not a word to his master. Then a maid hurried past him holding a wad of dirty clothing, and another holding a pile of soiled linen. He might not have been there, for all the interest he generated.

Mayhap he longed to be elsewhere so fervently he had made himself disappear. Absently, he touched his face. He *was* here, though. Wishing hadn't changed that.

As soon as he stepped into the great hall, he realized the busy servants formed only the edge of a whirlwind. In here, activity spun in ever-widening circles. At the center of the whirlwind stood Alisoun, trunks gaping open all around her.

Did she feel bruised and tattered by the pain of losing Philippa? If so, she showed no evidence of it now. The Alisoun he'd first met had returned: controlled, determined, in charge. As he listened, he heard her direct her maids to pack her trunks for travel, and slowly he digested the fact that she planned to depart.

Depart. Striding forward, he loudly demanded, "Where do you think you are going?"

For one brief moment, the movement in the great hall faltered. Then once again it commenced, more quickly, more emphatically, and everyone, it seemed, pointedly ignored his presence.

Everyone except Alisoun.

"I'm leaving," she said.

"Leaving."

"I hired you to keep me and my people safe, and this you failed to do. I have no use for you now."

The maid who hauled her night soil got more respect than she gave him. Worse, he feared he deserved her contempt, and the faint curl of inner shame translated itself into ire. "You forget, madam, that you are my wife."

She stood without moving, her hands curled loosely at her sides. "Try as hard as I can, I can't forget that."

She made him so angry! All calm disdain while he seethed with questions and dread. In as nasty a tone as he could forge, he asked, "What if I don't let you go?"

"But you're so good at letting people go." She spoke without expression, but somehow she made her opinion of him clear. "Look how well you did with Philippa."

He strode forward, furious at the implied accusation of cowardice. "What would you have me do? Let Osbern destroy my family to protect her?"

"Your family?" Alisoun laughed lightly. "What about your lands, the wealth which I brought you? Shouldn't you mention your anxiety for them?"

"I worked hard for what I have." Dismayed by his own defensiveness, he tried to explain. "I have the right to want to protect it."

That destroyed her equanimity. Fists clenched, eyes sparking, Alisoun said, "Aye, and be damned to the life destroyed when you do."

His fury rose to meet hers. "Who are you to so criticize me? A stiff, humorless, former spinster without a drop of love in your veins to sweeten your disposition."

Her momentary spark faded. "None at all," she agreed.

Her restraint only made him madder, and he lashed out. "I only married you because I felt sorry for you."

"And for the money," she reminded him. "Let's not forget the money."

"Damn the money." He meant it, too. "And damn you!" That he didn't mean, but the words had been spoken and he couldn't call them back.

The slight tremble of her lips, the downward tilt of her brows—aye, on her face for those with eyes to see was evidence of her anguish. "I have broken a vow I made before God—to protect Philippa. So I *am* damned, if that gives you pleasure."

"You made a vow before God to obey me, too." He expected her to defend herself, but Alisoun surprised him.

She declared her independence. "What is one more broken vow?"

"You hold our wedding vows invalid?"

"I hold them as unimportant." Lady Edlyn came out of the solar, holding Hazel, and Alisoun held out her arms for her. "I suppose we should be grateful you didn't remember the babe, or Osbern would have another helpless soul to torment."

"Nay!" But no one had heard him lie to save Hazel, and who among these accusers would believe him if he told them?

Alisoun still handled Hazel as if she were some foreign creature, but David thought Alisoun needed that child's comfort right now more than the child needed Alisoun's.

"I'll send you an allowance every month," Alisoun

said. "George's Cross will remain my primary residence, and when I've settled there you might think about sending Bertrade to me."

His gaze shifted to his daughter. She sat on her stool, shoulders hunched, knees drawn up, with Alisoun's kitten in her lap. The gown she'd worn so proudly had twisted sideways until it wrinkled in a tight circle. Guy stood behind her, leaning against the wall, his gaze fixed on the child.

"I offered to take her now, but she doesn't want to go. She still has an affection for you, of course."

"Generous of you," he muttered.

Alisoun dismissed him without a glance and went to Bert. Kneeling beside his daughter, Alisoun spoke softly, petting the cat in Bert's lap until the creature stretched luxuriously. Smiling with tremulous interest, Bert replied, then with a quick glance at him, her smile faded.

Rising, Alisoun commanded, "Do send her when you can. She deserves a proper upbringing."

He wanted to argue that she, with her inexperience, couldn't raise his child properly, but the servants distracted him as they snapped locks on the trunks and bound them with leather straps. This was moving too fast. "You can't have packed already."

"You needed almost everything I brought to Radcliffe, so I'm leaving it here. What I have at George's Cross will suffice me until I can send to market once more."

Ivo and Gunnewate each hoisted a trunk onto their shoulders and strode past him, paying him less attention than they would a cockroach.

Desperate to halt this relentless procession, David said, "You need protection on the road and these two have already proved themselves unworthy."

"My men are sufficient for the normal hazards of thief and brigand." Alisoun allowed Lady Edlyn to help her with her cloak. "No one stalks me now." With an unladylike snort, she said, "I suppose you could say you have done what you were hired to do. You removed the threat from my life." She walked past him to the door, her maids trailing after her. There she half-turned. "Good-bye, Sir David. I wish you health, life and happiness in the future."

"Wait!" He hurried toward her and found his way blocked by a gauntlet of irritated maids. Craning his neck, he called, "What about our child?"

"I will send you word when it is born, and if you wish you may come and visit. Beyond that you have no rights."

23

I hated to stay, but what was I to do? That little girl's world had collapsed on her, and she didn't really understand why. It wasn't as if I liked Bert. A stupid, scrawny thing, all scabby knees and big eyes, but she knew her sire had done something dreadfully wrong.

So when Sir David stumbled into the great hall after Lady Alisoun left, only three people remained to face him. Guy of the Archers, Bert, and me. Without waiting for anyone to speak, Sir David demanded, "What did you want me to do? Let Osbern murder Bert and destroy us all?"

"I didn't say a word," Guy answered, but he didn't have to. He made his opinion clear when he moved away from Sir David's reaching hand.

Sir David hesitated, then his hand dropped. "I didn't have a choice."

"If you don't mind," Guy said, "I have duties in the south tower with the men. The sewage pond is directly below, but even so the stench seems less intense there."

*He walked out of the great hall and we knew when he
stepped outside, because he slammed the door so hard
the very stones shook.*

*"Well, damn him, too." Sir David dropped into his
chair and looked around. "Bert! At least you didn't
want to go with her, did you?"*

*"Nay." But Bert didn't sound any too certain, and
she leaned over the cat in her lap.*

*Sir David observed the way she petted the animal, and
he snorted. "She even left behind the kitten I gave her."*

*"I asked for it." Bert scratched the kitten under the
chin. "It reminds me of my new mama, because it'll
scratch if you try to hurt it but it's all soft and clean and
cuddly if you're nice."*

Looking wretched, Sir David stared at his daughter.

"Daddy?"

*Bert whispered, but Sir David heard her. "What,
sweetling?"*

"Weren't you nice to my new mama?"

*"I was just sensible. I thought she liked sensible
men, but I hazard I was wrong." His hands curled and
uncurled. "What did she say to you?"*

"When?"

"When she knelt down and talked before she left?"

*"We talked about the kitty's name," Bert answered.
"She wanted it to have a name so I could tell her about it
in the letters we will write." Picking up the kitten, she
rubbed it against her cheek and it purred so loud in that
empty room I could hear it. "She liked the name I picked."*

*Sir David seemed incapable of speech, so I asked,
"What did you name it?"*

*"It's black with white, so I named it Clover after one
of the cows." Bert beamed at me through her tangled
hair. "Can you remember that?"*

"She named the cat." Sir David rubbed both his

*temples with his hands, then lifted himself with a roar.
"I need ale. Where's the ale?"*

*I ran to get it for him, and that was the last coherent
sentence we heard from him for the next drought-
stricken eight days.*

I was glad I stayed for Bert.

Sir David of Radcliffe opened his eyes and stared. This
time he knew where he was. Those large, horizontal,
treelike objects would soon resolve themselves into the
reeds on the floor of his great hall. The fond kisses
pressed on his ear were the gifts of his best hunting
dog, and the panting that surrounded him was only the
pack gathered around him for warmth. He'd woken too
many times to the same scene and the same sounds to
be mystified by them now.

Groaning, he tried to raise himself off the floor while
holding his head in his hands. It didn't work. Either he
could push himself erect or he could hold his head, but he
couldn't do both. And he really needed to sit up, because
he was going to puke. "Eudo," he moaned. "Guy."

No one answered. Probably they were too disgusted
with him to stay in the same room. And why not? He
could scarcely stay with himself.

"Bert?"

She was gone, too. Praise God for Eudo. Sir David
didn't remember much, but he knew that Eudo had
kept Bert entertained while her father tried to find
peace in the bottom of a jug of ale.

Too bad every time he looked into a mug, Alisoun's
face floated there, staring at him.

Of course, it was worse when he closed his eyes.
Then he saw poor, pathetic Philippa leaving, the pris-
oner of her own husband.

Was she still alive?

"Nay!" He flung up his hands to block the thought, and the motion brought up his dinner. Rolling away, he waited until the chamber stopped spinning. He held onto the bench, pulled himself up, and staggered to the door. Flinging it open, he stepped outside and lurched, blinded by the light. The sun hadn't been so bright and hot since last summer, and it was all the sun's fault when he missed the first step, caught himself, missed again, and tumbled down the stairs. As he lay in the dry dust at the bottom, he realized that if he hadn't been so drunk, he would have killed himself.

He wanted to see Bert, explain himself to Guy, and make himself a hero in Eudo's eyes once more. And in his own eyes, too. It seemed that mattered the most.

Listening, he heard voices, and he hoisted himself to his feet once more and started toward the training yard. He rounded the corner and saw Eudo with his arms around Bert, showing her how to shoot a bow. The sight brought David to a skidding halt.

"Sir David!" Eudo jumped away from Bert guiltily. "I was just showing her . . . "

Bert stared at Eudo as if he had gone mad, and David realized that while the lad found comfort in holding Bert, Bert thought his embrace nothing but kindness. David said, "Fine. My thanks. You've kept her entertained and done her no harm. I won't forget." Sitting down on a stump, he waved them on. "Go ahead. Let me see what she's learned."

As Eudo helped Bert place her arrow into the bowstring, David remembered that he'd held Alisoun just the same way, demonstrating how to shoot an arrow while absorbing her vitality. Now that vitality had disappeared from his life, and he had no one to blame but himself.

If it had been up to Osbern, he'd never have known what he missed. That worthless poltroon had tried to kill Alisoun before David had even met her. He'd tormented her, beaten Sir Walter, frightened her people, and David had done nothing to avenge her. David could think of little else.

It had taken eight days of trying to justify himself to himself, but now he knew. Alisoun had done what was right, and not what was proper. He had done what was proper, and not what was right. He had sent Philippa back to her husband and possibly to her death, because he was a coward, looking out for himself, fearing the king's wrath, trying to hang on to his possessions at the cost of his confidence.

He had a lesson to teach Osbern. He'd already learned his own.

"Did you see, Daddy? Did you see?" Bert stuck her face into his and pointed at the target. "I got close!"

"You did!" The arrow quivered in the fence behind the target, and David puffed with pride. "You're Daddy's brave girl, and I'm glad, because I've got something to tell you. Something to tell everyone at Radcliffe." He waved Eudo over. "You, too, but where's Guy?"

The children glanced at each other. "Guy?" Eudo's gaze slid away. "Why, I believe he had to ride . . . somewhere."

"Somewhere?"

"Somewhere . . . else."

David didn't need to seek any more explanation. Guy had left Radcliffe.

"Very well," he said. "Guy is gone, and I'm going, too."

"You're going?" Bert, his indomitable Bert, started to cry.

Pulling her onto his lap, David said, "I haven't really been here since Alisoun left, anyway."

"I know, but everyone keeps leaving." Bert put her head on his shoulder and bawled.

David hadn't known he could feel any worse, but he did now. He petted his daughter and wondered if Eudo would start crying soon. The squire seemed to be struggling with his emotions also, and David found himself explaining his actions to a lad and a lass. "I made a mistake. Now I'm going to go and fix it."

Bert stopped sobbing and started listening. Eudo tilted his head and narrowed his eyes.

"I'm going to go get Philippa back from her husband. The only way to do that, I imagine, is to—" he shuddered as he remembered the result of his last challenge, "—kill him."

He had the complete attention of both children now.

"There's a good chance I'll die in the attempt." He waited to hear Bert's yell, but she remained mute and he thought perhaps she didn't understand.

Eudo stammered with excitement. "I'll prepare and go with you."

"Go with me?"

"I am your squire."

"Don't you understand? I said I might be . . ." He noticed the eager, quivering tension of the lad, and he hadn't the heart to finish the sentence. "You are my squire, and I regret leaving you here, but I depend on you for something much more important than passing me my weapons."

Eudo withered, and David could see his thoughts. His first chance to participate in combat, and David denied him. "What do you require of me, Sir David?"

"It is a mighty quest which I lay on you, and I pray you are worthy of my trust."

"I'm worthy!"

Speaking slowly and clearly, David said, "Should I not return, I rely on you to take my beloved daughter to George's Cross, to Lady Alisoun."

Eudo's sideways glance at Bert told the tale. He wanted to fight in battle, not babysit a lass.

Taking his shoulder, David leaned close to Eudo's face and tried to impress him with the importance of this responsibility. "You remember the journey here, Eudo. It was dark and fraught with danger. There were wolves, and two children alone will attract thieves."

Now Eudo understood. He blanched at the mention of wolves and his hand went to his knife.

"But Guy is gone and I fear that, should Osbern kill me, he'll send men to take Bert—" David hugged her closer, "—and you can't allow that."

Indignant, Bert struggled against his grip. "I won't let them take me, Daddy."

"I know you won't, Bertie, but you'll let Eudo help you." With a lift of the brow, David indicated to Eudo the hazard he had set him, not just in the journey, but in the handling of Bert. "Eudo, there's no one else to do it. When Osbern sends, his knights will first tell of my defeat, then try to bribe my men. One of them will take the bribe and give Bert up. That's why I trust you, Eudo, and not them. You've proved your honesty to me."

Eudo's young mouth firmed, and David didn't care that the lad had no whiskers yet or that his voice occasionally squeaked. Knowing Eudo would care for Bert eased his worry. "You'll have to be wary and ready to slip away unseen." David took one of Eudo's hands in his. "This is going to be much, much worse than that thing in the graveyard. You'll be constantly frightened, but remember the nettles you planted in the rocks to protect Lady Alisoun from the archer?"

Eudo nodded.

"That's the kind of ingenuity that will get Bert to George's Cross."

"I'll get her to George's Cross, sir. I swear I will."

"I know you will. Once there, Lady Alisoun will take care of you."

Now Bert piped up and showed how little she truly comprehended. "Daddy, are you going to go fight that nasty man and get Philippa back?"

"I'm going to go fight him." And the memory of their last battle rose to haunt him. Taking a deep breath, he tried to calm the sudden pounding of his heart. "I'm going to try to kill him, because he deserves it. And I'm going to make it safe for Philippa to have her baby with her once more."

The children didn't hear his doubt. They only heard the magnificence of his goal, and their faces shone with pride and admiration.

Bert grinned, and Sir David saw the gap where she'd lost a tooth within the last few days. In his drunken stupor, he hadn't notice, but she forgave him—all because she loved him.

She said, "I know you'll save her. You'll come back, because you're the best warrior in the land and I love you a lot."

The faith she had! And Eudo stood with his chest thrown out and a great smile on his face, too. Crushing them in his arms, David said, "I love you both, too." Was love really so strong a bridge between souls? His granny had said it was. She said that even after his death, his love would continue, warm like a fire. Tentatively, feeling like a fool for entrusting this message to children, he said, "I want you to do one thing for me. Will you tell Lady Alisoun that I love her?"

If anything, they smiled more. "Oh, aye, Daddy, I'll tell her," Bert promised.

"I will, too, Sir David." Eudo started to walk away.

"Where are you going?" David asked.

"To get your armor and your weapons. Isn't that what your squire is supposed to do?"

"Aye. Aye, that's what my squire is supposed to do."

The carts started down the road from George's Cross to the village below. Laden with linens, with silk for a wedding gown and presents to please Edlyn's new lord, they represented the finest trousseau Alisoun could assemble for the girl who had grown to mean so much to her.

Edlyn stood, her feet firmly planted in the bailey, and looked around at the buildings and the keep as if she could impress the images on her heart forever. Impulsively, she turned to Alisoun. "Couldn't I stay until—"

"Until when?" Alisoun tried to smile, but her lips trembled too much. "Until Hazel grows used to me and accepts me as her mother? Until I have this babe? Until . . . until when?"

"You're just so alone," Edlyn burst out. "Heath is no substitute for Philippa. Hazel is no substitute for me. And Sir Walter . . . "

She hesitated. No one had spoken David's name in Alisoun's presence since they'd left that breeding ground of bitterness called Radcliffe. With a composure that no longer came naturally, Alisoun said, "Nay, Sir Walter is no substitute for Sir David, at least when I need companionship."

"He just seemed the man who could please you," Edlyn burst out. "Will you ever forgive him?"

"Nay." Just that one word, flat and final.

"I wish . . ."

"So do I, but wishing cannot mend a broken fence." Alisoun touched Edlyn on the shoulder. "Anyway, when I took you with me to Radcliffe, I told myself your bridegroom wouldn't notice another month, but you have to ride south before winter comes, for I believe he *will* notice another year."

"At his age, what's another year?"

Alisoun couldn't help it; she laughed at the puckish expression on Edlyn's face. Then Edlyn laughed, too, accepting her fate a little better.

"Hey!"

A man's shout interrupted them, and Edlyn's face lit up. "Hugh." His name was only an exhalation, but the joy in her voice vibrated through Alisoun. Glowing with youth and spirit, Edlyn waved enthusiastically at the man she loved with an unrequited passion.

Loping over, he stood next to them, a big, stupid youth who had no thoughts in his head beyond the security of George's Cross, his practice that day on the training yard, and his ambitions. Without even knowing it, he crushed Edlyn's hopes. "Are you leaving today? I hadn't realized." Enveloping her in a fraternal hug, he said, "God speed you on your journey, and I wish you the greatest happiness with your new husband."

"My thanks." Edlyn said it to his back as he hurried off.

"He takes his duty to protect my demesne seriously." Alisoun found herself making excuses to combat the woeful expression on Edlyn's face.

"What will he do when Sir Walter is able to resume his duties once more?" Edlyn asked.

"We'll knight him." Alisoun looked ahead to that day when she would have to make that decision, and it seemed like just one more burden placed back on her shoulders by David's perfidy. "Then I suppose he'll go looking for adventure and fortune."

"I suppose. And I suppose I'll never see him again. I suppose that's all for the best."

Edlyn's quiet agony as she said good-bye to her childhood dreams tore at Alisoun's heart. She tried to think of something to say, something to ease the pain, but her experience with such emotions was new. How could she help Edlyn when she couldn't even help herself?

Crossing her arms over her chest, Edlyn whispered, "Will I ever see you again?"

Alisoun could offer no more than feeble hope. "Perhaps someday I will go up to London with my children and we can meet there."

"You can't take Lord Osbern's child out where others can see her, and you won't leave her home."

Alisoun couldn't dispute that.

"So I *will* never see you again."

"We'll leave that in God's hands."

Edlyn nodded, her eyes dry, her gaze steady. "Aye, that would be best."

Once, not so long ago, Alisoun had been like a mother to Edlyn, and Edlyn had believed Alisoun could twist events to make everything right. She no longer expected that—she'd learned differently through these last long summer days—but she loved Alisoun none the less. Now they were women, united in grief and going their separate ways. Opening their arms to each other, they hugged. Then a groom helped Edlyn into the saddle and with a wave and a brave smile, she rode away.

At last Alisoun had seen her ambition for Edlyn come to fruition. The lass who had been terrified by Osbern's attack had been replaced by the young woman who went to get married. Edlyn now faced the grief of her life with stolid maturity. Yet Alisoun wished that the girl had not had so many ideals crushed, so many dreams destroyed.

If maturity was nothing more than cynicism and unhappiness, then it was highly overrated, and Alisoun herself wanted none of it.

Alisoun ran to the drawbridge and stood staring at the retreating procession.

Ah, there had been a time in Alisoun's life when she thought that if all people acted with maturity, the world would be peaceful, organized, and prosperous. Now she sought a return to that aloof state of mind, but the memory of her own hopes and dreams haunted her.

She hated David. Hate burned in her gut until she feared it would harm the babe, but still she couldn't tame her rancor.

Worse, she missed him. She wanted someone to talk to, someone who thought the same thoughts she did and shared the same values.

Not the same values, she corrected herself. She had thought they shared the same values, but he'd let Philippa go with her husband because he feared the loss of his lands.

And of his family. That inner voice, always fair, taunted her. He worried about Bertrade. He wanted to keep his daughter safe, and he would sacrifice anyone to do so. And he wanted to keep *her* safe, too, Alisoun grudgingly admitted. He had done everything he could to keep her safe: taking her to Radcliffe, mobilizing his forces there, protecting her even when she had refused him her bed.

So mayhap he had had a little justification for his actions.

But when she remembered Philippa's scars, her

anguish, her fears; when she remembered that lonely baby upstairs in her keep who cried pitiably for her mother—then she no longer thought him justified, and she wanted to do something, anything, to rectify this situation.

She heard a slow, shuffling tread and the tap of a crutch on the wooden planks behind her, and she turned at once to Sir Walter.

"You shouldn't have walked so far." She rebuked him. "And never down the stairs from the keep."

"I didn't walk all the way. I couldn't bear to be inside anymore, so Ivo carried me." Sir Walter's bruises had faded, the scars had drawn together and formed red and white streaks across his face, and he moved with great difficulty. He looked down toward the village to the tiny figure of Edlyn, and said, "We'll miss her, eh, my lady?"

"Dreadfully."

Balancing carefully, he tugged at her arm. "Come inside. I still find myself unconvinced that the duke of Framlingford will not retaliate against you, and I don't like you standing in such an exposed spot."

She didn't want to go, but she knew he was right. Osbern would no doubt brood on the wrong she had done him and would someday come back to take his revenge.

But only when he'd finished with Philippa.

She whimpered softly, but Sir Walter heard. "Would you help me, my lady? I find myself tiring more easily than I expected."

Blindly, she took his arm and helped him back into the bailey, and after a moment her choking sensation eased. One couldn't remain in pain all the time, and the act of helping Sir Walter seemed to bring solace.

She could, after all, successfully aid someone.

Sir Walter was speaking, and with an effort she tried to comprehend the words.

"I'm not the man I once was, my lady. I'll never walk easily and I'll never fight in battle again. Not only that, but I am humbled in spirit as well. You were right about the threat the duke posed, and I should have listened and done my duty rather than instruct you in yours."

He breathed heavily, and she realized he hadn't simply used his condition as an excuse to bring her inside. He did need to rest. She looked around, and the hovering Ivo rolled a tree stump toward them for Sir Walter to sit on.

She smiled at the big man who gave her his unquestioning loyalty and wished all men were so easily trained. Sir Walter had almost died learning that a woman could know better than a man, and David . . . in his ignorance, David had lost her.

But did he really care?

She and Ivo held Sir Walter's arms as he lowered himself onto the stump. With a grunt, Sir Walter settled himself, then with his gaze on his feet, said, "If you choose another steward for George's Cross, my lady, I understand, but there can never be another man who would truly be as dedicated to your service."

Now she realized the reason for at least some of his discomfort, and said hastily, "Sir Walter, I have failed in my duty to you if you think I would choose another man to care for George's Cross. You may not be able to fight, but you know the people, the crops, and you have the loyalty of the men-at-arms and the mercenary knights. I have no time to train another, especially since I have a one-year-old daughter to reconcile to her new home, and—" she looked at him directly, "—I will be giving birth in the winter."

He smiled. The attack on him had left him with few teeth and a mouth permanently split on one side, but she read his joy. "That is indeed a blessing, my lady, and I rejoice that the child will be legitimate."

She grimaced in pain at the thought of her marriage.

"I meant no disrespect," he added quickly. "Only that I doubted your attachment to Sir David, and I should have realized your wisdom."

"Wisdom." She chortled.

"Your activities are always wise and well thought out, my lady."

"I used to think so, too."

"Even taking Lady Philippa from her husband had its base in wisdom."

"*Now* you give me your blessing?"

"And if you think about it, you'll see it is wisdom to give up your grief about her recapture." She drew back, but he caught her hand. "There was nothing you could do about it. There was nothing anyone could do about it. A wife belongs to her husband, and you always knew that one day, he would capture her."

"I suppose I knew, but I hoped that Sir David . . ."

"You can't blame the man for recognizing an impossible situation and doing the best he knew how."

"He isn't who I thought he was."

"Who's that?"

"A legend."

"*He* never said he was a legend."

She didn't answer, because she knew it was true.

"You, lady—you usually think so clearly. What solution can you envision that would take Lady Philippa away from her God-given husband?"

She treated his question seriously. "I've thought about it and thought about it. I can't bribe Osbern. Even if he needed my money, he's the kind of man who would keep Philippa for the pleasure of tormenting her and knowing that her pain tormented me. I can't appeal to the king. He arranged the match himself, and he would never interfere between man and wife."

"And think of your estates. Your first duty is to them."

"I've lived my whole life for these estates, and I know now someone will always tend them. They are too rich to remain unclaimed for long." Almost to herself, she said, "Surely Philippa's life is worth more than any land."

"Ease your heart, my lady! Perhaps Lord Osbern learned his lesson during his wife's long absence and now treats her with honor she deserves."

She gave a bitter laugh.

Quickly he abandoned that fantasy. "It would take a desperate man who cared nothing for his life or his family to try and rescue Lady Philippa."

"Or a desperate woman." She said the words, it seemed, even before she thought them.

"A woman? Ha." As Sir Walter tried to struggle to his feet, Ivo rushed to his side and assisted him. "With all due respect, my lady, a woman's weapons are useless against the might of king and Church."

She was desperate.

"I'm going to the guardhouse now, and then I will retire."

Yet what was she supposed to do?

Sir Walter patted her hand. "If I may be so bold, I would advise you to resign yourself to Philippa's fate and submit to your husband your unquestioning obedience."

Don armor and ride to rescue Philippa herself?

"Ah, I see a spark in your eye." Sir Walter smiled, a wise lift of the lips. "I'm glad we had this talk."

"I'm glad, too." She smiled back at him, at ease for the first time in days.

He waved Ivo away and hobbled off on his own, and she waited until he could no longer hear her before she turned to her man-at-arms. "Ivo! Have we got any armor that would fit me?"

Ivo's lips moved as he repeated the question silently, clearly puzzled over the meaning. "Aye. There's an old leather breastplate."

"Is there a sword I could lift? Maybe a sharp knife?"

"Aye. There is." But rather than going to get them, he stood and scratched his hairy chin with an intent expression. At last he seemed to have comprehended something, and he asked, "Are we going t' get Lady Philippa from her husband?"

"*I* am." She needed him to get to Osbern's stronghold but she would not command him. "If you and Gunnewate wish to accompany me, I'd be grateful."

"There's nary a question that I'll accompany ye an' speaking fer Gunnewate, he'll go, too." His scratching fingers wandered down to his chest. "Pardon me, my lady, fer being forward, but I heard ye say ye're with child."

In sooth, she made this decision not only for herself, but for the life within her. Still, she knew what she had to do. With steady resolve, she answered, "No child of mine could want a mother tainted by dishonor and cowardice."

His fingers came to a halt and he nodded slowly up and down. "Aye, m'lady, ye're right about that."

She realized she'd been holding her breath as she waited for Ivo's opinion. A plain man, an honest man, he viewed the world without imagination and still he approved her plan. She needed no more benediction. "Then we have a journey to make."

24

The banners flying from the ramparts of Osbern's castle gave Alisoun her first indication of the obstacles she now faced.

"M'lady?" Ivo spoke in his slow, measured manner. "Isn't that the king's coat o' arms?"

"It is." She could scarcely believe her luck, although whether it was good or bad, she couldn't decide. "Henry is here. I should have known." Not many of King Henry's subjects had the wealth to feed and shelter the court during one of his summer tours, and she suspected Henry took a special delight in plucking the fruits of Osbern's wealth.

Gunnewate had ridden ahead. Now the dust stirred beneath his horse's hooves as he returned to report, "It looks like half the country's mustered in the bailey, m'lady, an' they're all yelling an' excited. A tournament, I'd say, but the stands are only half built."

"A fight, more likely." Alisoun fingered the blade hidden under her cloak. "That might make my mission easier." But now that the moment had arrived, her stomach twisted and rolled.

She was planning to kill Osbern. What had she been thinking? She'd never killed anyone. And how would she do it? By sneaking around and slipping a knife into his ribs? A paltry, cowardly battle for right, but if she challenged him—him, the king's champion—he would laugh and break her like dry kindling.

"Shall we go down, m'lady?" Ivo asked.

She saw that he had bared his weapons, and it occurred to her he had come prepared to fight and die. She could do no less.

"Aye, let's go." Ivo rode on one side of her, Gunnewate on the other, and she entered the castle like a warrior of old flanked by her faithful companions. Yet as they entered the outer bailey, no one challenged them. No one even seemed to notice. Everyone—servants, knights, lords, and ladies—were gathered in a circle around two figures, clad in fighting armor, who stood facing each other. From atop her horse, Alisoun had a view the others only fought for, but the warriors' helmets covered their faces and she knew not who they were. Nor did she care, for lifted above the throng on a half-built viewing stand sat King Henry. A few of his lucky nobles, the ones powerful enough to remain at his side, stood around him, and there she sought Osbern.

She couldn't see him.

"Want me t' find out where the duke is?" Ivo asked.

She nodded, and he urged his horse into the outer fringes of the crowd and toward a tree, laden with children who had climbed there to watch the combat. Stretching up out of the saddle, Ivo twisted the hair of a stableboy and the rumble of his voice rolled through the leaves. "Where's the duke o' Framlingford?"

The children all laughed, their high-pitched voices

full of scorn. The stableboy pointed at the warriors in combat. "There. He's fightin'."

"Who's he fightin'?" Ivo asked.

"That crazy man, an' they're fightin' t' the death."

Cold tingled in Alisoun's fingertips and at the tip of her nose as she overheard this exchange.

Ivo shook the lad. "What crazy man?"

"That crazy man, that one who walked up t' the king today, on the first day o' the royal visit, an' said he was goin' kill his champion."

Alisoun could no longer contain herself. "Why?" she shouted.

"He said t' avenge the death o' Lord Osbern's wife."

Red spots flexed and grew before her eyes. She gripped the saddle and fought to retain her balance. But she could still hear Ivo ask, "Do ye know the man's name?"

No one answered for a moment, then a girl's voice piped up, "They call him Sir David. Sir David o' Radcliffe."

David hated fighting. Whenever he found himself sweating beneath his hauberk, trying to see around a nose guard, gripping a sword in one hand and a shield in the other—well, then he knew how stupid combat really was.

Of course, that was while he was still afraid, before the exhilaration of battle had swept him up and carried him away. And every time he fought, he always feared that that glory would fail to seize him, and he'd have to fight on, cold with the cowardice that no one recognized.

Especially now. Especially facing Osbern. Osbern had defeated him before, and that gave him a powerful advantage over David.

Osbern knew it, too. In a voice designed to carry over the shouts of the crowd, he asked, "Did your wife force you to come?"

David saved his breath and stoically met the hacking of Osbern's sword with his shield.

Osbern didn't seem to mind David's silence. Lightly, he chatted, "She's a powerful woman, I warned you of that, and unless you train her properly at the beginning, you'll have no peace all your life long." He lost that congenial tone. "Ah, but I forget. You're going to die today, so you'll not have to worry."

Osbern's sword slashed toward David's neck, but David stepped aside at the last moment and the steel whistled through the air.

That angered Osbern, and he said, "A rather drastic solution to an unhappy marriage, isn't it?"

The crowd cheered when he lunged and his tip slid down David's shield and caught in David's chauss over his knee. He hadn't used enough force to pierce the chain mail, but the kneecap snapped sideways and David went down hard beneath the weight of his armor.

"Give it up, old man!" one of Osbern's knights shouted. "You're so slow you're boring us."

Turning his back on David, Osbern chided the heckler. "Such manners! And from one of my own men. Haven't I taught you respect for your elders?"

Even as the crowd laughed, David swung the flat of his sword behind Osbern's knees. Osbern toppled with a clatter of armor. The chanting of his people ceased, and a spattering of cheers rose from the crowd.

Mostly feminine cheers, David noted. Looking at his prone opponent, he experienced a deep visceral satisfaction and realized that once again, his pleasure in the fight had returned. So Osbern's taunts had been good for something. Leaning on his sword, he hoisted himself to his feet. "At least, my lord duke, I can stop your tongue."

As David had hoped, Osbern clambered to his feet in a fury. "My tongue will say as it pleases at your funeral."

"Mayhap so, my lord. Mayhap so." They squared off again, and this time, David noticed, the tip of Osbern's heavy sword shook just a little. He was rattled or tiring, or both, David hoped. Then the shock of taking Osbern's first blow almost broke his shield arm, and that hope faded.

Still, his practice with Hugh had paid off, for he met Osbern's blows with a supple defense and even placed a few of his own. He would have placed more, but he waited, for he'd fought Osbern once before and lost, and he knew his strategy now.

Aye, he knew it, but whether he had the skill and strength to counter it, only time would tell.

"I've had her, you know."

Osbern's gibe jolted David's concentration. "Had who, my lord?"

"Your wife. We played hilt and hair more than once."

Still uncomprehending, David watched Osbern swing the sword and he stepped aside. Then he asked, "Alisoun? Are you saying you swived her?" Before Osbern could concur, David burst into laughter. "I wouldn't brag about that if I were you, Osbern. Her maidenhead remained intact for me, so if you'd been there first, your blade must be as short as your reach."

Osbern jabbed at David's chest. The thrust slammed past David's shield and pierced his hauberk. David leaped away. Blood spurted once, then slowed to a trickle, but Osbern waited no longer.

He slashed at David, pressing him hard.

Laughter, David realized, could get him killed.

He concentrated on his work, but clearly Osbern had been toying with him before. Now Osbern was angry.

But that was good, David assured himself. An angry man didn't think clearly.

Then Osbern brought his sword up from underneath and smashed David's blade. The hilt jerked out of his hand and it went flying, and David looked at the tip of a sword pointed at his face.

"On your knees," Osbern commanded. "On your knees, and maybe I'll spare your miserable life."

"It's not worth sparing if I don't kill you," David said, but he did as he instructed. He remembered this from the last time. The humiliating defeat. The groveling. The magnanimous release.

But this time, Osbern wouldn't release him. They both knew it, but Osbern wanted to savor his full triumph, and David gladly would let him.

His whole plan depended on Osbern playing the role as it had been played before.

"Look at him!" Osbern called. The crowd hollered and whooped. "The former champion of the king, the legendary Sir David, on his knees before me." Slowly, his gaze still fixed on David, he lowered his sword. "Begging for his life! And should I give it to him?"

"But you haven't disarmed me yet." Moving with care, David drew his dagger from its sheath.

Osbern started laughing as hardily as David had earlier laughed. "What are you going to do? Slash my ankles with that?"

"Nay." David brought the point up under Osbern's hauberk. "I'm going to geld you."

Osbern froze. "Put that down."

The crowd quieted.

"You have the sword, my lord duke. You have the greater weapon. Why don't you use it?" David felt Osbern's muscles quiver as he considered it. "Of course, I'll cut until I hit bone, and I might die and you might live, but cold water will no longer hold any fear for you."

Osbern shifted. "So what are we going to do? Stand here until we rot?"

"Nay, my lord. You're going to surrender to me."

"Are you mad?" Osbern shrieked. Then he shrieked again as David shifted his weight forward and pressed the point closer to home.

"I don't think I am, but it's possible. After all, I'm half-hoping you swing that sword, so I can be the object of praise from all womankind."

"I'm dropping the sword." The fine steel blade thumped in the dirt. "I'm surrendering to you."

"Are you indeed?" David checked. Osbern's dagger remained in its sheath, but David made no demand that Osbern surrender it. Instead he stood and brought his dagger up under the chain mail coif to rest on Osbern's throat. "Take off your helmet."

Osbern started to jerk it off.

"Slowly, my lord. You don't want to alarm me, for I truly would like to kill you. You insulted and tried to murder my wife. You savagely beat your own wife. You're a plague on the face of England, and everyone would be happier without you."

Now Osbern moved with infinite care, and David smiled to see the way his chin trembled when it came into sight. Loudly, David asked, "Do you freely surrender yourself to me and grant me that ransom which I require?"

Glaring venomously, Osbern said, "I do."

"I demand custody of your wife, Philippa."

The crowd gasped and David heard King Henry calling, "What? What did he say?"

"She's dead." Osbern wiped his mouth with the back of his hand.

"Then we'll exhume her here and now and show King Henry how you treat the heiresses he gives you." David stepped away and turned his back on Osbern. "Let's do it now."

When he heard a woman cry out he leaped away from the blow of Osbern's dagger. While Osbern still hung off-balance, David shoved his own blade into the hollow of Osbern's throat.

Osbern was dead before he hit the ground.

Osbern's knights surrounded David before David could rearm himself. "The king's cousin," they shouted. "He's killed the king's cousin!"

Then something drove a wedge through the knights to David, and David saw Guy of the Archers, clad in armor and carrying enough weapons to decapitate half of London.

He promised, "We'll fight back to back, Sir David, until we can't fight anymore."

The knights around the king abandoned their posts and crowded forward to watch the fight, and if Henry could have done the same and still retained his dignity, he would have been off his chair and mingling with the crowd. As it was, he leaned forward, his hands clenched around the arms of the chair, his gaze intent on the combat. Alisoun seized her chance. Climbing onto the viewing stand, she drew her short sword and held it where the king could see it.

Henry never moved. Only his gaze flicked along the

steel glinting in the hot sun. He followed it to the hand that held it, then up to her face. She found herself gratified by his astonishment. "Lady Alisoun, what are you doing with that sword?"

"I'm holding you hostage." She spoke without inflection, concentrating on keeping the sword steady and hoping that her reputation as dispassionate would carry the king beyond his initial amused reaction.

It seemed to work. Easing himself back in the chair, he asked, "May I ask why?"

"I want you to command Osbern's knights to cease their attack on Sir David of Radcliffe and Guy of the Archers."

Henry's gaze flicked toward the field. "But Sir David and Guy of the Archers seem to be acquitting themselves well."

"Two cannot win against so many." She noticed that the sword had drifted down, and jerked it back up.

"At one time, Sir David defeated fifteen men to save my life. There are not more than twenty knights out there, and he has Guy of the Archers to protect his back." Casually, he inquired, "Why should you care about the fate of Sir David?"

She was holding a sword on Henry. So why should she be concerned that she had wed without his permission? Yet she was. To wed without the king's consent could sometimes be seen as treason. Stiffening her spine, she answered him with equanimity. "Sir David is my husband."

"He married you? I mean . . . you're married?"

His stunned surprise could hardly be called flattering. "We are wed."

"I knew Sir David could fight with the best, but I never imagined him up to the challenge of—" he looked her over, "—you."

"We deal with each other very well, but we cannot continue to do so if he's slaughtered in combat."

Gingerly, he pushed the blade away from his stomach. "Most felons stick the point somewhere and keep it there."

The tone of this conversation seemed almost too friendly, and she confided, "David told me if I ever needed to attack someone I should aim for the eyes, the throat, or the gut."

"So far, your blade has reached all three, and if it continues to droop, the future of my royal line is in danger."

She jerked the blade higher. "So will you order Osbern's knights to cease their attack?"

"I don't think I will have to. It seems my cousin was not well liked and his passing is welcomed by at least some who are here."

Alisoun straightened and stared.

Henry inched the blade away until the tip rested on the arm of his chair.

She didn't notice. She only saw as first one knight, then another, was removed from the fight by his woman. One by one each knight's wife walked into the fight, took her man by the arm, and pulled him out of the combat. All conflict faltered. No man could concentrate on his swordwork while a woman walked through the battlefield.

"The queen would be pleased with this demonstration of filial devotion," King Henry murmured.

"The women all know what Osbern was, even if the men didn't know or didn't care."

"A sharp reproach." Henry touched her wrist. "But possibly well deserved."

At last five knights were left facing David and Guy, and Alisoun murmured, "They must be unwed."

Henry laughed.

Now David and Guy assumed more aggressive stances and the five knights began to back away. "They'll not get far," Henry said. "Now we'll see some expert combat, and Sir David will win ransom from them, also. They'll learn a lesson that they'll not soon forget."

As Henry predicted, David and Guy disarmed each knight. Guy took the ransom from three of the knights, David from two, leaving them even in victory for the day.

Then David removed his helmet, and suddenly Ivo stood by his side. As Alisoun watched, she saw David's startled reaction to her man-at-arms' offer of service. He looked around and she knew when he spotted her, for his eyes narrowed to two tight bands. Then he accepted Ivo's assistance with every evidence of gratitude.

Ivo had deemed David worthy of his mistress at last.

Bare-headed, without his weapons, but still clad in his armor, David started toward the king. The crowd yielded for him easily and he walked with solemn dignity. Yet the closer he came to the stand, the quicker he walked. When he neared enough to speak, he demanded of Alisoun, "My lady, what are you doing here?"

The woman didn't seem to realize how his emotions rumbled at the sight of her. In that prissy voice that so infuriated him, she said, "The same thing you are, it seems."

"I doubt that." He leaped onto the stand, and his gaze fell to the shiny blade that rested on the chair's arm. "Why do you have a sword pointed toward our sovereign lord?"

Henry caught her wrist when she would have moved

the blade. "She served as my bodyguard when your performance distracted my knights." Waving his sheepish nobles away, he said, "Nay, nay, my lady Alisoun performed admirably in your absence. Just remain where you are for the moment."

"With your permission, my liege." David took the sword from Alisoun's fingers.

"It is good for a subject to ask my permission," the king mused. "Especially in matters of marriage."

He knew. The king knew. David wanted to slap his forehead and whimper. Instead he said, "When trapping a wily fox, my liege, a warrior must seize the creature at the first moment it is ensnared, lest it hurt itself in the struggle."

"I do not appreciate being compared to a fox," Alisoun said crisply.

"I do not appreciate having my wife hold a sword on the king," David answered just as crisply.

Henry stopped them with a chuckle. Turning to Alisoun, he held up three fingers and counted them down. "Wealth, breeding, and a devotion to duty. Were not those your requirements for a husband?"

Delicate color crept up Alisoun's face. "I discovered, my liege, that Sir David's devotion to duty outweighed his lack of . . . ah . . . breeding, and—" she coughed, "—wealth."

Henry lifted his brows. "So you wed him knowing full well he didn't meet your requirements?"

"I did."

"Then, Sir David, although it offends your lady wife, I accept your story of fox and warrior."

David stifled his laughter. Alisoun stood unmoving.

Henry sighed. "Although I pity you, Sir David, a wife who shows so little emotion."

The king's lack of perception shocked David.

Couldn't he see by the tilt of her chin that she was angry? That the slight tremble of her fingers signified weariness and relief? That the moisture that wet the outside corner of each eyes presaged her storm of grief at losing Philippa?

But no, Henry saw none of those things. He saw only two unlikely people bound together by wedlock, and he had decided to be amused rather than angered by their unsanctioned union. "I will fine you," he said. "Nothing more."

Familiar with Henry's constant need for money with which to finance his warfare, David winced. But he knew they had gotten off easily, and probed the king's mind once more. "Will I be imprisoned for killing your cousin?"

"Who?" Henry started. "Oh, Osbern. Nay, nay. 'Twas a fair challenge, and he did try to kill you after he had surrendered. Don't concern yourself." Henry must have noticed the way David stared, for he leaned forward and confided, "I mean, God rest his soul, I'll order Masses said, but he was older than me, and picked on me unmercifully when we were lads. He might have been obsequious after my coronation, but I knew the manner of man he was. His family is influential and wealthy, so I never dared do anything about him, but the kingdom is well rid of him—although you never heard such denigration from me."

David bowed, astonishment and relief warring in him, and his knees wavered in a sudden attack of weakness. The king thought David had done him a favor. All his fears—of losing his daughter, his wife, his lands, and his life—had been for naught. He had done what was right, and for that he had been rewarded.

He looked at Alisoun. Well, not rewarded, exactly. But he got to keep his wife.

Then she spoke. "If I may be so bold as to ask, my liege, what tale did Osbern weave to explain the death of his wife?"

Her softly spoken question jerked David away from his blossoming sense of triumph and back to gritty reality. In sooth, he did have his wife, but his wife had lost her dearest friend and she could, in fairness. blame Philippa's death on his failure to challenge Osbern at Radcliffe.

Alisoun could blame him? Hell, he blamed himself.

"No tale. He simply said she was away on another of his estates." Henry cocked his head. "So he killed the good woman I gave him, and the estate is not entailed to a male heir. Where shall I bestow it?"

David and Alisoun said it together. "Osbern left a daughter."

"Hazel resides with me at George's Cross," Alisoun said.

"Excellent." Henry rubbed his palms together. "Another heiress to marry off."

David barely restrained his groan. The king was, indeed, mad for marriage, and he doubted Hazel would pass her second birthday before she found herself betrothed. Then he remembered who had custody of the child.

Alisoun had experience in holding off unwanted suitors. Hazel would be safe until Alisoun decided she was ripe for marriage.

Holding out his hand, David asked, "So shall we go, lady wife?"

"I beg you, husband, to allow me to first find Philippa's maid and inquire about the details of her death."

David didn't want Alisoun to know. He didn't want her haunted by the gruesome details, but the king rose

and said, "A worthy plan, Lady Alisoun. It shall be as
you wish. In the meantime, may I offer my cousin's hospitality to you both. You're hungry and no doubt weary,
and now that Sir David is once again the king's champion I will require him to swear fealty to me."

David didn't want to stay. He didn't care how hungry or tired he was, he just wanted to take Alisoun to a
private place and ask if she would ever forgive his stupidity. Osbern's body had already been taken into the
castle chapel, where he would rest and not disturb
the royal activities. But Alisoun assuredly wanted to
say her prayers for Philippa, and so she followed
Henry off the stand, and David followed her, up the
stairs, into the keep, and up to the royal table set on
the dais.

The other nobles kept their distance, as the king had
commanded, while the servants hurried to their duties.
Osbern had died, but at this moment his passing had
little impact.

To Alisoun and David, Henry said, "I'll have you
each on one side of me when we dine. Appropriately, I
think, for the countess of George's Cross and the king's
two-time champion to flank the king while we toast
your newlywed status."

Alisoun agreed with composure, but David could
scarcely speak. He had never eaten at the king's table
before. He was only a knight, and although he could
fight, no one had ever thought him as worthy of more
than token respect. Now, because of Alisoun, the king
had seated him at his right hand.

When the squire approached with a basin of water in
which to wash, David plunged in his head and scrubbed
until the salt of sweat and the dirt of the road had disappeared. When he turned, he realized an unusual
silence gripped the hall. Wiping his hair with a towel,

he moved to Alisoun's side. "What's wrong?" he asked.

Alisoun gripped his hand as if nothing had ever come between them—or as if she didn't realize what she did. In a low tone, she said, "The servants claim to know nothing of Philippa's death, and one of them—" Alisoun broke off as the door from the undercroft opened.

Watching her, David saw her eyes get big, then with a cry she flung herself at the battered figure in the doorway.

"Philippa." She wrapped her friend in her arms. "Philippa, you're alive!"

25

"How's my babe?"

The pallor of the dungeon hung about Philippa, bruises marked her jaw, and one eye was swollen shut. But she was alive, Osbern was dead, and Alisoun resolved that nothing would threaten her friend ever again.

In an upper bedchamber, the two friends tried to realize that at last the threat to their lives and happiness had been destroyed.

"Hazel's healthy, but she misses you." Alisoun didn't mention the hours she had spent rocking the crying baby, trying to comfort the child desolated by the loss of her mother.

"I long to hold her in my arms once more." Philippa's voice trembled with eagerness, and the maids who fed and bathed her redoubled their efforts to please the mistress they had been forced to ignore.

"You'll have her soon," Alisoun promised.

"Aye, I will. Soon I'll leave this place behind, and I'll never come back."

Somewhere, somehow, Philippa had developed a steely determination to go with her earthy good nature. No one, Alisoun thought, would ever be given the chance to harm Philippa again. She might marry again—indeed, Alisoun thought Philippa was made to be married—but somehow Philippa would hold the balance of power. Going to her friend, Alisoun knelt at her side. "The thought of you in Osbern's hands haunted me."

Philippa touched her cheek. "You should not have been troubled. He loved me, you know."

"A dreadful, capricious love then." Alisoun held Philippa's hand against her skin and thanked God again for her miraculous survival. "Did he keep you in the dungeon the whole time?"

"He said he had to punish me for running away. I didn't care what he did, as long as I knew Hazel was safe."

"She's fine," Alisoun repeated.

"I'm leaving to see her as soon as a way can be prepared." Philippa turned her face up and let the maid swab her swollen eye with cold water. "Today. I'm leaving today."

Briefly, Alisoun thought of the king and his court who waited below in the great hall. Then she dismissed them. "I'll arrange a cart. I don't think you're strong enough to ride."

Philippa started to argue, then thought better of it. "Can we find me an escort?"

"Put on a clean gown, and I'll go speak to David about it. He'll find someone." Alisoun opened the door.

Guy of the Archers fell in as if he'd been leaning against the wood. Straightening, he said, "I'll do it."

Puzzled, Alisoun asked, "Do what?"

"I'll be the lady's escort. It would be an honor to reunite her with her babe."

Alisoun stared at Guy, then at Philippa as she smiled tranquilly from her place by the fire. "Have you been listening at the door?" she asked.

Guy didn't seem to hear Alisoun. He saw only Philippa, spoke only to Philippa. "Would it please your ladyship if I escorted you?"

She held out her hand. "My thanks, gentle knight. I would have no other."

Rushing to her side, he took her hand and knelt, and Alisoun felt suddenly superfluous. She stepped into the hallway and found David waiting, a peculiar expression on his face. Obviously he had been with Guy as he waited. "Do they love each other?" he demanded.

"I never suspected, but it would seem they do . . . or at least that they know they might love." Alisoun didn't know why, but after she said the words she blushed and lowered her gaze.

He sounded odd, also, his voice deeper and fraught with significance when he said, "They seem an unlikely couple, but I suppose love blossoms where it will."

Beneath his words lurked something unspoken which she didn't comprehend. Wouldn't comprehend. Instead she took refuge in briskness. "Since you are now in the king's favor, could you explain to Henry that Philippa longs to embrace her child and seeks permission to leave immediately?"

"*I'm* in the king's favor?" David's voice had returned to normal, and she risked a glance at him. Although his mouth formed a serious line, his eyes watched her faithfully and seemed to analyze her every movement. "You are also in the king's favor."

"How could that be? I held a sword on him."

"Badly." He dismissed her pretensions with one brisk word. "And you have done the one thing that was guaranteed to find favor in Henry's eyes." His sober mouth twitched into a smile. "You married me."

"I could have married anyone and gotten the same results," she snapped, unnerved by his scrutiny. Most people said they didn't understand her. David, on the other hand, seemed to understand her too well, and right now she wasn't sure she wanted him to fathom how she felt. She wasn't even sure how she felt, or why she insulted him.

He didn't take offense. "But no one else ever wanted to marry you, did they?"

"Too many wanted to marry me."

"Not you," he corrected. "But your estates."

She wanted to say that she and her estates were one and the same, but they weren't. Lady Alisoun was from George's Cross, but *she* was not George's Cross. She had separated the two entities forever when she'd decided to put her lands at risk to rescue Philippa.

And David . . . well, he wanted George's Cross, but he wanted her, too. She was not the bad medicine he had to take to gain claim to her lands, but an added jewel for his shield.

The saints knew he'd told her so in many ways; now she believed him.

She blinked. Had she been daydreaming? By Saint Michael's arm, she had. David had disappeared. She rushed after him toward the stairwell, but already she heard his voice in the great hall, begging the king to allow Philippa to leave at once.

She also had a duty to do, she reminded herself. She had to arrange transportation for Philippa, not chase after her husband for the purpose of useless chatter.

In fact, when she thought about being alone with David and speaking about their difficulties, she could only remember his half-tender, half-exasperated expression and wonder what it meant.

Still, she didn't want to return to the chamber which housed Philippa, and when she entered she knew why. Too much sunshine seemed to have penetrated the dim recesses of the room, and she had to call that glow happiness. She couldn't discern its origin—the glow permeated the stone walls, the beamed ceiling, the tapestries, and the wooden floor. On the other hand, she didn't look directly at Guy or Philippa or their rapture would blind her.

Calling the maids, Alisoun directed them on errands to prepare for Philippa's journey, and by the time the serving women had departed, David returned. "We're leaving at once," he announced.

"We?" Startled, Alisoun rounded on him. "Who's we?"

"Guy, Lady Philippa, you, me." David took her arm. "And Louis."

"You and I can't leave."

He hustled her out the door.

She tried to dig her heels in. "We must wait on the king!"

He kept a firm grip on her as they descended the staircase and bypassed the great hall. "He told us to go."

"On your instigation!"

David shrugged and held the outside door for Guy and Philippa. "Of course. I told him that Lady Philippa needed a heavy escort to George's Cross, because I had set the precedent for minor nobility to wed rich widows." Guy chuckled as he descended the stairs, and David grinned, quite proud of himself. "King Henry

almost fainted at the thought of losing dominion over
another one of his heiresses."

"You are a wicked man," Philippa said, her voice
rich with admiration.

"How can you approve of him?" Alisoun asked her. The
cart stood prepared, all their horses had been saddled, and
Ivo and Gunnewate stood stoically awaiting their depar-
ture. Obviously David had given commands in addition to
hers. "It is always best to pay court to the king when it is
convenient to secure yourself in his good graces."

"The king's good graces gave me Osbern for a husband. I no longer seek the king's good graces."

Philippa's outburst left Alisoun stunned and speech-
less, and David used the time to put her on her palfrey.
To Guy, he said, "We'll ride north together to George's
Cross, then Lady Alisoun and I will ride on to
Radcliffe."

"We will?" Alisoun said. "But I wanted to stay at
George's Cross and tend to Philippa."

"Did you?"

She didn't really. Her well-trained maids would
overwhelm Philippa on her triumphant return. But
Alisoun feared to be alone with David.

"It will be as my lady rules," he said, but his long
face belied his proffered agreement. "Like Philippa, I
long to see that my child is robust and thriving."

"Is Bert unwell?" Alisoun demanded.

"Nay, but I said farewell to her and warned her it
could very well be the last time I saw her, for I probably
rode to my death." He smiled wistfully. "I would reassure her now."

"Oh." He *had* almost ridden to his death. When
Alisoun thought how close Osbern's dagger had come,
the belated terror made her ill. When she thought about
Bertrade, her heart ached.

She could remain at George's Cross without David. Of course she could. But she didn't mention the possibility, because Guy and Philippa deserved to be alone.

Then she wondered where her former self had disappeared—the one who would have disapproved of a romance between a dowager duchess and a mere knight.

She guessed that Osbern had killed the former Lady Alisoun, for of all the men she'd ever met, only Osbern met all her requisites as a perfect husband. He had wealth, breeding, and a sense of duty, yet his evil deeds had scarred Philippa and Hazel and finally brought about his own downfall.

At David's hands. She looked at her husband. She had now put her life in danger for another, and she understood his former reluctance. She'd pointed a sword at the king's throat—and his chest, gut, and nether regions—and threatened him, and all the while her knees shook and her teeth chattered. She had known that with one cry he could have had her cut down, and she had discovered she couldn't have stricken him a blow even if it *had* saved Philippa's life.

She couldn't kill anyone. She was an errant coward.

But David had killed Osbern, thinking all the while he would die, if not at Osbern's hands, then as a victim of the king's vengeance.

She wanted to tell David how much she respected him for his courageous stand for justice, but she couldn't.

Not while Guy and Philippa could hear.

So she waited.

The travelers reached the village of George's Cross and said their good-byes. Guy and Philippa rode up to the castle. David and Alisoun rode north.

The silence grew heavier with every step.

He wanted to talk to her. He wanted to explain why he had allowed Osbern to take Philippa in the first place, and why he had gone to free her. He wanted to tell her that he had done what was conventional and he now comprehended the line she walked between compassion and propriety.

But Ivo and Gunnewate rode on their heels and he hesitated to speak in their presence. Even at night they weren't alone.

So the days had passed and too soon they topped the rise above Radcliffe. David stared at his beloved home without joy or hope. All the long journey together, he and Alisoun had said nothing but polite words. As far as he could see, they could continue like that forever. They could live their whole married life just as they'd passed the journey, both longing to speak, both weighted with the memory of their last quarrel and frightened to expose themselves once more.

Who would break the silence? David chortled in a sudden burst of acrid humor. How could he even wonder? Alisoun knew how to organize her castles; she had no inkling how to handle the intimacies of marriage. She who had so much in material wealth had never had someone love her, and he had to show her the way.

His destrier seemed to think so, too. Louis, who should have been in a hurry to reach his stable, lagged behind while Alisoun and her men rode on.

Alisoun glanced back, then waving Ivo and Gunnewate on, she returned to David. "Has your horse gone lame? A trek like this must be difficult for a steed of such advanced age."

Louis turned his head and looked at David, expressing equine disgust. Then, with a very human nod of conspiracy, he came to a complete halt. David sat with the reins held loosely in his hands.

"Is he in pain?" Alisoun asked. "Do you think he's thrown a shoe? Is he—"

She realized David studied her, and he saw the moment she stopped worrying about Louis, and started worrying about what David would say to her and what she would say to David.

"I have a question." He tried to ask casually. "Do you love me?"

Apparently he was not successful, for she drew back, and her palfrey took a few steps away. "Do I what?"

"Do you love me?"

If he was going to speak, he realized, she had expected him to speak of loyalty or honesty or duty. Something she understood. Something she had experience with. Instead he'd asked her a question which baffled her by its very unfamiliarity.

"Love?" She kept her back ramrod straight in the saddle. "To what kind of love do you refer? I admire you. I appreciate your finer qualities."

He gained confidence from her discomfort. "What about my lesser qualities?"

"Well, I don't admire *them*."

"But do you love me for them?"

"David." She leaned all the way back in her saddle. "I don't believe that people admire other people for their lesser qualities."

"I don't want you to admire me. I want you to love me." Her brow puckered, and he realized he would have to work for her comprehension. Leaning out, he held out his hand and slowly, warily, she took it. Then he asked, "How did you feel when I let Philippa leave with Osbern?"

Her face lengthened as she blanked all expression, and her fingers grew cold in his grasp. "I did not admire you."

"That's a lukewarm reaction to a man who would allow your best friend to leave with a man who would no doubt kill her."

Taking a deep breath, she admitted, "I disliked your actions."

"My actions? You disliked my actions?" How cleverly she separated him from his deeds. "How did you feel about me?"

"I . . . disliked you."

He stared at her in blatant disbelief.

She tried again. "I loathed you."

"You hated me."

She looked away from him.

"You hated me, but you're a rational woman who does what is logical, so you put me from your mind and concentrated on the future without me."

She tried to speak several times, and finally said, "Not exactly. I wasted a great deal of time thinking about how . . . how . . . "

"Aye?"

"How I'd like to take your liver and feed it to the cat."

"That's good!" She could be taught. "That's what I hoped you would say."

Her mouth dropped open just a little, and she shook her head as if confused.

"When you came to Osbern's castle and saw me fighting him, what did you think then?"

"I thought that you had seen the error of your—"

"I don't believe that."

Such bluntness came hard for a woman as steeped in diplomacy and as restrained in her passions as Alisoun, but she enunciated each word scrupulously. "I wanted to be undignified in my joy."

He grinned with relief and teased her. "Undignified in your joy, huh?"

"I wanted to jump up and down and yell."

She'd made a huge admission, but David was greedy. David wanted more. "All because you were glad to see me. Do you think you would have reacted with such unbridled emotional desire if another champion for Philippa had stepped forth?"

Her fingers curled, the tips brushing his palm. Her lips curled, her eyes going unfocused. "Nay. When I looked up, I knew I'd been waiting just for you." She stiffened, recalled to herself by her instinctive reply. "That is, I hired you to protect me, therefore I expected you to fulfill your duties."

"And you were ecstatic when I did."

"I was pleased, aye."

He sighed hugely.

"I was *very* pleased." Even before he showed his skepticism, she tried to express herself more clearly. "I was . . . proud. I was . . . delighted."

"Why?"

"Because you . . . "

She didn't want to say it. He could see how she struggled with her hurt and her pride.

But his Alisoun had courage, and at last she admitted, "You're my only hero."

A thrill skittered up his spine at her reluctant confession. They had come to the heart of the matter at last, and he wanted to shout, to dance, to jump Louis over the fences and make love to Alisoun in his herb garden. Instead he contented himself with doing what she would want. He spoke a simple, easy-to-understand sentence. "You *do* love me."

A series of emotions paraded across her face. Fear, amazement, vulnerability, and happiness.

He liked the happiness.

In a tiny voice, she asked, "How did you know? I didn't. And how did you know that you had to tell me?"

"I just thought that since I had to tell you you were with child, I might also have to tell you you were in love with me."

Bert and I stopped practicing with our arrows when we heard the first rumble of thunder. The sky had been clear and all of a sudden clouds rolled in! Well, we looked at each other.

"They're back!" I told Bert.

"I told you my daddy'd win," she said.

I wanted to shake her, but I couldn't take the time. We scrambled up the steps to the top of the wall walk and looked out past the village. There we saw Sir David's destrier King Louis galloping toward the castle with my lady Alisoun's palfrey running behind, and far off in the distance two small figures racing for the shelter of the forest as the rain moved toward them.

"I hope the wolves don't get them," I said.

The first big drops struck Bert on the nose, and she grinned, showing a big gap where two more teeth had fallen out. "They won't eat my daddy because he has his sword. And they won't eat Lady Alisoun 'cause she's too tough."

Bert was right. After the rain stopped, Sir David and Lady Alisoun walked all the way home. Then they ate, then they took a bath, then they went to bed for a long, long time.

That year, all of Northumbria brought in a harvest

that filled the barns to bursting. In the spring, Lady Alisoun delivered healthy boys—twins! Sir David almost split from pride, and to anyone who would listen he would recount the tale his granny told about how a great love warmed everyone around them.

We didn't need to hear the story. We were living it.

New York Times bestselling author

Christina Dodd

The Prince Kidnaps a Bride
978-0-06-056118-5/$7.99 US/$10.99 Can

Changed by his imprisonment to a dangerous man, Prince Rainger is determined to win back his kingdom—and the woman he loves more than life itself.

The Barefoot Princess
978-0-06-056117-8/$7.99 US/$10.99 Can

Since the powerful and wickedly handsome marquess of Northcliff has stolen the people's livelihood, Princess Amy decides to kidnap him for ransom.

My Fair Temptress
978-0-06-056112-3/$7.99 US/$10.99 Can

Miss Caroline Ritter, accomplished flirt and ruined gentlewoman, offers lessons to any rich, noble lord too inept to attract a wife.

Some Enchanted Evening
978-0-06-056098-0/$6.99 US/$9.99 Can

Though Robert is wary of the exquisite stranger who rides into the town he is sworn to defend, Clarice stirs emotions within him that he buried deeply years before.

DOD1 1206